W9-ACX-483

From the Start

No Longer the Property of
Hayner Public Library District

RECEIVED
MAY 1 8 2015
By_____

HAYNER PUBLIC LIBRARY DISTRICT
ALTON, ILLINOIS

OVERDUES 10 PER DAY, MAXIMUM FINE
COST OF ITEM
ADDITIONAL $5.00 SERVICE CHARGE
APPLIED TO
LOST OR DAMAGED ITEMS

HAYNER PLD/ALTON SQUARE

Books by Melissa Tagg

Here to Stay
Made to Last
*Three Little Words**
From the Start

*e-novella only

NO LONGER THE Property of
Hayner Public Library District

RECEIVED
MAY 2 5 2015
By

HAYNER PUBLIC LIBRARY DISTRICT
ALTON, ILLINOIS

OVERDUES 10 PER DAY. MAXIMUM FINE
COST OF ITEM
ADDITIONAL $5.00 SERVICE CHARGE
APPLIED TO
LOST OR DAMAGED ITEMS

From the Start

Melissa Tagg

BETHANYHOUSE

a division of Baker Publishing Group
Minneapolis, Minnesota

© 2015 by Melissa Tagg

Published by Bethany House Publishers
11400 Hampshire Avenue South
Bloomington, Minnesota 55438
www.bethanyhouse.com

Bethany House Publishers is a division of
Baker Publishing Group, Grand Rapids, Michigan

Printed in the United States of America

All rights reserved. No part of this publication may be reproduced, stored in a retrieval system, or transmitted in any form or by any means—for example, electronic, photocopy, recording—without the prior written permission of the publisher. The only exception is brief quotations in printed reviews.

Library of Congress Cataloging-in-Publication Data
Tagg, Melissa.
    From the start / Melissa Tagg.
        pages cm
    Summary: "Kate Walker writes romance movie scripts for a living, but her own broken engagement has left her disillusioned and believing true love isn't real, could a new friendship with former NFL player Colton Greene restore her faith?"— Provided by publisher.
    ISBN 978-0-7642-1307-6 (softcover)
    I. Title.
    PS3620.A343F76 2015
813'.6—dc23   2014041330

This is a work of fiction. Names, characters, incidents, and dialogues are products of the author's imagination and are not to be construed as real. Any resemblance to actual events or persons, living or dead, is entirely coincidental.

Cover design by Dan Thornberg, Design Source Creative Services, and Paul Higdon

Author represented by MacGregor Literary, Inc.

15 16 17 18 19 20 21   7 6 5 4 3 2 1

To my siblings:
Amy, Nathanael, and Nicole
I love you guys.
Tons. :)

1

*H*ow in the world had rain earned such a romantic rep? Kate Walker tipped the collar of her jacket and burrowed her chin against the chilly afternoon's heavy breathing. Chicago's usual sticky late-August warmth had gone into hiding today—saggy clouds and a veil of gray creating the perfect backdrop for the swoon-worthy embrace playing out in front of her.

The dashing hero holding tight to his girl in the middle of the park, swinging her in a circle as she laughed with abandon. Oblivious to the rainfall, the both of them. And then . . . the most magic moment of all.

The kiss.

Kate folded her arms.

"I know—sentimental fluff, right?"

She turned at the whispered voice beside her. Oh yes, the guy in the unzipped hoodie and ripped jeans who'd found her wandering around the movie set a few minutes ago. Couldn't have been older than twenty-two, and yet, as he'd led her to the tent under which the hushed production crew for *Love Until Forever* did their work, he'd talked as if he'd been in the filmmaking biz for decades.

"Say again?"

Raindrops pelted the plastic overhead, and a camera on a dolly scooted along the park's border. Back behind the tent, a rope separated those with set badges and the few dozen onlookers currently getting a behind-the-scenes peek at what might be Kate's last project.

"That's all these quickie made-for-TV features are. Fluff. The kind tucked in between *60 Minutes* and the local news. Nothing memorable, but it's a career start, right?" He flashed a smile that assumed she agreed. "I have film-school friends who'd kill to already have any AD credit under their belt."

Associate director. *And he has no idea who he's talking to.*

She didn't know whether to laugh or sigh or just roll with the punches while insult and embarrassment duked it out.

Guess she couldn't blame the kid. Kate rarely showed up on set—didn't generally have reason to visit. She'd only come today at her agent's request. Marcus called this morning, asking her to meet him here, said he had news.

Funny little word, that. *News.* So many possibilities crammed into four letters.

If only she could still the pecking voice in the back of her mind. The one daring her to hope that maybe, just maybe, this time the news might be good. But better not to get her hopes up.

After all, in the thirteen months since she'd sold her *Love Until Forever* script, she'd racked up a pile of rejections high enough to give the Sears Tower a run for its money. Scratch that—the Willis Tower. You'd think she'd get the name right, considering she'd had to take a part-time job there, doling out tickets, just to make ends meet.

How had so much changed in just a few short years? From multi-script contracts and her first book deal to standing in the rain, hoping against hope Marcus might have the kind of news that saved careers and made possible things like, oh, paying the mortgage on the cute brownstone in the cute neighborhood she used to think she could afford.

"Cut!" The director's call ordered.

Where is Marcus anyway?

The AD poked her with his elbow. "Hey, I don't think I gave you a chance to introduce yourself. You are . . ."

"Kate Walker." She pulled her hand from her coat pocket and held it out. "The writer of that sentimental fluff."

His grip on her palm went lax. "I, uh . . . I . . ."

The burst of laughter from behind them—of course Marcus chose that moment to show up—cut off the AD's sputtered reply. That and a glare from the director that told her he hadn't appreciated the chatter on set. She gave the AD an awkward "See ya" and made her escape, deserting the cover of the tent.

Spatters of rain pricked her coat and caught in her hair for only seconds before footsteps splashed in a puddle beside her and a shadow rose overhead.

"Skulking away, are we?" Marcus's joking voice accompanied the tapping of raindrops on the umbrella he now held over them.

"I can't believe you laughed."

"Oh, come on. It was funny." Marcus tugged on her elbow, pulling her to a stop. With his reddish hair and stubborn freckles, he'd always reminded her of a grown-up Opie. "He's a newbie know-it-all. Everybody's like that right after college."

"He's cocky—that's what."

"Of course he is." Exaggerated sympathy dangled in Marcus's voice.

"He doesn't know what he's talking about."

"Of course he doesn't."

But he's right.

There they were again, the nagging whispers she could never quite hush—roused from temporary rest by the AD's prodding.

You promised you'd write something important. But here you are, thirty years old . . .

Marcus's umbrella rattled as a gust of wind chugged over the blocked-off street edging the park. "Walker, you're not actually bothered by what that guy said, are you?"

She was saved from answering by the director's yelped instructions from the tent. "Start again from the kiss."

She turned back to Marcus. "You said you had news?"

"Not out here. It's raining, and I can't take you seriously when you're wearing that coat."

"What's wrong with my coat?" She cinched its belt as they started walking again. Maybe a little much for late summer—even a cool summer—but she'd take any chance she could get to wear the tweed trench coat with the oversized buttons and turned-up collar. It had character.

"It looks like something a reporter or detective would wear in an old-time movie. I feel like I should call you Ace and start talking really fast."

"Do it and you'll only encourage me to wear it more, my friend. As for the rain, a few sprinkles never hurt anyone."

Especially not lovers on the brink of happily ever after. Not that she'd know all that much about that. But the hunky actor and his costar currently repeating their kiss for the cameras . . .? The weather couldn't touch them.

Score one for waterproof makeup and extra-hold hairspray.

Kate stopped abruptly, gaze suddenly and unwillingly stuck on the staged love scene in the park. The brilliant green of a Midwest summer edged up to moody skies, the park's border of towering cedar, maple, and walnut trees fidgeting in the wind. She barely noticed Marcus bumping into her. Hardly felt the pull of the breeze in her hair. Heard only the hush of a whispered memory.

"This is right, Kate. Don't you feel it? Come to Chicago."

One prodding smile. One long kiss. One naïve decision.

The moment snapped as the actors in front of her parted.

One broken heart.

She blinked.

"Kate?" Marcus nudged her with his elbow, his umbrella tilting at the movement and sending rivulets of water down its curve. "You okay?"

"Just cold." She dusted the last specks of her stray memory away with a shake of her head. "It's Gene Kelly's fault, you know."

"What's whose fault?"

"He did that tap number in a pretend downpour. It's the reason everybody thinks rain is romantic. Thanks a lot, *Singin' in the Rain*."

"You are cold *and* kooky, Kate."

She shrugged. Speaking of kooky, though . . . under the soft glare and watchful eye of set lights, the actors in the park were still . . . well, acting. Which didn't make sense. According to the script she'd written, the kiss ended the scene. Ended the whole movie.

Concern picked its way in as the director's call sounded from the tent once more. The starring couple broke apart—assistants appearing from opposite directions to offer umbrellas and drinks—and a buzz of activity filled the set, cameramen shielding their equipment and someone barking orders at the props guy.

"Let's go inside." Marcus steered her toward the house kitty-corner from the park. From the outside, the two-story structure looked like any other house on any other Midwest street. Pale blue siding, white shutters to match the white porch.

But Kate had wandered around the set enough to know the inside of the house was a maze of half-built rooms, shallow staircases, and hallways that led nowhere.

All for show.

Unease wriggled through her as their shoes clomped over the rain-splotched porch steps, same questions as always setting her on edge any time she gave them mental space. Had she built a career as fake as this set? Just like the house's flimsy foundation of wood and plastic—nothing concrete or permanent—had she settled for less-than by peddling ideals she didn't put much stock in personally?

Romance.

True Love.

Happily Ever After.

Not to sound cynical, but . . . yeah. Right.

Marcus abandoned his umbrella on the porch, and Kate followed him under the doorframe and into a living room that could've graced the cover of a Pottery Barn catalog. Colorful throw pillows perfectly arranged on a beige couch. Framed photos on redwood end tables. Patterned rug reaching to the point in the room where the décor stopped and set lights began.

Marcus motioned for her to sit, then shrugged out of his raincoat and ran one hand through his hair. The movement carried a reminder.

She pushed a pillow out of the way and lowered to the couch. "How's Breydan?" She shouldn't have waited so long to ask.

Marcus released a sigh, settled into the rocking chair opposite her. "Okay. Last round of chemo next week. We're praying this does the trick, once and for all."

It put things in perspective, remembering Marcus's little boy. She traced the stitching on the pillow beside her. Her concerns about her career were nothing when stacked up to a word like *cancer*. A child like Breydan. *And Mom.*

"Which reminds me—you're coming to dinner Thursday night, right? Breydan wanted me to make sure."

At her nod, Marcus smiled, took a breath. By the time he released it, he'd switched gears. Kate could tell—pressed lips, hesitance in his eyes. Sometime in the past five years, their professional relationship had morphed into a friendship. She usually appreciated that.

But it added an awkward angle to business discussions. Especially . . .

Her hope dissolved even before Marcus spoke.

Especially when the news wasn't good.

"The network said no. Again." She supplied the words for him. He nodded.

"Okay." She said it slowly, humbling reality loitering in the word.

"It doesn't make any sense. You took home an Emmy. I'm as shocked as you."

Except, if she was honest, Kate wasn't that shocked. It'd been four, almost five years since the Emmy win. And her screenplays had felt forced and dry for a long time now. Which was probably why that scene she'd just watched being filmed had detoured from her original script. Then all those rejections . . .

The warning signs had practically stood in front of her belting out an ominous concerto. But she'd plugged her ears and looked the other way.

Marcus leaned forward, elbows on his knees and concern spelled out in his furrowed brow. "I know this isn't the news you wanted to hear. It's been a hard year."

She pictured little Breydan then. Propped up in a hospital bed. Pale and thin, but with a heart-melting smile powerful enough to reach past all the disappointment in the world. No, she wouldn't pout about this. "It's okay. It's fine."

And the truth was, once she got past the whole blow-to-her-pride thing, maybe it really would be. Okay, that is. Because hadn't she been telling herself for years now how wonderful it'd feel to someday write something meaningful? Full of impact. Strong.

To feel as if her words had weight and her characters, depth.

Cottony, tentative hope tiptoed in. What if this was her chance? What if this latest rejection was the nudge she needed to finally branch out and . . .

And what exactly? She'd been trying to define her blurry dream for so long, but it never quite came into view. Which is probably why she was still floundering around, writing stories that felt less and less true with every year that passed. Because she didn't have a clue what came next. What was a girl supposed to do after her heart dried up and took her creative spark with it?

I just need an open window, God. Just a sliver of sunlight to remind her He had a plan even if she didn't.

"This is a temporary setback, Kate. You'll write another script, and it'll get snatched up, just like that."

"But what if I—"

The buzz of her cell phone interrupted her. And maybe it was rude, but the temptation to escape this discomfiting conversation got the better of her. She pulled it from her bag and checked the display. New York?

She stood, mouthing a *Sorry* to Marcus. "Hello?"

"Hi, this is Frederick Langston. Is this Katharine Walker?"

Frederick Langston. A name she had seen so many times in Mom's handwriting. A name she had written out herself only weeks ago.

Dear Mr. Langston, I know this letter is out of the blue and I hope you don't find it too strange, but . . .

"That's me."

"I got your letter, Ms. Walker. We need to talk."

〜⌒

An expectant buzz hovered over the gaggle of reporters and photographers gathered for the press conference Colton Greene never should've had to give.

One stupid decision.

And now here he was, six-foot-three frame constricted by a suit and tie and folded into a metal chair, facing off with the media, who would most likely forget about him after today. Manager on one side. Coach on the other.

Make that former coach.

"It's not a death sentence, Greene."

If his manager meant the statement as a dose of encouragement, Colton wasn't swallowing. He closed one palm over the microphone in front of him. "Easy for you to say. I heard Caulfield's moving up the roster this year. You'll be repping another starter this season."

Used to be Colton was Ian Muller's biggest client. Sure, Colton had spent the bulk of his eight years in the NFL as a backup, bouncing from team to team as if caught in a never-ending game of career hopscotch. But finally—*finally*—he'd hit his stride three seasons ago. Like magic, he'd led the team two wins deep into the play-offs. First time in a decade they'd made it that far. Then two seasons ago, conference champions.

What he wouldn't give for the story to end there. Colton fingered the collar jabbing into his neck as Ian stood.

Okay. Show on the road.

Except not quite, because instead of moving behind the table-top podium, Ian looked down at Colton. "We've had this discussion a thousand times already. There's announcing, speaking gigs, your book contract. After the year you've had, a memoir will land you on the bestseller list just like that."

Ian palmed Colton's shoulder, leaning over. "You turned your life around once. You can do it again. Which is why we're here today. You're going to show the sports world—*your* world—you may be off the field, but you're not out of the game."

"Cute, Muller. Someone should put that on a motivational poster."

Ian straightened, pinched grin in place for the cameras, but not enough to mask the irritation underneath. And he probably had every right to be annoyed. Colton had been sulking for months. Maybe he *should* buck up, see this press conference as the start of something new rather than the end of a dream.

Easier said than done, though. Like throwing a pass into triple coverage. You could tell yourself it'd work out all you wanted, but that didn't stop the doubts ready to tackle the last of your confidence.

Don't think football. Think about Lilah. His one ray of hope in all of this. Hadn't she said, all those months ago, his career was the reason their relationship wasn't working? Well, after today, he no longer had a career. Which paved the way for the plan he'd dreamt up last night, when dread over today's announcement demolished any chance at sleep.

He slid his hand into one pocket, felt the velvet of the jewelry box that'd been mocking him from his bedside stand for eight months now. No longer. He'd do what he had to this morning, and tonight he'd talk to Lilah. Make everything right.

"Afternoon, everyone. Thanks for coming out today." Ian spoke into the mic extending from the podium. "We'll make this brief with time for a few questions afterward. Colton?"

Colton stood, far too tall for the wimpy podium, and as he took his place behind the mic, the flash of cameras whited out the already stark walls. Nerves, the kind he was way too seasoned to be experiencing, dashed through him.

"Hey, everyone. I'm sure you can guess why we're here today. I wish it was for a better reason." Glimpses of familiar faces poked through the haze of camera flashes. His gaze landed on a writer from *Sports World*, the one who'd been so sure all last season Colton would lead the Tigers to the Super Bowl. "I saw that column you wrote a couple months back predicting I'd be ready to play again by training camp, Crosby. Wish I could prove you right."

Crosby returned his nod, a mix of sympathy and resignation in the movement.

"But the truth is, I'm not ready to play. And unfortunately, according to my doctor, knee and shoulder specialists, surgeons, and probably every patient at St. Luke's who ever heard me groaning my way through physical therapy, I'm not gonna be ready. Not for this or any season."

And then came the pitying hush he'd known was coming. Lasted barely a second before more camera snaps, only long enough to blink. But it was enough to tighten his jaw and set to twitching muscles that had already been tested to their limits during months of therapy. *Just finish the speech*.

"This has been an amazing journey, one for which I'm incredibly grateful. I'm thankful to Coach Johnson, coaches Peterson and Dreck, my teammates . . ." The list spilled out just like he'd rehearsed, his navy tie batting the skinny mic, knuckles turning white as he gripped the podium.

"It's been a great privilege playing for this team and this city. And though it's ended much sooner than I would've liked, I'm carrying good memories into my future."

My future. Ian had instructed him to add extra verbal punch to those last words.

Instead they'd come out sounding slight and unconvincing. Ian was probably itching to kick him. Guess he just wasn't any good at faking it.

And that was the real reason he was here, wasn't it?

Because he hadn't been smart enough to leave his emotions on the sideline and focus on the game.

"You've got to ask yourself what Greene was thinking, going in for that tackle."

"Never a good idea for a QB to try and play hero after an interception like that, not unless the game is on the line. Which it wasn't up to that point."

"He's always had an impulsive streak. Saw that in his days playing college ball at the University of Iowa. But today? That was pure recklessness."

He could still hear the drone of voices from the TV in his hospital room. The sports analysts dissecting the fourth-quarter mess of what would turn out to be his last game.

Good memories? Sure, they were there somewhere. Just hard to find under the one that nagged him day in and day out, reminding him that the only one he had to blame for his future without football was himself.

He reached under the podium, fingers closing around a bottle of water. Almost done. He unscrewed the water bottle.

"So today I . . . I . . ." Water sloshed over the edge of the bottle and puddled on the table. *Say it.* "I'm regretfully retiring from the game of football." Almost before the words escaped, he lifted the bottle and gulped down a drink, thankful for the distraction as he mentally grasped for composure.

And then Ian was standing, acknowledging Coach Johnson, who replaced Colton at the podium and said something about Colton's contributions to the team and how they'd miss him and *blah, blah, blah.*

And Colton was back in his metal chair, shoulder aching and the sharp pang in his knee he'd almost gotten used to taunting him under the table.

Then came the questions.

Did his injuries require future surgery?

How long had he known his career had come to an end?

Had he still been hoping to make a comeback while in PT all these months?

Eyes to the clock at the back of the room. Ian had promised they'd cut this off at the thirty-minute mark. Only five minutes to go. At least no one had asked about—

"About the play that caused your injury—"

The last swallow from his now-empty water bottle slid down his throat, his gaze riffling through the room until it landed on the source of the question. Blond hair in a high ponytail, gray pantsuit, youngish, standing in the middle of the pack. Didn't recognize her.

"I believe that's been fairly well covered by you all. Many times." Uneasy chuckles fanned through the room. "Listen, it was a bad pass. Great interception by Fallon. I saw him take the ball down the field and my instincts kicked in. Yeah, maybe I should have let him go, but it's football, folks. The point is to not let the other team score."

A few grins peppered the crowd, and for the first time since that brutal game, he almost felt . . . heroic. Or at least justified.

But the feeling died in an instant as the glaring memory of that failed pass pressed in, along with the reminder that it wasn't his first intercepted throw of the game—but his third. The result of going into the evening game unfocused and ticked off. When the Eagles' corner had picked off the pass, he'd simply lost his mind. Anger took over, and he'd gone after the defender in a desperate flying leap that ended with him at the bottom of a pile.

Cocky, stupid, and, worse—as he'd realized when his throwing shoulder hit the turf—dangerous.

The reporter cocked one eyebrow. "Yes, well, you probably

saw some of the headlines—the ones speculating that your on-field actions were the result of your off-field turmoil."

Oh, now that was a craftily worded sentence if he ever heard one. What outlet was this reporter with anyway? "Was there a question in there somewhere?"

Another round of tense laughter, but to her credit, the reporter held his gaze. "I suppose if there was, you're not answering."

The challenge in her voice was unmistakable—as was the warning in the look Ian shot his direction. *Don't engage. Stay on topic. And whatever you do, don't mention . . .*

"Look, if you're talking about Lilah Moore, it's true. We went through a bumpy patch right before that play-off game." *Oh man.* Ian's expression was shooting bullets. Colton would probably find himself without a manager after this.

But what did he have to lose? Lilah—former actress turned political activist—had already walked out of his life, turned him down before he even had a chance to propose that January day. Annoying thing was, he couldn't even hate her for it. If there was a chance of getting her back, he'd rush at it like so many defensive linemen had rushed him over the years.

And that's when the idea took hold. Crazy, impulsive . . . scattered pieces of his once-shattered hope slowly forming into a whole picture.

The ring box in his pocket felt suddenly weighty with significance. Maybe there was a reason he'd brought it this morning. Some kind of divine foreshadowing. Not that he'd been much good at praying lately, not since all the prayers about his injuries seemed to go unanswered. But what if God was opening a door?

What if he won Lilah back right now, in front of the cameras and everything?

If he could just find the right words.

"So you *do* credit your performance in that game to your high-profile break—"

"I credit my performance to a bad pass." He avoided looking at Ian. Instead made eye contact with the nosy reporter who he just might thank if this turned out well. "As for Lilah, she's . . . she's an amazing woman."

She really was. In addition to her political activities, she still directed Colton's foundation—not that they'd gotten very far turning the foundation into anything worthwhile. He'd mostly started it last year because that's what other athletes did. But if anyone could make something of it, Lilah could.

"Even after all these months, I . . . I still . . ." *I still love her.* The words stalled in his throat, hazy uncertainty fogging over him. *Say it, Colt. Make the grand gesture.*

Why couldn't he get the words out?

And then that same reporter. "Well, have you talked to her since her engagement?"

A thudding silence dropped like an anvil.

"To Ray Bannem. The governor's reelection campaign manager. Have you spoken with her since the news broke last night?"

Another camera flash.

"I . . . have not."

Lilah? Engaged?

To someone else.

Hadn't his world already tilted enough?

Congratulate her. Say you wish her the best. Smile. Don't let them see . . .

But all he could do was stand, empty water bottle tipping and rolling down the table.

"I believe we're done here."

2

Kate probably would've lost this game regardless. But with Frederick Langston's words ping-ponging around in her brain, her demise was a certainty.

"I know it's a crazy thing to ask. A long shot. And an expensive one at that. But after I got your letter—"

"Stay on the road, Katie."

Breydan's laughter bounced into her thoughts, and she angled her Wii remote, eyes latched on the TV in the eight-year-old's bedroom. "I'm trying."

On the flat screen, Breydan's car whizzed past the finish line. He dropped his controller, lifting skinny arms into the air. "First place." The futon they sat on barely shifted at Breydan's movement.

"Every stinkin' time." And then, just like it had for the past four races, the game cut her off before she had a chance to finish the course. "You know what I'm going to do? I'm going to buy my own Wii, practice in my free time, and next time, I'm so gonna win." Or at least steer well enough to complete the race.

"It's not my fault I'm good at Mario Kart and you're not."

"Why, you . . ." She reached out as if to tickle him, then instead leaned in for a side hug. He tried to wriggle away, feigned an annoyed protest, but then—just like she knew he would—gave in and let her squeeze.

When she finally released him, Breydan looked up at her, brown eyes brimming with playfulness despite the circles of purple underneath. "Another race?"

His bald scalp and tiny frame might have been his standout features to anyone else, but to Kate, it was still Breydan's gap-toothed smile that captured her heart without fail. She reached for her remote. "Another race, for sure."

And not only because she'd lose to Breydan a hundred times if it made him happy, but also because she'd heard an unfamiliar male voice drifting from the kitchen when she arrived at Marcus and Hailey's.

They thought they were so sneaky, didn't they? Another blind date. And a surprise one, at that. At least she'd been able to escape up to Breydan's bedroom before Hailey had a chance to whisk her into the kitchen to meet their latest scrounged-up Prince Charming.

And here she'd been hoping to snag some alone time with Hail. Advice. She needed advice way more than she needed a man. Because while she'd been praying for an open window, in one short phone call with Frederick Langston, God had gone and blown the walls off her house.

And she had no idea what to do.

"You ready to go, Brey?" Hailey appeared in the doorway of Breydan's bedroom. "Your ride's going to be here any minute. All packed?"

Breydan stood and walked to the twin bed nudged up to the opposite wall, its football-patterned comforter matching the rest of the room's décor—football-shaped lamp on an end table, framed posters. "Katie doesn't want me to go." He picked up his backpack.

Kate rose, palmed his head as if it were a basketball. "Oh, I'll get over it and forgive you, B-man. This once."

Breydan's focus flitted from Kate to his bag and back to her. "It's just . . . Luke is the only friend whose house I ever get to go to 'cause he's sick too, so his bedroom is all sterile and stuff. But I don't have to go."

"Don't be silly, mister. Go to your sleepover."

He dropped his bag and barreled into her for another hug—the full thing this time, bony arms extending around her waist. "Thanks, Katie."

"Count yourself lucky," Hailey said, picking up her son's bag and shaking reddish bangs from her forehead. "Anyone else calls her Katie and they get clobbered."

"I'm special." Breydan said the smug words into her stomach, squeezed again, and then backed up.

"Oh wait. Can't believe I almost forgot." Kate reached for the messenger bag she'd plopped on the futon and pulled out a blue-and-orange jersey.

"No way. Peyton Manning?"

"Of course. You did say he's your favorite, right?" Wouldn't surprise her if she'd gotten it wrong. Football was a language she didn't speak. But for Breydan, she'd do anything—including sitting through a game that made about as much sense to her as Swahili.

Breydan was pulling the jersey over his T-shirt when a honk sounded from outside. "That's my ride. Thanks for the jersey, Katie. Luke's gonna be so jealous." He slung his backpack over his shoulder and raced from the room, the sound of footsteps thumping down the stairs tracking his movement.

Hailey stuck her head into the hallway. "Don't forget to say bye to Dad on the way out." She turned back to Kate. "I think dinner's almost ready."

Kate narrowed her eyes at her friend. "You guys will never give up, will you?"

Hailey flipped straight hair over her shoulder, then bent down to pick up one of Breydan's abandoned plastic footballs. "Don't know what you're talking about."

Kate folded her arms. "I know an ambush when I see one. Or in this case, hear it." And even if she hadn't already heard the man's voice, there'd been the soft lilt of jazz music trickling through the first floor. The fancy setup of the dining room table. Both Hailey and Marcus in nice clothes.

And she, in her oldest jeans and barely enough makeup to count. Lovely.

"Sending Breydan away, though? That was low."

Hailey tossed the football into a toy-filled net hanging in one corner of the room. "Hey, for the record, we didn't invite Rhett until *after* Breydan got asked to the sleepover."

Rhett, huh. "So many *Gone with the Wind* references just went through my head I don't even know which one to pick. I should just leave."

Hailey shrugged, striped sundress swaying around her ankles as she continued picking up Breydan's room. "Fine with me. Means more garlic breadsticks and baked ziti with sundried tomato pesto for the rest of us."

Kate froze in the doorway, blinking to adjust to the hallway's dim lighting.

"Gotcha, didn't I?" Hailey laughed.

Turning around, Kate grimaced. "You don't play fair, Laramie."

Hailey stopped in front of her, freckled cheeks spreading with her grin. "It's simply a matter of knowing one's opponent. I happen to know you eat lettuce straight from a bag most days. And by 'straight from,' I mean you don't even bother with a plate. Just pour the dressing in the bag and stick a fork in."

"That's called efficiency." And a good way to avoid dishes.

Hailey nudged her out the door. "It's called desperation. Besides, Marcus vouches for this guy."

She moved toward the staircase, slid one palm along its polished banister as she made her way down. "Marcus is my agent, not my matchmaker."

"We could've had you married eight times over by now if you weren't so stubborn." Hailey's words punched the air behind her. "It's been six years since Gil, Kate. You gotta move on one of these days. Don't you think—"

Hailey cut off as Kate stilled at the bottom of the steps, icy hurt sharpening through her. She caught sight of herself in the mirrored entryway hutch—brunette hair trickling from a messy bun. "That's not fair, bringing up Gil. You know what that does to me."

Dredged up a knotty mess of emotions—that's what. Seriously, a therapist could have a field day exhuming her graveyard of Gil-related memories.

In the mirror, she saw Hailey drop onto a stair and sigh. "You write romance for a living. Don't you ever want to take a chance on finding your own?"

Kate looked toward the living room, where sunset spilled through tall windows and stained the opposite wall in reds and oranges. Mom used to say the fiery sunsets were her favorite.

"Go write something important."

She couldn't think of Mom without thinking of her words. Eight years hadn't done anything to diminish their pull. If only she'd found some way to live them out.

Now—maybe, finally—she had, thanks to Frederick Langston. That is, if she could conjure up the funds. It meant putting scriptwriting on the back burner for a while. That and the half-dozen half-written sophomore novels wasting away on her computer.

She lowered to the stair beside Hailey. "It's not romance I'm looking for."

"Isn't there even a little piece of you—"

"Nope." Gil had rubbed the sheen off that once-sparkly possibility, left only rusty disinterest in its place. "Hail, I got this call the other day. When I was on set with Marcus. From the development director at the James Foundation."

Hailey shifted on the stair. "That's the foundation your mom helped start, right?"

"Not just helped. She wrote the grant application and made the presentation that got them five hundred thousand in federal seed dollars." She'd named the foundation after the verse in James in the Bible—the one about taking care of widows and orphans.

The Italian aroma wafting from the kitchen pulled a hungry growl from Kate's stomach. She'd done her best to support the foundation. Even in the lean months—when she'd burned through her last advance and had to beg for extra hours at the Willis—she'd managed to continue sending small checks.

Because of Mom. Because she believed in the foundation's work. Because it made her feel a part of something.

"So why'd he call you?"

"They need a writer. For three months. In Africa."

Three months traveling through six countries, documenting the nonprofit's work building health centers and training medical professionals, with special emphasis on pediatrics in communities with orphanages. At the end of it, she'd help write an extended annual report that would be packaged for donors as part of the foundation's forty-year anniversary.

"*We had a federal grant to cover the project but it got yanked away,*" Frederick Langston had explained. "*But then I received your letter.*"

The one she'd written on a whim on a day when she'd been missing Mom. A letter simply to thank the foundation for carrying on the work Flora Walker had begun, asking if there was anything she could do to help—freelance writing, perhaps. *Something important, something that matters.*

Mr. Langston had answered her letter in a bigger way than she'd ever imagined. Called it a sign and offered to change her life—at least for three months. But something told her three months would be enough. Because it was a beginning—a first step toward fulfilling her promise to Mom.

The one reality still tethering her hopes to the ground? Money.

"Africa. Whoa."

"I know. The really exciting thing is, Frederick said I would have time to work on my own interviews and writing while I'm there too. My head's spinning with book ideas. Gritty, real-life kind of stuff. I'd come home with so much material."

The whole thing felt weighty and important and . . . and everything her current life of writing romance wasn't.

"I'm sensing a *but*."

"They can't pay me. They'd cover my lodging, but that's it." No income for three months. Expensive plane tickets. Meals. And a mortgage and car payment and health insurance that wouldn't stop just because she'd left the country. She'd have to give up her job at the Willis Tower, too.

"You can't let money be what holds you back."

"I spent almost all my savings buying my house. And I haven't sold a script in over a year."

Hailey stood. "Okay, new game plan. I'm going to go back to the kitchen and let your date off gently. Then, over dinner, you and Marcus and I will come up with a way to get you some money. If we all put our heads together, we can come up with something."

"But Rhett—"

Hailey waved one hand. "Honestly, he's only twenty-five. And he's super tan. You'd look like you ran through a cloud of chalk dust next to him."

Kate groaned and flopped back on the stairs. "Wow, I'm old and pale."

"And don't forget broke."

"It's so nice to have such an encouraging friend."

Hailey patted her head. "Hey, you're lucky to have me. I don't just set up dates for you—I break them when necessary. I'll be back." Her laughter lingered as she disappeared down the hallway.

Kate pulled herself up, torn between guilt and relief. What if the guy back in the kitchen was nice? Maybe she should tell Hailey to let him stay. They could eat fast, end things early.

She stood, Hailey's name on the tip of her tongue, but the chirping of a text message cut her off. She let out a breath and pulled her phone free from her purse. *Logan?* Her brother texted about as often as she trimmed her hair. Which was twice a year *if* she was feeling like an overachiever.

Have you talked to Dad or Raegan tonight? Can't get ahold of them.

She paced from the stairway to the living room and tapped out a reply.

No. But Dad's on every committee in town and Rae has like 3 jobs. Just try later.

Her phone rang only seconds after she pressed Send. She lifted it to her ear. "Wow, a text and a call in one day, bro?"

"You haven't heard."

Why was there near panic in Logan's voice? "Heard what?"

"A tornado hit Maple Valley thirty minutes ago. They're reporting massive damage. I can't get ahold of anyone, and . . ."

Her heart hammered.

"I'm worried, Kate."

❧

The banging on his apartment door wrenched Colton from a blurry dream and hard sleep. He tried to lift his head, but the weight of it roused a throaty groan and sent his face back to his pillow.

Except the leather under his cheek wasn't a pillow. He opened one eye. Coffee table. TV. Fireplace. He was in the living room?

The pounding on his door continued, almost in sync with the throbbing at his temples. Another moan, and he turned onto his back, the ceiling fan's whir overhead brushing his hair over his ears. Why had he slept on the couch?

And why did he feel like death?

And who at the door couldn't take a hint?

Probably the same person who'd been calling and texting incessantly since the press conference days ago. "Go away, Ian." He croaked the words, tongue heavy and head thumping at each syllable.

And that's when last night finally came into partial focus. The bar. His third night in the place. The drinks. The guy on the end stool. Had they fought? He lifted his hand to his jaw, winced at the sting of pain when he felt the tender spot.

Oh man, it'd been years since he'd been in a bar fight.

"It's Logan. Let me in, Greene."

Logan Walker, his college buddy—the only friend who'd spent more time at his side in the hospital than Lilah.

Lilah. Over. For good.

Another knock.

"Just a sec." Colton stood, bare feet shuffling over the sheepskin rug covering his living room floor. The hammer in his head continued its pulsing as he made his way to the front door. He glanced down before opening the door—jeans, T-shirt. Same clothes he'd worn to the bar.

He pulled the door open. "Let me guess. Ian called you."

"Didn't have to." Logan pushed past Colton, dropped his phone and keys on the entryway table, and made for the living room.

Colton closed the door. "Make yourself at home."

"Don't get sarcastic on me or I'll deck you. Again." Logan abandoned his suit jacket over the back of the couch, then made quick work of opening the patio blinds and pushing the glass door aside.

Colton squinted against the assault of sunlight. But the fresh air? Had to admit that felt good. "Wait, deck me again?" He worked his sore jaw. Logan had done that?

Logan turned. Blue tie, white shirt, pants as uncreased as Colton's were wrinkled. And for a moment, shame pushed past the pounding in his head. That his friend—good, respectable, always-do-the-right-thing Logan Walker—was seeing him like this.

Hung over. Bruised. A mess.

"I didn't want to hit you, but you insisted on driving."

"You punched me. I-I thought . . ." He ran a hand through shaggy hair. "There was this jerk at the end of the bar. I don't remember exactly . . ."

"Two of you got bounced before you could get into it. Bartender took your keys, said my number was the only favorite in your contacts."

Yes. Because he'd finally deleted Lilah from the list. Apparently all those times she'd visited him at the hospital, the constant checking in as he worked his way through physical therapy—none of it meant what he'd thought: that there was still a spark of life in their relationship, that she still cared.

No, apparently she'd only stayed in touch due to her work with his foundation, all the while moving on with her personal life.

Which felt worse? The physical ache that seemed to have a grip on his entire body, or the humiliation slogging through him?

Logan only stared at him as Colton slumped onto one of the stools at the peninsula counter dividing the living room and kitchen. "Guess I should say thanks."

"Don't thank me. Just tell me what you were thinking." Logan rounded the counter and entered the kitchen. He reached for a coffee mug hanging from a peg in the wall and slid it under the Keurig. "I know your life hasn't been a load of fun lately, but getting drunk in a seedy bar? Picking a fight with a stranger?" Logan started the coffee maker. "That's the kind of thing you stopped doing five, six years ago. Thought you'd gotten it out of your system."

Elbows on the counter top, Colton rubbed his eyes. "I didn't pick the fight. I remember that much." The Keurig gurgled to life. "He recognized me, made some joke about headlines and Lilah . . ."

Logan waited until the coffee finished, then set the mug in front of Colton. "Drink up."

Colton obeyed, liquid hot and bitter in his throat.

"So it was about Lilah." Logan ran in the same political circles as Lilah, had actually been the one to introduce Colton to Lilah—recommended her for the job heading up the Colton Greene Foundation. Which was a joke in and of itself. Between Colton's career—and then the loss thereof—and Lilah's political activist work, they hadn't even picked a cause to focus on. It was a foundation without a purpose.

A little too similar to the man it was named after.

Logan started a second cup of coffee, then turned back to Colton and pressed both palms on the counter. "I heard about the engagement. Have you talked to her?"

Colton shook his head, looked up from his already half-empty mug. She'd stopped calling after her fourth attempt went unanswered. "You?"

"She's worried about you, Colt. We both are."

"Yeah? Well, don't be." He threw back the last of his coffee.

Logan pulled the second cup of coffee from the Keurig, but instead of drinking from it, set it in front of Colton—hard enough that liquid sloshed over the edge. "Clearly you need another."

"Walker, I appreciate the ride home last night. But you can leave now."

Logan's eyes narrowed. "You know what you're reminding me of? The sullen kid I met freshman year of college. Such a huge chip on his shoulder you'd think the entire world was out to get him."

Colton pushed his stool away from the counter. "I'm sorry the fact that my career and the woman I thought I was going to marry being ripped from me at the same time means I'm a little worse for the wear—"

"Worse for the wear? Dude, you smell like a distillery."

Colton jerked off the stool so hard it tipped and dropped to the floor. He skulked to the patio door.

"Listen for a minute, will you? I didn't just stop today to check on you. I wanted to tell you about my dad."

Colton froze, fingers in place on the screen door's handle. He hadn't seen his friend's dad for years. Not since college. But the man . . . Well, he was a good guy. Took Colton under his wing during Colton's years as Logan's dorm-mate at the University of Iowa.

Colton had no doubt the man was a big part of the reason he'd eventually been able to sneak free from the grip of childhood shadows.

Oh, they were still there—dark and hazy as always—but he'd finally stopped peering into them. Trying to remember . . .

Yes, Case Walker's influence had had something to do with that. "What about your dad?"

"There was a tornado last night, major damage. I spent the whole evening trying to get ahold of my family. Dad sprained his shoulder."

Colton let out a breath he hadn't realized he was holding.

"I'm heading back to Iowa for a few days to help out. Taking Charlie with me. Thought maybe you'd want to come along. Get out of LA. Clear your head. Besides, Charlie misses you."

For the briefest moment, the thought of his friend's three-year-old daughter was almost enough to lend a hint of a smile to Colton's face. Almost. "Don't know."

"Well, I've got a flight this afternoon, so make your decision fast."

Colton nodded, opened the screen door, and stepped outside onto his sun-warmed wooden balcony. Below him, palm trees surrounded his complex's recreation area, the sound of splashes and laughter lifting from the pool below.

He propped his elbows on the balcony railing and sighed. Shouldn't have lost it with Logan. It's not like he had an abundance of friends. And with no family and now Lilah out of his life, he should hold tighter to the few he had.

It's like he was eighteen again. Alone. Aged out of a foster system that had never wanted him anyway.

He heard movement in the kitchen through the screen door. Cupboards opening, a pan rattling. Had Logan decided to cook or something? *Good luck finding food, Walker.*

His phone suddenly blared to life from his pocket. Didn't have to look at it to know who was calling. He slid it out and lifted it to his ear. "This is Colton."

"Wow, you answered. Color me shocked."

"What is it, Ian?" He glanced into the apartment, saw Logan pulling a carton from the fridge. *Huh, I have eggs?*

"Okay, fine. Skipping the small talk. Got a simple question for you: You going to pull yourself together or not? Because I don't have time to waste, Greene. I've been busting my butt trying to line up appearances, sponsorships—anything to keep the last of your career alive. But if you're going to continue ignoring my calls while partying at night, let me know now so I can stop putting my rep on the line for you."

Colton turned back to the balcony railing, the fog in his head finally starting to clear—probably from the coffee and the late-afternoon sunshine.

The flint in Ian's tone.

"Ian—"

"I heard about last night. And the night before. And the night before that. If you want even a hope of salvaging your career, you've got to clean up your act. Now."

"What career? I'm done. Washed up." He could still taste the doctor's sour words: *"If you keep playing, you'll do the kind of permanent damage we can't fix."*

Colton Greene. Unfixable.

Sounded about right somehow.

"You still have your foundation."

With Lilah at the helm? How was he supposed to handle that?

"And you'd make a great sports-show host, Colt. I've been saying that's your obvious plan B ever since the injury. You've got the looks and the talent. But nobody's going to take you seriously if you can't pull yourself together."

Colton ran one hand along the wooden railing, pulled back with a jerk when he felt a splinter poke his palm.

"So that's my question: Can you pull yourself together? Yes or no?"

"Yes."

"That wasn't even close to convincing."

Colton closed his eyes and tipped his head, the heat of the sun, his sore jaw, Ian's pushing . . . all of it demanding a deep breath and forced calm. *He's only trying to help.* "Yes, Ian. What do you want me to do?"

"Lay low for a while. Stay out of the spotlight."

The smell of the eggs Logan must be frying drifted outside, along with the memory of his friend's offer. *"Heading to Iowa . . . come along. Clear your head."* There were probably worse places to lay low than Iowa.

Ian's voice cut in. "One more thing. You've had a book deal on the table for over a year. It's time to get serious. Publisher's getting antsy. You've fired two ghostwriters."

Colton stiffened, apprehension beating through him. "Didn't fire them. Just didn't work out."

It had sounded like such a good idea at first, the book. After all, he had the life story people liked to read. Rowdy D1 quarterback with the painful past and bad-boy image, drafted right out of college, always in trouble during the off-season. Then just like that, during his second season in the NFL, he turns his life around after his friend coaxes him to church on Christmas Eve.

The friend . . . Logan.

But he hadn't realized when he'd signed that book contract what it'd mean, working with a writer. Hadn't known they'd dig so deep. Poke and prod at shadows he'd rather not illuminate.

"One bestseller of a sports memoir could rewrite your reputation and jump-start your future, Colton. You need this."

36

Ian paused, his forceful stretch of silence driving his point home. "I emailed you details on a couple other writers. We have to nail this thing—I'm talking book drafted in a month or two. They've already pushed the release date back twice. They're not going to do it again. Choose a writer. I want a name by Monday. Otherwise I'll pick for you."

Colton closed his eyes against the sunlight, clawing humidity slithering over his skin. "Fine." He'd review the information. Probably on the plane trip to Iowa. Yes, sometime between stepping outside and Ian's ultimatum, he'd made the decision—he'd go with Logan.

He had to. Because something told him if he didn't, he'd find himself in another bar tonight. And on the couch again tomorrow. Same headache, same blurred thoughts.

That Christmas Eve memory further away than ever.

And the gnawing question impossible to ignore—who was Colton Greene anymore without football?

～◦

The shimmer of a full moon shone like a beacon's gaze over the rolling landscape, heavy Iowa wind rustling through cornfields crowded with lanky stalks that bent and rose in waves. Kate turned her Focus onto the gravel lane that led to Dad's acreage, nighttime painting a blueish tint over the rustic wood exterior of the house just now coming into view.

Home.

She hadn't planned to make the drive today. When she'd talked to Dad and Raegan on the phone this morning during her breaks at the Willis, they'd both insisted she hold off. Especially since she'd already been planning to come home for the Labor Day festival in a few days—which might not be happening anymore.

But as she'd worked in the closet-sized office, handing out tickets to the elevator she'd never bothered to ride herself, she hadn't been able to shake the anxiety of the night before, of those few tense hours waiting to hear if everyone back home was okay. The three hundred and seventy-five miles between Chicago and Maple Valley somehow gaped wider and wider with each hour that passed.

A treacherous storm had endangered her family and pummeled the community that'd never stopped feeling like home.

And she wasn't there.

By the time she punched out, she'd made the decision: She'd pack her car, hit I-80, and make the seven-hour drive during what was left of today.

Of course, today had slid into tomorrow about an hour ago—which meant she'd be arriving to a slumbering household. She pulled into the driveway and parked by the basketball hoop standing guard at the edge of the cement. Always her brothers' first stop whenever they happened to be home at the same time. Their cousin Seth usually joined in, too. He'd lived with Dad and Raegan for over a year now.

Drawn shades and closed blinds blocked all the front windows of the house—all but one. Her window, second floor, curtains pulled aside, as if the house slept with one eye open. Kate grinned as she stepped from her car, warm breeze skittering over her bare arms. She made quick work of unloading her suitcase, entering through the door she knew she'd find unlocked at the side of the garage, hunting around for the house key Dad usually kept hidden behind a decorative wood *Welcome Home* knickknack on top of the fuse box.

She slid the key into the doorknob, a trill of delight vibrating through her even as travel weariness chipped away at the last of her energy. There was just something about this place . . . and the uncanny way it untangled knotty emotions before she'd even entered the house.

An apple-cinnamon scent wrapped around her as soon as she stepped inside, as familiar as the lineup of shoes in the entryway. She lugged her suitcase up the split foyer's few steps, careful not to bang it against the wall, and treaded into the living room.

She didn't have to turn on any lights to know the spacious room probably looked much the same as it had last Christmas—minus the ornament-laden tree. Brown leather couch with throw pillows in earthy shades, fireplace mantel packed with family photos, a smattering of books and magazines splayed across the coffee table. The living room opened into a dining room, where tall patio doors peeked out on the moonlit backyard.

Thump.

Kate froze at the sound coming from upstairs. Who had she woken? Her fingers tightened around her suitcase handle as she waited.

Silence.

She let out her breath and padded toward the stairway, up the steps, then down the hallway leading to her bedroom. She stopped off at the bathroom—brushed her teeth, traded her contacts for glasses, and debated whether to dig around in her suitcase for pajamas. She was already wearing comfy cotton shorts and a T-shirt. Close enough.

Within minutes, she stood in front of her bedroom door and turned the knob—slowly. Pushed the door open—slowly. No creaking. *My room. My bed . . .* her luxurious, full-of-pillows, antique king-sized canopy bed. The one she'd have in her town-house now if it wasn't way too big.

She abandoned her suitcase just inside the bedroom door and walked to the bed. She couldn't see much—only shadows in the dark.

Did it smell different in here? Sort of . . . musky? Masculine? *Huh*. Maybe Dad was trying out a new air freshener.

She slipped off her glasses and laid them on the bedside table. Inched back the covers, lowered onto the mattress, pulled up her feet . . . stretched, rolled . . .

Hit a wall. A warm . . . muscled . . . *moving* wall.

The sound of springs bouncing joined her breathless gasp as the man—*WHAT?*—flew from the bed. The sudden movement and her own panic ended with her snarled in sheets and then thudding to the floor, too shocked to even squeal.

"What . . . in . . . the world?"

Yes, definitely a man's voice. And not Dad's. Or Seth's.

She kicked free of the sheet that'd come off the bed with her, shoved her hair from her face, and looked up. A man's form stood frozen on the other side of the room.

He was in my bed. He was in my bed and he's not wearing a shirt. He was in my bed and he's not wearing a shirt and now he's coming over here . . .

She scrambled backward and bumped into the bedside table, knocking her glasses to the floor. She grabbed and fit them in place, then jumped to her feet.

"Are you hurt? Did you hit your head or anything when you fell?" He rounded the bed. "Are you going to scream?"

Like she could play twenty questions when her heart was Fred Astaire–ing it up inside her chest.

Fight or flight? Fight or flight?

She slapped at the light switch on the wall, but instead of the light turning on, the ceiling fan hummed to life. The man in the bed must've heard her huff of frustration, though, because he reached for the lamp on the bedside stand, dim light pushing against the dark.

And then he was standing in front of her, all six-foot-who-

40

knew of him. Gym shorts. Sandy hair tousling under the fan's whirring. Eyes so ridiculously blue-green the Pacific might as well give up. The faintest scar carved into the corner of one eyebrow, however, probably expelled him from flawless territory.

"Uh . . . hi?" Sleepy confusion huddled in his voice.

Her heartbeat finally began to steady. "Who are you and what do you want?"

The man's sheepish discomfort shifted into an almost-smirk—great, add dimples to the list—and he brushed a pillow feather from his shorts. "Who am I and what do I want? Did I wake up in a poorly scripted detective show?" He raked his fingers through his hair.

"You're not my dad. Or my sister. Or my cousin—"

"Astute."

She folded her arms now. "So who are you?"

"Colton Greene." He said it as if it explained everything.

"Is that supposed to mean something to me?" Actually, now that she thought about it, maybe it did sound at least a little familiar. Did he live in Maple Valley? Was he some friend of Seth's? A visitor she'd heard Dad talk about?

He tipped his head to one side. Shrugged. "Well, anyway, I'm a guest. Not an intruder or anything."

"Why should I believe you?"

"Uh . . . because I was asleep." He drawled his words. "I'm not wearing a shirt. What kind of thief comes in half-dressed and goes to bed instead of, like, making off with the china and silver?"

"I don't know. Could be your MO."

He mimicked her folded-arms pose. "All right, you nailed it. They call me the Narcoleptic Burglar." He did droll amazingly well. "Now whatcha gonna do?"

Was sinking into the floor an option? "Listen, you . . ." *You what?* Come on, she was a *writer*. Shouldn't the whole sentence-forming thing work better than this?

He cocked one eyebrow, waiting, his amusement so obvious it was practically a third person in this little exchange.

But that's when her bedroom door flung open and Raegan spilled into the room. And Logan.

Wait . . . Logan?

"Kate!" Raegan flung herself at Kate for a hug. "We heard a thump and voices and . . ." She stepped back, eyes widening. "You met Colton."

Colton stepped forward. "Oh, she skipped the meeting part and went straight to getting into bed with—"

He clamped his lips together when Kate threw him a glare. Which she promptly turned on Raegan when her sister let out a snort. And then on to Logan. "What are you doing here? Aren't you supposed to be in LA?"

Logan pulled her into a hug. "Nice to see you, too, sis."

"You could've told me you were coming home." Despite the annoyance in her voice, she hugged her brother.

"Thought it'd be fun to surprise you when you came home for the festival." Logan glanced at Colton. "Sorry we gave Colton your bedroom, but this is the only one in the house with a king-sized bed. Guess you got a bigger surprise than planned."

Bigger indeed. The man was the size of a lumberjack. Or a linebacker. Or . . .

Her mind hitched on that last thought. Linebacker. Football. *Ohhhh. Colton. Greene.*

It wasn't Dad she'd heard say the name. It was Breydan. All those times when he talked to her about football. Showed her the bobbleheads of his favorite players that lined the windowsill in his bedroom.

Somewhere in the recesses of her obviously not so quick-on-the-draw brain she'd known Logan had a football player friend. But apparently putting two and two together took extra skills in the muddle of a post-seven-hour drive.

Colton Greene. The NFL quarterback. The one in the headlines.

In her bedroom.

"So now do you believe I'm not a burglar?" He lifted one corner of his mouth in a half smile she might've called half-cute if she wasn't wholly mortified.

Raegan laced her arm through Kate's. "C'mon, let's go wake up Seth and have a late-night snack. We've got a tub of cookie dough in the freezer."

They were nearly out the door when Colton's voice sounded behind them. "Welcome home, Kate."

Welcome home, indeed.

3

*A*ll right, Charlie, what we're doing right now, it's between you and me and good ol' Aunt Jemima here. That's it."

The sound of a man's deep voice stopped Kate in her tracks, just shy of turning the corner that led into Dad's kitchen. The rich aroma of coffee had been enough to lull her from sleep and lure her down the hallway. But in her just-woken-up state, she had somehow forgotten that it wasn't just family staying in the house.

It all came flooding back now. The football player. Logan and Charlie. And the incident that newly topped her list of most embarrassing moments. Crawling into bed with Colton Greene. What were the chances anyone in her family would ever let her live that one down?

Colton's voice carried to her now. " . . . can't tell your dad since he's such a health nut. So this stays a secret."

What stays a secret?

Kate inched forward, carpet tickling her bare feet, and peeked around the corner. Adorable three-year-old Charlotte stood at the island counter on a chair. Though Logan's adopted daughter didn't resemble the Walker clan—not with those reddish Shirley Temple curls and green eyes—that didn't alter her rank as family darling.

Next to Charlie, Colton held a bottle of syrup, lifting it higher and higher as he poured it over a plate piled with waffles, Charlie's giggles mixing with the sound of trilling birds outside the window over the kitchen sink.

And oh, the sound of those giggles. . . . Charlie still didn't talk much—a fact that had to concern Logan. But she didn't have to form sentences to make obvious her affection for Colton. Her upward gaze was downright adoring.

Apparently this wasn't the first time the man had interacted with her niece.

"All right. Syrup—check. Walnuts and banana slices—check. I can't think of anything we're missing." Colton dabbed his finger through the syrup and licked it off. A navy blue T-shirt stretched taut over shoulders that seemed even wider this morning. "Anything else you want with your insanely unhealthy breakfast?"

Instead of answering, Charlie mimicked Colton's taste of syrup, licked her lips, and grinned up at him, pink-and-white polka-dot pajamas hanging loose over her toddler frame. *Hello, Kodak moment.*

Colton bent his legs to stand eye level with Charlotte. "You can tell me if there's anything else you want, honey."

His gentle words balanced in the air, and for a moment Kate thought Charlotte might actually respond verbally. *Come on, Charlie. Let us hear your voice.*

Instead, Charlotte leaned over to kiss Colton's cheek and then wrapped her arms around his neck. He responded immediately, pulling her the rest of the way to him. "It's okay. You'll talk when you're ready. Besides, we're already simpatico, you and me, words or no words." He tapped her nose, then shifted her around to his back. "Piggyback ride to the table, m'lady."

Kate hugged her arms to herself, a disconcerting warmth wiggling through her, along with the realization that she couldn't go into the kitchen looking like this. She still wore the clothes she had slept in—baggy blue pants that didn't quite reach her ankles and a T-shirt. Her brown hair spilled from a messy ponytail, and her glasses kept sliding down her nose.

"Oh, hey, I know what we forgot," Colton said, snapping his fingers as he rose from setting Charlie down at the table. "Whipped cream." He moved toward the fridge, jeans and bare feet visible now.

Uh, yeah, she'd come back for coffee later. Like after she'd dressed properly. Put in her contacts. Traded bedraggled for at least halfway put together.

But Charlie picked that moment to look away from Colton, her jade eyes hooking on Kate's peeking around the corner. Next thing she knew, Charlie was clambering from her chair and hurling herself toward Kate.

Instinct opened her arms for her niece, knees bending. When she rose, she brought Charlie with her. "Charlie Walker, my favorite girl in the world." Over Charlie's shoulder she saw Colton's expression move from surprise into a half smile that carved dimples into his cheeks.

Okay, so maybe there were worse things than being seen in her pajamas. She tightened her arms around Charlie, gaze roaming around the room—stainless steel appliances, a collection of pots hanging over the center island, swirls of beige, copper, and brown in the floor's ceramic tiling. Granite counters and cherry cupboards wrapped around the room.

Streaming rays through the patio doors filled the open space. In the distance, the sun lit the rural landscape that embraced the spot Mom and Dad had picked to build their house—a few miles outside Maple Valley, a rolling ravine covered with a tangle of blue ash, buckeye, and shagbark hickory trees descended into a twisting creekbed.

Her gaze pulled back at Colton's cough. He stood in front of her now, can of whipped cream in one hand, damp tips of his hair evidence he'd recently showered. But hadn't shaved. A perfect five o'clock shadow covered his chin and cheeks. "Hey."

"H-hey. Hi. Morning. Good. I mean, good morning."

He reached forward to ruffle Charlie's hair. "Let me guess: The talking thing—doesn't work so well pre-coffee."

"Astute." She repeated the word he'd used last night.

Oh, that smile. No wonder he'd landed on as many entertainment magazine covers as sports mags—a tidbit she'd learned from Raegan as they had stood around the kitchen munching on cookies with Logan and Seth into the wee hours of the morning. She'd heard all about how Colton had turned into the NFL's media darling in the past few years, landed a starting spot when the Tigers' former QB got injured. How he'd been the stuff of Super Bowl predictions.

How it all ended with an injury last season. Apparently he'd just announced his retirement earlier this week. Is that why he'd come to Iowa with Logan?

Instead of joining them in the kitchen last night, Colton had insisted on clearing out of Kate's room. Once he'd transferred his stuff into Beckett's old room, he'd never come back out.

Kate lowered Charlie to the floor now. "You know Logan would develop a permanent tick if he saw what you are feeding his daughter."

Colton's nose wrinkled as he cast a guilty glance toward Charlie's plate. "It's not that bad of a breakfast."

"It is if you're planning to top it with that." She nudged her head toward the canned whipped cream.

"What's wrong with this?"

Charlie climbed back into her chair. "If you've gone to all

47

the trouble to make waffles, it's only right to top them with real whipped cream."

Colton looked from Kate to the can back to her. "Didn't know Logan had a gourmet chef for a sister."

"Ha! Hardly. It's just that when it comes to waffles, well, I have standards." She moved to the fridge.

"Then I really don't know how to tell you this. . . ."

She ducked her head in the fridge and spotted what she'd hoped to find. She pulled out the carton of whipping cream. "Tell me what?"

"I didn't make those waffles. They're from a box in the freezer. The only thing I did was toast them."

"Colton Greene." She let her jaw drop in exaggerated shock and shook her head. "I'd scold you further, but truthfully, breakfast is the only meal I do with any kind of style. Lunch and dinner . . . it's all PB&J and mac 'n' cheese. Still, I think I'd better introduce you to the joys of real whipped cream." The sound of Charlie's fork scraping against her plate sounded behind them. Kate pointed to the pantry. "You get the powdered sugar, I'll go hunting for the hand mixer."

Only minutes later, she had the mixer going and the cream was starting to fluff. Beside her, Colton took a drink of the coffee she'd poured. Sputtered. "What the—"

"Dad must've made it." Kate's voice rose over the mixer. Her own mug was already half-empty. "He likes it muddy."

"Muddy? Try swamp-like." Colton motioned to the bowl. "You do realize by the time you've got that ready, Charlie will be done eating."

"It's the principle of the thing. Little more sugar."

He lifted the bag of sugar and poured until Kate signaled for him to stop. She felt his gaze on her as she scraped the beaters along the edge of the bowl.

"You're the sibling who lives in Chicago, right?"

"Yep." A city she'd never expected to end up in. Writing stories she'd never expected to write.

And for the hundredth time since that call from the foundation, bubbles of hope rose up and floated through her—though the reality of her financial situation poked at them.

"So family order . . . Logan's the oldest, then you, then the other brother—"

"Beckett. He's twenty-eight. Lives in Boston." Lawyer on his way to partner.

"And then Raegan."

"Yes, she's the youngest." Which meant she put up with her fair share of ribbing about her baby-of-the-family status and the fact that at twenty-five she still slept in her old daybed in Dad's house.

"And Seth . . . ?"

Kate turned off the mixer. "Cousin who's more like a sibling. He moved back to Maple Valley about a year ago, opened his own restaurant about a month back." And because he'd poured so much of his own money into starting the business, he'd been living in Dad's basement to save on rent. She unfastened one of the beaters from the mixer and handed it to Colton.

He blinked. "I'm supposed to lick that off?"

"Proving a point here, Greene."

He shrugged, took the beater, taste-tested her creation.

She folded her arms. "Well?"

"Fine, it's better than the stuff in the can. You were right."

She leaned one elbow on the counter, licked off her own beater. "What was that last part? Couldn't quite hear you."

His blue eyes narrowed. "I'm not saying it again." He reached one hand toward her face, and Kate jumped back.

"What are you—"

"You've got whipped cream in your hair."

49

Kate stilled, nerves fidgeting through her as Colton brushed out the whipped cream with his fingers.

So close. And oh, he smelled like . . . soap and pinewood and flannel.

"What's going on in here?"

They both jumped as if kids caught loitering where they shouldn't be, and Kate's gaze flew to the figure standing in the opening between the kitchen and the living room.

Arm in a sling, face bruised, form slighter than she remembered. *What . . . why?*

"Dad?"

~~~

Colton had thought the downed trees and flattened fields they'd passed on the way from Case Walker's house into town were bad. But this?

His gaze hurtled around the kitchen of The Red Door, the restaurant Logan's cousin had opened in the historical bank building that swallowed up one corner of Maple Valley's downtown. Storm-tossed debris littered the space—chunks of wood and brick, layers of dust covering the long metal counter in the middle of the room and the black-and-white-checkered floor. A late summer wind, heavy with humidity, crackled through the plastic tarp partially covering the hole in the back wall.

And a tree trunk—gouged through the wall.

"Whoa." The word slipped out on the heels of Logan's gasp.

Seth Walker nudged broken glass out of the way with his foot and perched against the tiled counter top that lined the wall opposite the wreckage. His hair was lighter than Logan's, and he stood an inch or two shorter, but the Walker resemblance was there. "It looks bad, I know, but trust me, it could've been so much worse. Not twenty minutes before the twister hit, I was sitting at that desk."

The one at the back of the room now split in half by the tree.

Logan picked up an overturned chair. "Thank God you and everyone got to the basement."

Seth nodded. "It's a miracle no one in town was seriously injured."

The image of Case Walker slipped in then. The shock on Kate's face when she'd seen her father walk into the kitchen an hour ago, all bruised and wearing that sling. No one had told her the man had dislocated a shoulder in the storm? She'd gone white as that whipped cream she'd just made.

And he'd had the uncanny urge to reach out for her—just to make sure she stayed steady on her feet. Which was funny, really. From his two brief exchanges with her, Kate Walker didn't seem like the fainting type. Plucky and strong willed, yes. Feeble, no.

Still . . . he hadn't missed the dismay rimming her shock.

"So the main goal today is to get the tree out of here," Seth said, pulling off his Maple Valley Mavericks ball cap and stuffing it in his back pocket. "Problem is, pretty much every piece of equipment in town is in use, since everyone's in storm-repair mode. Cleanup crews are focusing on residences and public buildings first. I could wait, but I'd really like to get the place reopened sooner rather than later."

Logan walked over to the tree. "If it wasn't such a beast of a tree, we could just lift it."

Odd to see Logan like this—dressed in old jeans and a faded T-shirt. Had he ever seen his friend in anything other than a suit?

"If we had a chainsaw, we could cut it up and get it out in pieces. Case already loaned his out, though, and the two stores in town that sell them are sold out." Seth eyed his cousin, then Colton. "But, uh, I did find a couple axes in Case's shed. I know chopping wood probably wasn't what you expected when you offered to help."

Logan was already moving his shoulders, as if loosening up in preparation for the manual labor. "I don't mind. You?" He tossed the question to Colton.

After the week he'd had, swinging a sharp tool at an inanimate object sounded awesome. He'd just have to be careful of his bad shoulder. "Put me to work."

"All right, then—the axes are out in the truck. But let me show you the rest of the place first."

They followed Seth through a swinging door into the restaurant's main eating area and Colton gasped for a second time—only this time out of appreciation.

It had the perfect inviting atmosphere—soft lighting and a fireplace in the corner, redwood ceiling that reached down to amber-colored walls. Unique touches like the cubed shelves displaying coffee mugs on one wall and the cobblestone base of the order counter.

"Oh man. This place is incredible." The impressed tone of Logan's voice matched the admiration clinking around Colton's thoughts.

The outside of the business, as he'd seen when they drove up, had just as much personality—the words *First National Bank* still etched into its gray cement, intricate cornice swirling above the entrance and at each corner of the sloping roof, a jutting brass sign with the name of the restaurant . . . and of course, the bright red door.

"Not gonna lie. I'm happy with how it turned it out." Seth gestured across the room. "In here you wouldn't even know a tornado hit."

So this was what vision looked like. The kind born and nurtured through determination, effort . . . success.

Colton used to know what that felt like.

"How long did the place sit empty before you bought it?"

Seth skirted around black-topped tables now, moving toward the front door. "Six or seven years. The city was on the brink of tearing the place down. There were days over the past year when I thought it'd never come together, but somehow it did. And honestly, I think it's the fact that it wasn't a cakewalk getting to opening day that's been helping me take the storm damage in stride."

Colton reached around to rub the crick in his neck that had been hassling him ever since he woke up that morning. Probably the result of spending the night in a twin bed he barely fit into.

Which made the decision he'd come to last night just before finally drifting off to sleep all the more logical: He'd help out with whatever storm repairs he could today—which he now knew meant playing lumberjack—but then he'd catch a flight back to California. If not tonight, then tomorrow.

He didn't belong in Maple Valley.

He'd felt it last night as the Walkers gathered in the kitchen, their laughter drifting upstairs to where he lay in Logan's younger brother's old bed. He'd felt it this morning as he watched Kate hug her father and joke around with her siblings and cousin as they trickled from their bedrooms one by one.

He felt it now . . . as he looked around Seth's restaurant, wondering what it'd be like to know not even a tornado could topple his dream.

Seth pushed through the front door. "Be back in a minute with the axes."

Half an hour later, sweat beaded on Colton's forehead as he angled his arms behind him, then forward—the thwacking of the ax digging into wood vibrating up arms. On the other side of the massive tree trunk, Logan took his turn. Across the room, Seth paced, cell phone at his ear, smile spreading over his cheeks.

"Look at him," Logan said, breathing heavy after his last

swing. "Flirting with his girlfriend while we chop a tree that's already down."

"How do you know that's who he's talking to?"

"See the smile on his face? If that doesn't spell *lovesick puppy dog,* I don't know what does. Word on the street is he's had a girl stashed in that apartment upstairs all summer."

"She wasn't stashed and she wasn't there all summer." Seth's shadow formed over the tree trunk. Must've gotten off the phone in time to hear Logan's last comment. "Get your intel right. She stayed at your dad's."

Logan leaned his elbow on the end of his ax, wiping one palm across his forehead. "Raegan told me all about it. Turns out our boy Seth has been emailing a girl constantly—like multiple times a day—for a year. And then she showed up here on opening day. Hasn't left since."

Seth shook his head, red creeping into his cheeks. "Wrong. She went home to Michigan end of last week."

"And then came running back as soon as she heard about the tornado. According to Raegan, the whole town's been waiting for the two of you to admit you're crazy about each other."

Slithering heat snuck through the tarp and slapped against Colton.

"Now you see what I have to deal with living in Maple Valley, Colton." Seth's phone rang again. He checked the display but didn't answer. "I don't even know why this town bothers with a newspaper. Talk spreads like poison ivy. Trust me—you so much as walk down Main Ave with a girl, and the local busybodies will have you coupled up in no time. Dare to have dinner with her in public, and you might as well start ordering wedding invitations."

Colton let out a laugh, then lifted his ax. "Don't worry, don't think I'll be here long enough to give the gossip line any romantic fodder."

Although he couldn't help the dollop of a memory that dropped in just then—of Kate Walker standing next to him, fingers wrapped around that beater and cheeks rosy on either side of her smile. Morning sunlight had brushed gold streaks into her hair and dotted matching flecks in her eyes.

And there, just for a moment, all thought of ditching Iowa had thinned away into nothing.

But why? Because for a few minutes a pretty girl had made him forget about everything he'd lost in the past year? No, he wasn't about to lose his focus. *Get back to LA. Choose a writer. Get the book done. Figure out what's next.*

Seth's phone rang out again, and this time he lifted it. "Sorry, probably the insurance company. Gotta take it, but I promise I'll take my turn with the chopping after." He moved away.

Logan lifted his ax. "Actually, Colt, speaking of your not being here long . . ." The sound of splitting wood erupted.

"Yeah?"

"My dad seemed older today. Don't you think?"

"Bruises and a sling could do that to anyone." But Logan had a point. Back in college, Colton used to think his friend's dad looked exactly like John Wayne from those old westerns one of his foster dads used to watch. Same height and bulky build. Same etched face that seemed more laugh lines than wrinkles.

But this morning, he'd appeared . . . tired.

Colton swung his ax.

"Did you see Dad's backyard? The tarp covering the roof? And apparently the depot he works at received more damage than anyplace in town. Then there's this restaurant. I think Seth has it in his head that he'll be opening up next week. But he's got to rebuild a wall. Fix plumbing. Have an inspection." Logan stilled. "There's so much. Too much. And with campaign season heating up . . ."

Colton read the frustration in his friend's eyes.

"I can't stay." Logan leaned one elbow on his ax. "But you could."

Whoa, wait. "Logan—"

"My father needs help. Seth needs help. I'd stay if I could."

But Colton couldn't stay either. He had a book to write and a career to revive. He couldn't put all that off to . . . what? Be a handyman in Nowhere, Iowa? Even if he did genuinely feel for Case and Seth and all the residents of this little town, he couldn't. "Sorry, man. I don't think . . . " He fumbled for an excuse, settled for lifting his ax.

"Why not? What do you have in LA to go back to?"

The force of his ax burying itself into the tree shook through him, pain slamming up his bad shoulder.

And Logan's words—stinging.

Of course I have things to go back to. His condo. What was left of his career.

Which is what?

The book project.

Which you could do from anywhere.

He looked at Logan again, took in the desperation clinging to his features. He was just trying to help his family. Which was so . . . Logan. How had the guy held on to his good streak after all he'd been through? Losing his mom and then just a few years later, so suddenly, his wife. Thrust into single parenthood while juggling his speechwriting career.

And it wasn't just his family Logan reached out to. How many times over the years had he come through for Colton? Especially this past year, after the injuries. And he'd never once asked Colton to return a favor.

Until now.

The pain in Colton's shoulder pulsed now. It'd be weeping

for ice by tonight. Nevertheless, he lifted his ax once more. And realized he didn't have a choice.

~∂

"How could you not tell me, Rae?" Kate whisper-shouted the question as her sister slid into a seat next to her at a table in Seth's restaurant.

Somehow her cousin's place had become the gathering spot for tonight's impromptu town meeting—during which the residents of Maple Valley would decide whether or not to move forward with the end-of-summer festival they always held on Labor Day. Two days from now.

Hilarious, really, that there was even a choice to be made here, considering the torn-apart state of the town. But that was Maple Valley. Resilient, even after a tornado took a bite out of it.

Resilient or maybe just crazy. Then again, this was the town that'd once moved forward with its live Nativity at Christmas, even after one of the teenage wise men had accidentally burned down the makeshift stable. The town that nabbed any and every excuse to hold a fair or fundraiser or put on a fireworks display.

"Not tell you what?" Her sister tucked a strand of hot pink hair behind her ear. Raegan had always had a style all her own—pierced eyebrow, at least a dozen thin bracelets crammed onto one wrist, bright hues streaked into her hair. She was the only one of the siblings to inherit Mom's lighter coloring—blond hair and blue eyes—instead of Dad's darker features.

"About Dad getting crushed by a beam at the depot." Chatter buzzed through the room—snippets of conversation about wrecked garages and missing lawn furniture—and the bell of the restaurant's entrance jingled in a steady rhythm of arrivals.

"He wasn't crushed." Raegan shook her bangs out of her eyes. "And he didn't want me to say anything. You know how Dad is."

No, she knew how Dad *was*. Former military man turned international diplomat. Ambassador who'd served at the foreign office in London and later—after marrying Mom—in New York City at the UN building. Sometimes still seemed like a different life—those early years on the East Coast.

They'd moved to Iowa when Kate was only seven—the first time Mom got sick. But even then and through all the years that followed, Dad had retained his solid nature and soldier-like stature. And yes, of course *that* Dad would've refused to tell her about his injuries.

This morning, though, he'd looked like a different man. Exhausted. Weakened. The sight had sliced through her, even as she grinned and barreled in for a hug, careful to avoid the sling.

"You should've told me."

"You were already planning to come later in the weekend. He didn't want you changing your plans."

Up front, Milton Briggs, longtime mayor, pounded a gavel on the brass cash register that sat on a counter.

"Hey, careful, that thing's an antique," Seth called from across the room.

Amazing to think her cousin—the one who'd job-hopped his way through his twenties, restless and discontent—had created this space. It had the class and ambiance of a downtown Chicago restaurant with the comfortable feel of a small-town diner.

"All right, folks, let's get this meeting started." The mayor stood on a chair—probably a good call since he barely reached over five feet. What he lacked in height, though, the man made up for in personality. Ruddy cheeks, bushy eyebrows, always a story or joke for the prompting. In addition to serving as mayor, he also ran the town bakery, nearly as much a fixture in Maple Valley as the bustling Blaine River that ran through it.

"I think everybody knows why I called this meet—"

"Can't hear you from the back," a voice called.

Milt tried again, barely a notch louder. "I think everybody knows why—"

"He needs a microphone," a woman from two tables over said. "Folks—"

Milt was interrupted again, this time by someone claiming she had a megaphone in her car.

"Who keeps a megaphone in their car?"

Oh, Kate recognized that voice. Lenny from the woodshop, right?

"If you had seven kids, you'd keep a megaphone within reach at all times, too."

"All right, all right." Milt lifted his arms to quiet the crowd. Nothing doing. "Five-minute intermission while Mrs. Carrington retrieves her megaphone."

Kate turned to Rae. "We didn't make it thirty seconds into the meeting before a break."

Raegan grinned. "It's times like this I just love this town."

"It's quirky."

"It's home."

True. And yet, Kate hadn't lived here since college. And now she was contemplating leaving Iowa even further in the rearview mirror. *Africa.*

How many times had Mom talked over the years about taking a trip across the Atlantic, seeing the fruit of all the work she'd put in back when she'd helped start the James Foundation?

Taking that trip felt a hundred kinds of right.

But the money. It had become a nagging refrain she couldn't shake. She needed to sell a script. A book. Something.

Now that she was home, though, it was more than finances yanking at her. There was also the wreckage in Dad's yard. All the work to be done to clean up from the tornado. The depot . . .

"How bad is it really, Rae? Dad's depot, I mean."

Dad's depot. It's what they'd been calling the Maple Valley Scenic Railway and Museum ever since Dad took it over. One of Iowa's only heritage railroads, it was a huge part of what made Maple Valley the charming tri-county tourist stop it was, its fourteen-mile passenger ride a picturesque nod to simpler days gone by.

"Pretty bad. The roof was completely ripped off. Boardwalk's gone. And it runs on a skeletal budget as it is, so I'm not sure he's going to get much help from the city on repairs. There's talk . . ." Raegan's shoulders slumped. "Well, there's talk that, if it can't get fixed and reopened in time for the fall season, it might not reopen at all."

But the town loved the depot and all its history. *Dad* loved it. And after all he'd given up when Mom got sick . . .

The colors of sunset streamed into the room through long windows fronting the restaurant—pinks and yellows. The front door jingled. Probably that lady with the seven kids and the megaphone.

"There's some concern about the river, too," Raegan added. "I guess the dam up in Dixon took a hit."

Which meant the fear of flooding—always an ominous concern for their riverfront community. Worry knit through her, and threaded into it a kinship with the people seated all around her.

You could stay.

The thought had whispered through her all day. What if she hung around for a couple weeks? Helped out at Dad's place, at the depot, here at the restaurant. Took some time to think about her future—pray.

Her move to Chicago after college had been so impulsive—the result of Gil's urging. She'd turned down an internship in DC and everything, a choice that'd left *what-if* imprints all over the back of her mind.

Maybe this time, on the brink of another major life change, she should ease into the decision. Try to figure out whether such a bold move lined up with God's desires for her future.

Easier said than done, though. It was hard to hear God's voice over the demands of her own heart. Or the memory of Mom telling her to go write something important. Or her agent and bank account and Frederick Langston and . . . The list could go on and on.

"All right, we can get started again." Milt called the meeting to order for a second time, and the crowd hushed. "My thanks to Seth Walker for letting us use his place for a meeting space. Electricity still isn't working at the city building."

Appreciative murmurs spread through the room, and Kate turned her eyes toward Seth once more. He seemed like such a part of this place. Like Dad. Settled and sure.

Even Raegan, with her part-time jobs and lack of college degree and hesitance to move out of Dad's house, had an assurance about her.

Her focus shifted to the man standing next to Seth. Colton rubbed one shoulder absently, shifting his weight from foot to foot, clearly ill at ease.

"You should've seen them working in the kitchen today," Raegan whispered. She must've followed Kate's gaze. "It was like something out of *Seven Brides for Seven Brothers*. All they needed were flannel shirts and a song or two."

Colton wore a baseball cap now, pulled low over his eyes. Trying to stay incognito? Probably smart. Once word got out that a former NFL quarterback was in town, he could say good-bye to any sense of privacy.

Although surely he wouldn't be in town long. He likely had television appearances and commercial shoots and whatever else celebrity athletes did.

Milt was still talking into the megaphone about the aftereffects of the storm, the pros and cons of moving forward with Monday's parade and festival. But Colton now edged his way along the wall and toward the kitchen. Where was he going?

When he hadn't reappeared ten minutes later, Kate gave in to her curiosity, abandoning her seat and as inconspicuously as possible following the path Colton had taken.

She found him near the walk-in freezer. He stood with his back to her, the outline of muscle clear under the light of the hanging fixture overhead, something draped over his shoulder. An ice pack?

"Hey, Colton."

He turned with a jerk. "Whoa, you keep freaking me out." He held the ice pack against his right side, barely hiding a grimace as he moved his arm. "I mean, this wasn't quite as bad as crawling into bed with me—"

"That horse is dead, Greene. Its body is already decomposing. There's not going to be anything left to beat soon."

"You took that cliché to new and gross territory, Katie."

"Uh, it's Kate."

"No one ever calls you Katie?"

She shook her head. No one except Breydan. Not since Gil.

"But your full name's Katharine, yeah?" At her questioning look, he went on. "Logan told me after I asked him how he ended up with a middle name like Flynn. You're all named after old Hollywood stars."

She nodded. "My mom loved classic movies. I pulled double-duty, though. Logan, Beck, and Rae just have middle names in honor of Mom's favorites. But me, I got Katharine for a first name—after Katharine Hepburn—and my middle name is Rose, after Hepburn's character in *The African Queen*. Mom used to call me Rosie."

"Rosie. I can see that."

Silence settled between them then. He was probably wondering why she'd followed him to the kitchen. She was wondering herself. "Shoulder hurting?"

"Turns out the lumberjack thing wasn't so great for the injury." He shrugged, another wince on its heels. "Plus, I figured if I stuck around that meeting any longer I'd get roped into riding a float or something." He gave her the full grin now, and goodness, if it didn't yank every nerve inside her to attention. *Distance. Need. Distance.*

She took a step backward, the drone of Milt's voice drifting in. "Well, if you want an escape, I was thinking about heading over to the depot after the meeting. I haven't seen the damage yet. It's only four or five blocks away. We could skip out early." Although why Colton would have any desire to see a little depot that barely counted as a regional landmark, she didn't know. "That is, if you want—"

"I do." He set the ice pack on the counter top.

Okay. All right, then. So they were leaving. She moved toward the tarp that covered the hole in the wall, pushed it back enough to step through, then waited as Colton hopped onto the grass beside her. With the last of the sun's light tucked away, a blanket of navy blue covered the sky, first stars like a nubby pattern.

Kate slipped her hands in the back pockets of her jeans as she moved toward the sidewalk. The pathway dipped toward the river that bordered the eastern edge of the town square and cut Maple Valley in half.

They continued down the path that traced the river, their shoes pattering over the cement and the occasional hum of lamplight reaching into the quiet. Up ahead, the Archway Bridge reached across the moonbeam-streaked ripples of the river. Over to the west, a series of storefronts watched their movement behind glass window eyes.

A firefly swooped past her ear. "It was nice of you to spend all day helping Seth. Especially considering you didn't even know him until yesterday."

Colton shrugged. "But I've known Logan a long time."

"And Charlie?"

"I covered for Logan and Emma once when their babysitter flaked out. I let Charlie jump on my bed and introduced her to Pixy Stix. She's liked me ever since."

The mention of Logan's wife pricked Kate. Two years since the car accident. And still so hard to believe at times that her sister-in-law was really gone. That somehow Logan managed alone out in California.

Colton cleared his throat beside her. Well, not completely alone.

They came to the bridge, and she angled toward it. "We call this the Archway Bridge. 'Cause it arches."

She didn't miss Colton's stifled chuckle.

"This area floods a lot, which usually forces a couple of the bridges to close, but there's only been one time I can remember when the Archway was barricaded—which literally cut off one side of town from the other. I was seventeen and got trapped on the west side, our house being on the east. Had to stay at a friend's house that night."

The river's lapping floated up from below as they crossed the bridge, the wood underneath their feet echoing with each step. Why was she babbling on about the bridge?

"When are you guys heading back to LA?"

"Not sure about Logan, but I'm . . . staying."

The bridge gave way to another span of sidewalk that reached toward the edge of town and the depot in the distance. "You're staying?"

"Through the end of September, at least. Logan asked, and

I'm not exactly busy at the moment. I guess there's some big event at the depot in a month or so."

"Depot Day—usually the last weekend in September or first weekend in October."

"Right. I'm going to help your dad get ready for that."

He was staying. For a whole month.

"You?" His arm brushed against hers.

"Actually I was thinking of sticking around, too. I'm between writing projects—"

Colton stopped. "You're a writer?"

She turned back to him. Why the surprise? "Yeah."

"Books?"

"One." Could he see her cringe? One book for a small press that had probably only contracted it because of Gil's connections. "Mostly screenplays, though. Made-for-TV features. I'm not out there writing impassioned speeches like Logan. Although, I did win an Emmy. Once." She didn't know why she'd added that last part. Why she'd given in to the sudden, illogical desire to impress the man. "Sounds more notable than it was, though. This town, my family, I think they view me as a big-shot movie writer, but what they don't know is I've got enough rejection letters to fuel the world's biggest bonfire and I'm not sure what to write next and I finally have this opportunity to do the kind of writing I've always wanted, but no money to make it happen and—"

And why in the world was she telling him this?

Their footsteps quieted as they reached the grass, the depot appearing ahead of them.

"Kate, do you see that?"

He pointed to the depot, and she followed his gaze. A dot of light bounced in the depot's window, like a firefly bobbing and weaving.

"Someone's in there. Should we call the cops?" Colton reached into the pocket of his jeans.

Kate let out a laugh. "Or we just go in and tell whatever teenager is pulling a prank to leave."

"*Or* we call the cops."

"Every cop in town is probably back at the meeting. By the time we call in, whoever's inside will be gone."

She started walking again, slowing as she neared the oblong depot and the steps leading up to its front door. *Ohhh.* The poor building. The storm had peeled back its tiled roof, and the once-charming pale yellow siding was now stripped and scratched. Shutters hung askew, and the wraparound boardwalk was so damaged it was nearly nonexistent.

"It looks awful."

But when she looked over at Colton, he wasn't staring at the building so much as peering through its half-open front door. She once again followed his gaze . . . and saw what he saw. The figure standing at the cash register. Completely focused, messing with the cash register.

"Stay out here, Kate," Colton whispered.

"It's just a kid. We can—"

Only she never had a chance to finish her response. The kid suddenly darted from behind the counter and barreled through the front door, glass windows rattling as the door smacked into the wall.

And Kate found herself thrust against Colton, his arm reaching out to pull her close, out of the way of the intruder's barging run. By the time she got a glimpse over his arm, the kid was already disappearing into the night.

4

*C*olton had suffered broken bones more fun than this.

"I swear, Walker, this is the last time you rope me into something like this." He spoke into the walkie-talkie that a couple decades ago would've made his eight-year-old self feel like a spy or maybe a soldier. Instead, today he only wanted to chuck the thing out the window of what he was told was a Dodge Ram.

But who would know underneath all the plastic drapery and tinsel of the ridiculously overdone parade float overhead? A cramp tightened through his leg and pinched up his back. His six-foot-three frame wasn't meant for this tiny space. Hello, claustrophobia.

"What kind of town holds a parade less than a week after a devastating tornado?"

"Dude, if you're sticking around, you might as well get used to Maple Valley shenanigans." Logan's voice oozed smug even through the crackle of the walkie-talkie.

"One month, Walker. I said I'd stay a month." And up until Saturday night, he'd had a hard time believing it'd actually take that long to help Case Walker repair the depot. But then he'd seen the state of the place.

He'd watched as the shock of seeing the museum building in complete disarray traveled over Kate's face—shattered glass and tipped display cases, dents in wainscoted walls, downed beams, and everywhere, antiques and mementos tossed around.

In those few minutes of quiet as she picked her way through the wreckage, well, he would've agreed to stay a year.

It was only later that the idea had hit him. He'd mulled it over yesterday while seated at the end of the Walkers' pew in church.

He was going to be here until October. Kate was considering extending her stay.

He needed a writer.

Kate was a writer . . .

Not only that, she was in between projects and apparently in need of money.

Is it crazy? Or was it an answer to the prayer he wasn't sure he'd even prayed?

Colton now peered through a rectangle opening that gave him his only view of the outside world. No peripheral vision. No escape from the heat filling the cab like helium in a balloon. If this torture didn't end soon, he'd pop. "I hate parades. And whatever happened to simple floats on trailers? This isn't the Macy's Thanksgiving Day Parade. I don't see Dick Clark anywhere."

Static accompanied Logan's laughter. "That's New Year's."

"What?" He felt the telltale buzz of an oncoming headache.

"Dick Clark hosted the Times Square New Year's ball drop, not the Macy's parade. He died, though. It's some reality TV guy now. Keep up, bro. Over."

"Stop saying *over*." Was it possible to physically melt in here?

"Ten-four. You survived how many tackles and you can't survive this?"

The mixed smell of burnt oil and antifreeze wafted through

the cab. He wiped beads of sweat from his forehead. "Not funny, Walker." He tried to stretch his legs, knuckles tightening over the steering wheel.

"Do the people at ESPN and *Sports Illustrated* know you whine so much? Some ex-Tiger you are."

Despite the suffocating heat, something cold and sharp iced through him. He dropped the walkie-talkie, heard it plunk to the floor. Tried to breathe through the fumes roiling up from the truck's engine. What had been a minor pulse in his temple now throbbed around to the back of his head.

"Colt?" Logan's voice crackled through the walkie-talkie once more.

He nudged the thing under his seat with his foot. From what he could see out the pretty-much nonexistent windshield, they'd almost reached the end of Main, which meant this fiasco was nearly over. Then he could squeeze out the escape hatch of a door, and if he was lucky, slip through the parade crowd undetected. Maybe find Kate somewhere in the mess of people. Test out his idea on her.

The first hint of trouble outside the float rumbled in then—someone shouting, a jerk of the truck bed. His left foot found the brake as the walkie-talkie crackled once more from the floor. "Greene, get out."

"What?" But of course Logan couldn't hear him.

"Get out of the truck. There's smoke . . ."

Didn't need to hear more than that. He yanked the vehicle into Park and reached for the door handle, squinting against glaring sunlight as he unfolded from the cab. A clamor of shouts surrounded him, parade organizers hurrying to the float's side, as a cloud of gray rolled from the truck's hood.

And for one stretching and unwelcome moment, in a sudden and swift backward drifting, the past twenty years slipped away. He was nine. And everything was black and silent, as if he'd been sucked into an eerie bubble, only the smell of smoke existing alongside him in the darkness.

But then, just as quickly, the whirring blast of a fire extinguisher jerked him away from what, in its blurry, mysterious state, couldn't even count as a memory. Someone was spraying the front of the truck as float riders jumped to the ground.

Colton blinked. Breathed. Begged the shadow back into its hiding place.

In the background, the marching band continued its blaring rendition of "This Land is Your Land."

"Colton!"

It wasn't Logan running toward him, but Raegan. Her purple Converse shoes slapped against the pavement as she hurried to him.

"I'm all right." Outwardly. Inside, the jolt of the murky flashback that couldn't have lasted more than a couple seconds still burned him. How long had it been since one of those hit?

"When a flashback comes on, write it down, Colton. Every detail. Everything you can remember." Dr. Traborne. Why could he so clearly recall that voice while the images the psychiatrist had tried to lure into focus in therapy session after session remained hazy and remote?

"I can't remember any of it. Don't you understand, I can't . . ."

"You're completely white." Raegan stopped in front of him now, concern in her eyes. Wasn't she supposed to be on the rec center float a few vehicles back? "I don't know what happened. You were rolling along and all of a sudden someone saw smoke or steam or something come from the front of the float. Must've overheated. At least you're near the end of the parade."

A posse of men, including Logan, now worked together to

roll the float to the side of the road. And the parade carried on, slithering toward the bridge he and Kate had crossed two nights ago on the way to the depot. This town was weird.

But at least he was free of the deathtrap.

He rubbed a hand over the chin he hadn't bothered shaving today. "Well, guess I get out of driving the rest of the route."

"Guess so." Raegan tucked her hands in the back pockets of her shorts.

He tipped his sunglasses over his eyes as the marching band shifted into a drum-line routine. Kate jogged over then, hair flopping behind her in what he'd come to realize was her usual ponytail. Although she'd left her hair down for church yesterday, in unruly waves that reached past her shoulders.

"I know you were complaining about the parade, Greene," she said as she reached them. She propped her hands on the waist of her faded jeans. "But you didn't have to start an engine fire to get out of it."

"Hey, if I was going to purposely start a fire . . . A, I wouldn't have waited until the end of the parade, and B, I would've done a better job than that little display of smoke."

Raegan laughed. "I'm not sure how comfortable I am with the fact that a man sleeping under our roof is bragging about his fire-starting skills." She blew a bubble with her gum. "My float's getting away without me. See ya."

She ran back to the parade, leaving Colton and Kate alone. He now glanced around the stretch of street and grass that made up Maple Valley's center. Its downtown wrapped around the green town square in a quaint arrangement of buildings—some brick and some paneled. Old-fashioned brass signs and colorful awnings reached toward the lampposts lining the sidewalks.

"Damage doesn't look quite as bad when there are so many people crowding the square, does it?" Kate said.

He turned to her. "I'm surprised so many people came out after a week like last week."

"Oh, Maple Valley loves its parades. Part of what gives us our eccentric charm. That and the fact that we probably have more antique stores per capita than any town this side of anywhere."

"Guess I know where to come next time I want an uncomfortable chair."

"And make sure not to miss the display of historical doorknobs at Moser's. It's the highlight."

He laughed, then paused under the shade of an old oak tree stripped of half its leaves but a survivor of the storm nonetheless. "Listen, Kate, I've got a question for you. More like a favor to ask. It's kind of . . . big."

"If it's to switch back bedrooms, I've only offered about a thousand times already."

Barely an exaggeration. But no way was he stealing the woman's space. "Bigger than that. You've written a book before, yeah?"

All the ease left her expression, replaced by a wariness she tried to hide behind a nonchalant shrug. "One."

"How'd you like to write another?" Wait! Should he have run this by Ian first?

"I don't understand." She wrinkled her nose, a dusting of freckles he hadn't noticed before now obvious in the sunlight.

Ian told me to find a writer. She's a writer. And something told him working with Katharine Rose Walker would be about a hundred times more enjoyable than any of the professional ghostwriters Ian had dug up.

He lifted his sunglasses to his forehead and met Kate's eyes. "Not just any book, Rosie. *My* book."

"Trust Maple Valley to turn a cleanup effort into a party."

The statement of amusement came from the lithe girl with the blond hair Seth had introduced as Ava Kingsley—the woman who, according to Raegan, had swept their cousin clean off his feet.

Kate clapped the dirt from the work gloves covering her hands. "I thought you were a newbie, but clearly you're already well acquainted with the quirkier facets of Maple Valley." She reached for a gangly branch, hefted it up, and tossed it into the growing pile in the middle of the town square.

The city had cancelled all its Labor Day events except for the parade. But then someone had come up with the idea of doing a massive bonfire tonight—a fun way of cleaning up the storm-flung branches and debris.

A celebratory spirit hovered in the air as community members worked together to clean up the park. Someone had set up an apple-cider table over in the corner, and a big-band tune piped through the speakers around the band shell.

Ava threw a handful of sticks into the woodpile. "I may have only been in town a month, but I've been trading emails with Seth for a year. I've heard plenty of stories about this town."

Oh yes, Raegan had recapped Seth and Ava's long-distance friendship turned budding romance for Kate on her first day back in town. It was the kind of story that would've made for a good film script.

And that was all it took—one fleeting thought about writing—to tow Colton's crazy idea back to the forefront of her mind. Truthfully, it'd been there all day—daring her to come up with one good reason why she should say no.

One good reason? I can come up with a dozen.

For starters, how about the words that chased her around anytime she remembered back to her first book: *Colossal flop.*

73

The harshest of the few reviews her book managed to garner had pulled out all the stops. Then there was the fact that she'd never even read a sports memoir, let alone considered writing one.

But she owed Colton an answer—had promised him one by the end of the day. He'd apologized for needing such a quick response, but apparently he had an antsy manager and a looming deadline breathing down his neck.

Kate pulled the sweatshirt from around her waist and tugged it over her arms. Only the third day in September, and already autumn was hinting at an early appearance. The day's warmth had trickled into cooler temps as night approached.

An engine rumbled into the buzz filling the square.

Ava dragged off her work gloves. "Oh good, the fire department's here. I don't know whether to be comforted or concerned by that." She flashed a grin. "And there's Seth."

Kate's cousin walked across the lawn. He high-fived a guy who'd been working and laughing with Raegan for the past hour, then spotted Ava, his smile the stuff of Disney cartoons.

"I gotta say, the two of you would be awfully convincing leads in a Heartline movie."

Ava hugged her arms to herself. "Ha, except I'm no actress."

True, considering Ava probably couldn't have hidden her giddy expression if she tried. Seth reached them, pulled Ava to his side, and planted a kiss on her temple. "My girlfriend has finally met three of my four cousins. Now we just need to get Beckett home."

Ava dressed simply—jeans and tee, baseball cap and work boots. But it was the blush in her cheeks and the way she leaned into Seth that caught Kate's attention. "Well, it took a tornado to get Logan and Kate home. You just need another natural disaster."

"If the river floods like everyone's worried it will, we just might get it."

Behind Seth one of the Parks and Rec guys arranged the last of the firewood and pulled out a lighter.

"Is it really that bad?" Kate asked. "The river, I mean?" It was high, sure, but flooding was usually a bigger concern earlier in the summer.

"If the dam in Dixon bursts, yeah, it's really that bad." Seth kissed Ava again, the lightness in his voice not at all a fit for his words.

"Hopefully that's an unlikely *if*." Ava grabbed Seth's hand. "C'mon, let's get some cider. Come along, Kate?"

"That's okay. Already had two cups." And she was feeling a bit like a third wheel. She watched the pair walk away hand in hand.

"Cute couple, right?"

Raegan.

"Everything finally came together for Seth. Gives me hope." The bonfire flared to life—first small flickers of orange that lapped in the wind and scooted along the kindling, then full-on flames. She turned to her sister. "And speaking of cute couples, who's the guy?"

Raegan followed Kate's pointing to the man her sister had worked alongside ever since they arrived at the square. "You don't know Bear McKinley?"

"Bear? As in lions and tigers and . . ."

"Yes, Bear. Guess it makes sense you don't know him. He moved here five or six years ago. Good friends with Seth."

"And you. Clearly." She attempted a knowing wiggle of her eyebrows.

"Stop that or I'm going to start calling you Twitchy."

"I'm just saying, you guys were laughing and talking and hobnobbing all coupley-like."

Raegan fisted her waist. "You're home for, what, seventy-two hours, and already you've joined the busybody express?"

Kate threaded her arm through Raegan's and turned her toward the fire. "All right, I'm sorry."

"Just because Bear is ridiculously handsome. And sings and plays guitar. And is beyond smart—you should hear him talk history and politics and . . ." Raegan took a breath. "None of that means I have a crush on him."

Kate smiled. "Of course not."

"Shut up."

"Hey, I agreed with you."

They watched the fire for quiet minutes, the activity around the town square seeming to slow as the growing fire spread its light and warmth. Both familiar and unfamiliar faces dotted the circle of people around the bonfire.

Home.

"So what're you going to tell Colton?"

"Hmm?"

"About the book. I know he asked you. He told me yesterday after church he was going to. You're going to do it, aren't you?"

So his request hadn't been impulsive. He'd put thought into this. "Me? Write a book about football? A sport that interests me about as much as the periodic table."

Raegan nudged her with her elbow. "Not about football. About him. I've heard you say a thousand times you wish you could write something real. Gritty and real life—those were your words. Can't get much more real life than a memoir."

She *had* said that. Over and over until she sounded whiny even to her own ears.

"Plus, think about the money."

"The money?"

"Kate, he's Colton Greene, not Joe Schmo peddling a life

76

story no one will ever buy because no one has ever heard of him. This would be a guaranteed bestseller."

"He's . . . he's really that well-known?"

Raegan's laugh was half chuckle, half snort. "Yes, he's really that well-known. And from what I read on Google, he's got the kind of life-turnaround story people love to read. Trust me."

"You Googled him?"

"You didn't?"

Life turnaround.

Money.

"Thing is, last time I wrote a book, it got panned. And all those rejections . . ." She turned to face Raegan. "Besides, writing a sports memoir is as far away from the kind of writing I'd like to do as what I'm already doing."

But it wasn't just that. It was . . .

It was Colton. Something about him—he unnerved her. He . . . she . . .

Fine, she was attracted to him, okay? Possibly for the first time since Gil, a man—one she didn't even know, had only met three days ago—had captured and held hostage her attention. The way he interacted with Charlie, spent an entire day helping Seth, drove that ridiculous float, pulled her to him the other night at the depot . . .

The heat of the fire warmed over her cheeks.

There was an edge to him, too. An intriguing broodiness under the surface she'd sensed from that very first night in her bedroom. Without even trying, Colton Greene had done a number on her curiosity and her common sense.

And it scared her.

"Kate, how many times have we had this conversation? You talking about how dissatisfied you are with your writing. Wishing you could do something different, write something different?

But you never do anything about it." Raegan folded her arms. "You're the one who's chosen to keep writing movies. And for the record, whatever you say, they've been great movies. Dad and I have watched every one. I'd bet money Logan and Beckett have, too."

"They're sappy love stories."

"They're heartwarming and fun. But that's not the point. You could've switched gears at any time. You could've finished another book or gone and gotten a job writing for a nonprofit, or . . . or I don't know. Now you've got an opportunity that could make your dream possible and you're thinking of walking away?"

Raegan had never talked to her like this—never scolded her in such blunt terms.

"If you're going to dream, Kate, commit to it. Don't just talk about it."

"Easy for you to say. You don't even have—" She clamped down on the harsh words she never should've let escape.

Too late.

The bonfire crackled and together with the boney old oak tree overhead cast shadows over her sister's face.

"Just because I'm not off in a big city with a big career like you and Logan and Beckett doesn't mean I don't have dreams."

She tried to reach out for Raegan's arm, but her sister stepped back. "I know, Rae, I shouldn't have—"

"And even if I didn't, I'd rather not have a dream at all than be too scared to pursue the one I've got." And with that, Raegan turned and walked away.

~⌒つ

Colton marched into Logan's room. "I asked her to write my book."

Logan dropped a pile of folded clothes in the middle of the floor. "Man, announce yourself, will you?"

Colton plopped onto Logan's perfectly made bed—the corner of the top quilt folded over to make room for his pillow. Very Logan-esque. A suitcase lay sprawled open at the end of the bed. *Wait* . . . "You're packing?"

Logan picked up the clothes he'd dropped and set them in the suitcase. "Candidate got a last-minute fundraising gig and they need a speech on energy policy drafted by Friday."

Hints of Logan's childhood flavored the room—two walls painted bright red, a framed Iowa Hawkeyes poster hanging on the back of his closet door, a bulletin board over his desk barely visible behind ribbons and awards, photos and newspaper clippings. And on the desk, a photo of all four Walker siblings, arms draped over each other's shoulders, and goofy faces pointed at the camera.

What would it have been like to grow up in such a close-knit clan?

"You work too much, Walker. You ever think of taking a real vacation?"

"Not sure that word's in my vocab."

The wry humor in Logan's voice didn't match the fatigue in his eyes. A better friend would've noticed Logan's exhaustion before now—wouldn't have spent so many months wrapped up in his own miseries, miseries that probably seemed more like luxuries to someone who'd lost a wife and never got a break for more than a couple days at a time.

Logan added a pile of socks to the suitcase. "So what about your book?"

But instead of answering Logan's question, Colton flipped the suitcase closed. "How are you and Charlie doing? Really?"

His friend paused, shrugged, surprise registering in his

expression. Maybe, too, discomfort. Uncharted territory, this. Too often in the past, their friendship had been about Logan bailing Colton out of trouble. Had Colton ever taken the time to turn the tables?

"We're fine."

"You do realize *fine* is generally code for *horrible?*"

"Who says?"

"Everyone who's ever said 'I'm fine' while feeling anything but."

Logan rubbed one hand over the opposite arm, breeze fanning into the room from the open window, and then crossed the room to pull the chair from his desk. He sat backward in it, arms drooping over its back. "We are fine most of the time. Work is busy, but good. Charlie's healthy and happy, has a great nanny. And her pediatrician said the not-talking thing can be normal sometimes for kids who don't have older siblings to mimic."

"But?"

"I'm burnt out," Logan admitted in a low tone. "I barely see my daughter. I still have days when some random, stupid piece of my brain convinces me, just for a second, that Emma's going to walk through the door. That she's not really gone."

He said it all without taking a breath. No pauses.

But Colton could feel the sharpness of his friend's hurt all the same. If only he could find words to meet the moment. *Like Norah used to.*

He sucked in a breath. Where had that come from? He hadn't thought of his old social worker in a long time—her closet of an office, the easy way she'd had of rounding her desk, draping one ebony arm over his shoulder, and landing on just the right words.

"It's going to get better. I have to believe that," Logan said now. "Because I've got a daughter, and she's going to have a good life, no matter what."

"Of course she is. You both are." The assurance seemed trite, lacking.

Seconds passed and Logan straightened. "Hey, you really asked Kate? What'd she say?"

"That she had to think about it. Probably means *no*, right?"

Logan swiveled in his chair for a few hesitance-filled seconds. "Kate could use a career break. Maybe this is the perfect thing for both of you. But . . . she's my sister, Colt."

His mouth went dry. "I know."

"She's got hurt in her past, and none of us want to see it repeated."

Logan couldn't seriously be implying what he thought he might be. "Dude, I asked her to co-write a book with me. That's it. Besides, after Lilah . . ." He'd had enough with women for the moment. Too distracting. Case in point, that last game, the injuries he still iced every night. "You can trust me, Walker. Strictly business."

Logan stood. "Yeah?"

Footsteps pattering through the hall sounded from outside Logan's room. "Will you believe me if we shake on it? Spit in our palms and all that?"

"Unnecessary. And also gross."

The footsteps stopped, and both men looked to the open doorway. Kate. Out of breath. "Hey. Hi."

"Where've you been, sis? You smell like a fire."

She ignored Logan's question, gaze on Colton. "I'll write your book."

He stood. Opened his mouth. Closed it. Opened it again. "You'll write my book."

"I'll write your book."

"You'll write my book."

"I'll write—"

"Sheesh, broken record, anyone?" Logan flipped open his suitcase. "This just in: Kate's gonna write Colton's book."

"And it better work out well, because I just called and quit my job at the Willis Tower."

Colton only grinned.

And was still grinning seconds later when Kate left just as abruptly as she'd arrived. When he finally turned, it was to see Logan drilling him with raised eyebrows.

"Like I said, strictly business."

5

There was something soothing about painting a building. Sorta like watching the mowing of a football field. Rhythmic. Peaceful.

Five days in Maple Valley and Colton had started to get used to the slower pace. Especially in the past couple days of helping Case Walker at the depot in the mornings. Yesterday he'd spent almost the entire day working with the older man to strip peeling paint away and prime the walls for fresh color.

"Probably dumb to paint first, considering all the other repairs," Case had said yesterday. "But sometimes getting something presentable on the outside makes braving the inside easier."

Colton dipped his roller into the paint tray at his feet, then checked his watch. Two hours until he was supposed to meet Kate downtown. Their initial meeting to talk about the book. For the first time since he'd signed the contract with the publisher, honest to goodness interest in the project sparked through him. If he worked fast, he could get this wall done before heading out.

"Whoa, it really is Colton Greene, right here in Maple Valley."

He froze, paint roller lifted midair, heard the tap of paint drops hitting his old running shoes as he turned. And then the snap of a camera.

So much for peaceful. A disgruntled cough rumbled up his

throat, and his displeasure must've shown on his face, because the woman with the camera took a step back and lowered her arms, expression stopping somewhere between awed and apologetic.

"Don't worry, I only took the photo to prove to our sports reporter I actually met you. He didn't think I'd have the nerve to track you down."

Sports reporter? So she *was* media. And he'd thought he could escape all that hype tucked away in Iowa.

"You're quiet." The woman pushed brown bangs out of her eyes and dropped her camera into the bag slung over her shoulder.

"Actually I'm busy." He turned, dipped his roller into the pan at his feet. Early afternoon sunlight glistened in the blue paint and reflected off the silver of the plastic pan.

"And curt."

He didn't miss the hint of surprise mixed with annoyance in her tone. And for a sliver of a second, guilt needled him. His mom may have died two decades ago, but time hadn't dulled the memory of her voice drilling manners into him until "please" and "thank you" became second nature.

Even as a rambunctious kid, he'd been able to pull off polite when he needed to. Like during endless interviews with potential adoptive families—more often than not the look on his social worker's face letting him know, good manners or not, it wasn't happening this time either.

Poor Norah. He hadn't realized it back then, but he now had no doubt those going-nowhere interviews had been as hard for her as they were for him.

Weird, second time in a week Norah had come to mind.

Colton slicked blue paint over the rough wood of the depot. When the roller ran dry, he turned once more.

Still there.

"Sorry. Is there something I can do for you?" He dropped

the roller into the pan. "Besides help you prove a point to your sports reporter?"

She smirked. "Goodness, that was something close to a smile."

"Who *are* you?"

"Amelia Bentley. I'm actually here to talk to Case about an article on the railroad. We always do one this time of year right on the cusp of fall—which is when the railroad gets the most business. But when I saw you . . ." She shrugged, jade eyes glinting in the midafternoon sunlight. "Well, can you blame me for asking if you'd ever consider gracing the local newspaper girl with an interview?"

"Can't blame you. But can't do an interview either."

Because he'd promised Ian. *Lay low. Stay out of the spotlight.* 'Course, did a local paper even count as the spotlight?

And speaking of Ian, it was probably about time he returned one of his manager's half-dozen calls ever since Colton's stilted text Monday night.

Good news. Snagged a writer. Name's Kate Walker, sister of a friend. Staying in Iowa while we write the book. Draft by October.

He still wasn't entirely sure what'd swayed Kate's decision about the project. Most likely the money. Regardless, it was kind of great, really, how it'd all worked out. Like God had known Colton and Kate were the answers to each other's problems, said *voilà,* and parked them both in Iowa.

What had that pastor at Case Walker's church said Sunday? Something about keeping your eyes open and trusting God to show up. Maybe that's what'd happened.

His gaze drifted now to the railroad tracks ribboning over gravel. How long had it been since he'd asked God to show up? Not to grant a request or get him off a hook or heal an injury but to simply show up in his life?

He looked back at Amelia, her attention moving from his half-completed paint job to the sign that welcomed visitors to the depot. Case had told him the Maple Valley Scenic Railway offered afternoon rides, dinner car rides in the evenings, morning runs on Saturdays. "Well, at least I tried." She tipped her sunglasses over her eyes.

"And don't forget, you've got a picture." He grasped for a tinge of friendliness, made himself smile again. She wasn't pushy, he'd give her that.

"Ah, Amelia, you're here." The now-familiar polish of Case's voice sounded in sync with the clapping of his footsteps on the boardwalk as he came around the depot.

"Sorry I'm early. But I thought I'd get a few photos before our interview."

"No apology necessary. Take all the photos you want. The 2-8-2 Mikado steam locomotive just got a washing down—she's all pretty if you want to start there. Meet you in the office in ten minutes?"

Amelia nodded, shot Colton one more look of curiosity, and stepped from the boardwalk, moving toward the orange-and-black locomotive Case had pointed to.

Case gave an exaggerated wink. "She's single, Greene. And a looker."

"Only I'm not looking." And if he was, he wouldn't look here. Because Maple Valley was a pit stop on the way to whatever came next. A new life.

Which meant he had to get better about tempering the piece of him still yearning for his old life. The one where he got to play the game he loved for a living, be a part of a team, something big. And, yeah, the life where spectators and their admiration filled him with pride and purpose. Maybe that was wrong to admit, but there it was.

Besides, when it came to women, he obviously had a thing or two to learn. Twice now he'd completely misread Lilah—counted on a future together she clearly didn't. Back in January when he'd first planned to propose, only to have her break up with him before he got the chance. Then just last week, when he'd been so sure her months of checking in on him as he recovered from injuries and surgeries meant her feelings were still alive.

Obviously he couldn't have been more wrong.

He started to reach for his paint roller again, but Case's hand on his shoulder stopped him. "Son, I know Logan asked you to stay. Worried about his old man."

"Oh, but no—"

"Don't try to deny it." Case's eyes narrowed even as his lips pressed into a grin. "My kids are helpful and considerate, yes. Subtle, not so much. But I'd hate to think you're stuck here if you'd rather not be. My arm may be in a sling, but I'm not helpless."

Few days ago, *stuck* might've been exactly how he felt. But something had changed the other night in Logan's bedroom. When Kate said yes. Like knotted rope shaken loose and finally usable.

"I'm glad to be here, sir." He couldn't help the show of respect tacked on to the end of his statement. Ever since he'd first met Case Walker, back in college, when Logan's parents had come to the college for Parents' Weekend, he'd felt an instinctive sense of respect for the man.

"In that case, glad to have you."

Colton picked up the paint roller. "Plus, it worked out pretty well—meeting Kate right when I needed her." He said the words nonchalantly, but Case's sudden quiet, the flicker of something unreadable in his eyes, stole Colton's ease. "Not needed *her* so much as needed a writer. And if you're worried about . . . I mean, if you think I . . . ." Discomfort crawled up his spine. "It's like I already told Logan. Strictly business."

Case's surprise chuckle echoed in the open space behind the depot. "Ha, that's not at all where I was going. I was going to congratulate you on convincing the girl who went to no more than two football games her entire high school career to write your book." He slapped Colton on the shoulder, sending dots of paint from the roller in his hand to the wall. "But as long as we're on the subject . . ." He took the paint roller from Colton and set it down once more.

"I promise, strictly—"

"Ease up, kid. Truth is, my elder daughter could use just the opposite of business. She'd kill me for saying so, and Lord knows I'd wallop anyone who intentionally hurt her. But if you could manage to get *her* to treat your working together as anything but business, I'd have to be impressed."

"Sir, are you saying—"

"I'm saying have fun with the book project. Kate could use a change of pace, and clearly, so could you. Now where's that reporter?"

He stepped away, leaving Colton to let out a breath. Talk about a surprising turn in conversation. Didn't matter what Case said, though—whether he was joking or not. Colton had promised Logan.

And he'd promised himself. No more distractions. He'd write this book. He'd follow through on his plans to stay in town long enough to see the depot reopen.

Then he'd return to his real life, the career that just might hobble back into existence if this book was the success Ian predicted. Speaking of which . . .

He pulled out his phone. Ignored the slew of texts. *Might as well get the argument over with.* He pressed the speed dial for his manager.

Ian picked up on the second ring. "Not a good idea, Colt."

"Afternoon to you too, Muller."

"If you'd answered one of the four times I called earlier, I'd be all over the laid-back greetings. But my patience is down to zilch."

Colton moved away from the depot wall, tall grass brushing underneath his feet. "Fine, then, what's not a good idea?" As if he had to ask.

"Asking a woman you've known all of two seconds to write your book."

"Almost a week. I've known her almost a week. And I've known her family a lot longer. They're good people."

"Condoleezza Rice. Shirley Temple. Nelson Mandela. My mother. All good people. None of whom should be writing your book."

"Pretty sure at least two of the people on your list are dead." Colton paced along the building, swallowed up in its shadow. "Now, if you really could get Condi Rice, I might reconsider this whole thing."

Not even a hint of amusement in Ian's grouchy pause or his sighed question.

"Does this woman know anything about football? A single thing?"

Colton rolled his eyes and rubbed one palm over the back of his neck. "I'm sure she can spell the word. That's a single thing."

"Greene."

He paused, softening his tone. "Ian, you're looking out for me. You always do, and I'm grateful for it—even if I've done a lousy job of showing it lately." He leaned one hand against the wall, then jerked away when he realized he'd stuck it in wet paint. "I know you want what's best for my career. Thing is, I'm certain . . . this is it."

"Has she ever even read a sports memoir? How do you know

she's not just in it for a slice of your fame? Or is this about you? How hot is she?"

His tolerance fizzled. "It's like this, Ian. This isn't about me being stubborn or unreasonably unbendable. It's about being convinced it's the right thing." Colton's fingers closed into a fist, wet paint smudging over his fingers. "You want me to do a book—only way I'm doing it is with Kate Walker."

～⌒～

"So my mocha is the quarterback and the cinnamon shaker is a wide receiver?" Kate hunched over the coffee shop table, notebook in hand and focus on Ava Kingsley's makeshift field.

Her cousin's girlfriend had offered to teach Kate the basics of football the second she'd heard about Colton's book project. Which was about ten minutes ago when they'd bumped into each other at Coffee Coffee.

Yes, that was really the name of the little storefront coffee shop nestled at the corner of the city block that faced the river. The interior made up for the name's lack of creativity—one brick wall ornamented with eclectic artwork, tables of varying heights dotting the floor space, colorful mosaic backsplash running the length of the counter.

Ava pushed her blond ponytail over her shoulder and nodded. "Yes, and all these torn-up napkin bits, they're the opposing team's defensive line. Their goal is to stop the offense from gaining yardage."

A coffee machine rattled and hissed in the background. "And the offense needs to gain ten yards within four downs to keep possession."

"Right."

"Such a weird sport. Who came up with the idea of downs?

Why'd they decide you only get four? Who thought it was smart to have so many guys on a field at once? It's so messy."

And somehow she had to learn to write intelligently about it. Maybe this wasn't the best idea ever. But it was too late now. She'd called Frederick Langston this morning and agreed to the trip to Africa. After his initial burst of enthusiasm, he'd given her the details.

She would go to New York City soon after Thanksgiving, work with the team heading to Africa for a couple weeks, complete an orientation, and plan the specifics of the project she'd be writing. Then she'd go home for two weeks over the holidays and leave for Africa shortly after the New Year.

So much for easing into it—taking time to think and pray. But this wasn't like her impulsive choice to follow Gil to Chicago. And Africa, the foundation, Colton—all the things pulling her toward this decision—they weren't like Gil. Besides, what was there to think about? Colton and his crazy idea had plopped into her life right when she'd needed money. If that wasn't God saying "Go for it," what was?

Ava shook her head now. "It's not messy if you know what you're looking at. It's like reading music. Someone who doesn't get notes and scales and clefs looks at sheet music and it's a bunch of gobbledygook. But for someone who reads music, everything on the page has a purpose. Just like all the guys on a field. They've got a position and a specific role to play."

Like characters in a story. *I don't have to master the sport. Just fake it well enough to convince readers. And reviewers and peers and sports geeks.* She swallowed, mouth suddenly dry, chalky worry clouding any earlier confidence.

Kate reached for her drink. Caught Ava's eyes once more. "What?"

"What are you doing with my quarterback?"

She winced as she swallowed, her too-sweet mocha now luke-warm. "Sorry." She replaced the cup. "You really like football, don't you."

"If by *like* you mean *emphatically adore*, yes. I actually used to help coach a college team. Unofficially, that is. When it didn't turn into an actual job, I ended up here."

"With Seth." Kate grinned. "So . . . you're going to keep helping him at the restaurant long term?"

"For now. Maybe, um, you know . . . forever."

"You don't miss coaching?"

"Oh sure. But it's kind of fun—refreshing, too—to be part of someone else's dream for a while, instead of so obsessed with my own. Now, enough about me. " Ava moved the cup closer to a stir stick.

Hmm, what position had she said the stir stick was? Hiker?

"So the play starts with Stick Guy hiking the ball to the mocha who's then going to look for the open cinnamon shaker. Or, if he sees an opening in the napkin line, he just might run it himself." Ava looked up. "Got it?"

Kate stared at the table, now just a clutter. She shouldn't have agreed to this. If she couldn't pull off a romantic screen-play—supposedly her area of expertise—what made her think she could write a compelling memoir about a man she hardly knew who played a sport she didn't understand?

Ava waved her hand over the table. "Pay attention, girl. I'm saving you from having to read *Football for Dummies*. Don't you want to surprise and impress Colton with your football knowledge?"

Colton. He'd be her saving grace, right? He could massage all the football scenes in the book. Her worry stilled. "Did you watch many of Colton's games?"

Ava reached for the strawberry smoothie she'd conveniently

not included in the improvised field lineup. "Are you kidding me? He was one of my favorite players."

"What was he like?"

"Loose cannon, really. He's pretty big for a quarterback, so he was great at breaking through a line. And even though his pass percentage wasn't out of this world, once in a while he'd pull off this incredible throw at the last minute. I think that's why he was so fun to watch—you never knew what he was going to do."

"Couldn't that also be seen as a weakness, though? I mean, from a coach's perspective?" Or any perspective. An image of Gil slid in then—the day *he'd* done what she never expected, told her everything she'd thought about their relationship was wrong.

"*We never should've been more than teacher and student, Katie.*"

"*But you said—*"

"*I said a lot of things I shouldn't have.*"

The blaring of Ava's phone interrupted the memory. "Sorry, gotta answer this. Outside, apparently." She pointed to the sign hanging on one wall. A picture of a phone with a slash through it.

As Ava disappeared out the front door, Kate plucked her mocha from the table and rose. Might as well get a refill while she waited, do something to silence Gil's voice, still annoyingly crystal clear in her memory.

The barista behind the counter fiddled with the handle on one of the machines as Kate approached. The woman let out a frustrated groan. "Stupid thing."

"Everything all right back here?"

The girl spun, the ties at the back of her apron hanging loose. "If by 'all right' you mean a disaster in the making, then yeah, absolutely." She swiped at the strands of jet-black hair dangling over her face, leaving a trail of coffee grounds along her cheek. Pierced nose, skull-shaped earrings, college aged. "Any minute now the midmorning rush is gonna show up, and here I am with a broken espresso machine and—" She broke off as the machine rattled once more.

"What exactly constitutes a rush in Maple Valley?"

The barista—Megan, according to her nametag—shoved up the sleeves of her black-and-white-striped shirt, scowl deepening. "You'd be surprised. If we ever ran out of coffee, this town would go into a collective shock. Bunch of caffeine-deprived zombies roaming the streets." She abandoned the machine. "What do you need?"

Hm. Not big on service with a smile, it seemed. "Uh, well—"

"I'm the only one working this afternoon, so spit it out."

Kate glanced behind Megan to where the espresso machine sputtered once more. "Look, I've worked in a coffee shop off and on over the years. I know the equipment. Can I take a look?"

Doubt—or maybe confusion—brushed over Megan's face, but she motioned to the waist-high swinging door that led behind the counter. "Be my guest."

Kate skirted around the counter corner and inspected the machine. Oh yeah, easy fix. She fiddled with it until it looked right, then stuck a cup under the spout and turned it on.

But instead of gurgling to life the way it should have, the machine spat, hissed, and in a fit of malfunction, water gushed like a fountain. A shriek slipped out, joined by Megan's voice behind her.

"I thought you said you knew what you were doing."

"I thought I did." Liquid slapped at her face, drops sliding down her neck and splotching over her shirt. "A little help?"

"If I knew what to do I'd have done it ten minutes ago."

The distant chiming of the bells over the entrance joined the noisy moment. Kate plunged one hand into the mess of equipment, palm clamping over the spot spewing water. Lot of good that did. Now it just spurted through her fingers, spraying every direction.

"Unplug it." She closed her eyes against the jetting water. Good thing she hadn't tried too hard on her hair today. It framed her face in matted strands. *And please tell me the mascara I flicked on this morning was waterproof.*

Megan yanked a cord, and seconds later, the flow of water slowed . . . and fizzled to a stop.

"Trouble, ladies?"

Nooo. Of all people?

She and the barista turned in sync as the espresso machine gave one more chug. And there stood Colton, black hoodie hanging loose over a black-and-white-checkered button-down, the perfect picture of ease and enjoyment.

"No trouble at all." Kate drawled the words, daring Colton with crossed arms and narrow eyes to tease any further.

But it wasn't enough to drain the amusement from his smirk. "So if I ask for an espresso, there's no problem?"

Cheeky man.

"You can order anything but espresso." Megan gave a toss of her hair and pinned him with a glare. "What'll it be?"

He glanced back and forth between them. "Actually I was just meeting Kate—"

Megan shook her head. "You come into the shop, proceed to laugh at us—"

"I didn't actually laugh."

"And then you don't even have the courtesy to buy anything?"

Kate stifled a giggle as Colton's focus darted to the menu. "Cappuccino. Medium."

"Fine. It'll be ready in a minute." Megan turned with a huff.

Kate angled around the counter and followed Colton as he

inched away. He leaned in when she reached him. "I don't even like cappuccinos. She intimidates me."

"Don't worry. You're not alone." Kate smoothed her hands over her jeans, sudden tremble of unwelcome nerves making an appearance.

Which was silly. Because all they were going to do was sit down and talk about his book. Figure out a game plan, how they were going to turn an idea into reality within a month. Shouldn't matter that he towered over her, seemed to gulp her up in his shadow in an illogically enjoyable way.

"Talked with my manager today, by the way. Gave him your agent's contact info. Should have a contract for you in a few weeks."

Wow, her own experience in the publishing world might've been short-lived but it was enough to know things usually happened in months, not weeks. *They're fast-tracking it*. Because of her. Because Colton had picked her to write the book that could make or break his career.

And he was just standing there now, a thesaurus full of synonyms that added up to ridiculous amounts of handsome. And she, with her coffee-stained shirt and a gripping certainty that she couldn't hope to live up to his expectations.

Colton shrugged out of his hoodie then, just as Megan called out from the counter. "Cappuccino."

Colton brushed past Kate, reached for the drink, and handed Megan a ten. "Keep the change." He turned back to Kate.

"Trying to buy her off?"

"What are the chances she spit in this?" With his other hand, he held his hoodie toward her.

"Do I look cold?"

"No, but, uh . . ." He nodded at her shirt, covered in water and coffee grounds.

She looked from Colton to the hoodie and back to Colton. "I can't do it."

"I know it's too big. You'll swim in it, but—"

She shook her head. "I mean the book. I don't know what I was thinking. You need someone who knows how to write a sports memoir. Who can tell the cinnamon shaker from the stir stick from the napkin bits."

"You lost me, Rosie."

"It's Kate, and I'm not your writer, Colton." Even if, for no reason that made any sense, she suddenly really wanted to be.

"I think you are." He held his hoodie out to her once more, waited until she finally accepted it. "And if it's football that has you worried, don't worry. I've got a plan for that."

～～つ

The energy of the Mavericks players radiated from their cluster around the fifty-yard line, reaching over to where Colton watched from the fence outlining the field. They were running in place, knees high, and palms clacking against their thighs with each step.

Arms slung over the metal fence, Colton felt the itch of his own pent-up aggression. Yeah, he might fit in a workout most days—a physical therapist-approved regime, of course—but it was nothing like the feel of suiting up and training with a team, the mingling smell of mowed grass and exertion fueling his focus.

Next to him, Kate fiddled with the zipper of the hoodie he'd loaned her. It hung on her frame, draping over her like a blanket. "So watching a high-school football practice is going to teach me all I need to know?" The zipper stuck halfway up.

"Not even close, but that's not the point."

She yanked on the zipper. "Then what is?"

"Getting you into the spirit of football. You don't have to know the sport to write my book. Just appreciate it. I'll take care of the jargon and technical stuff." He leaned in to help her with the hoodie, giving the zipper just enough of a jerk to loosen it, then pulled it upward.

In the background, the shrill of the coach's whistle cut into the rhythm of the players' kicks and grunts. "Give me fifty push-ups, followed by two laps. Then water up before we get to work."

Colton paused, two fingers still closed around the zipper underneath Kate's chin. The wind played with her hair, and afternoon sun highlighted the uncertainty in her eyes.

"Colton Greene. I thought that was you."

Colton blinked and dropped his hand, then turned to see the coach ambling his direction. The man stopped in front of him, athletic frame tempered by the silver hair poking from underneath his hat and reading glasses sitting low on his nose. He tucked his clipboard underneath one arm.

"Coach Leo Barnes." He jutted one hand over the fence for an awkwardly angled handshake.

Colton nodded his head toward Kate. "And this is Kate Walker."

"Oh, I know Kate, all right. Had all four Walkers in high-school government class."

Of course. Because he was in small-town Iowa, where it really wasn't exaggerating to say everybody knew everybody.

"Good to see you again, Mr. Barnes."

"I think you can get away with Leo now, kid. Or Coach." He turned back to Colton. "I'm trying real hard to play it cool, but gotta admit to feeling star struck. I was at the playoff game where you threw that seventy-yard pass. Smoother than a Bing Crosby ballad. Made it look effortless."

Effortless, or the result of some mighty good luck. Either way, it was the best game of his career, no question. "Good-looking crop of players you've got out there." They sprawled across the grass, on hands and toes, pushing themselves up with bent elbows.

Coach Leo nodded. "They're not half bad. Whined their way through hot summer practices, but now that it's cooling off and the season's about to begin, they're shaping up."

Colton could still remember the jolt of crisp morning practices at the University of Iowa—so different from fall in California. He'd forgotten how much this Midwest state had grown on him in those four college years—games on dark evenings when the chill turned his breath white, the sky so wide open and clear it was as if the stars watched him play.

If junior high and high school had stretched like one long desert, college in Iowa had been the first step into an oasis that offered new life. One finally mostly free of haunting half memories. He had his old social worker to thank for it—she'd forced him to complete all those scholarship applications. The University of Iowa had made the best offer.

"I should tell you I'm usually a stickler for closed practices," Coach Leo said. "Got a couple parentals who think they're coaches. Enough to drive a man nuts." The coach pulled off his cap, swiped the back of his hand over his forehead. "This town and its football. Doesn't go all *Friday Night Lights* or anything, but Maple Valley sure does love the game. Enough so that, if I let it, practice time would turn into a spectator event."

"Sorry, we can take a hint." Colton pulled his arms off the fence.

Coach Leo released a chuckle as he fit his hat back over silver hair. He had a weathered face—the kind wrinkled by smiles and probably endless hours of sun-soaked marathon practices. Considering his size and those linebacker shoulders, the man must've played football back in the day. And if Colton had to guess, he'd bet the slight ridge in Leo's nose came from a long-ago nasty hit.

"Don't be an oaf, Greene. Not kicking you out. Just saying if you're gonna stay, maybe try out the other side of the fence. I could use a guy like you."

"Say again?"

"Not that I could pay you or anything. The school's athletic budget is bare bones as it is. But surely you miss the game. Word on the street is you're sticking around awhile. Why not come hang out at some practices? The guys would get a kick out of it."

"I'm not a coach, Coach." And yet . . . what might it feel like to dip his foot back into the game? To feel a part of a team again? The camaraderie, the sense of belonging. The thrill of competition.

He might not be able to play himself—a punching reality that still smarted if he thought too long on it—but look at Case Walker. The man had boasted the kind of career few men attained. Honorable. Bold. Admirable. Serving his country first in a war, then in an office.

And yet he'd had to walk away from the life he'd built when his wife got sick. He'd found a way to make a new life for himself. Amazingly, he seemed content.

What if Colton could do the same?

"You're thinking about it." Behind Coach Leo, his players rose in trickles to begin their laps.

"Maybe."

"Hey, isn't that . . ." Kate's voice rose and fell, her eyes on the field, recognition sparking through them. "It's the kid from the depot. The one who broke in."

He followed Kate's gaze, landing on a player hefting himself from the ground.

"You're talking about Webster Hawks?" Coach lifted bushy eyebrows. "Don't tell me he got in trouble."

"Not exactly. He didn't steal anything." Because he hadn't had time. No, the moment the kid had seen Kate and Colton he'd frozen at the cash register, an alertness about him, enough that Colton had practically witnessed his mental wheels turning as he assessed the situation—the doorway, Colton, Kate. And then he'd darted with a wildcat-like quickness and perfect footwork. "What position does he play?"

The coach's forehead wrinkled underneath the bill of his cap. "He's new—transferred this year when he was placed with a foster family. Said he played secondary at his old school."

Foster family. Colton's gaze found Webster once more, now tracing the edge of the field in lanky, even strides. Put a ball in the crook of his arm, and he'd be a ready-made carrier. He could just feel it. "I think he's your receiver."

"You don't even know if he can catch."

"You can teach a player to catch. But reading the field and making your move, there's an instinct there. I think Webster might have it." Colton tipped his sunglasses over his eyes. "'Course, it's just my gut speaking. I'm no coach."

"You could be."

He felt Kate's eyes on him, her interest mingling with his own.

"Look, I've got an idea." Coach turned, waved down Webster, now rounding the goalposts. "Hawks, come here."

The kid jogged over, breathing hard, and as he approached the curiosity in his expression shifted to something closer to unease. Did he recognize Colton and Kate from Saturday night? "Yeah, Coach?"

"This is Colton Greene. Hear you had a bit of a run-in the other night."

Webster's attention flickered from Colton back to Leo.

"He thinks you're a wide receiver. What do you say to that?"

The kid shuffled his fingers through shaggy hair. "Dunno. Except first game's in a few days. Isn't it a little late to make a change like that?"

Colton couldn't help cutting in. "Not if it's a smart change."

"Normally I'd balk at another guy telling me how to arrange my roster, but Greene here is a special case. And he sees something in you." Leo leaned against the fence. "I have a feeling he might be willing to work with you. Test out his gut and see if I should have you on offense after all. That right, Greene?"

So that was the coach's idea. Launch the proposition right in front of Webster so Colton couldn't say no.

But who said he wanted to? Webster might be standing there with arms folded and chin jutting, trying for all the world to don a nonchalance that said he didn't care, but Colton had worn the same forced indifference after years of foster-home hopping. He could feel the undercurrent of Webster's wariness as clear as the wind now rattling through the bleachers behind him.

That's what insecurity did to a kid—the kind that came from wondering how long *this* bedroom in *this* house with *this* family would last.

And he found himself nodding. "Sure, I could—"

"Coach, you want me to play receiver, I'll do it," Webster jutted in, a hardness in his eyes. "But I don't want to be anybody's special project." His jaw tightened. "I got another lap to do."

He turned on one foot and shoved off, the force of his movement like an Olympic swimmer pushing through a wall of beating water. Even angry, Webster displayed the athletic bent for a larger role on the team. He passed his teammates now finishing their laps and flocking to the water cooler propped on a table on the sideline.

Leo let out a sigh. "I have a feeling he'll get home tonight, realize he just said no to one-on-one coaching from an NFL quarterback, and kick himself."

Ex-quarterback. Colton shrugged. "Can't blame him. I might feel weird, too, if I was singled out."

"Why don't you stick around anyway, Colt?" Kate asked the question softly. "Take up Coach Leo on his offer. Help with the team some. We can meet back up later and—"

"Don't think so."

Questions—probably the kind he didn't want to answer—hovered in her eyes. "But why—"

"Thanks, Coach, but I've got a book to write and repairs at the depot and . . ."

Working with Webster was one thing, but he couldn't hang out on the sidelines playing pretend coach to kids running the field with their whole future ahead of them.

It'd be too close to watching the person he used to be.

And too much of a reminder that he'd never be that person again.

6

He won't talk about himself, Rae. How am I supposed to write a book about a guy who won't talk about himself?"

Kate dropped three quarters into a cheerleader's hands and picked up a cup of hot chocolate. How was that teenager staying warm without a jacket in the day's low temps? The first of autumn's leaves scampered across the town square now, stirred by a nipping wind that seemed to forget today only marked the end of September's first full week. No Indian summer this year.

"But you've spent the past three nights sitting on the porch with the guy. I thought you were interviewing him." Raegan paid for her cocoa and stepped away from the table set up in the square.

"I was. But all I've got are notes about his favorite games and memories of teammates. At this rate the book's going to turn out little more than a glorified *Sports Illustrated* article." A swirl of clouds knotted overhead, crouching low in a sky more gray than blue.

Raegan sipped her drink, then wrinkled her nose. "Blech. They didn't get this mixed well. Powdery hot chocolate. Mom would not approve. Remember how she made it?"

Oh yes. Thick and so sweet just half a cup could put a person in a diabetic coma. "At least we successfully participated in Booster Club Friday and did our part to help the cheerleaders afford new pompons."

Booster Club Friday was always the first weekend of the school year. School let out early, and the town square played host to tables and booths and, of course, the football player auction, during which community members "bought" players for an afternoon of volunteer work.

"Yep, now all we have to do is use the money Dad gave me to buy a player. He said to get someone who looks like he'd be good at shingling a roof. How are you supposed to assess that skill by just looking at a person?"

They walked toward the gathering of townspeople fanning around the band shell, Coach Leo's auctioneer voice rattling over the square. "Don't know, but you better hurry up and pick someone. There are only a few players left." They stopped at the edge of the crowd. "I still don't see why I needed to come along to this, though."

She should be helping Dad at the depot. Or clearing the mess of branches and storm debris still littering the backyard. She'd felt compelled to come, though, when Raegan asked. Ever since their argument at the bonfire, she'd been looking for ways to smooth things over with her sister.

Raegan poured the rest of her hot chocolate in the grass and tossed the cup in a bin. "Believe me, you'll be happy you came. Today is going to be . . . rewarding." The hot pink scarf fluttering under Raegan's chin matched the streaks in her hair.

"You sound like a personal trainer trying to get someone to do push-ups." What wasn't her sister telling her?

"This will be way more fun than push-ups. Trust me."

"Can't. Not when you've got the same look in your eyes as that time you convinced me to perm my hair in high school."

Raegan clapped her hands together. "Oh, my goodness. I forgot about that. Your hair was so short back then. You were like the brunette version of Annie." Raegan's burst of giggles competed with Coach Leo's auctioneering. "And then your date showed up with his head shaved and it was just too perfect. Annie and Daddy Warbucks off to the prom."

"And this would be why I can't trust you. Because you're still mocking me for something that happened thirteen years ago."

Raegan clamped down on her laughter and leaned in. "You're right. That was ages ago, and I've got much newer material to work with."

"If you say one word about me getting into bed with—"

Raegan held up one hand. "Fine, not a word. But you were talking about him. Finish spilling."

"Nothing more to tell. He won't talk about himself. Period." Kate swallowed the last of her watered-down cocoa.

"Next up, we've got T.J. Waring." Coach Leo's booming voice echoed through the park.

"Ooh, the Waring kid. His dad owns a roofing company. Hello, obvious choice." Raegan waved her hand in the air. "Fifty bucks!"

Kate ditched her paper cup and crossed her arms. "You ever stop to think this town could get in trouble for auctioning off kids for work? Like child labor or something?"

"They're high-school guys. I don't think they like to be called kids." Raegan flapped her hand again. "Sixty-five!" She continued bidding until she'd secured her purchase for ninety dollars. "Mission accomplished. And for ten bucks less than what Dad sent me with. Almost thought Lenny Klassen might outbid me, but behold, the power of a pouty smile."

"You're shameless."

Raegan counted out nine ten-dollar bills and pocketed the

tenth. "And ten buckaroos richer." She turned to Kate then, the buzz of Leo's voice continuing in the background. "So here's a question about the Colton thing. Why not just research the guy? He's famous. There can't be much about his past that hasn't hit the Internet."

Rain clouds tussled overhead, and Kate zipped up her black fleece. "I don't want facts, Rae. I want stories, anecdotes, memories. I want to know what shaped him, turned him into the man he is now." Her gaze sought him out—standing across the square, leaning against the old oak tree, bulky arms folded. Surprisingly, he'd bid on one of the team members earlier—Webster, the one who'd rejected his offer to practice together earlier in the week. "He's interesting. One minute he's joking around, teasing, loaning out his hoodie. The next he's . . . broody."

Like when Leo had asked him to coach and he'd refused so swiftly she'd have thought *coach* was code for skinny-dipping in the Blaine River. Colton had barely said a word the rest of that night.

"And with Miles Venton going at eighty bucks, we've reached the end of our squad." The coach pulled his mic off its stand. "But not the end of our event. Boys, bring up the baskets."

Wind wrangled through the square. Kate slid a glance to Raegan. "Baskets?"

"Kate, this is where I'm going to need you to remember I'm your sister and you love me."

Suspicion plunked in. Up front, a bunch of guys from the team climbed the stairs to the band-shell stage, four or five baskets each dangling over their arms. "Talk."

"Couple years ago, the boosters needed to raise extra money to replace the marching band uniforms. So they tacked on a basket auction." Raegan's explanation released in a *whoosh* of words. "Girls put a basket together, guys bid on it, they go on a picnic or a date in the evening or whatever. Everybody had so much fun, it became an annual thing."

"And."

Raegan backed up a step. "And I made a basket for you."

"What?"

"See, there's this guy—"

"Nope. Uh-uh. Not happening." She turned.

"He's sweet and nice and a math teacher." Raegan followed her, grabbing her elbow. "His name is Sheldon."

"First up, we have a basket that's so heavy I'd be willing to bet there's a pan of lasagna inside."

Sheldon. Somewhere in this crowd was a guy named Sheldon who Raegan had talked into buying her basket. A basket she hadn't even put together for a date she didn't want.

"You can't leave, Kate. I gave him fifty bucks."

She halted, mouth gaping as she spun. "You *paid* him?"

"Well, I . . . I just wanted to make sure . . ."

Oh no. No, no, no. A flash of blue caught her eye then. *Colton.* Still standing under that tree. *Yes.* Before she could talk herself out of it, she jogged toward him, skirting around Raegan, out of breath by the time she reached him.

"Hey, Ros—"

"I'd tell you it's Kate, but clearly you're ignoring that, and it doesn't matter anyway because I don't have much time and I need to ask you a favor."

His dimples curved with his smile. "So what's up with this basket thing? Like something out of a prairie novel."

"You read prairie novels?" She shook her head. "Beside the point. Please, Colt. Please, please, please, bid on my basket."

His grin turned into a laugh. "Can't. Word on the street is there's a math teacher in the picture."

"Raegan told you?"

"She's super excited about it. Told me she packed this gourmet meal and everything. I know all about the dude." He placed one hand on her shoulder, tease lighting his eyes. "And look, don't let the fact that the guy has a pet iguana bother you. I'm sure he doesn't sleep with it or anything."

"You're not serious."

"Completely serious—except for the gourmet meal part. I think I saw her put a box of Pop-Tarts in your basket."

Kate narrowed her eyes. "Colton—"

"Oh, hey, if I'm not mistaken, that's your basket up for grabs right now."

Coach Leo's voice bounced through the park, and Kate whirled to see him holding a small basket with a blue ribbon.

She turned back to Colton. "Bid on my basket, Greene."

"You kidding? It's the tiniest one up there. If I was going to bid, I'd bid on that huge one that probably has a steak dinner inside."

"Save me from the math teacher with the iguana. Please."

"Fifteen dollars!" The call came from somewhere in the middle of the crowd, a nasally voice.

Colton's expression turned apologetic. "Shoot, only fifteen? That's a low start." Her glare cut off his chuckle, and he sighed. A long, exaggerated sigh that whispered over her cheeks. "Fine." He lifted his hand. "Twenty-five bucks."

"Thirty." The same voice from the crowd.

"Kate." Raegan appeared at her side, phone in front of her.

"Thirty-five." Colton winked at her.

Raegan pulled on her elbow, tugging her away from Colton. "I know you're mad, so I thought I'd do you a favor, and all I could think to do was get you some quick answers on Colt."

"What?" Her gaze darted to Colton—he was bidding in the fifties now—and she stepped farther away.

"I think I know why he doesn't want to talk about his past."

"Not the time, Rae." Kate's voice came out a hiss.

"Trust me, you need to read it." Raegan thrust her phone at Kate.

"Trust you? After you dragged me to this thing and tricked me into—" Her argument cut off as her gaze landed on the headline of the article Raegan had pulled up on her phone.

Two Dead in Train, Car Collision

She sucked in a sharp breath.

Heaviness filled Raegan's eyes. "Read it."

In the background, Colton's voice mingled with that of the other bidder. Kate took the phone, scanned the opening paragraph, pieces coming together in snippets.

Deadly crash.
Alan, 32, and Joan Greene, 30.
Declared dead at the scene.

And beside the paragraph, a photo of a barely recognizable car, flipped on its side. On a railroad track.

"Eighty-five dollars," Colton's voice called from mere feet away.

Kate kept skimming the article, compassion expanding inside her until it almost physically hurt.

"One hundred bucks."

She looked at Colton, then Rae.

"Read to the end."

Kate lowered her gaze to the article once more, cold air slinking up the sleeves of her fleece and raising goose bumps on her arms.

Also found at the scene was the couple's nine-year-old son. He was treated for minor scratches at Lake County Memorial

Hospital. He is currently in the care of Lake County Human
Services.

Oh, Colton.
"One hundred twenty-five."
Found at the scene.
What did that even mean? She looked at the photo. If he'd
been in the car, how could he possibly have survived? But what
would he have been doing out of the car?
"One hundred twenty-five dollars to Colton Greene. Going
once."
Colton flashed a smile her way, but she dipped her head to
avoid his gaze. And swiped the tear from her cheek.
"Going twice."
He'd watched his parents die.
"Gone."

Colton had no idea how this was going to go down—or
what had possessed him to do this. Webster Hawks sat in the
passenger seat of the truck Colton had been borrowing from
Case Walker for the past week, arms crossed and head turned
to the window. Not exactly a picture of eager anticipation.

But he didn't have a choice—Colton had bought and paid
for five hours of the kid's time. What he'd originally thought
was going to be his only buy of the day. Until Kate had come
begging. He couldn't have said no if he'd wanted to.

Wished he could figure out why she'd gone quiet, though,
after he'd finally won her basket. He'd teased her, told her he
expected to find an amazing dinner in that basket when they
met back up later tonight.

She'd barely laughed.

The first drops of rain splattered on his windshield now as he turned into the parking lot that edged up to the high-school football field.

Good. A rainstorm should make the afternoon interesting if nothing else.

Although he probably shouldn't be happy about the rain—not when worry about flooding was the biggest news in Maple Valley at the moment.

"Those clouds are almost black," Webster huffed. "What are we going to do if it pours?"

Hey, so the kid knew how to talk. "Same thing we'd do if it was sunny and clear skies." Colton shifted into Park and reached around for the football on the backseat. He tossed it into Webster's lap. "Play some catch."

Minutes later, they'd passed the ticket stand and made their way onto the field, what had been a sprinkle of rain now a drizzle.

"Why are you so convinced I need to play wide receiver?"

Colton pulled on his windbreaker as they walked. "You were itching to ask me that the whole drive here, weren't you?"

Webster only grunted.

"That night when we caught you breaking in at the depot, you knew we were coming in, but you kept picking the lock of that cash register for a few seconds. Methodic, completely focused." Was that pride on Webster's face now? *Hmm.* It was probably better not to make the kid think Colton admired his efforts at burglarizing. "A receiver has to have the ability to block out all distractions. You need single-minded concentration."

Webster stopped. "And you think I've got it?"

"That and you're quick on your feet." He zipped up his coat. "And you're a bit of a drama queen."

Webster's eyes narrowed, but the hint of a grin tugging at his mouth gave away the laughter he held in. "False."

"All I'm saying is, most of the receivers I know like attention. They want the ball in their hands and the game at their mercy."

"You think I want attention?"

"You tell me. Why else does a kid pick a train depot of all things to burglarize on a night when half the town is hanging out just a few city blocks away?"

Webster didn't respond. But to his credit, he didn't look away, either. Nor did he swipe at the rain now running in rivulets down his face.

"Toss me the ball and head down to the twenty-yard line."

"Fine. But if it starts to lightning, I'm out." He chucked the ball at Colton.

Colton caught the football with a light hand. When Webster reached the twenty-yard line, Colton lobbed the ball his direction. Like he expected would happen, the ball slicked through Webster's hands and landed in the grass.

Clouds shadowed the field, and the rain shifted into a hearty downpour. Wind chugged in gusts over the open space.

Colton grinned. Perfect. The storm was their opponent this afternoon. No, not the same thing as defenders rushing at Webster. But a good object lesson all the same. "Throw it back."

Webster threw a perfect spiral, and through sheets of rain, Colton connected with it. Seconds later, he returned it. This time Webster's focus latched on to the ball and he snagged the catch. And so they continued for five minutes. Ten.

"I can't believe you paid fifty bucks just to play catch," Webster called.

For that, Colton made the kid run for the next one. But instead of making the catch, Webster slid in a puddle of mud. He let out a curse and slapped the ground before standing. Mud clung to his legs, and by now, the rain had soaked clean through his shirt and track pants.

For the next ten, fifteen, twenty throws, Colton sent Webster racing around the field. When a distant peal of thunder shook the sky, Webster missed another catch and chased the ball to the twenty-yard line.

"Forget the thunder, Hawks. No lightning yet. Focus. Watch the ball, feel the sideline. Watch where your toes come down and stay inbounds."

And then, as he lifted his arm to send the ball sailing toward the sideline, came the moment Colton had been waiting for all afternoon. A grunt of resolve from Webster. A determined steeliness in his eyes, in his stance, in the way his whole body seemed to zero in on the ball.

He pumped his legs, moving in a spurt of speed that knew its target. He jumped, hands the perfect cradle for the ball as they closed around it, then tucked to his side. Webster came down, shoes sinking into wet grass mere inches from the sideline.

And then he ran.

Past Colton, past the fifty-yard line, toward the opposite goal post, not even another growl of thunder slowing his pace.

And Colton tasted rain as his surprise turned into a smile.

So worth it.

The thought caught him off guard, bumping into him like a defender he didn't see coming. But it was true, wasn't it? It was worth it to see a kid who reminded him of himself running like he had something to move toward.

Webster reached the end of the field and slapped the ball to the ground. "Bam."

"I'll be more impressed when you do that with half a defensive line chasing you down." The wind carried his yell down the field. Hopefully Webster heard the impressed tint to his otherwise sarcastic words.

Webster swiped the ball from the grass, made as if to send

it back to Colton, but jerked to a stop. Colton shook wet hair from his forehead, peering through sheets of rain. "What is it?"

Webster looked at his wrist, fiddled with—what? A watch? Wristband or something?

"Dude, what's the holdup?"

When Webster didn't respond, Colton shrugged and started toward the kid, trying to ignore the tightness in his knee he'd noticed ever since they started playing.

When he reached Webster, the kid was unfastening what was indeed a watch. He held it up to his ear. Tapped it.

"Not waterproof?"

Webster lifted his face then, and Colton nearly tripped on the anger written in his eyes. Over a watch? Didn't even look like that nice of one.

"Can I see it?"

Webster only chucked it to the ground. "What next?" All the energy, all the bravado, gone from his voice.

"What's wrong? If it's the watch, there's probably a store in town we can take it to. Or—"

"We gonna throw some more or what? 'Cause if not, I'm out. Not like I really wanted to be here anyway."

The chill in Webster's voice sank under Colton's skin. "If you don't care about this, fine. No sense wasting your time and mine."

"What? You've got better things to do? You don't have a team. You don't have a girlfriend. You don't—"

Colton lifted one palm. "Enough." How in the world had a broken watch started this?

Webster stepped closer. "You think because we've both done the foster-kid thing we're the same or something? We're nothing alike. I read about you. Your parents died in a freak accident but before that they probably cared about you, right? Most parents do—that's what I hear." He yanked off his soaking wet shirt.

The kid had no idea what he was talking about.

No idea.

"Know what my mom loved? Shooting up." He slapped his shirt to the ground, leaving it in a muddy wad as he skulked a few steps away.

"Web—"

He turned, lifted up both arms. "I'll play receiver if you want. But eventually the season will end and I'll graduate in a couple years and age out of the foster system—and then what? Land a huge scholarship like you did? Go All-American? Get drafted? Right."

Why couldn't Colton find words to ease or at least acknowledge the pain he heard in Webster's hurled words? Another moan rumbled through the sky, and then the first crack of lightning.

And Webster stopped his pacing. Squared off with Colton. "Even if all that happened, look at you." He sized Colton up in one angry swoop, eyes narrow, gaze dark. "One dumb move on the field, one injury, and you're done. At the end of the day, it's just a stupid game. Can't depend on it anymore than you can a drug-addict mom."

He swiped his shirt from the ground, flung it over his shoulder, leaving spatters of mud and rain to trail down his back as he stalked away.

And Colton to face the razor-sharp truth in his words.

~o

Surely Colton wasn't standing her up.

Kate scanned the length of the gravel lane reaching from Dad's house, now ribboned with puddles. Dusk had chased away most of the afternoon's storm clouds and now wisped through the sky in chalky pastels. *Where are you, Colt?*

Maybe he'd been joking when he told her he'd meet her tonight for the requisite evening picnic. Maybe she'd been too preoccupied with the contents of that article to realize Colton didn't actually expect her to make sure he got at least something for money he'd spent on her basket.

Maybe she'd let herself look forward to tonight too much . . . for reasons that didn't make any sense. She couldn't let herself get distracted now—not when she was on the brink of living the dream she'd locked away for too long. Not when she'd already missed her chance once—because of a man who'd turned out to be as false as her hopes for their future.

The creak of the screen door whined behind her, and footsteps—Dad's, she just knew—padded over the porch boards. "He'll be here."

She set down the picnic basket that had doubled in weight since she snatched it from the table in the band shell. "It's not like it's a big deal if he doesn't show up. It's just a silly town tradition."

Dad's hand settled on her shoulder. "He'll be here." A few seconds of quiet later, Dad shifted and drew out Kate's gaze. "Katie, I need to tell you something. I've had a phone call . . . from Gil."

She swallowed, tasted sour displeasure. "Gil?" He'd only met Dad a few times—once when Kate was still at ISU, and then when Dad had come to Chicago to visit her. Why would he . . .

"He said he's tried to call you."

He had? "I must not have recognized the number. I don't usually answer if I don't recognize the number." And she was even worse about listening to her voice mails. "Please tell me you hung up on him."

"Believe me, I wanted to. But I could hear sincerity, desperation in his voice. I didn't make him any promises. Only told him I'd tell you I heard from him. Pass on his number."

"I'm not calling him, Dad."

He nodded. "That's your choice. Understandable. But I have to wonder—"

"I don't." Did she sound hard and unfeeling? Could Dad blame her if she did?

The rumble of Dad's old truck, the one he'd loaned Colton for the duration of his stay, saved her from finishing this conversation. She didn't want to talk about Gil. Didn't want to think about him—or why, after all this time, he suddenly needed to talk to her. Dad patted her back. "Told ya Colton would come. Have fun."

Kate leaned in to kiss his cheek, then reached for the picnic basket. She hurried down the porch steps and walked to the truck. But when she opened the passenger door, it was to see a hardness in Colton's face. "Hey."

Her greeting fell flat.

"Should we talk about where we want to do this picnic?" *Or why you look like you just came from a funeral?*

"Let's just drive."

"Okay." She handed him the basket, climbed into the truck. Her eyes connected with his when he handed the basket back. And though he blinked and looked away just as quickly, she still saw it—the flicker of turbulence in his eyes.

Hurt. Raw and unmistakable.

His name was on the tip of her tongue, a question just waiting to be asked—what had happened in the hours since she stood with him in the town square? But he jerked the truck into reverse before she could speak, gravel crumbling under the tires, puddles splattering, and hesitation overriding her curiosity.

They were half a mile from Dad's before he finally spoke. "Sorry I showed up late."

"No worries." A lie, really. Because that's all she'd been doing as she stood on the porch. Worrying that he wasn't going to show up. Worrying about the fact that she was worried.

It's not like we're friends. Not close ones anyway. He doesn't owe me an update on his whereabouts.

"By the way, as a thank-you for buying my basket, I moved all your stuff back into my bedroom. I'm back in Beckett's."

"Kate—"

"Don't even try to argue. I've seen you rubbing your neck constantly. You can't sleep in that little bed in Beckett's room any longer. It'll turn you into a permanent pretzel. Besides, it's fun playing musical bedrooms." She waited for him to laugh or argue again or something. Nothing. "I take it . . . it wasn't the best afternoon ever."

The rural landscape passed outside in a blur of green and gold and brown. Triplet silos rose in the distance, and even with the truck's windows rolled up, the grainy scent of field dust and wet grass mingled. "Not the best."

"We don't have to do this, you know. We can go back to the house."

His momentary quiet convinced her he was about to agree. But a stretched-out pause later, he shook his head. "No. I paid good money for this picnic."

"You sure?"

And then he smiled, a smile that seemed an effort at glossing over the past five minutes—maybe his whole afternoon. "Pick the place and steer me the right direction, Rosie Walker."

Gravel shifted to pavement under the truck's tires. "What do I have to do to get you to call me Kate?"

"I can't help it. You look like a Rosie."

"Do not. Rosies should have pretty curly hair and wear sundresses and . . . and pink lipstick."

Colton laughed and loosened his grip on the steering wheel. "You have curly hair."

"I have unmanageable tangles, and I can't remember the last time I wore lipstick."

"Well, you blush on command. That seems like a Rosie-ish trait to me."

"I do not."

"You do. I could make you blush right now."

"Colton—"

"You look very pretty tonight, Katharine Rose Walker, even if you're not wearing a sundress or pink lipstick."

"Thank you, but I'm not going to blush." Too late, because she could feel the heat climbing into her cheeks.

"I saw a picture of your mom in the hallway back at your dad's. You look so much like her, it's uncanny."

She stilled, any joking argument lost in a breathless moment of soft surprise. "I never thought I looked much like her. Raegan's the one who got her blond hair and blue eyes."

Colton moved his gaze from the road to her. "You got her smile."

If she was blushing now, the warmth came from a place deep inside her. His words filled a hungry space she hadn't even recognized until now.

Colton returned his focus to the road. "And her nose."

Her laughter poked at the weight in the air between them, and he joined in, a sound she could get used to, if she were honest. Deep and rumbly and . . .

"So where are we going? I'm just driving aimlessly, but I'm starving."

The idea slid in as soon as she looked out the window. "Pull over here."

"You want to eat in a ditch?"

"Nope, just pull over."

He obeyed, parked, took the basket from her lap, and seconds later they stood at the side of the road. She pointed toward a corncrib—metal cylinder with a cement base—squatting on a hill in the middle of the field.

Colton shrugged. "Not exactly a picnic table, but I can go with it."

Tall grass swished through their feet as they made their way toward the field. The ground was still damp from the afternoon storm. "We used to play in this field when we were kids. Beckett's best friend's parents live just down the lane. We'd come here and play house—although if you ask him, he'd lie and say we played war or cowboys and Indians or something."

Kate angled around an abandoned tire, avoiding slabs of wood and scrap metal to reach the corncrib. Colton climbed up its cement base first, then reached down to help Kate up. She bumped against his chest before steadying.

He looked down at her. "Here's a question that'll make you laugh. What's a corncrib actually used for?"

Kate's laughter knocked into the quiet. "Oh, you are so not a Midwesterner. But shouldn't you know this? You went to college in Iowa City."

"Yeah, but I was consumed with football and partying, not expanding my ag knowledge."

Partying, that's right. She'd read a few more articles about Colton this afternoon. Okay, more than a few. Once she'd started Googling, she couldn't stop. She'd read about his college success, his reputation as a wild card on and off the field, then his sudden lifestyle change a couple years into his career with the NFL. He was even quoted in one of the articles, crediting his turnaround to newfound faith and a friend who, in his words, had knocked sense into him.

She had a feeling Logan might be that friend.

Colton walked a circle around the inside of the crib now, long stride easily crossing over the opening cut through the crib's concrete base. Thin metal bars, halfway orange with rust, wrapped around the roofed bin.

"Corncribs are used for storing and drying out corn after the harvest. The crib is open so the air can dry out the corn and it's raised on cement so pests can't get it. Like rats or mice."

"Rust and rodents. And this is where you want to eat dinner?"

She nodded. "And if you're lucky, I might tell you all about combines and barns and irrigation, too." She nudged a board with a nail sticking upward out of the way. "Careful of all the nails out here. Tetanus just waiting to happen."

Colton stopped in front of her. Man, he was tall. And big. And why couldn't she stop herself from reacting to him? It wasn't just his appearance. It was the way he'd fit into her hometown so quickly, how he woke up early to clean up debris in Dad's yard and then spent all day at the depot. It was the way he obviously cared about that kid on the football team. It was the hurt she was convinced lurked underneath. *I like you more than I want to, Colton Greene—so much more than I should.*

"So should we eat?"

Right. Food. The picnic. The reason they'd come out here. Yes, they should eat. Probably on opposite sides of the crib. "Not just yet. I have to show you the best thing about corncribs first." *Bad idea, Walker. Don't draw this out. Eat and leave before your common sense goes any further underground.*

But she couldn't obey her own conscience. Instead she walked to the edge of the crib, gripped its metal bars and motioned for Colton to join her. "The view's great if you get high enough."

She started climbing, metal rattling with each movement, Colton at her side. They stopped three-fourths of the way up, feet propped in between bars, fingers curled around metal at eye level.

And the view was just as she remembered—a patchwork of farmland stretching like a never-ending quilt. Over to the west, a blacktop road cut through shadowed fields, the pale colors of sunset tinging everything with blue.

"There's the depot over there." She pointed. "Couple miles south is Hanson's Apple Orchard. Best cider you'll ever taste."

"I like this. My own personal tour guide of Maple Valley. What else do I need to see while I'm here?"

"Well, we've already talked about all the antique stores. Oh, there's this huge green house on the west side of Maple Valley. It's the coolest house in town. Has this circle driveway and all these lilac bushes on one side, a little balcony off the attic. I don't think anyone's lived in it for years, but I love to drive past it. The whole place just seems magical to me. Sounds silly, but I love it."

"What's the inside like?"

"No idea. Never been inside."

"It's one of your favorite spots in town and you've never been inside?"

"Like I said, silly, I guess." She pointed to a cluster of trees. "Over there's the ravine behind Dad's house. You should walk down there sometime. There's this creek with a bridge. It's where Dad took Mom on their first date. Mom was new in town, and she didn't go to prom, so Dad turned that little bridge into their own dance floor. Decorated it with lights and everything." She stopped. "Sorry, I'm rambling."

"I don't mind the rambling. I like hearing about your family."

Because he doesn't have one of his own. A chilly wind reached through the corncrib's bars to scrape over her cheeks. "Colt, I . . ." The confession dangled for a moment before she released it. "I read about your family. Your parents, the accident."

123

He looked away, breeze sifting through his hair. "Research. I get it. You're writing my book. You need the facts."

The cold of the metal bars turned her fingers icy. "Do you . . . remember it?"

She saw the tightening of his jaw before she even finished the question. His eyes turned stormy.

"Let's eat."

"But—"

The clanging of metal interrupted her as Colton began his descent. She'd wrecked things.

She started her own downward climb, riffling for words to erase her last question. Or would it be better to keep pressing? After all, like he said, she was writing his book—his story. This was a vital part of his story, wasn't it? Maybe it would be good—

Her thoughts cut off as her foot came down on something sharp, her squeal slicing in sync with the pang. Colton was at her side in a second, gaping along with her as she held her foot up, nail and board sticking out from the bottom of her shoe.

"Are you okay?"

"I've got a nail in my foot."

"Right, dumb question."

She steadied herself with one hand against the corncrib's wall while Colton bent over. "It's not in very deep. Just pull it out." She was shocked more than hurt. Thank goodness for her tennis shoes.

"You sure?"

"Well, I'm not sure what the advantage would be in keeping it in there."

Colton's expression hovered between amusement and uncertainty, but he bent once more and without warning yanked the nail from her shoe. He helped her sit down then, pulled off her shoe, her sock, and inspected the bottom of her foot. His fingers tapped over her skin, soft, gentle. So much more affecting than that nail had been.

She gulped in a breath of air. "It hardly hurts."

"And it's not bleeding very much. Now see, if you'd been wearing a sundress and flimsy shoes, this could've been much worse." He tied her sock around the wound and then, before she could protest, stuck one arm under her knees and the other under her back.

"What are you—"

He hoisted her up. "We need to get you to the ER."

"It's not that bad, Colt."

She could feel his breath on her forehead. "You're the one who was talking about tetanus earlier. You need to get a shot."

"You don't have to carry me."

He ignored her and kept walking, arms snug around her, the warmth of his chest heating through her. And he thought she'd blushed earlier.

"I ruined our picnic." First her prying questions. Now this.

"You didn't ruin a thing." He dipped into the ditch, then climbed up to the road, stopping at the car. "Hey."

That one word came out raspy and serious, and she lifted her head to meet his eyes. The stormy gray had disappeared, leaving an oceany blue green. "Yeah?"

"Does it really bother you when I call you Rosie?"

Not even a tiny a bit. "You paid a hundred and twenty bucks for a meal you still haven't gotten to eat. You climbed up a corncrib. You told me I look like my mom. You just carried me to the car. You can call me anything you want, Colton Greene."

7

*C*olton had three minutes to make an impression that may or may not pave the way for his future career as a TV sports analyst.

A career he hadn't realized was on the horizon until Ian's frenzied phone call.

He laced his fingers together to keep himself from fidgeting as activity buzzed around him. A lone cameraman fiddling with a lens. A lawn away, Iowa State University's Jack Trice Stadium rattling with the sound of fans filling the bleachers for the ISU vs. Iowa game. A heady wind carrying the aroma of tailgaters' barbeques.

And a woman with a press badge whisking past him, but not before brushing his cheeks with some kind of powder. Ian hadn't told him this gig required makeup.

"How far away are you from Ames and how quickly can you get there?"

He'd barely roused from sleep enough to answer Ian's call this morning, let alone provide a geographic update. But somehow, within thirty minutes of receiving the news that Ian had landed him a quickie interview with an ESPN affiliate before today's game, he'd been on his way—a borrowed tie around his neck, an old suit jacket of Logan's pinching his shoulders,

Case's warning to be careful of deer running across the road in his head.

And Kate in the passenger seat.

She waved at him now from behind a cameraman. Her denim jacket was unbuttoned to reveal a green-and-blue-plaid shirt and a yellow scarf around her neck. He still wasn't sure how she'd ended up coming along. Only that she'd followed him around the house, one room to the next, as he hurried to get going.

"I didn't know you wanted to be a sports analyst."

"Not sure I do. But my manager thinks it's a good idea. That's what a lot of retired players end up doing."

"Do you like talking in front of a camera?"

Not at all. *"I like talking football."*

Eventually she'd wound up in the truck with him and they hadn't stopped talking the entire forty-five-minute drive to Ames. They'd laughed about last night, that trip to the ER, how the tetanus shot had hurt worse than the nail had. It was as if this morning had become an extension of the evening before—the late night out on the porch, finally eating that picnic meal she'd packed, conversation flowing as naturally as the sunrise they'd almost stayed up to see.

It'd been a good night. One of the best he could remember in his recent past. Made all the better by the fact that she'd never turned back to the topic of his parents, the accident.

"You ready for this?" Link Porter, anchor for the cable sports affiliate, plopped into the canvas chair next to Colton.

"Ready as I'll ever be." Colton propped his feet on the bar running along the base of his chair. At least there was only one camera for the short pregame segment—that would be better than the flock of reporters he used to face off with during post-game media appearances. He'd never grown entirely comfortable with the stare of cameras. But this is what athletes did when their playing days came to a close, right?

It's the closest he'd get to the life he used to know.

"Nippy one today." Link rubbed his hands together. The former Tigers tight end, retired now for twenty-plus years, wore his signature lime-green tie and a practiced smile that displayed bleach-white teeth. His silver-blond hair was gelled to a near wax. "I don't know why anyone would willingly choose to live in the Midwest, cold as it gets."

Colton watched as Kate jutted her hands back into the pockets of her jacket, hopping in place against the chill of the afternoon. She'd insisted on watching the interview rather than finding her way to the fifty-yard-line seats they'd been given. Sunshine poured like liquid light over a crystal blue sky. "Oh, I don't think it's so bad here."

"Wait 'til the first blizzard. You'll wish you could eat your own words."

Though Link's affiliation with the Tigers had ended two decades before Colton had come on the scene, he'd met the man a few times over the years. He'd waffled between admiring him for managing to hold on to his celebrity and wondering if the spotlight felt as good on such a different stage.

"Can I ask you something, Link? This sports-show hosting thing—you like it?"

"I've been doing it for twenty-some years, haven't I?"

"Was the transition hard, going from playing to watching and talking?"

A faint streak of condescension colored Link's laughter. "You kidding? I was nearly forty when I retired. My body was ready for the break."

That was the difference, then. Link had played until he was ready to quit. Colton's end date had pounced too early.

A guy whose press badge said *Maury* rounded the camera and adjusted his headphones. "All right, gentlemen, we're on in ten."

Colton's feet fumbled over the bar under his chair and hit the ground.

Link shifted to face him. "Look, son, if you're nervous, don't be. Gonna be over before you realize it's started."

Easy for him to say. For Link, this was just a routine pregame spot. No biggie.

For Colton, it was the first real break he'd had in months.

Except that wasn't exactly right, was it. There was landing in Iowa and meeting Kate and knowing he'd found the perfect writer for his book. There was the fact that he'd spent the past five days helping Case Walker out at the depot—actually doing something worthwhile, contributing. There was the inkling of hope forming inside him since coming to this so-called flyover state. An inkling that hinted this past year, what he'd considered a slew of endings, might also contain a surprising beginning.

"Ten. Nine. Eight." Maury began the countdown.

"Oh, I almost forgot to ask. Do I look at you or the camera as I talk?"

"Seven. Six. Five."

Link spoke through an unmoving grin. "Both."

"Three. Two."

"But how—"

Maury dropped his arm.

"Good afternoon, folks, Link Porter here, getting pumped for what's looking to be a hot game on a cold day in Iowa. I've got Colton Greene with me, former quarterback for the LA Tigers and also an alum of one of the schools readying to battle it out on the field today. Good to have you with us, Colt."

"Good to be here, Link." There, he'd made it through his first line.

"Now, I'm not going to bother asking you who you're rooting for today, considering you played all four years of your college career as a Hawkeye. Started for three years, All-American as a junior and senior. Should be fairly obvious where your heart is today."

Colton rubbed his palms on his dark jeans. Shoot, could the camera see that? "Fairly obvious, yes, but we're in Cyclone territory, so I'm probably better off not flaunting my loyalties."

Link's chuckle could've come straight from a laugh track. "Well said. Let's talk on-field strategy. If you're Coach Hardy, what are you saying to the Hawks right now?'

Colton looked to the camera. This is where instinct should take over. Where he should forget the monitor and tiny lapel mic stuck to his collar.

But instead, nerves he'd refused to give in to earlier chose this moment to march over his practiced bit. *Coach Hardy . . . talk about ISU's defense . . . point out Iowa's penchant for running the ball*. They'd gone over this before the taping.

"If I'm Coach Hardy, I'm . . . I'm probably talking defense, telling my quarterback . . . um, my quarterback . . ."

"Starting QB is Bobby Emmanuel," Link cut in. "Senior whose sixty-four-yard pass cinched the deal against Kansas State last Saturday. Did you see that game, Colton?"

"Uh, no. I didn't."

Link's smile never wavered, but impatience flashed in his eyes. "Back to defense. We've only seen this ISU team a few times so far this season, but they defend well against spread offense. Do you think we can say the same for the Hawks?"

Sunlight glared against the camera's glass lens. Colton blinked. Felt his stomach churn. "I do, Link."

He was blowing this, the few words that attempted to rise up his throat meeting with the taste of sour anxiety before they could make it out.

"Focus on the faces." Ian's voice, from the dozens of press conferences he'd sat through.

But his manager's advice didn't work as well here. Not when the face he was supposed to be looking at belonged to a seasoned professional who probably regretted agreeing to Colton's involvement in this segment. But then, as Link said something about the team's standings this early in the season, Colton caught sight of Kate in his peripheral vision.

Only for a second, but long enough to take in the encouragement in her expression.

"—which is why I'm convinced, despite their similar records going into this game, we might see ISU easily rise to the top today."

"I'm not so sure about that, Link."

Link could barely veil his disapproval. "No?"

"The Hawkeyes have had two wins coming into today, yes, but neither were the blowout we all expected. I think today they have something to prove, and they could surprise us in a big way."

Two whole sentences and not a single stutter. Relief slid in—but not enough to erase the pummeling embarrassment of his blunders.

Seconds later Maury signaled, the red light on the camera dimmed, and Link leaned back in his chair as he accepted a thermos of coffee from a passing crew member. "Well, that's that."

Maury's expression held even less approval than Link's.

Colton pulled the wired mic from his shirt and handed it to the woman standing in front of him. Same one who'd awkwardly strung the wire up his shirt in the first place. The cameraman was already pulling down his equipment.

"So, uh, we're good?"

Link downed a swig of coffee. "We're good. Enjoy the game."

That really was that. "Well, thanks. Maybe I'll see ya again sometime."

Neither Link nor Maury hid their doubt. And all the hope he'd placed in this three-minute segment released, like water from a bullet-hole-strewn bucket. He shook Link's hand, then found Kate waiting where she'd been the whole time.

There was too much perk in her smile, too much bounce in her "Great job."

"I can't remember which of the Ten Commandments says not to lie, but I'm pretty sure you just broke it."

Kate looped her arm through his, leading him away from the site of his humiliation. "Nuh-uh. You really did good. Especially there at the end."

Only there at the end. Ian had said he'd stream the interview, was probably back in LA sitting stone-faced in front of his flat-screen.

"Come on, let's go find our seats and watch the game, and you can tell me why I should care about this game."

"It's the biggest rivalry in your state. That's why you should care."

"I actually meant the game of football in general."

"Why are you trying to hurt me?"

Laughter danced in her eyes.

"You're going to watch the whole game, Rosie, and by the end, you'll love it. Or at least appreciate it. I'm going to make sure of that." And maybe, in the process, he could forget about the embarrassment of the past three minutes—and the fact that he may have just blown his future.

Again.

Kate had one goal in bringing Colton to the Twister Tavern: cheer the man up.

And so far, it was working. "Yeah, baby, twenty-nine baskets. Whoo!" She spun from the arcade basketball game tucked into the corner of the restaurant where she'd spent half her Saturday nights when she was in college.

"I can admit that's impressive." Colton eyed the basket at the end of the net-lined game. "But I should probably tell you I've set records on this game, oh, like a hundred times. We actually had one of these back in our dorm at Iowa—"

"Shh." She clamped one hand over his mouth. "You're still in ISU territory, and after our loss today, you can't just start flinging around your questionable loyalties."

He grinned behind her hand. "Fine. But watch . . . and learn." He turned, stuck a couple quarters in the machine, and proceeded to blow away her twenty-nine baskets with forty-five of his own. He whirled back to face her with a cocky smile. "Whatcha say now, Walker?"

That if it meant more of those grins, she'd happily lose again.

That very possibly the last screw holding her common sense together had just twisted free and now clinked through her all loud and disconcerting and impossible to ignore. *Get a grip, Walker.*

"I say it's unfair. I haven't had dinner yet."

"Fine. We go eat, then rematch."

She followed him back to the table, where a waitress was just now delivering their food. A plate heaping with French fries and a burger for Kate. Basket of ribs for Colt. She plopped into her seat and immediately dropped a napkin in her lap. "Come to momma."

Colton grinned at her over his pop glass. "You never struck me as the burger and fries type."

"You've only known me eight days. There's a lot you don't know." She dragged a fry through her ketchup and took a bite.

Amazing how little this place had changed since college—new menus, maybe, updated ISU pendants and team photos occupying wall space, but same old wood-backed booths and checkered tablecloths. Waiters and waitresses still wore the red-and-yellow aprons she remembered and the *e* in the *Cyclone City* neon sign over the bar flickered like always.

She reached her fingers around her burger. "Holy cow, this thing's huge."

"Ha, holy cow. Funny."

"What? Oh . . . yeah." Another glance at her burger. A moment's hesitation.

"Not funny?"

"I love my meat, but I prefer not to think about where it came from."

But at least Colton laughed as he lifted a glazed rib. He had a nice laugh. A rich, tenor sort of sound. And it wasn't something she'd heard much during the football game. Oh, he'd tried—put on a good face. Took time to explain to her the ins and outs of what happened on the field. Argued halfheartedly with her about their opposing alma maters. Cheered when his team pulled off a game-winning touchdown in the last minutes of the fourth quarter.

He'd even let her interview him during halftime, more game memories and notes for the book she'd better start writing one of these days.

But she'd sensed the persistent internal grimace he couldn't shake ever since that interview. He was beating himself up over it, she knew. He'd put so much stock in that one impromptu opportunity.

Not all that different than her and the James Foundation.

Maybe that's why she'd found herself suggesting they grab an early dinner in Ames before heading back to Maple Valley. A good barbeque joint could work miracles, right? Except maybe she shouldn't have picked a place with television monitors hanging in the corners, all tuned into cable sports.

They ate in silence for a few minutes. She waited until he'd half finished his ribs before treading into conversation. "Colton, what did you do when you weren't playing football? Before the injuries, I mean."

He looked up from his plate. "Um . . . sleep?"

"Surely you had some outside interests. Hobbies. Causes. Friends." *Girlfriends.* It was the closest she could get to the question she wanted to ask. She'd read about Lilah Moore online—rising star in the world of California politics. And according to the articles she'd read, not only the director of Colton's foundation but also his longtime girlfriend.

Until she'd dumped him the day of the game that ended his career. Apparently she was now engaged to someone else.

Colton reached for his glass but instead of taking a drink fiddled with his straw. "Football's been my life since high school. It didn't leave a lot of room for anything else."

"It's just . . . I can't write an eighty-five-thousand-word book solely based on game highlights, Colton. You don't want to talk about your childhood. You don't want to talk about your personal life."

She could feel him stiffening, even from across the table. Perhaps this was the wrong time to bring up the subject. But they weren't exactly swimming in time to get this project done. His manager wanted a draft by early October. The foundation wanted her in New York for a couple weeks of orientation in November.

The deadlines were beginning to eat at her.

A waitress glided past, carrying a plate sizzling with something straight from a frying pan. "I'm really glad you're the one writing this book, Kate. I want it to turn out well. I need it to turn out well. But there are some things . . ." Ice cubes clattered against the edge of his glass as he twisted his straw. "There are some things I'm not going to talk about. Not even to you. Couldn't even if I wanted to."

Couldn't? What did he mean by that? And why did she feel like a wall had just gone up, mere seconds wiping away the past week of a gradually forming friendship that'd surprised her with its ease—the past twenty-four hours spent almost entirely in each other's company?

What's the story you don't want to tell, Colton?

The more time she spent with this man, the less she felt she knew him.

But the more she wanted to.

"For a while, I did a lot of speaking."

She blinked. "Huh?"

"You asked what I did outside football. I took some speaking gigs. I volunteered at a homeless nonprofit. And I spoke at schools, some church youth groups—that kind of thing."

She lowered her hamburger, recognizing his remark for the attempt it was. "But how . . . ?"

"You're wondering how I could have spoken to groups, considering how badly the interview went." At the far end of the restaurant, someone tapped the jukebox, and a whiny country ballad glided over the room. "I'm completely comfortable up on a stage in front of three hundred kids. But put a camera in my face and I freeze up. Don't know why."

And he was hoping for a future as a sportscaster? "What did you talk to students about?"

Colton dropped his wadded-up napkin in his now empty

basket. "Making good choices. Staying in school. In the words of my oh-so-tactful manager, we took advantage of my reformed-bad-boy image." He rolled his eyes as he mimicked his manager's voice but then shrugged. "It was good, though, the speaking. Feeling like I was doing something important. If I had to have such a lousy childhood and make dumb choices later on, nice to have something good come from it."

"When in your lousy childhood did you discover you had serious football skills?" She thought he might balk at that question, like he did every other time she'd asked about his past.

Instead, he fixed his gaze somewhere over her shoulder, thoughtful remembrance gliding in his blue irises. "The first foster home I stayed in lasted four months. One day my case manager showed up. She said the family had decided it wasn't working. I'd have to go back to a transitional home." He leaned his chin on his fists. "It's weird, I can still feel the vinyl of her Pontiac Grand Am. I took a lot of rides to and from temporary homes in that thing."

Kate slid her plate away, pulled into his memory.

"So we drove away from that house, and Norah—she was my case manager—took me out on this country road. Told me life hadn't been fair to me, and she wouldn't blame me for being angry. And she parks next to this old barn, pulls a box out of her trunk. It had all these figurines inside it—glass, old, ugly. Said she had planned to give them to Goodwill but suddenly had a better idea for them."

In the background, the country song drifted into the smooth lilt of an old Elvis ballad. "Next thing I know, she's chucking a figurine at the barn wall. Hands me one and tells me to throw it. We emptied her entire box."

Colton looked up now, gaze flickering as if traveling from the past back to the present. "Anyway, after that, she asked me if I played any sports. Said with my throwing arm, I should try baseball."

"Baseball?"

He grinned. "She's a baseball fanatic. So I went out for it just for her. I went out for pretty much every sport over the next couple years. Football was where I excelled."

And it had become his escape. A coping mechanism. Like throwing glass against a barn wall.

Their waitress stopped at their table then, cleared their plates, and left the bill. When she left, Kate cleared her throat. "Thanks for telling me that, Colton."

He shrugged. "Should fill in a few of those eighty-five thousand words at least."

"Have you kept in touch with Norah?"

"Not too much. She's sent me some cards over the years. I sent her tickets to that last playoff game in January. We didn't part on the best of terms—I was such an angry kid back then. Didn't realize at the time how lucky I was to have her. Not every foster kid ends up with a case manager like that."

"Is that why you bought Webster at the auction yesterday? Trying to be an influence in his life the way she was in yours?"

He lifted his shoulders once more. "Or I just miss the game so much that I'd play catch even with a kid who can't stand me."

Maybe. But she doubted it.

"Excuse me. You're Colton Greene, aren't you?"

Kate looked up to see a college kid standing at the edge of their table, hopeful eyes ogling Colton. Colton nodded.

"Guys, I told you it was him," the student called over his shoulder.

And for the next ten minutes, she watched Colton sign autograph after autograph, pretending he wasn't thrilled.

While she pretended she wasn't getting attached.

When was the last time he'd been this out of breath?

Colton pumped his legs as he tore after Bear, over grass and stray leaves. His focus darted between the ball in Seth's friend's hands and the deck chairs across the Walkers' front lawn, marking off the end zone.

"Get him, Rae!"

Raegan was several yards ahead of Colton, and just as Bear was about to reach the makeshift end zone, she stretched out to grab his arm.

Kate's whooping a few feet back joined his own cheers.

"Oh yeah. Take that, Bear McKinley!" Laughter simmered in Raegan's voice as she yanked the football away from the guy whose size fit his name.

"That's my girl," Case called from the porch, lifting his root beer with the arm not stuck in a sling.

A tepid breeze skated over Colton's face as he turned, grain dust from the field across the lane floating in the air. Kate lifted both hands for double high-fives, her hair in straggles around rosy cheeks. "Now aren't you happy you ended up with two girls on your team?"

He could barely feel the badgering ache in his knee, its futile reminder that this was pretty much the only form of football he'd be playing anytime soon strangely void of its usual punch. "Hey, I wasn't unhappy to have the two of you on my side." He elbowed her. "I knew we could take on Seth and Bear and Ava."

This is what a Sunday afternoon should look like. Patchy sunlight filtering through clouds and tree branches over a rambling stretch of grass. Church clothes long since traded in for outdoor wear—sweatshirts and jackets now discarded on the porch steps.

And friends he hadn't known more than two weeks split into

teams for very possibly the most unorganized game of touch football he'd ever played. Bear gave Raegan a playful punch in the arm as she sauntered past.

So maybe yesterday's gig hadn't gone well. Maybe he'd looked ridiculous sitting next to a TV veteran like Link Porter and stammering in front of the camera.

But for these few sunny hours, none of that mattered. All that mattered was getting the old football he'd found in Case's garage down the lawn and past those hunter-green lawn chairs.

And once the game was over, well, he already had plans for the rest of the day.

He placed one palm on each sister's shoulder as they huddled. "Okay, ladies, last possession and clearly our opponents don't think we've got a shot."

Kate pulled a band from her pocket and gathered her hair into a ponytail. "I say we try a double-reverse play. It was so sweet yesterday when the Hawkeyes did that. All those hand-offs—so tricky but so perfectly executed. Like a complicated but flawlessly composed sentence."

Colton tasted his own delight. "I have never liked you more than I do right now, Kate Walker."

An alluring flash flickered in her bronze eyes. "Let's try it."

As Kate reached for her water bottle, he took the ball from Raegan. "Much as I admire your pluck, it might be a bit much to pull off. Let's do a simple fake. Raegan, you run up the left side, and I'll make like I'm gonna throw. Kate, you come around behind me and be ready for the hand-off. You're going to take it down the field."

"You kidding? They'll be all over me."

Colton shook his head. "Nope. Bear only has eyes for Rae, and—"

Raegan sputtered. "Um . . . what?"

"And Ava's been the interception queen all afternoon. She'll try to predict where I'm going to throw and head there."

Kate folded her arms. "But Seth—"

"He's just as useless as Bear. Trust me, he won't be watching you. You've got this."

"Hurry up, Greene," Ava's smug voice called.

Doubt brushed a frown over Kate's face. "If anyone runs it, it should be you, Colt."

"Uh-uh. It's all you. Now line up, Walkers."

Kate sighed and took her place in front of him, Raegan off to the right. Kate leaned over for the hike. She snapped the ball, Raegan took off . . . and the play came together just as he'd described. His fingers brushed Kate's as he handed off the football, and he saw the blend of resolve and glee curl over her as she found her opening and spurted forward. Seconds later he cheered as she flew toward the end zone and made her touchdown.

"That's my other girl!" Another yell from Case.

Raegan hooted and punched Bear's arm, and Seth and Ava let out twin groans. Kate was still out of breath when Colton reached her, her ponytail loosened from the run and her cheeks red.

"Told you the fake would work." He slung one arm around her shoulder as they headed toward the house.

"Yeah, yeah, you were right."

"I was also right about the game—admit it. You totally see the beauty of football now, yeah? It's your new favorite sport? You'll never miss another Super Bowl?"

The breeze embraced her laughter as she matched his pace. "I can appreciate it, okay? Good enough?"

"For now. I've still got a few weeks to turn you into a fanatic." Although it felt like too short a time. Days he'd once thought might drag here in Iowa had instead raced by in their fullness.

Kate stopped, reached up to rub her eyes. "I got some dust or an eyelash or something in my eye."

He turned to face her. "Need me to take a look?" Her hair smelled of vanilla—or maybe coconut—and she blinked.

But instead of rubbing her eye again, she dropped her hand. "Why do you love football so much, Colt?"

"I like learning plays. I like the simplicity of the objective, but the intricacy of getting there." He shrugged, finger grazing the side of her brow as he studied her irritated eye. "Favorite was calling audibles. Those moments in a game when I'd study the field, the defense. I'd get this feeling in my gut. Last-minute change of plans. It was . . ." He paused, his trail of thoughts suddenly off course. "Exhilarating."

She blinked again, gaze speckled with self-conscious uncertainty. "I . . . uh . . . I think my eye's fine."

It was his turn to blink. "Right." He swallowed, stepped back, realized everyone else had already gone inside, and cleared his throat, grasping for the composure he'd somehow lost in the past sixty seconds.

Logan's sister.

Who looked way too great winded with a football tucked under her arm.

Strictly business.

He started up the porch steps, trying to ignore the awkward tension that'd dropped like precipitation, despite a cloudless sky. Seth and Ava dropped onto the loveseat in the living room when he entered, and Kate and Raegan took up opposite sides of the couch.

"Hello, Sunday afternoon nap," Bear said as he settled into the recliner.

"No sleeping allowed." Colton stood in front of the group. "I've got plans for us." He beckoned to the pile of DVDs stacked on the built-in shelves next to where the TV hung over the fireplace.

Kate's eyes narrowed. "Please tell me those aren't what I think they are."

"I asked your dad if he had any of your movies. Turns out he has them all." Colton grinned. "Someone make popcorn. We're having a movie marathon."

"Already on the popcorn," Case said as he passed through the room toward the kitchen.

"Which one should we watch first, Rosie?"

"Rosie?" Seth draped his arm along the back of the loveseat.

"Main character in *The African Queen*. Katharine Hepburn's first color film," Colton explained. "Only role Humphrey Bogart ever won an Oscar for."

Everyone stared.

"What? I listen when Rosie talks." He fingered through the DVD cases. "Whoa, Mario Lopez starred in one of your movies? The *Saved by the Bell* guy?"

"Colt—"

"Ooh, is that the one with the girl from *Full House*, too?" Raegan jumped up from the couch. "Heartline loves to cast old '90s TV stars. Kate's met most of them, too."

"Guys, I really don't want—"

"Ooh, ooh!" Raegan pulled a case from the middle of the pile. "I love this one. It takes place in Charleston. And for once, they filmed on location. It was right after Kate won her Emmy, so they spent a little more making it, and—"

Kate jumped to her feet, cutting Raegan off. "Eye's still bothering me. I'm gonna go . . . " Her voice dragged in time with her feet, and she disappeared from the room.

Colton pulled the DVD case from Raegan and opened it. "Charleston it is." He popped the disc in the player, picked a spot on the couch and sat. But when Kate still hadn't returned by the time the opening music faded, he turned to Raegan. "What's taking Kate so long to come back?" he whispered.

Raegan looked from the screen to Colton, bit her lip. "Uh, I'm not sure she is coming back." Raegan's long sigh sent her bangs fanning, and he tilted his head in question. The smell of popcorn wafted from the kitchen. "She's embarrassed by her movies. Always has been."

"But I thought . . . I planned this for her." Had thought it'd be a fun way to show his appreciation for yesterday. Get the gang together to admire her stuff. Make her feel good or special or something.

Bad call, Greene.

He rose, angled between the couch and loveseat, and headed toward the second floor. He found Kate in Beckett's bedroom. She stood next to the tabletop desk, framed picture in her hand.

"Hey, you. You disappeared."

She'd taken out her contacts and now wore her glasses. She looked good both ways, but the glasses made her look extra writerly. Studious.

Cute.

He swallowed the thought, came up beside her, and glanced at the photo she held. "Your mom and Beckett. Is that San Diego?"

She nodded. "When each of us turned thirteen, Mom took us on a special weekend trip—just her and us. And we could pick anywhere in the continental US. Beck picked San Diego."

"Where'd you pick?"

She set the photo back down, an imprint of dust marking its spot. "New York City. I wanted to see her foundation headquarters."

"The one you're going to Africa for?" She'd told him about it yesterday on their way home from Ames, in words that released so fast she couldn't have hidden her excitement if she'd tried. He'd fallen asleep last night trying to picture her in a little village in a dusty desert.

"Yeah. Did I tell you my mom helped start it? She wrote the grant that got it off the ground. I've read the thing once or twice—saved a copy of it. Pages and pages of statistics and strategic plans and case studies. It's a masterpiece."

"I'm gonna guess you've read it more than once or twice."

"Crazy thing is, my mom never planned to be a nonprofit leader." She turned to Colt. "Mom wanted to be a medical missionary. Went on a trip to Ethiopia in high school and decided her calling was to be a doctor and move to Africa. She was pre-med in college, applied to med school twice, but never got in."

"So the foundation was Plan B." He perched on the corner of the desk.

Kate nodded. "If she couldn't be a doctor herself, she wanted to help make it possible for others. The foundation opens clinics and helps train locals to be doctors, nurses, and paramedics. It's amazing to think about—this random, regular woman from Iowa, starting a foundation that now, almost forty years later, is still going strong and doing incredible work. She didn't do it alone, of course. But still."

The wistfulness in Kate's voice tugged at him, understanding wedging into the space between them. What had sounded out-of-the-box to him yesterday—the idea of her up and leaving the country for three months, a short-term trip at least temporarily upending her writing career—suddenly made sense. This trip to Africa wasn't a whim. It might've come out of the blue, but she'd been waiting for it, craving it.

This was her personal NFL draft. "I think you take after your mom more than you know, Kate."

She didn't look convinced.

"I know I only met your mom a couple times back in college. But I think maybe the way you saved a copy of that grant she wrote, well, that's what that pile of DVD cases out in the living room would've been to her. And is to your dad."

She tried to let out a sarcastic laugh, but he cut her off with a raised hand. "I'm serious. You can write them off if you want, be your own harshest critic. But they're pieces of you. They're something you created, and that gives them value." He dipped his head toward her. "Plus, from what I hear, they're pretty great stories."

"They're *love* stories, Colton."

"I like love. Most people I know kinda do." He pushed off from the desk, only inches between them. "But if you really, really don't want us to watch any of your movies, I'll go put a stop to it right now. I'll insist on watching the Patriots-Broncos game."

Kate's gaze wavered behind her glasses, hesitancy waltzing with what might be appreciation. She lowered her arms and tucked her hands into the pouch of her hoodie. "That game'll be a blowout. With both Martin and Christoff out, the Pats will get slammed."

He felt his jaw slacken.

"What?" Kate's glasses slipped down her nose as she glanced at Colton and smiled. "I listen when you talk, too." She started for the door. "Raegan's right. The Charleston one is the best. I hope that's the one you chose."

He followed her from the room.

Logan's sister. Strictly business.

8

"Oh, Kate, thank goodness you're here."

Raegan's panicked voice was the first thing to greet Kate as she stepped out of her car. She'd parked halfway down the block from the coffee shop, having arrived downtown at her sister's beckoning. The shadow of storefronts reached over her and across the street, piles of sandbags lay strewn at the river's edge.

"Whoa, we're sandbagging already? We're that worried about a flood?"

"That's not what I'm talking about. I'm talking about this." Bangles jiggled and clinked at Raegan's wrist as she pointed down the block, toward the line of people stretching from the coffee shop entrance. She could feel the fidgety tension even from here.

"Is there an impending coffee shortage I don't know about? Is this like a bank run back during the Great Depression? Like in *It's a Wonderful Life*?" And what did Raegan expect her to do about it?

"Don't joke, Kate. It's not pretty." Raegan tugged on her arm and pulled her to the sidewalk. "Maple Valley only retains its quaint charm so long as all its citizens are properly caffeinated. Without it we're the queen's court in *Alice in Wonderland*. Everything gets very 'off with your head.'"

"Dramatic much?"

By now they'd reached Coffee Coffee's entrance, the disgruntled crowd riddled with scowls. Raegan pushed her toward the door.

"We can't butt in line, Rae."

"We're not butting in line. You're going to go help man the counter. You've done the barista thing before."

"But I—"

"Please. For the sake of our entire community's sanity. Help us."

The smell of coffee and something pumpkin greeted her as Raegan shoved her through the door. The line that ended outside reached to the front counter inside. One lone woman ran the cash register, hair slipping free from her braids and frazzled expression matching her frantic movements.

"That's Amelia Bentley. She works for the newspaper but picks up a few hours here, too."

"Why's she working alone?"

"Apparently Megan went home sick."

Megan, the angry emo girl? Kate sighed and unzipped her jacket. "Fine, I'll help for a while. But only for a while." Because she was supposed to be writing the opening chapter—chapters, if she was lucky—of Colton's book today. She had to come up with something to send his manager soon.

She slipped behind the counter and found an apron hanging over a peg. "Help is here."

The woman behind the cash register punched at its keys. "You don't how much of a lifesaver you are. I was about to curl up in a ball and cry."

Thirty-five minutes later, the line of customers had finally dwindled to its end. Kate sighed and slumped against the back wall. "For a minute there, I thought we were going to have a riot on our hands. Especially when we ran out of pumpkin bread." The customers had emptied the glass display case.

And if Kate never made another mocha in her life, it'd be too soon.

Amelia untied the apron at her waist, then held out a hand. "Time for proper introductions. I'm Amelia. I work at the paper. And sometimes here. Though if Megan ever leaves me alone again, I'm turning in my resignation."

Kate accepted her handshake. "Kate Walker."

"Raegan's sister. The one who's writing Colton Greene's book."

"One and the same." Planning to write anyway. And after last weekend, she finally had something to write.

Why then, every time she'd sat down in the past couple days since then, had her fingers frozen over her laptop keys?

"Which makes you just about the luckiest girl in town. Everybody's talking about him. And if he hadn't turned me down for an interview, I'd be writing about him, too."

"Between the tornado and possible upcoming flood, you'd think people in this town would have enough to talk about." Sunlight gushed through the shop's front windows, and Kate lifted her hand to shield her eyes. Even from here, she could see the river glistening across the road, its waters lapping higher than usual. "So what happened to Megan anyway?"

"Took off sick. So sick she shouldn't have driven herself home. But I don't think she has any family in the area. Not many friends either."

From what Kate had seen of the girl, it wasn't too surprising.

"I'd go check on her, but if I put up a Closed sign, that riot might actually happen."

Kate glanced at the computer bag she'd abandoned when she took up residence behind the counter. She really needed to write.

But if Megan was that sick . . . and she didn't have anybody . . .

Decision made. Kate untied her purple apron and slipped it over her head. "I'll go. Know where she lives?"

"Yeah, only about a half mile away. I'll write down the address for you."

Ten minutes later, Kate pulled up in front of an old Victorian house that'd been remodeled into two residences. Painted cotton candy pink, it stood out from behind a sprawling willow tree. Soooo pink.

Kate double-checked the address on her scrap of paper—143B. West side. Kate got out of her car and in seconds stood atop the open porch of the old house. It took three rings of the doorbell before the door swung open.

Megan's raspy "What?" was pure irritation. Her nose was red and her green eyes glassy, surrounded by dark smudges.

"Uh . . . hey. You look awful."

"Gee, thanks. Is that all?"

The girl wore a quilt around her shoulders and held it in place underneath her chin.

"You're sick?"

"No, I just like playing Superman when I'm by myself."

Even with a hoarse voice—and probably a fever, too, if the redness of her cheeks was any indication—she still pulled off effortless snark. But she'd said she was by herself. And that was enough to tug a maternal instinct in Kate. She brushed past Megan.

"Hey, what are you doing?"

At first glance, the entrance of Megan's house was about what she would've expected from someone her age. Band posters lining the wall against the open staircase leading to the second floor, a few items of clothing draped over the railing, and a laundry basket sitting on one of the steps.

But then she entered the living room. And stopped. It was like walking into a greenhouse—plants, so many of them, such a variety. Draping from end tables and wall shelves. Covering a window seat and lining the fireplace mantel.

Megan shuffled into the room behind her.

Kate turned, catching a glimpse of the shock on her own face in the mirror behind Megan.

But Megan only shrugged. "What? So I like plants."

"How do you take care of all of them?"

She sneezed. "Water and sunlight. It's not rocket science."

Kate stuck her palm on Megan's forehead. "You've got a fever, girl. Do you have any Tylenol?"

"I've been taking it all day."

And clearly that's not the only thing she'd been doing today—not if that ice cream bucket by the couch meant what she thought it did. The thought of stomach flu germs was enough to make her shudder.

"Yeah, I wouldn't want to be here either." Megan dropped onto the couch. "But you're the one who barged in. I don't even know you."

"You should go to the doctor."

"They'll just say it's a virus and tell me to wait it out."

"Have you eaten anything today? Do you need groceries? Or more Kleenex? I could go to the store. I could get you some NyQuil—that stuff's a miracle in a bottle."

Megan shook her head, dark hair tumbling from a messy bun, and lay on a pillow. "I'm fine." She tucked her legs underneath her quilt. "Except for the fact that I have no idea why you're here."

Kate lowered onto the loveseat. "I was at Coffee Coffee. Amelia said you went home sick. She was worried about you."

Megan closed her eyes. "I'm fine. Just needed rest. I'll go back in a few hours."

"Pretty sure no one's going to want you serving their coffee. You should probably call your manager and take the rest of the day off."

"Don't need to call."

"You can't go back to work."

She opened one eye. "I don't need to call because I am the manager. It's my place."

Okay, forget the plants. This surprise won. "Wait, you're saying you *own* Coffee Coffee. You're what, twenty years old?"

"Twenty-one."

"Twenty-one and you own and operate your own business."

Megan must have heard the *How?* in Kate's voice. She lifted her head to perch it in her hand. "My grandmother left me an inheritance. To put it delicately, I'm loaded. Or was, until I bought Coffee Coffee."

"That's putting it delicately?"

"Lucky for me, unlike a lot of inheritances that don't kick in until a person's twenty-one, my grandma stipulated that I receive the money when I turned eighteen."

She tightened the blanket around her shoulders. "I . . . I think she must've known when she finalized the will that my homelife wasn't all that . . . homey."

Megan sneezed again, and Kate fished for a Kleenex box she'd seen peeking out from underneath a curling plant. "Mind me asking how so?"

"Oh, I wasn't abused—nothing like that. My parents are both doctors, actually. Really busy. Rarely home. When they were, I usually felt like I was in the way. You ever get the feeling you grate on somebody just by being around them?"

Uh, yeah, she could think of someone. As in someone in this room. As in not a plant.

Megan finished her tea, then set her mug on the coffee table. "Anyway, it's not a sob story or anything, but I made the mistake of telling them when I was seventeen I didn't want to go to college. They got mad. Next thing I knew I was graduating high school with no plans but a bank account that gave me options."

"So you bought a coffee shop?"

"Not right away. I traveled for a few months, wasted more money than I care to think about. Followed a guy to Maple Valley, which was stupid, but ended up okay because I saw the coffee shop was up for sale and everything clicked."

"You are one surprising kid, Megan."

Megan flopped back onto her pillow, as if spilling her backstory had sapped her energy.

"I'm going to make you soup." Kate stood. "Kitchen's that way?"

"You really don't have to."

"I know I don't."

She was halfway through the next room—more breakfast nook than dining room, with an antique-looking round table and wooden chairs—when she heard Megan's raspy voice call her name.

She poked her head back into the living room. "Yeah, Megan?"

"Thanks." When Megan closed her eyes and pulled her blanket up to her chin, she didn't look like a saucy twenty-one-year-old business owner but a girl unknowingly hungry for something much more than soup.

Kate lingered in the doorway, watching Megan's soft breath fan her bangs for another minute before turning once more.

She found Megan's kitchen well stocked—much more so than she ever kept her own. Organized, too. She located chicken broth and a bag of egg noodles. A chicken breast in the freezer and celery and carrots in the fridge. A good-sized pot in the drawer underneath the stove.

She worked in quiet—only the sound of her knife bouncing against the cutting board and a woodpecker outside the window over the kitchen sink for background noise. And then, the *ding* of her phone. Signaling an email. Which she waited to read until she'd set the chicken broth boiling on the stove.

And then wished she hadn't read at all.

Gil. Because apparently he just couldn't leave her alone.

She jumped as the sound of boiling water spilling over the edge of the pot on the stove hissed into the silence.

❧

If Ian didn't stop grumbling soon, Colton was going to hang up on him. It'd be a first.

It'd be a relief.

Colton stepped out of the car, clamping down on the desire to defend himself against Ian's irritation. A tangle of gnarled leaves was visible under the car's tires.

"It shouldn't have been hard. Three minutes of poise, talking about the game you know inside and out."

Did Ian not realize he was upset enough at himself after his poor performance on Saturday? It was the same battered feeling he used to get after bad game days, especially early in his career, when the overwhelming desire to prove himself had tailed him like a dogged stalker.

In front of him now, the two-story home where Webster's foster family resided gobbled up the bulk of its lot, flanked on both sides by smaller, ranch-style houses. Sure beat some of the run-down sorry-excuses-for-a-house placements he'd found himself in during his nine-year stint in the foster care system.

And from what he'd heard from Coach Leo and Case Walker, the Clancy family was a good one. He leaned against his car as he waited for Ian to finish his tirade. Who knew whether Webster was home—or would even agree to see Colton if he was.

If only he'd been smart enough to actually look at his phone before answering it when it'd started ringing on the way over.

"If you're done with the lecture, I've got someplace to be."

"This isn't a lecture, Greene."

"Then what is it? You know I've never been good in front of a camera."

"You've done dozens of press conferences."

"This was different."

"Why?"

Frustration beat through him. He ducked his chin into the high collar of his fleece pullover. "I don't know." But it was. Somehow he'd managed to get used to groups of cameras and bullet-like questioning from reporters all at once. But there was something different about one camera in his face . . .

Like the difference between running a play on the football field with his whole team, versus running the field alone.

A dog barking in a distant yard cut into the otherwise quiet of the neighborhood. Colton let his pause stretch.

He could hear Ian's forced exhale loud and clear. When his manager finally spoke again, his tone was low, his pacing steady. "I've got a full client list, Greene. You've always been one of my best. A favorite. But my patience has its limits."

"Ian—"

"I want to help you land on your feet in a post-team career. I really do. But if you're bent on sabotaging yourself, there's nothing I can do."

Colton straightened, a gust of wind raking over his hair and stinging his eyes. "What are you saying?"

"I'm saying you need to decide what you want, and you need to decide soon. No more flaking out or it might be time to find yourself a new manager. I don't like saying it. But there it is."

Yes, there it was. An ultimatum in plain, unmistakable terms.

He pushed away from his car and started up toward the Clancy house. The smell of someone burning the first of autumn's leaves drifted over the sidewalk. "I understand."

"Do you?"

"Yeah." If Ian didn't believe him, he'd just have to prove it. He'd practice or something. Go buy a camera and have Kate play reporter and learn to put up with the stare of the lens.

"Fine, then." Ian didn't sound convinced. "Oh, and by the way, call Lilah back sometime, will you? She's been trying to get ahold of you. You've got to make some decisions about your foundation."

They hung up and Colton let out a long sigh as he climbed the Clancys' porch steps, the creak of the stairs under his Nikes setting off a round of barking inside the house. He pressed the doorbell.

"Hush up, Rocky." The scolding came in sync with the screen door opening, hinges squeaking. A woman appeared in the doorway, bright red hair peeking out from underneath a Maple Valley Mavericks baseball cap. "I am so sorry about our crazy dog. You'd think Rocky had never seen another human being."

Behind her, the little dog yapped and jumped. "As in Balboa?"

"No, as in Colavito."

"The baseball player. Nice."

"We take our sports seriously around here." She reached down to snatch the puppy up. He gave one more bark, then quieted. "I told my husband we should've opted for a snake or lizard or something, but nooo. He had to have a dog."

"I like that your options were between a dog or a reptile."

She grinned. "You're that football player, aren't you?"

"Guilty as charged. Colton Greene." He held out a hand, then gave a sheepish grin when he realized she couldn't shake it with the dog in her arms. He dropped his arm to his side.

"Laura Clancy." She stepped aside to let him in the house. The smell of what had to be chocolate chip cookies engulfed him, his stomach suddenly reminding him he'd missed out on dinner, having stayed late to help Case at the depot. "Nice of you to bid on Webster last week. Him being new in town and all, I wasn't sure he'd be a quick pick."

Laura spoke as Colton followed her into a living room—worn but comfortable furniture, end tables crammed with framed photos, a slew of dog toys spread on the carpet.

"Is he around? Mind if I talk to him?"

"Sure, down in the basement. Follow me."

She led the way through a dining room—wall shelves crowded with trophies and more family photos—into the kitchen, then to a doorway at the back. She opened it and ducked her head inside. "Hey, Web, you've got a visitor."

Only silence rose up from the stairway leading down.

Laura turned, sighed.

"I'll head down, if you don't mind."

"Please, have at it."

His feet padded over the carpet-covered steps as he descended into the basement, air cooling around him. He spotted Webster right away, hunched over a notebook sprawled atop a desk.

He paused at the bottom of the steps. Should he go in further? "Hey, Hawks, it's me."

Webster didn't even glance up.

"I texted you."

"Got homework."

Colton nodded slowly and glanced around the room. When Laura Clancy had said *basement*, he'd pictured wood paneling and shag carpet. Maybe a futon for a bed and pipes running overhead. But this was a nice setup. Carpet couldn't be more than a couple years old, light-colored walls, a high ceiling, and recessed lighting took away any basement feel to the room. Flat-screen TV and desk complete with iMac weren't too shabby either.

And yet . . .

Even as nice as it was, he couldn't help wondering if Webster might feel isolated down here. Maybe in the Clancys' effort to provide him a space all his own, they didn't realize that what kids like Webster really wanted—whether they realized it or not—wasn't so much independence but inclusion.

Belonging was a tough enough sense to conjure up when all the rest of the world seemed to be divided into family units and you were on your own. It was all the more difficult to grasp onto when feeling like the odd man out in the latest foster home.

Not that he faulted the Clancys. Their hearts were obviously in the right place.

"I just came by to drop this off." He reached into his pocket and pulled out the watch Webster had left in that puddle of mud on the field. He'd stopped by the jewelry store downtown this morning—had it fixed.

Webster stopped writing, still didn't look up.

Colton set the watch on the desk next to him.

Webster's quiet expanded into something thoughtful. He picked up the watch, ran his thumb over its face. "My dad's. Only thing of his I've got."

Colton had thought it might be something like that. He stayed silent, waited while Webster fit the watch over his wrist. And then, "I heard there's a joint downtown that has good pizza and old-school Pac-Man."

Webster finally looked up, an unspoken thank-you written all over his face. "Quarters?"

"We'll get some on the way."

Webster stood, grabbed the sweatshirt draped over the back of his chair. "Fine. Let's go."

✌◯

"It's called an intellectual property transfer agreement."

"Uh, Beck, you want to explain that minus the legalese?" Kate sat atop the pink bedspread in her bedroom.

Well, Colton's bedroom for the past almost-two weeks. But hers once more for the moment—because if she was going to face that email from Gil, she needed the familiarity.

Even without Colton home, though, this room tingled with his presence. The hoodie he always wore draped over the corner of the antique vanity's mirror. A pair of running shoes, laces splayed, abandoned next to the bed. The brace he slipped over his knee when he went running.

She remembered thinking that first night that Colton was way too big for this small room. And this small room way too pink for such a . . . man.

But now, looking around the room, it wasn't the pink she saw, but all the ways he'd settled in. And it wasn't just here in this bedroom he'd made himself at home, but here in Maple Valley. In less than two weeks, he'd become a fixture at the house and the depot, Seth's restaurant and the coffee shop, the hardware store, even church.

Colton Greene, the professional football player from California, had carved out a place for himself in her hometown, of all places.

"I get the feeling you're not listening, sis." Her younger brother's usual patience carried over the phone, and the box springs creaked as she shifted to cross her legs.

"Sorry. You're right. Start over?"

"Basically, it's a contract in which both parties agree about the specs of the IP—intellectual property—and about the value. You would, in essence, be saying 'I no longer claim any ownership or right to this story idea, what's been written so far, or any further development of the story.'"

Intellectual property transfer. It sounded cold and impassive. Empty of emotion.

But if she was going to grant Gil his request, that's exactly how she wanted it.

Kate reached for the mug of Earl Grey tea she'd carried into the bedroom with her. The teabag string still sagged over the edge of the cup, and the water-warmed glass heated her fingers. As she took a drink, the email she hadn't meant to memorize replayed itself.

> I wanted to talk to you about this in person, Katie. I've called you, your agent, even your father. I don't blame you for not wanting to talk to me. Please believe me, I wouldn't insert myself back into your life if it wasn't important.
>
> It's about that script we were writing together when . . . everything went down. With your permission, I'd like to finish it. But it was your script as much as mine. So I'd like to do this the right way.

All this time—the phone calls, the voice mails, the emails. And all he'd wanted to talk about was a writing project. Cruel déjà vu—that's what this was.

"Assuming both parties agree on the terms, it would be a fairly fast process," Beck was saying now. "But if you feel the IP is higher in value than the other guy or if you want to add a bunch of conditions to the agreement, I suppose it could become more drawn out."

With one hand, Kate balanced her mug on her knee. "No, if I do this, there isn't going to be anything like that. I want quick and easy. Open and shut. Bing, bang, boom. Done and done." She tapped her fingernails against her mug with each phrase. "Over and out."

"You done?"

"Yes."

"So this is a script we're talking about, right? Screenplay?"

She sighed, replaced her mug on the bedside stand, and flopped backward into the pillows behind her. "Yes, it's a script."

A half-written script that Gil had apparently dug up a few weeks ago when he was cleaning out his old office. She'd been so tempted to immediately delete the email. Just like that, make it disappear from her inbox and hopefully her memory.

But something stopped her as her finger hovered over the key. Why this script? Why now? And why was he going to such great lengths to get her permission to finish it?

"So why are you transferring the rights of something you've written? Why hand it all over to the co-writer? Wouldn't the writing credit be good for your career?"

The subtle, spicy scent of Colton's aftershave lingered in the sheets and comforter beneath her. "Beckett, I'll be honest with you if you promise not to flip out."

"Why does it matter if I flip out? I'm in Boston. I can't do too much damage."

She pictured him, probably sitting at the antique desk in his apartment, catching up on work. Except for his glasses and the slight curl to his hair, Beckett looked so much like Dad did in photos at that age.

"The other writer is Gil."

His pause was a wordless lecture. "You're serious. Gil. That slimeball?"

"Slimeball might be a little over the top." But she smiled all the same.

"He led you on, his student, almost ten years younger than him, for almost a year."

"I wasn't his student by the time we actually started dating."

"He wined and dined you. Convinced you not to take that internship in DC and move to Chicago. And then, pow, one day he surprised you with the news that he was already married."

Her muscles tightened and a lump in the mattress underneath poked at her side. "I don't need a history recap, Beck. I was there."

Besides, Beck didn't know everything. He didn't know, for instance, how much Gil had helped her on her book. She'd worked so hard on it throughout her senior year of college, an almost frenetic desperation to finish it before Mom died. Gil had revised scenes and proofread and gotten it into the hands of that editor he knew.

For all the ways he'd hurt her, it hadn't all been wining and dining.

She reached under the comforter to pull out whatever it was bunched up underneath her. Another hoodie. How many did Colton own?

"Yeah, well, now that I know this piece of info, I say you make Gil buy you out of your part in it. I'll rep you. If he really wants the script, he can have it. But we'll make him pay. We'll make him pay good."

"Lawyer Beckett, you frighten me." She tossed the hoodie to the end of the bed and sat up. "Look, this was just an initial info-gathering phone call. Gil wants to talk. Figured I'd like to go into the conversation prepared."

"Why talk to him at all? Let your agent handle it."

"Thanks for the help, Beck." She closed her eyes. The long day had sapped her energy . . . and her desire to argue this out.

"Is that your way of telling me to butt out?" When she didn't answer, he sighed. "I know I'm just your *younger* brother. It's Logan's job to give the advice."

"And yet, you're the one I called."

162

"Right. So just be careful, okay? Be smart."

They hung up minutes later and she lay back on the bed. Maybe Beck had a point. Maybe contact with Gil was a bad idea. It'd taken so long—*sooo* long—to let him go after finding out their relationship was nothing but a sham.

She closed her eyes again. It felt so good to be in her own bed. She could fall asleep here . . . felt herself drifting . . .

The sound of the front door closing rang through the house. Kate jerked. Darkness dimmed the room, and warmth from her bed's comforter, her pillow, enveloped her. She'd fallen asleep. What time was it?

Dad had said he was working late at the depot. Had Raegan come home?

Footsteps sounded down the hallway, longer strides than they would be if it was Raegan.

Colton . . . She jerked up in the bed. She couldn't let him find her in here, waking up from a nap . . . in his bed. But the footsteps were nearly to the door.

She jumped from the bed and slipped into the bathroom connected to the room.

Whyyyy? Why are you hiding?

Because she didn't think well two seconds after waking up—that's why.

Colton's steps sounded in the bedroom.

Just explain to him you had a silly yearning to visit your bedroom.

Right. That didn't sound ridiculous at all.

She heard Colton walking toward the bathroom. *Shoot. Shoot, shoot, shoot.* She jumped into the tub and pulled the shower curtain over the opening.

Hiding in the bathtub in her own bathroom. This was one for the family vault of mock-worthy memories.

Colton walked into the bathroom. Paused. Maybe he was just grabbing a Kleenex or something. He'd be leaving soon . . .

Except no, because suddenly his arm snaked into the shower and reached for the faucet. Water rushed over her feet, and then—*oh no*—he twisted the knob to start the shower.

Water squirted at her face and over her clothes, and it was all she could do not to scream or sputter. And panic welled in her. She couldn't stay here. Not with Colton on the other side of the shower curtain, probably getting undressed. *Undressed.*

But where could she go?

Bad idea, Walker. Bad, bad idea.

But before she could figure out what to do, the shower curtain flung aside and she immediately closed her eyes. "Don't do it, Colton." Her voice pitched to a squeal. "Don't get in."

"Chill, Walker. I'm dressed."

She opened one eye, gaze traveling from the floor up. Bare feet. Jeans. Shirt. Smirk. "Y-you . . . you knew I was in here." Water streamed over her face and slicked down her arms.

Colton bent over to turn off the water, then pointed above her. "Light does this crazy thing, Rosie. It's called forming shadows."

"You knew I was in here and you still turned on the water." She shook her head in slow motion, eyes pressed to slits. "You're mean."

"But at least I'm not wet."

"Why, you—" She lunged for the bottle of shampoo on the shelf inside the shower and in one smooth motion had it open and pointed at him, soapy liquid blasting him in the chest.

"Miss. Walker. How could you?"

While he was still looking at the soapy mess she'd made on his shirt, she reached for the faucet and turned the shower on, then angled the nozzle at him.

"You're getting the whole bathroom wet."

"I'm saving you a load of laundry."

He climbed over the tub edge, laughter bouncing off the tiled walls, and fought her for the nozzle, both of them now completely soaked and bubbles floating in the air.

"Never start a water war with a Walker, Colton."

He barreled against her, pushing the nozzle away from his face. "You forget I'm a lot bigger than you."

She was giggling like a kid, completely trapped against the shower wall. He reached behind her to turn off the water, the strawberry scent of the shampoo filling the space and steam clouding the air around them.

And so much laughter.

Until, finally, they quieted. Only the dripping of water and the sound of the bathroom's overhead fan.

And her heart suddenly hammering in her chest.

She looked at Colton, saw the rapid pace of his breathing. *What were we thinking?* And why was Colton looking at her like—

"I should go."

She clambered out of the tub, grabbed a towel from the shelf on the wall, wrapped it around her shoulders, and all-out fled from the room.

She reached Beckett's bedroom door just as Raegan's voice called for her.

"Hey, sis, did you—" She broke off, staring at Kate's wet clothes. "What happened?"

"Long story." Or not so long. But *"I just had a water fight in the shower with Colton"* would invite more scrutiny than she could handle.

She took in Raegan's appearance then, the slump of her shoulders and the frown pulling at her mouth. "What's wrong?"

"They're planning to close the depot. The city council decided to put it to a vote. All Dad and Colton's work will be for nothing."

9

"Dad? What in the world are you thinking?"

Kate's words came out sputtered and uneven as she jogged from her car to the cover of the train depot's jutting overhang. The depot's recent paint job made it fairly glow against its hilly backdrop. Flecks of autumn color—red and yellow and orange—were just beginning to poke through the canopy of green and brown covering the landscape.

And there was Dad, denim-clad legs visible halfway up a ladder perched on the wooden platform in front of the depot. The overhang hid the rest of him.

Kate slipped the hood of her sweatshirt from her head as she reached the depot. She still wore her pajama pants. Hadn't even taken the time to put in her contacts. She'd hoped to find Dad this morning before he left the house, but a torrent of emotions mixed with overnight storms had kept her tossing and turning past midnight.

Do not think about Colton. Do not think about water fights in showers.

This morning rain still twirled downward from portly clouds—their underbellies lit by stray lightning and a pastel sunrise. She stopped at the foot of the ladder, nudged up her glasses and tipped her head. "Really, Dad? Working on outdoor light fixtures in a storm? Aren't you asking to get electrocuted? And with one arm in a sling?"

He grunted, unscrewed a bulb, and glanced down. "Catch."

Next thing she knew, the old bulb dropped, and she jerked to catch it.

"And for the record, young lady, the sky's barely making a peep right now. More chance of me falling off this ladder and breaking a leg than getting electrocuted."

Kate propped one slipper-clad foot on the ladder. "That's comforting."

About as comforting as hearing this old depot and museum might be closing. Would be, according to Raegan and, apparently, the city council.

How could they just give up on the place? After all the work Dad had put in. All the history this little building housed.

Metal scraped against metal as Dad screwed in the new bulb overhead. He nodded his head in satisfaction and climbed down the ladder. Faded jeans and a flannel shirt—so different from the military uniforms and tailored suits he used to wear.

Same grin, though, even if weathered by surrounding lines.

"So?" he asked, one eyebrow raising—a trait he'd passed on to only Beckett. Kate used to spend hours in front of the bathroom mirror, attempting to pull off the same expression. "What has my night owl up so early?"

She tipped her head toward the building. "This place. You. Wondering what you're going to do."

His lips pressed together, and he reached for the ladder, wood clacking as he folded it together. He hefted the ladder with one hand, and Kate jumped in to secure its other end.

They carried the ladder around the corner of the building, toward the shed attached to the side of the depot, where they stopped as Dad dug in his pocket for the keys.

"You are going to do something, aren't you?"

Lingering raindrops slanted in, dotting her sweatshirt. She waited while Dad put the ladder away and relocked the shed. When he turned, she recognized the determination in his expression. Oh, he might dress differently, might've retired from government service years ago. But he was still solid as a tree. Like that oak giant in the town square that'd refused to bend in the tornado.

"It's the council's decision, Katie. It's expensive to keep up the depot—maintain the rail and the cars. And now with all the damage . . ."

"But you and Colton have been working like crazy. Colton said he thinks you can have it ready for Depot Day."

"If they vote to close it, there's not going to be a Depot Day this year." A windy gush hurled wet air their way, and Dad patted her shoulder, turning her toward the depot's back entrance.

"But surely the businesses in town will be upset. The depot's a tourist draw, Dad." The scent of lemon and pine enveloped her as she entered the building.

"A tri-county draw, at best. And unlike the antique stores, it isn't even open all year round."

The light from frosted glass sconces along the walls mingled with soft sunlight to showcase the work Dad and Colton had done in recent days. Pale green covered the upper half of the walls wrapping around the room, while rich walnut wainscoting reached up the lower half. One end of the room opened into the small, now-dark eating area where the depot served ice cream in the summer and hot cocoa and apple cider during chilly fall months.

The wooden floor still showed nicks and grooves from decades of foot traffic and the recent storm. None of the glass display cases had been replaced yet, and the walls seemed empty without shelves full of knickknacks, old passenger books, and railroad paraphernalia.

But it was beginning to look as she remembered.

"Come on back to my office. You haven't had your morning coffee yet."

"How can you tell?"

Dad grinned. "Your forehead's all pinched."

She followed him past the raised ticket booth that had windows open to both the inside and outside. "That's because I came here hoping we could come up with a plan to save the depot. Instead you seem . . ." *Completely at peace, actually.* And it didn't make sense.

He led her into his office in back—little more than a closet, really. No oversized mahogany desk and matching hutch like he'd had back when they lived out east. Barely room for a small rolltop and a couple padded chairs.

She lowered into the chair edged into a corner while Dad pulled a mug from atop the desk.

"I'm surprised Colton isn't here yet. He's been getting here by seven most mornings." Dad peered inside the cup, then used the edge of his shirt to wipe it out.

Kate smothered a smirk at his cleaning method. "I've been worried the time we've spent working on his book was taking away from his time helping you."

"Not at all. He's a hard worker, that one. And more than a little handsome, according to Rae." Dad reached for the coffeepot at the corner of his desk. "Though, truthfully, if I was going to pair him with one of my girls, it'd be you."

"Dad."

He turned on an innocent smile and handed her the mug. "What? I've thought the two of you would make a good match from the start. Can't a man make an observation?"

"Play matchmaker, you mean?"

"Potato, po-tah-to." He poured his own cup of coffee. "And for the record, by 'from the start,' I mean since I first met him—Parents' Weekend at Iowa. Logan called up a couple days before to ask if we could include Colton in whatever we ended up doing that weekend—seeing as how he didn't have family visiting and all."

"That sounds like Logan."

"And I'm telling you, soon as I met him, I thought, Katie needs to meet this kid. Flora thought so, too. We talked about it all the way home from Iowa City. I thought you'd be a good pair because he had a Beatles poster hanging on his side of his dorm room. Remember when you went through that Beatles-obsessed stage?"

"I was fourteen." She sipped her coffee—Dad's usual thicker-than-syrup brew.

"That was just my first impression though. Later in the weekend I decided his sense of humor was a perfect match for you."

"Dad—"

"Now your mom, her reasoning was entirely different."

"Don't want to hear it." Except she absolutely did. There was something therapeutic about talking about Mom. About sitting in Dad's office, seeing Mom's picture on his desk, just talking.

Even if the subject matter had warmth flooding her cheeks. *Nah, that's just the coffee.*

Right.

"She thought you'd have cute kids together."

And of course she chose that second to take a drink. She choked, felt the bitter liquid scorch down her throat, and sputtered. Couldn't even scold Dad, not the way her windpipe tightened in mortification.

"Ah, Katie, you're way too easy to embarrass."

"I'm not embarrassed, Yente. Emma Woodhouse. Dolly Levi. Pick your fictional matchmaker of choice."

"*Fiddler on the Roof* and Jane Austen's *Emma*, but I'm stumped on the third one."

"*Hello, Dolly!*, Dad. You should know this. I watched the Barbra Streisand version a thousand times as a kid."

"And always got a sore throat from trying to sing like Louis Armstrong. Now I remember." Dad laughed and regarded her for a moment.

Then, thank her lucky stars, he apparently decided to have mercy on her, because he let the subject of Colton drop and settled into his chair.

"Can't we talk a little more about the depot, Dad? Can't we at least try to do something?"

He sipped his coffee, letting her request hover in the air for stretched-out seconds before finally answering. "Listen, Katie, I'm your father, not one of your scripts. You don't have to fix things for me."

She set her cup down. "I'm not trying to—"

He interrupted her with only a look. Took another drink. "There's something God's been teaching me over the past decade or so—this idea of letting go. Not good at it, never have been. Probably what made me a good soldier and ambassador. But I'm in a different place now. More and more I'm seeing the value in stepping back and waiting. Discerning when it's right to hold on and when it's right to loosen up and let go."

He set his cup on a coaster atop his desk. "If it's time to let go of this old place—no matter how much your mother loved it or all the memories attached to it—then I don't want to waste time holding tight to a season in my life that's hit its expiration date."

Despite their softness, his words landed with a thud, sending plumes of surprise fogging through her.

"But . . . if it closes, what will you do?"

"I'll do whatever comes next."

"You don't have a plan?"

"Tell me, Katie, when has having a plan ever translated into things going exactly the way you expected?" He leaned forward then, fatherly gaze somehow gentle and firm at the same time. "I'm not saying we should go through life all half-cocked and clueless. But a little flexibility, a little wait-and-see—I'm coming to see that's healthy."

That sounded nice, but the problem was, Kate hadn't had a plan for years. Not since Gil turned her life upside down. For six years, she'd simply been doing the next thing, writing the next script, scrounging up the next part-time job to fill in the financial gaps.

Now she finally—*finally*—had a real plan. And she wouldn't trade it for all the flexibility in the world.

"Dad, I—"

But his office door burst open, cutting her off. And there stood Colton. Winded, smiling.

"I've got a plan." His gaze darted from Dad to Kate, focused expression wavering for just a moment. "Nice pajamas."

She only rolled her eyes.

Dad stood. "For what?"

He grinned. "Saving the depot."

~~~

He'd pulled it off. He couldn't believe he'd actually pulled it off.

Colton looked around the sprawling yard of the railway depot, satisfaction welling inside. At first, he hadn't been sure Case Walker was all that keen on his idea for pulling together the last-minute event, inviting the media, and probably drumming up the best publicity the railway had seen in decades—maybe ever.

Kate had been the clincher. She'd jumped at his idea the second he presented it. Cajoled her father into going along with it. Went with Colton to the city offices to convince Mayor Milt and the rest of the town's leaders.

Now here they were, three days later, the field behind the depot packed with cars, and the lawn crowded with people. Maple Valley, for all its quirks, knew how to throw a party.

Best of all, he'd counted three television crews and at least four reporters with notepads and cameras. One radio station had even set up a live broadcast.

And it hadn't cost the city budget a dime.

"Dude, I feel like I've stepped back in time instead of just flown across the country." It was Joe Kemper who spoke, a former teammate from Colton's first year in the NFL. The now-retired tight end had led a team Bible study back before Colton had shown much interest in faith. But that had never stopped Joe from inviting him.

And then there was Greg Williams, the quarterback who'd played backup behind Colton back at the University of Iowa, and Darrell Clapton, a former Tigers teammate. Four NFL-ers, Seth and his friend Bear, and a handful of other men from town were going up against the Mavericks football team in the city's first ever train pull.

The smell of barbeque from The Red Door drifted over the lawn. Seth's girlfriend, Ava, led a crew of volunteers serving food behind a six-foot table. There had to be a few hundred people, at least, covering the lawn in gathered clumps—eating, chatting, casting interested glances toward where Colton stood with his friends on the boardwalk. The dinner train rested on its tracks, like a proud performer waiting for its turn in the spotlight. Eager fans had made generous donations to join the NFL-ers for a dinner excursion after the train pull. Across the expansive lawn the depot gleamed almost as if it, too, had been made up for the occasion.

Overhead, roaming clouds blurred the sky's blue.

Please, God, just let the rain hold off. Maple Valley needs this.

And please let his shoulder and knee hold up, too. It'd been days since he'd needed to ice either one. But if anything was going to aggravate his injuries, attempting to pull a train car— even just a foot—could do it.

"I can't believe you've been in Iowa for weeks." This from Greg. "If I'd known you were here, I'd have brought my boys over from Cedar Falls to meet you. They still can't believe I once played with *the* Colton Greene."

Colton let out a laugh. Greg said it like Colton was synonymous with one of the Manning brothers. "You should've brought them today."

"Too last minute, unfortunately."

That had been Colton's concern about the whole event. But Maple Valley thrived on spontaneity. And with the publicity, the tourist traffic in town, surely the city council would agree keeping the depot open—at least for the rest of this year—was a viable option.

"You guys about ready?" Kate ambled toward them, brown eyes sparkling in the sunlight. She, more than anybody, had poured herself into making today happen.

"Ready as we'll ever be."

They began the walk to their train. Case had picked two empty freight cars for the event.

Kate sidled up to him. "Nice scarf, by the way."

He glanced down at the thing. "Raegan made them for the adult team. She said tan was the manliest color of yarn she could find at the craft store."

"My sister crochets?"

"Either that or she hired out the labor. So who are you rooting for?"

Dimples creased her cheeks as she grinned. "I'm torn. On the one hand, the Mavericks are my team, you know? My school. But you guys have my cousin and Bear."

His jaw dropped with exaggerated shock. "Excuse me?"

"And you, of course."

He folded his arms. "Good, because I am your co-writer after all. Which I believe means you owe me at least a little loyalty."

"Speaking of which, I read those paragraphs you added to chapter three. You're a good writer, Colt."

"Eh, years of practice."

"Practice?"

He stopped, realizing he'd said more than he meant to. And if it was any other day and any other person, if something crisp and fresh as the almost-autumn air around him hadn't grabbed hold of him, he would've clammed up and not said another word.

Instead, with a kind of abandon he hadn't felt in years, he went on. "After my parents died, I couldn't remember the accident. Not any of it. DHS required that I go to therapy. Therapists made me journal. I had notebooks full. Dozens."

The clutter of voices around them, the music piped in from speakers someone had set up, all faded into the distance as Kate watched him. "You still don't remember."

He shook his head.

He did, however, remember what'd happened to the journals. The day Norah had called him in for that last meeting, after she'd closed the manila folder with all his case paperwork and told him he was no longer a ward of the state, she handed a box full of his notebooks to him.

He shoved it back at her and walked out of the room.

He'd been such a jerk to the one person who'd cared.

"Colton?"

He met Kate's eyes. "Yeah?"

"I'm rooting for you."

Simple words, but he had a feeling they would stick in his head, fill him up on soul-hungry days.

"Greene, get over and join the huddle." Joe Kemper's voice pushed into what had become a moment anchored with import.

"I better go."

Kate leaned forward to straighten his scarf. "Pull hard."

He jogged over to his teammates, Joe's pep talk already in motion. "We've got something they don't, men."

"What? Gray hair?" Darrell, the oldest of the group, joked.

"No, experience."

Colton watched Kate move off to the side, joining Raegan and Case and the other spectators.

"Sorry to break it to you, Kemper," Greg said, clapping his hand on Joe's shoulder, "but I've never pulled a train before. Does anyone even know how much these things weigh?"

"No idea, but the point is, we've played in championship games. And you don't get to championship games without intense focus and teamwork. Look at them." Joe pointed to where the varsity team, in full uniform, gathered at the parallel track. "They outman us and outweigh us. But what was it you were telling us about the team on the way to town, Greene?"

"They haven't found their footing. They don't gel yet. Lost their first couple games."

"Men, *we* are going to gel. Let's take our places."

Colton started toward the train with the others but stopped short, looked back at Kate. "One sec, guys."

He ran over to her, unwinding his scarf as he did.

"Too hot?" she said as he reached her.

He draped it over her neck. "You wear it. For good luck."

As he hurried back to the train, he felt the first drops of rain. He joined the rest of his team, picked up one of the chains Case had attached to its base.

And then the whistle blew and the yelling began. He gripped his chain and pulled, Joe's shouts egging him on with the heaves and grunts from the men around him. "Pull!" Joe's voice.

He pulled. And pulled. Like playing tug-of-war against a giant with no idea if they were making any progress.

A raindrop caught in his eyelash, and he blinked to flick it away. Joe called again. "Pull!" He felt the sharp pang in his shoulder but gritted his teeth and let his muscles roar.

"Pull! All together."

Minutes passed, how many he didn't know. But soon they'd found a rhythm, pulling as one until eventually the freight car's tires finally squealed. Metal rubbed against metal as the rain picked up.

"We're doing it. Pull!" Joe again.

Colton's shoulder would hate him in the morning, but they were going to do this.

And right as the sky broke open and the downpour began in earnest, the cheers of the crowd let him know they'd finished. He let his chain drop, muscles burning and sweat mixing with the rain that slicked over him. His team whooped and smacked each other on the back, and he looked over to see the high school team close to finishing their own pull.

But that wasn't the moment of victory for Colton. No, that came when he spotted Kate jumping up and down, smile as bright as the sky wasn't. Next thing he knew, she was in front of him. "The scarf worked."

He lifted her off her feet, into a hug that had to have taken her as much by surprise as him, rain and cheers wrapping around them.

More shouts broke out as the high school team finished their pull.

But he couldn't make himself turn. Couldn't stop looking at Kate, drinking in the sight of her—her smile, hair whipping around her face, the flicker of unadulterated delight dancing in her eyes.

"Kate."

"Thank you, Colt. For doing this for the depot and Dad and the town. Thank you."

Instead of pulling away, she buried her face in his neck.

And he knew the truth in that moment—he hadn't concocted this plan, called in his friends, and worked twelve, fourteen hour days the past three days just for the sake of the depot. Or Case.

He'd done it for Kate. Because of how much it meant to her.

And how much she'd come to mean to him. Maybe it was all the time spent together. The way she had of seeing past his exterior, his fame, his failures, to the memories and vulnerabilities he usually kept buried.

In just a little over two weeks, Kate had unearthed in him a longing he hadn't realized he even had—to be known, seen. Not as California DHS Case 174—the foster kid who'd lost his parents and teen with a penchant for trouble. Not as number 18—quarterback for the LA Tigers.

But just as Colton. The guy who'd finally done something right.

She lifted her head then, gaze locked with his.

Then jumped when Case Walker's voice barreled in. "Anyone who wants a train ride, we're taking off in ten."

The first second Kate could manage, she escaped to the dinner train's bathroom—a space that made the walk-in closet back in her townhouse seem cavernous. She'd already used a tissue to wipe away the worst of her rain-smudged makeup. But now that she had access to a mirror, she wanted to see the real damage.

\The train's movement rumbled under her feet, and she steadied herself against the sink before braving a look in the mirror.

"Delightful. Just . . . delightful." Yes, she'd gotten rid of the mascara smears, but in the process had cleared away whatever was left of her makeup. But surely the fluorescent light bulb over the mirror exaggerated her pale skin and circle-rimmed eyes, right?

"Psst, Kate, you in there?"

"Uh, yeah, Rae."

"Let me in."

"How do you know I'm not . . ." *Oh, never mind.* She unbolted the door and Raegan squeezed in. "What do you need?"

Raegan's hands clamped onto Kate's shoulders. "Ohhh . . . my goodness. Oh. My. Goodness."

"I really look that bad?"

Raegan jostled her shoulders. "No. I'm talking about that scene outside. With the scarf and the hug and *Colton*."

The train jolted underneath then, and Kate knocked into the wall behind her. A rush of claustrophobia squeezed her. "I don't know what you're talking about."

Bold-faced lie. That moment in the rain . . . Well, she couldn't talk about it now. Didn't want to. Something had happened in that moment, and she wasn't ready to shine a spotlight on it for anyone else. Never mind that it'd happened in front of half the community. And cameras.

But for now, she wanted to hold it close. It wasn't only that hug, it was what he'd told her before the pull. Offered her a glimpse of his past that couldn't have been easy for him. And then the way he'd looked at her. Like today, this whole thing, was his gift to her.

Except, oh, what was she saying? *You can't do this, Kate.* Couldn't let a two-week friendship balloon into something unreasonable in her imagination. She was setting herself up for hurt.

He's going to go back to LA. I'm going to go back to Chicago. Then New York. Then Africa. She had to rein her heart in now, before it leapt too far from her control.

"You're so good at playing dumb, big sis."

The sarcasm lacing Raegan's tone did nothing to quell the annoyance rising in Kate. "And you're so good at reading into things."

Raegan's lips curved. "Come on, it was plain as day, obvious to everyone who saw it. Dad noticed. Seth noticed. Someone wearing a blindfold would've noticed."

The pungent aroma from the potpourri in the dish at the corner of the sink threatened to overwhelm Kate's sense of smell. Too much. Too small of a space. "Why would anyone be wandering around blindfolded?"

"I don't know. Why do you deny what's in front of your face?"

Kate folded her arms. "Which is?" She shouldn't have asked.

"You and Colton. Sparks. And not those flimsy sparklers that last like three seconds. I'm talking fireworks. *Ka-boom.*" She made little exploding motions with her fingers.

"I think you made your point. And you're wrong." She tried to reach around Raegan for the door handle, but Raegan moved to block it.

"Rae—" Kate's cell phone vibrated in her pocket. Probably Marcus. Again. He'd called at least four times in the past couple hours. *Patience.* She'd promised him an update on the book project this weekend. But it was still the weekend.

"Why are you acting so annoyed? I should be the one who's upset. I met Colton first. I should have first dibs on a crush—"

"I don't have a crush on him." Great, and now her voice had gone shrill. That would go a long way toward convincing Raegan.

"Don't worry, I'm not mad. If you two weren't so adorable together, I might be, but—"

"Raegan." She practically screeched her name.

Kate closed her eyes. Took a breath. Angled around to turn on the water—white noise—then reversed to face Raegan. "What you're insinuating, Rae . . . It's not funny to me." She spoke slowly, letting each word fall and hopefully hit its mark. "You can surmise whatever you want about Colton's and my . . . friendship. But keep it to yourself."

Confusion wrinkled over her sister's face. "*Why* are you reacting like this?"

The train jerked again. "In the span of a year, Colton has lost the person he thought he was going to marry and his football career. He's got a past that makes our own loss of a parent look like a walk in the park." She saw Raegan flinch at that. Had she gone too far? "And he's got a million other things to worry about right now—he's trying so hard to focus and move on. The last thing he needs is a distraction. So forgive me if I don't find it funny to joke about a friendship that just can't be more than a friendship. It can't."

Raegan seemed to shrink under Kate's harsh words, the bright light over the sink highlighting each wince. The chug of the train, muffled voices from outside, and the water slapping against the sides of the sink filled the momentary silence.

"It's just . . . not funny to me." She repeated the words, softer now.

When Raegan didn't respond, Kate reversed once more to

turn off the water. She leaned over the sink, hands propped on the edge, hair flopped over her shoulders.

"You go ahead and tell yourself all that if you like."

Kate's head jerked up at Raegan's surprising words, the hard glint in her tone. She met her sister's eyes in the mirror. They'd emptied of remorse and turned steely. Kate pivoted. "What?"

"Tell yourself it's Colton and all the things he's dealing with that you're concerned about."

"Of course I am."

"Oh, I'm sure you are. But only because you've trained yourself to flip the Off switch the second you recognize any romantic inkling in yourself. You're an expert at putting up walls, Kate. News flash: Gil happened almost six years ago. I know it hurt, and I know a person's first instinct after something like that is to do whatever they can to avoid it ever happening again, but I—"

"Stop it, Rae. Stop doing the psychiatrist thing." Her phone buzzed in her pocket again. *Oh come on, Marcus.*

"I'm not doing the psychiatrist thing. I'm doing the sister thing!" Raegan gave her exclamation space to dangle in the air before speaking again. "And if you were honest, you'd admit the one you're looking out for is you."

She couldn't take any more of this. Kate brushed past Raegan, pushed the door open, knocking it into another passenger. She muttered an apology and glanced both ways down the train car. On one end she saw the backs of the heads of Colton's NFL friends, a slew of ogling cameras.

The other direction appeared empty.

Easy decision.

"Kate."

"I don't want to talk about this anymore, Rae. Not here." Not at all.

Her phone dinged, letting her know Marcus had left a voice mail this time.

She hurried past the person she'd hit with the door and emerged into the light of the open space, blessedly clear of people. Sunlight streamed through the car's windows, the beautiful scenery outside begging for attention.

She tried. Sinking into a maroon seat, her gaze gulped in the tree-filled rises and falls on either side of the scenic bridge they now crossed.

But the landscape did little to cool the heated emotions simmering in her. Raegan didn't know what she was talking about.

Kate yanked off the scarf around her neck—Colton's scarf— and pulled her phone from her pocket. Five missed calls from Marcus. She should probably listen to his voice mail.

"There you are." Colton plopped down in the seat across from her. "Couldn't figure out where you'd disappeared to, considering there's not really anywhere to go on this train. Unless you were trying to pull some kind of Lone Ranger stunt and ride on top of the train."

Why did he have to talk in such easy tones, the kind reserved for friends and confidantes and people who shared inside jokes? And why did he have to be so ridiculously good-looking?

And why are you even trying to deny what Raegan saw?

"Why are you looking at me like that?"

She blinked. "Like what?"

"Like . . ." He drew out the word. "Forlorn. Like how I'd feel if you told me you still didn't appreciate football, even after all my time teaching and training—"

"We've gotta stop, Colt." The words rushed out before she could pull them back.

"Stop . . . ?"

Her fingers tightened around her phone. "Just . . . stop. This. Whatever."

His brow furrowed. "I'm trying really hard not to be dense here, but you're going to have to give me a little more to work with."

Instead of buzzing, now her phone trilled. Text message. She glanced down. Marcus. Of course.

But then she read the message. Sucked in a breath so sharp she could almost feel it land with a pang in her stomach.

PLEASE answer your phone, K. It's about Breydan.

10

*W*hy were hospitals always so cold?

The beeping and murmuring of a collage of machines surrounding Breydan's bedside filled the small room. The hospital bed swallowed his tiny form, the white of his skin matching both the sheets and the walls.

Despite her long sleeves, Kate felt goose bumps rise to the surface of her skin, and she swallowed. Hard. An attempt to keep whatever was swirling in her stomach—a fast-food breakfast, an oversized fountain drink, and fear—in place.

"The doctor is a little more optimistic this morning." A thread of hope, frayed and bare, hung in Marcus's voice. "He thinks . . . maybe, if his fever comes down . . ."

Kate grasped for rigid confidence. "It will."

She couldn't take her eyes off Breydan. So still. If not for the lines on one of the monitors, she would've wondered if he was even breathing.

"I can't believe you got here so quickly."

Seven hours in the car hadn't felt quick. It had felt like one of those dreams where you were trying to run away from something, or toward something, but weight slogged your steps.

Marcus turned. "And I *really* can't believe you brought Colton Greene with you. You should see all the nurses gawking at him."

It was more like Colton had brought her. He'd watched her return Marcus's call—was that just last night?—in the dinner train. Reached forward to grasp her hand the second he realized something was terribly wrong. And when she'd hung up and explained, he'd insisted on being the one to drive her to the hospital in the east Chicago suburb.

How he'd stayed awake as he drove through the night, she had no idea. But he wouldn't let her take the wheel even once. Maybe sweetest of all, about an hour into the trip, as they'd turned onto Interstate 80 near Des Moines, he'd glanced over at her, hesitated only for a moment, then asked if she'd like him to pray.

The tears she'd held back ever since the phone call had threatened once again, and she could only nod.

It'd been a simple prayer. Short. No flowery words or drawn-out pleas. But sincere. She'd tried to sleep after that, might have dozed off once or twice, that scarf of his under her head like a pillow. But Marcus's words replaying in her head made complete rest an impossibility.

"He had a sudden reaction to one of his medications. Fever, seizures. And with his immune system . . . It's bad, Kate. I think you'd better come. . . ."

She leaned over to brush Breydan's hair from his forehead. "Can you imagine how happy he's going to be when he wakes up and gets to meet Colton?"

"He's going to be just as happy to see you." Marcus squeezed her arm. "I'm going to go find Hailey. She was looking for coffee."

He turned to leave, but she called a question over her shoulder. "Did you see where Colton ended up?"

When they'd arrived at the hospital, he'd dropped her off at the canopied entrance. *"I'll figure out where to park and find you. Go on in."*

"Yeah, he's in the waiting room. I told him he could come in, but he thought maybe you'd want some time alone." Marcus studied her for a moment. "Want me to send him in?"

"Only if he's not napping."

Marcus nodded and left the room. Kate turned back to Breydan.

She pulled a teal chair up to the bed and lowered, then slid one hand forward, skimming the surface of the bedsheets until her fingers connected with Breydan's. His were limp, cold. Which didn't make sense, considering the fever Marcus said was raging through his body.

Nothing about cancer made sense.

"Hey, little man."

Only the drone of a machine answered her.

"I need you to wake up soon, all right? We have so many more Mario Kart races to play."

She traced his tiny knuckles, slipped her thumb under his palm.

"I haven't had much chance to practice lately, but one of these days I'm going to win a race." A tear tracked down her cheek. "Just you wait . . . One of these days . . ."

She was rambling now, repeating herself. But how else was she supposed to keep herself from falling apart.

Not fair, God. Not. Fair.

More tears now. They landed on the white bedsheet. She swiped her hand underneath her eyes. Sniffled.

"Kate?"

Colton's hand on her shoulder felt as warm as Breydan's did cold. And in less than a second she was on her feet, buried against him.

～⌒〇

If Colton did nothing else tonight, he'd convince Kate to get some sleep.

He rubbed his palm over the steamed-up mirror in Kate's

first-floor bathroom. His shower had heated the little room and eased at least some of the tightness in his muscles caused by seven hours in the car and then most of a day in a waiting-room chair. Both his knee and shoulder throbbed—whether leftover pain from yesterday's train pull or so many hours cramped in a small space, who knew.

Worth it, though. Worth the pulsing in his knee and the exhaustion.

Kate had needed him. And it felt good to be needed.

They'd spent most of the day at the hospital, but finally, as Breydan continued to sleep and afternoon drifted into evening, he'd talked Kate into going back to her townhouse for the night. Her friends, Marcus and Hailey, had promised to call if anything changed with their son.

Colton dried off his hair with the red towel he'd found in the cupboard under the sink, then hung the towel over the bar along the shower door. He'd already slipped on the black Adidas pants he'd thrown in a duffel before leaving Iowa. Now he pulled on a white T-shirt with the Hawkeyes logo across his torso.

The ring of his cell phone sounded from his bag. He plucked it out and lifted it to his ear. "Hello?"

"What is it with you and being unreachable these days?"

Ian. "I take it this isn't the first time you've tried calling me today?" He'd barely looked at his phone all day.

"I know Iowa's in the middle of nowhere, but come on, is cell reception really that bad?"

He stuffed his car-wrinkled clothes in his bag. "I'm not in Iowa."

"Then where are you?"

"Chicago."

"You're joking."

"What part of me telling you I'm in Chicago is funny?" Why was he being so short with Ian?

Because every time he calls, it feels like an intrusion.

He stilled at the thought, looking back at himself in the bathroom mirror. Was that true? Had he started getting so comfortable in Maple Valley that reminders of the life he'd left behind had drifted into unwelcome territory?

"It's not funny, it's ridiculously coincidental, is what it is. I've had a few job leads for you. One in St. Louis, one in Miami, the other in Chicago."

"Really." Why couldn't he muster up more interest? This is what he'd been hoping and praying for.

Except not lately. Man, he hadn't prayed about his career in days, maybe weeks. He'd prayed about that train pull yesterday—that it'd turn out well and encourage people he'd come to care about. He'd prayed about his book. Today, he'd prayed like crazy for that little boy in the hospital.

But not about sponsorships or speaking gigs or sportscaster jobs. The things he was supposed to be caring about.

"I was going to pursue the Miami one first, but now that I know you're in Chicago, I say we move on it. It's a regional sports show that's looking for a football analyst. Called Sports Circle. Good numbers, good ratings."

Colton dropped onto the edge of the bathtub. "Sports Circle. Chicago."

"I know it's not east or west coast, but it's a good market. Frankly, I was going to call you lucky if we could snag you something in Kansas City or Minneapolis. Chicago was more than I was hoping for."

Chicago. Wind. The Bean. Bears, Cubs, Bulls.

His brain riffled through Windy City trivia.

Kate.

He lurched. Hard enough that he lost his balance and thumped into the still-wet tub. But the water seeping through his pants and the fact that his legs now dangled over the tub's rim didn't stop the thought from completing itself.

Kate lives in Chicago.

Or, did, when she wasn't in Maple Valley. And until she left for that Africa trip she'd told him about.

"What just happened? You fall over or something?"

Maybe realizing he might have an open door to the town where Kate lived shouldn't make much difference. But it made all the difference.

The bathroom's fan rattled overhead as he pulled himself up from the bathtub. "Okay, I'm interested, Ian. So what happens now?" He pulled the shower curtain over the bathtub and picked up his duffel.

"We get you an interview set up. Sooner rather than later. Maybe even tomorrow."

His bag slid off his shoulder and thumped to the floor. "Can't do tomorrow."

"Are you kidding me? You're already *in* Chicago. If there's a God, he's doing a good job lining up all your ducks for you."

Except that God hadn't brought him to Chicago for a job interview. He'd come because there was a kid in a hospital with cancer. He'd come because Kate needed him.

"This kind of thing isn't going to come around again soon, Greene. Two of Sports Circle's last five anchors landed at the NFL Network. One at ESPN. If this isn't fate doing some fancy footwork, I don't know what is."

The sound of Kate's movement in the kitchen clattered in—cupboards opening and a pan scraping against a burner. He'd promised to take her back to the hospital first thing in the morning. Wait with her as long as it took for Breydan to wake up.

If he wakes up. Nobody would ever put voice to that thought, but the fear of it had to be pummeling Kate's friends . . . and

Kate. And there was no way he was leaving her to deal with that alone.

"I'll make the call first thing in the morning, see when they can get you in."

"Ian, no. Not tomorrow. Not so soon." His voice came out gravelly and firm.

Ian's pause pulled taut, tension as clear as if he stood in the bathroom with Colton. "You know what—do what you want. Take the interview or don't. But if you don't, then I think it'll be time to rethink our working relationship."

Colton closed his eyes and leaned over the sink. Being dropped by his manager? That'd be the final death knell for his career. And something told him it wouldn't do any good to tell Ian about little Breydan. Or Kate. Or why he needed to be here.

Ian wouldn't understand how someone Colton had met less than a month ago could be worth missing the perfect job prospect. How could he? Colton didn't understand it himself.

He only knew being here, with Kate, felt right. It felt right in a way nothing had since the last time he ran a ball down a field and cleared the end zone.

He realized then that the line had gone dead. So that was that. He jerked his duffel bag from the floor and dropped it over his shoulder. Looked at himself once more in the mirror. Clean and freshly shaven, only the faintest circles under his eyes hinting at last night's lack of sleep.

And something else. *Peace.* The kind that came from making the right decision, putting someone else first.

When he emerged from the bathroom, the aroma of food wafted over him. Breakfast food. His growling stomach reminded him now how little he'd had to eat today—vending machine food and hospital coffee.

He padded across the living room, dropping his duffel bag

on the couch, and found Kate in the kitchen. She had her back to him and apparently hadn't heard him walk up. Which gave him time to take in her appearance—brown hair tousled and damp, baggy pink flannel pants, white T-shirt.

He didn't realize he was staring until she turned, shrieked. "Whoa, Colt."

"Sorry." He held up both hands. "Sorry."

"For a big man you walk awfully quiet." She turned back to the sizzling frying pan.

He stepped up to the stove, stomach rumbling at the sight of the food. Scrambled eggs complete with a rainbow of vegetables. French toast on a square stovetop griddle. A bowl of grapes nearby on the counter top.

"You didn't have to go to all this work."

He caught a whiff of her hair as she reached for a spatula. And he'd thought the food smelled good.

"Wasn't much work at all. And besides, breakfast food is a thing with us Walkers. Family comfort food of choice. We all have our specialties." She moved the eggs around the frying pan with a spatula. "Beckett is the pancake king. Logan can make an omelet seem like a religious experience. Raegan, she's extra creative with fruit salads."

Colton snuck a grape from the bowl. "Does your dad have a specialty?"

"Mini quiches."

"You're kidding."

"Not even. Seriously, you should see him line mini muffin tins with Pillsbury dough." She giggled. First laugh he'd heard from her all day.

"And what's your specialty, Rosie?"

She wrinkled her nose at his use of her nickname, then slid her spatula underneath a piece of French toast. "This right here. Might just look like any old French toast. But I'll tell you my secret if you want."

"I want."

"I smash up some Captain Crunch and add it to the batter." She pointed out the empty cereal box sticking up from the trash bin.

"Genius."

She waved her spatula like a wand. "I'm no Julia Child, but I do have my strengths."

While she dipped additional pieces of bread into batter, he glanced around the smallish kitchen. White cupboards and stainless-steel appliances against bold blue walls. A peninsula counter jutted from one wall, the open space above it looking into the living room, where beige furniture faced a corner fireplace.

It was a comfortable home, clean and uncluttered, but not without touches of Kate. The hanging shelf in the hallway with a line of books about classic films. An antique typewriter on a slim table edged against the entryway wall. And a smattering of family photos throughout the first floor.

When he turned back to the stove, he caught Kate watching him. "What?"

"My kitchen seems so much smaller with you standing in it."

Funny, when he'd been thinking how much bigger his world felt with her in it.

"I can't believe you hung around the hospital the entire day."

"I was exactly where I wanted to be. Besides, I had some good reading material."

"Oh yeah?"

"Yeah, just a sec." He strolled back to the living room and pulled the book from his duffel bag. "A little something I picked up from the Maple Valley Public Library."

She turned from the stove, mouth forming into an O as soon as she saw the cover. "Oh, Colt, no."

"What? It's this great book by this famous author I know."

"Please tell me you aren't really reading it."

The French toast on the griddle sizzled behind her. "I'm a hundred pages in. I like it."

"It's overbearing and pretentious." She'd always dreamt of writing a book—her once-romantic bent revealing itself in the love stories she scribbled in notebooks as a teenager. College, however, had convinced her she needed to up her literary game. Write something high-minded and lyrically decadent.

Which might not have been a bad thing if the story had come even close to connecting with readers. If it had sounded even a bit like her own voice.

"I like it."

"It barely sold three hundred copies, and the few reviews it managed to get weren't flattering."

He laid the book on the counter. "All right, so it reads a little heavy. But I still see touches of you in it. I did wonder one thing, though." He opened the book to the beginning—the dedication page. Two simple words: *To Gil.*

Kate eyed first the book, then him. "He was a university professor and a co-writer for a while. We were . . . close."

Close like how he was close to Logan?

Or close like how he'd been to Lilah?

And, wow, this was the first time he'd thought of Lilah in he didn't even know how long.

She turned back to the stove, pushed eggs around the frying pan. "Things didn't end so great between us. I gave up this amazing communications internship opportunity in DC to stay in Chicago and help him with a TV movie script he was writing. That's how I ended up falling into writing for Heartline." She moved to the griddle, struggled to slide her spatula under a piece of bread that had sat too long. "But I got a big honking surprise the day I found out he'd been married the whole time I knew him."

Colton came up beside her, gently took the spatula from her, and took over with the French toast. "He sounds like an idiot to me."

There was a wry edge to her laughter. "I think I deserve the title, too, though. I mean, I gave up DC for a guy who really hadn't made any firm commitment to me. Yes, he helped me get a book published—and at a very young age. I wanted to get it done before my mom passed. She died before it released, but at least she got to read the final version." She rushed through the explanation, an effort at holding emotion at bay.

"I think it was all that time working on the book with Gil during my senior year plus the pain of Mom's death right after graduation that just completely clouded my common sense when it came to him. So I followed him to Chicago. But how dense does a person have to be not to realize there might be a reason he always wanted to meet at my place, never took me anywhere we might run into mutual acquaintances?"

He flipped over the piece of toast, one side nearly black. "You're not dense, Kate."

"Well, anyway, I thought he was a thing of the past. But he's been trying to get back in touch with me lately."

Colton pointed the spatula at her. "Don't do it."

"You sound like my brother."

Yeah, well, he didn't feel like her brother. She smiled up at him, strands of still-damp hair framing her face.

"So I was thinking we'd eat in front of the TV," she said, a catch in her voice that matched the pulsing of his own nerves.

"Monday night football?"

She rolled her eyes and pulled the spatula out of his hands. "I was thinking an old movie. You are woefully uneducated when it comes to the classics."

He didn't care what Ian said. He was right where he was supposed to be.

~～♥

Kate awoke to the faintest rhythm thumping from somewhere. And the warmest, most comfortable nest of pillows and blankets she'd ever experienced. Like a cocoon, this bed, if only she had any sense of where she actually was.

She opened one eye, then the other and peeked over the blanket pulled up to her neck.

Wait . . .

That wasn't a blanket.

And this wasn't her bed.

And that rhythm . . .

She felt her eyes bug but swallowed her gasp before it could squeak out. That was a heartbeat under what she'd thought was a pillow. *Colton* . . . And it was his arm wrapped around her like a comforter. His legs stretched out in front of him, propped on her coffee table beside their empty plates from last night.

Her own legs were tucked underneath her. She was curled up in a ball next to him. And wearing his hoodie.

Slowly, like a blurry Polaroid coming into focus, scenes from last night drifted in. Dinner of French toast and scrambled eggs in front of the TV, black-and-white movie they'd hardly paid attention to. The glow of her electric fireplace. The scrapbook Colton had found on the shelf underneath the coffee table—full of childhood photos and memories she recounted as they flipped through the pages.

And her book. He'd brought it into the living room at some point and showed her the lines he'd underlined. Oh man, if there was ever a way to steal a writer's heart . . .

And then the best part. He'd gone and torn out the dedication page and wadded it up.

"Colton, that's a library copy."

He'd only grinned. *"So I'll pay a fine."*

Wasn't long after that he'd slipped his arm around her shoulder and pulled her close. She'd shifted to lean against him. And then . . .

Then apparently fallen asleep.

And now she couldn't think of anything she'd rather do than let herself drift back to sleep. *So warm . . . so comfortable . . .*

But the second she closed her eyes, the ringing of a cell phone cut into her haze of sleepiness. Colton's, sitting on the coffee table. He didn't twitch a muscle. Poor man must've been exhausted last night after not sleeping the night before.

As gently as she could, she slid out from underneath Colton's arm, grabbed his phone and padded from the room. She couldn't figure out how to silence the thing fast enough, so instead she tapped into the call and lifted it to her ear. "Hello?" she whispered the greeting as she trailed into the kitchen.

"Uh, this is Ian calling for Colton."

"I'm sorry . . ." Her voice came out froggy. She cleared her throat and tried again. "Sorry, this is his friend Kate. He's asleep." Great. She didn't want to think about what the person on the other end of the phone probably assumed. Ian—that was Colton's manager, right? "I can wake him up if I need to."

"I'd hoped his common sense would return by morning. But if he's still sleeping at nearly noon—"

"Noon?" She somehow managed to whisper and shout at the same time. She'd told Hailey and Marcus they'd be back at the hospital by midmorning.

"Look, maybe you can talk some sense into him. I was able to get an interview set up for him at the station. They're expecting him there at one o'clock. I've called three times this morning."

And they'd slept through every one.

He had a potential job prospect? Here . . . in Chicago?

She abandoned the coffee filters she'd pulled from her cup-board and walked to the peninsula dividing her kitchen and living room. Colton still hadn't moved a muscle.

"What do you mean, talk some sense into him?"

"He refused to do the interview today. I don't know what's gotten into him lately."

Why would he refuse . . . ?

Because of me. That was it. He didn't want to leave her alone, and so he'd said no to what could be a game-changer for his future.

She couldn't let him do it.

"I'll talk to him," she said softly.

"Good. I emailed the station address and all the details to him, so just tell him to check his inbox. Tell him he'll regret it if he misses out."

She tapped out of the call and paused for only a second before calling the taxi company. Then she paced back to the living room. Morning light filtered through the bamboo blinds over her front window, painting stripes of gold over Colton's sleeping form.

"I've said it before and I'll say it again," she whispered. "You're a good man, Colton Greene."

She bent over and nudged him until he woke up. His eyelashes fluttered as his eyes opened. Oh, this man put to shame every mascara model she'd ever seen. "Wake up, sleepyhead."

"Don't wanna."

She was tempted to plop beside him on the couch, muss his hair, and tease him into consciousness. But there wasn't time. "Rise and shine. The day's a-wasting. Time to hit the ground running. Early bird gets the worm." She jiggled his arm. "I'm running out of clichés."

Suddenly his feet thumped to the floor and he sat up straight. "Wait, is it Breydan?"

His hair stood every which way, and a night's worth of stubble covered his cheeks. "I haven't heard about Breydan yet. You need to get up and change and get to your interview."

She grabbed his hand and jerked. Nothing—dead weight. "Gonna need a little help here."

"Interview?" he repeated, still holding her hand.

"Your manager called just now. He wasn't in the detail-sharing mood, but I got the gist. And apparently you've got an interview. In about an hour. You are not missing this, Colton Greene."

And suddenly he was on his feet, grim expression on his face. "Nope. Not happening."

"Yes, it is, but you have to hurry. Taxi's already on its way. I'd take you myself, but even after this many years of living here, I'm the worst at navigating traffic." She ran her hands through the knotty tangles of her hair.

"Kate, I said no last night to Ian, and I meant it. I want to be here for you. We can reschedule the interview when—"

"You don't know that." She pushed his duffel bag at him. "Go change."

"I'm not abandoning you."

She paused, his words sinking in, sweet to the taste, like hot chocolate warming its way down to her stomach. She stepped back around the couch, stood right in front of him, and lifted her palms to his cheeks, like a mother to a child.

Only with the way she had to tip her head to look up at him, with every nerve in her body suddenly alert, motherly was about the last thing she felt at the moment. She swallowed.

"Colton, you are not abandoning me. You're walking through an open door." She waited, hoping her words sank in. "Now go get dressed."

Something in her tone must have convinced him. Because even

though he opened his mouth to argue once more, he closed it just as quickly, then disappeared into the bathroom.

While he changed, she gathered up his things—the book from the library, his phone, his wallet. He emerged from the bathroom in less than ten minutes, wearing the same jeans he'd worn yesterday and a polo. "All I had with me," he said as he met her near the front door.

"They'll understand."

She dumped the library book into his duffel bag.

"Kate—"

"Cab's here." She handed him his wallet, his phone.

He stuffed them in his pocket. "Kate."

"Oh, your sweatshirt." She shrugged out of it, tucked it in his bag, then reached up to straighten the collar of his shirt, brush his hair off to the side. "All right, you're all ready to go." She slung his bag over his shoulder for him.

And then stood on her tiptoes.

And kissed him.

And froze, lips pressed against his and brain screeching. *What. Are. You. Doing?*

She jerked back and landed on her heels, the surprise plunking through her matching Colton's wide eyes. "I don't know why I . . . I was just caught up in . . . it was . . ."

His grin could have melted an igloo.

The cab honked.

And with a "Good luck" that came out in a squeak, she pushed him out the door.

11

And this is where you'd spend the bulk of your time when you're actually in the studio."

The kid showing Colton around the Sports Circle studio couldn't have been older than twenty-four, and next to him, Colton felt ancient.

"You said when I'm actually in the studio. So most of the time I'd be . . . ?"

"Out covering stories. At games. It's a travel job, for sure. The dude you'd be replacing—Carlton Jennings—he always said there were two things he could count on in life: tax season sneaking up on him and being gone on weekends."

Colton glanced around the studio's main room. It was so small. The blue desk with the sprawling glass surface filled up most of the room. A matching blue background with the gray-and-white Sports Circle logo covered one wall. Lights and camera equipment crowded the rest of the space.

"It's no ESPN, but it's not a bad place to work," the kid said. When he fiddled with the security badge he wore around his neck, Colton caught sight of his name. Landon.

He still couldn't get over how fast this had all happened. Ian's call last night. Kate waking him up this morning, insisting that he take the interview. The missed night of sleep as they drove to Chicago and the rush of this morning meant his brain was more fuzzy than focused.

Well, if he was honest, it was actually Kate's kiss that had him less than attentive now. So hilarious, the shocked look on her face when she'd pulled back, as if she couldn't believe what she'd just done. *Hilarious and awkward and . . . awesome.*

He grinned now, just thinking about it.

And if that taxi hadn't been waiting at the curb, if she hadn't practically shoved him out the door, it wouldn't have ended with that one little peck—that was for sure.

"So anyhow, our core viewership is Chicagoland, but it's a regional show, so we've got viewers in a six-state area."

Colton gave his head a small shake. Forced his attention back to Landon.

"We hit a ratings record last month. We're hoping to keep holding strong this month. Of course, with Carlton Jennings leaving us, that's a concern, but if *you* come on board, that could shoot us higher than we've ever been. Do you have any questions?"

Yeah, how did the guy breathe when he talked that fast? "Hmm. I guess . . . what's your role exactly on the show?"

Landon fiddled with his security badge. "Oh, ha, probably would've been nice to tell you that. I'm an intern—at this point little more than a glorified fact-checker for you—well, if you get the job, but come on, how could you not?—and your co-host. Her name's Stella. You'll like her. Just never do a Marlon Brando *Stella!* yell around her. She doesn't take it well."

Colton looked around the studio again, caught sight of a promotional poster with Carlton and Stella's faces smiling back at him. She looked nice enough. He tried picturing himself in Carlton's place. Tried imagining weekends spent on sidelines, instead of out on the field. Evenings in the dim lighting of the studio, chatting with an audience he'd never see.

He could do this job, couldn't he? So maybe it wasn't what he'd ever imagined—talking about the game he loved rather than playing it. So maybe he'd never warmed to talking to a camera. That didn't mean this couldn't work.

And in the past hour, somehow he'd come to want it to work. Much more than he had before. And the reason had nothing to do with abstracts like success or fame or career . . . and everything to do with a woman who'd kissed him an hour ago.

Maybe the thought should worry him—considering his recent past. Considering Lilah, how all that had ended for him, and not all that long ago.

But Kate wasn't Lilah. And he wasn't the same person he'd been a month ago.

"Colton Greene?"

The voice came from down the hallway, and both he and Landon turned. A lanky man with a wiry frame, something like impatience clinging to his features. He held out his hand. "Jerome Harving, executive producer for Sports Circle."

Colton accepted the handshake. "Nice to meet you, sir."

"Landon, thanks for giving the tour. Much appreciated."

The intern picked up on the dismissal in Harving's tone. "Cool to meet you, Greene. Uh . . ." He glanced at Harving. "Can I get an autograph before you leave?"

"Sure. I'll stop at the front desk before I head out."

Landon retreated, leaving Colton and Harving alone in the main studio. Glass windows along one wall peeked in on dark offices, and quiet permeated the space.

"Midday is always the slowest around here," Harving said.

"I appreciate you fitting me in so last minute."

"Yes. Well."

Okay, Colton wasn't imagining things, was he? Harving seemed about as interested in this interview as a restless kid in an art museum.

"Let's sit," the man finally said, motioning to the cushioned swivel chairs behind the anchor desk. When they were seated, he laced his fingers together atop the desk. "Why do you want to be a sports analyst, Colton?"

"Well, I love the game of football, Mr. Harving, and—"

"Jerome."

"Jerome. And I believe I have the experience at all three levels—high school, college, professional—to be able to talk about it intelligently and add value to the conversation." It was a canned answer, courtesy of Ian's email. But it was the truth. If Colton could talk about anything, it was football.

As long as he could get over the stare of the camera.

Jerome seemed to study him for a few moments. And then, "I'm going to level with you, Greene. We've done a slew of interviews, and I was literally a few minutes away from calling our lead candidate to offer him the job when your manager called. He's got the looks, the appeal, and the talent to fill Carlton Jenning's shoes."

So was there a point to this interview? "I understand—"

"But you've got one thing he doesn't. Name recognition. I wasn't sure that was enough to go back to ground zero, but I'm smart enough to listen to a studio head when he gives a direct order."

Not one for subtlety, apparently. Colton was here because the studio head wanted him here. Not this producer. No matter. "Well, like I said, I appreciate the opportunity."

Jerome glanced around the room. "I already know the facts about you. I know you don't have much experience with this kind of thing, save a pregame appearance last week in Iowa."

Colton had to work not to wince. Had Jerome seen that?

"We could spend an hour talking personalities and vision for the show and yada yada, but I haven't had lunch yet, and at the end of the day, none of the rest of that stuff matters anyway. What I really need to know is if you're any good in front of the camera. Unfortunately, your manager didn't have anything in the way of audition tapes."

Right, because he hadn't filmed any audition tapes. Because he'd spent the past weeks repairing a depot and writing with Kate and sinking into life in a town that had begun to feel like home.

Which was crazy. He didn't belong in Iowa, did he?

"We're going to have you do a test read right now. I've got a guy to run the camera." Jerome pointed. "Over there's the teleprompter. I'm going to head back to Sound. The lights will turn on in a sec, and whenever you're ready, start reading."

Oh wow, this was more than he'd expected. *Focus. Don't think about the camera. Just read the words and talk.*

The lights suddenly flashed on, beaming straight into his eyes. He blinked.

And then the words on the teleprompter started moving. *Just read.*

"Today's schedule includes a fiery matchup between two of Chicagoland's historic rivals . . ."

The light—it was making his head throb. And the words on the screen—he couldn't keep up. Worse, the camera seemed to glare at him.

"Keep going, Colton." Jerome's voice sounded from somewhere behind the brightness. "You're doing fine."

"You're doing great, Colt. You're a star. Let me take your picture." The voice from his past jutted into his focus.

A flash of light. The squeal of metal on metal. Another voice floating in the background. Arguing.

They flashed like snapshots through his mind, somehow vivid and blurry at once.

And jarring, leading him right up to the edge of memories that had been so very out of reach for so very long, and—

"Colton."

The voice yanked him from the precipice, and he blinked, hard. Realized he breathed as if winded and clenched his fingers at the edge of the anchor desk. He saw the white of his knuckles, felt the jolt of reality.

The studio lights blinked off.

"Is something wrong?" Jerome Harving, speaking from behind the camera, disapproval heavy in his voice.

"I'm . . . I'm sorry." He stood, sharp pain shooting up his knee and reaching toward his chest. "Can I . . . can I have one moment?"

Somehow his feet carried him away from the desk and out to the hallway, having no clue whether Jerome okayed the exit. He slumped against the wall in the hallway, heaving for breath. *What* was *that?*

Another breath.

Even in its fogginess, it was a fuller, clearer flashback than he'd experienced in years, similar to the kind that had pinned him in therapists' chairs and sent him home with indistinguishable nightmares as a kid. But why now?

The camera.

Think. He closed his eyes, allowed the flashback to replay. *"You're doing great, Colt. You're a star. Let me take your picture."*

Not Mom's voice. Not Dad's . . .

The trill of his cell phone cut in, and like a man drowning, he grappled for the saving distraction. "Colton Greene."

He was aware of the studio door opening, Jerome stepping out.

"Colton, it's Coach. I hope I'm not interrupting anything, but Laura Clancy thought you might be able to help. Webster Hawks has been missing for seventeen hours."

"Webster's . . . missing?" Shock snapped him from the daze of his flashback.

"He didn't come home last night. They've been looking ever since. Police are involved now. I thought maybe he might've reached out to you."

Colton's mouth went dry. "I haven't heard from him."

As Leo's silence expanded, dread rippled through Colton.

It didn't make sense—not after how well Webster had been doing the past week. They'd practiced together three, four times. Coach had even been talking about letting him play as a receiver at the homecoming game this week. Why would Web take off now?

Harving tapped his foot. "Greene, we've got limited time here."

"Coach, if you hear anything, let me know, all right? I'm in Chicago, but I can hit the road now."

"You don't have to come."

"I want to." He'd catch a flight or something, never mind Harving's glare. He hung up. "I'm sorry, Jerome, but I've got to leave. Can we reschedule this?"

"I've already put my lead candidate on hold. I need someone in that anchor's chair in two weeks. I don't have time to reschedule." The man's chin jutted. "If you walk out on this interview, the door closes."

Colton took a breath. "Consider it closed, then."

~⌒∂

"I saved the best for last." Kate leaned over Breydan's bedside, canvas bag in her lap now nearly empty of all the items she'd picked up on her way to the hospital. Sports magazines. Deck of cards. A board game Kate was hoping Breydan didn't already have.

And the football. She held it up so Breydan could see it from his prone position on the bed. "Now I didn't get this at the store. This comes all the way from Iowa. Signed by Colton Greene himself."

The man she'd kissed this morning. Oh, she could wring her own neck. What had she been thinking?

Okay, she hadn't been thinking. She'd been caught up in the moment, that's all. The flurry of helping Colton get out the door to that interview. Like a mom getting a kid ready for school.

Right, like there was anything maternal about that kiss.

"I can't believe it." Breydan's soft voice drew her back.

Watching his white lips struggle to form a smile was enough to sting her heart, and if she wasn't careful, the pools of liquid forming in her eyes would escape. She tucked the ball between Breydan's arm and his body, trying not to notice his skin-and-bones condition. Failing.

"He . . . was . . ." Breydan licked his lips and tried again. "He was really here?" He traced the laces of the football with one finger.

"He was. He had to leave, but he really wanted to talk to you. He told me to tell you—to promise you, actually—that one day when you're feeling better, he's going to play catch with you with this very football."

"He's awesome."

You don't even know. "He certainly is, Brey."

His finger stopped moving along the surface of the football, and he closed his eyes. Less than a minute later his hand dropped to the sheet. *Sleeping. Good.*

"God, please." The whispered prayer had become a mantra

in the past couple of days. They seemed to be the only two words she could muster.

And maybe that was okay. She'd tried elaborate prayers with Mom in the beginning, somehow convinced the right words might make the difference.

But no. It seemed God didn't work that way.

She wasn't really sure how God worked.

Her desperate prayers were more habit than heartfelt. Church had become routine. If she was honest with herself, her faith had stalled right alongside her writing these past years.

Elbows on the edge of the bed, Kate leaned her forehead into her hands, fingers combing through the hair she hadn't bothered to fuss with today.

"Kate?"

She lifted her head as Marcus stepped into the room, bringing the smell of coffee with him. He pulled a chair next to hers and handed her a tall, covered cup. "Hailey found a coffee shop about half a block away."

The hot liquid warmed her hands through the paper cup. "You guys didn't have to bring me any." But, oh, how glad she was that they did. Saved from the hospital sludge.

"And you didn't have to drive seven hours to be here."

"I wanted to. You guys are like family. You know that, Marcus."

His gaze drifted to his sleeping son, worry like a stormy current in his eyes.

What could she say to encourage him? "The doctor seemed more optimistic when he was in here earlier, don't you think?"

Marcus's nod was nearly void of conviction. "I'm losing hope, Kate."

She set her coffee cup on the bedside table and turned to him. "He's going to make it through this. The doctor said—"

"I know he has a solid chance of making it through *this*

episode. But he's only nine." Marcus's eyes welled. "He has decades of checkups and possibilities of reoccurrence in front of him. And at any time, the dumbest sickness or infection or, man, a medication, could take him down again."

He raked both hands through his hair, dark circles around his eyes matching the mental fatigue clinging to his every word. "If I could trade places with him, I would. I'd do it in a second."

She'd heard Dad whisper the same words once. She'd been home on college break, up late studying—not so much because she needed to but because that night Mom and Dad had sat all four siblings down to tell them the news. Mom's remission had ended. The cancer was back.

And this time, it was much, much worse.

She'd thought the rest of the family was sleeping when she'd wandered to the kitchen for a glass of water. But on her way back to her bedroom, she'd heard Mom and Dad's soft words as she passed their room. Through the slit in the door, she'd seen Dad holding Mom.

"I wish we could trade places, Flor. It should be my turn. It should be me."

"It shouldn't be either of us, hon. We should have four or five more decades together—"

"Whoa, five decades? You were planning to live past one hundred, then?"

They'd laughed. How had they been able to laugh?

"But even if I only get five more weeks with you—"

"Don't say that, Flor. I can't even handle—"

"—or five days, it's not the length of time I want to focus on. It's the with you part. You are the best thing that ever happened to me. Which I realize may be the most cliché statement ever—our writer daughter would find some better way to put it—but there it is. You. Are. The. Best."

Kate had padded the rest of the way down the hallway then, wondering how in the world a person's heart could feel so full while broken into so many pieces.

Marcus sighed now, palms on his knees, eyes still locked on his son. "Sorry, I . . . I guess I just needed to say the words. Admit to at least one person that I'm past the point of . . . of courage or hopefulness. I can barely even pray."

"You don't have to apologize."

Why couldn't she find the words to comfort her friend? Why couldn't she be like Colton had been last night, saying just enough to quiet the tempest inside her?

"You know, Marcus, I think . . . I think it's not wrong to ache or feel hopeless. Your beautiful, amazing son is in a hospital room fighting for his life. What parent wouldn't feel emptied of hope at a time like this?" She tasted the salt of her own tears. "But there are people who are hoping for you, holding you and Hailey up. Let us do that. Let *us* hope for Breydan's tomorrow and next week and next year. You just focus on him *right now*. On being his dad who loves him right here in this moment. "

Tears trekked down Marcus's cheeks, landing on his collar, on Kate's hands as she covered his.

She stayed in the room for a few more minutes, a few more whispered words and tears. Waited until Marcus moved to sit in the chair closest to his son's bed.

Her footsteps tapped against the floor as she left the room, giving Marcus space and time alone with Breydan. Emotion hiked through her, and she slumped against the wall outside the room.

Please, God.

And then a voice. "Kate? Katie Walker?"

Her gaze jerked up.

Gil.

❧

"I can't tell you how much I appreciate this, Case. It had to have been a huge interruption in your evening."

The passenger seat window of Case's Ford truck was cold against Colton's knuckles. He leaned his head against the headrest, greasy hamburger and fries not settling so well in his stomach. Probably due to the ridiculousness of the last forty-eight hours—a seven-hour drive, a night without sleep, a day nabbing restless naps in a hospital waiting room, followed by a too-short night, a frustrating interview, and then a last-minute flight.

But heading back to Iowa had been the right choice.

Case Walker shook his head and dropped a wadded-up wrapper in the fast-food bag between their seats. "If it was an interruption, it was a good one. Ever since the tornado, my life has been taken over by depot repairs and constant work. Felt good to ditch the Valley for a few hours."

Colton had nabbed a spot on a plane leaving Chicago for Des Moines around five-thirty p.m. He'd figured he'd just rent a car in Des Moines and drive back to Maple Valley. But he'd texted Kate about his plan, and she must have alerted Case, who had insisted on meeting him at the airport.

Now it was just past eight and they weren't far from town. They'd driven through a McDonald's at the last small town when Colton's growling stomach had given away his hunger.

"Well, all the same, I really appreciate the ride. Part of me isn't sure why I felt the need to race home."

Especially now. They'd still been in the Des Moines airport's parking lot when the call came from Coach. Webster had finally shown up. Apparently he'd gotten in a fight, didn't want to show up at the Clancys' with a black eye. But after a night sleeping in temperatures that felt more like late than early autumn, he'd decided to come home instead of spending another night in the elements.

Outside Colton's window, a combine with beaming front lights moved across a field in the distance. Moonlit shadows wove in and out of rows of corn waiting to be harvested.

"Wish I knew why Web chose now to get in a fight and disappear and scare his foster parents half to death. I know how tough it is constantly adjusting to a new foster family." He shifted in his seat, seat belt lancing into his chest. "But he seems to fit in real good with the Clancys. And on the field, I'm telling you, Case, he's something else. A little inconsistent at the moment, but when he's on, he's on."

Case pulled off the highway and onto the blacktop that would eventually lead into Maple Valley. Another fifteen miles or so to home.

Home. When had Maple Valley taken on that description for him? It was only supposed to be a temporary stopover. Like a rest stop at the side of an interstate, where you got out of your car, stretched your legs, grabbed a coffee. But eventually the time came to slide back into the car and move on.

He propped one elbow on the passenger door's armrest, cool night frosting through the window. The contents in his stomach continued to rumble. "Then again, maybe it makes complete sense that Webster would pick now to act up. Look at me—my game was peaking when I basically self-sabotaged."

Case glanced over, sloping moonlight highlighting the lines on his face and the thoughtfulness in his eyes. "Do you remember much about your injury?"

"Quite a bit actually. Which is amazing considering how hard I got hit." And considering his having no memory of the other traumatic moment in his life.

Every now and then dreams still carried him back to the

game. To the seconds right before the throw. If he closed his eyes even now, he could still see it all unfold.

He'd known even as the ball left his hands, it couldn't hope to reach its target. It wobbled in the air, and as the sea of players parted, his focus landed on the defender who seemed to appear from nowhere.

Interception.

Anger hammered through him. Helmet hits and grunts, pads pounding into each other—all the sounds that together formed the field's constant choir. But all he could see was number 24 from the opposing team, leaping to catch the ball, then landing and spurting forward.

In milliseconds, he scanned the field. Realized there wasn't a single Tiger who could catch 24. Not one man open to make the tackle or chase him down.

Only me.

Emotion and regret and livid irritation at his own failure fueled his burst of movement. He found his route, around a pile of black and orange, past the first defender, eyes on 24 . . .

And in an instant, his quest came to a crushing end as two linemen barreled into him from opposite sides. He felt the wrench in his back upon impact, tasted blood as the hit sent his entire body airborne.

Knew as he slammed into the grass—shoulder first, knee smashed between helmets and pads and body weight—this could be it. Probably was it. The injury that'd end it all. He heard his own yell as if from a distance.

And then . . . nothing.

Until the beep of a hospital monitor. And the whisper of confusion. Lilah's voice. *"He's waking up."*

Except . . .

Colton opened his eyes. Up ahead flashing red lights pulled

him back to the present and announced a train nearing the place where the back road intersected with rail. His stomach churned.

"You all right, Colt?" Case.

Had that really been Lilah's voice? He squeezed his eyes closed, trying to remember. He hadn't actually seen her that first day he woke up, had he? And the voice in his memory . . .

It was lower. Older.

"Colton?"

It wasn't Lilah. "Not feeling so good. Probably the fast food."

Red-and-white-striped barriers lowered into place, and Case slowed the truck. "Do you need to get out?"

The lights of the oncoming train chugged into sight, its whistle piercing the air. Colton unfastened his seat belt, hand to the door handle. "Think so." His groaning stomach sent him from the car, toward the grass at the side of the road. The sound of the passing train, its panting movement and wheels grinding against the metal track, covered Colton's heaves as he lost his dinner.

Case was at his side before he was done, crouching down with one hand on Colton's back and handing him a water bottle when it was over. Colton drank half the bottle in one long swig and stood.

"Wow, sorry about that."

Case shook his head. "No need to apologize."

Was it the fast food that'd messed with his stomach? Or something else?

The train's snaking form huffed around a bend and out of sight, leaving only the lifting crossroad barriers in its wake. The crossroad's lights flashed to a halt. Silence, except for the cicadas humming in the field.

"I don't know what I'm doing."

Case stuck his hands in the pockets of his jacket. "Right now

I think getting back home, maybe finding some 7-Up, might be a good idea."

Colton capped his water bottle. "I mean with my life. I walked out of an interview today. Just chucked it all. Ian has these plans, but I don't think they're going to work out. I'm a football player, not a TV show host. There's the book, yeah. But I'm . . ." *Lost.*

The rumble of the combine approached, its headlights roving over the road. And then Case's voice, thoughtful slowness in his words. "Colt, how much do you know about Raymond Berry?"

Huh, random question. "Wide receiver. Played for the Colts back when they were in Baltimore, right? Fifties and sixties?"

Case nodded, leaning against his truck. "And then he went on to coach. There's a story about him. First day as the Cowboys' receivers coach, he's working with the rookies and demonstrating how to run a sideline route. The guy was notorious for his precision and practice ethic. So he runs the route, makes his usual practiced number of steps, cuts toward the sideline . . . and he lands a foot out of bounds."

Colton took a drink of his water and nodded. "Happens."

"Not to Berry. He says, 'Guys, either the hash marks are wrong or this field's too narrow.'"

"Based on one demonstration?"

Case nodded. "So they get a tape measure and Berry's proven right. The practice field was eleven inches too narrow."

Colton finished his water. "That's hilarious. And a cool story."

"And rife with analogies. If I were a pastor, I'd whip it out once a year. You can talk about living a life of precision. You can talk about boundaries. You can talk about taking the time to notice when life just feels off." Case glanced over at him. "But for you, Colt, the story isn't about the lines. It's about the eleven inches."

"Not sure I understand."

Case pulled his hands from his pockets. "You're playing on a field that's too narrow, son. You marked off boundaries for your life and decided only certain things fit inside. Namely football and all its trimmings. And when those things dropped away, you felt like you'd gone out of bounds."

That's exactly how he'd felt. Not just out of bounds, but off the turf altogether. Directionless.

"But I'll tell you what I think." Case took Colton's empty water bottle and tossed it in the backseat of the truck. "I think God might have eleven more inches for you."

"Which means . . . ?"

Case rounded the truck bed, looked over at Colton, and shrugged. "There's more."

"That's it? Just a vague *more*? I'd kinda like to know what's in those supposed eleven extra inches."

Case laughed and opened his door. "You will. Give it time, give it thought, give it prayer."

"And in the meantime?"

"Get in the truck so we can go home."

Home. Colton got in the truck.

12

Kate used to imagine this moment. What she'd say or do if Gil suddenly reappeared in her life.

But she'd never expected it to happen in a Chicago hospital. That she would meet him on the cancer floor.

Gil now pushed a perspiring red glass toward where she stood at the edge of the table in the cafeteria. "Diet Coke. Still your drink of choice?"

They hadn't spoken for more than two minutes when they'd met in the corridor outside of Breydan's room—had that really been five days ago?

Gil hadn't said it, but she'd known as soon as she'd seen him—his thin frame, the purple under his eyes, the tufts of silvery black where a full head of hair used to be—he wasn't at the hospital as a visitor. He was a patient.

She slid into the vinyl seat across from him now. "Diet Coke, yes." He'd even remembered the slice of lemon.

"Thanks for agreeing to meet. The most I was ever hoping for was a reply to my email. Never thought I'd actually run into you. And here of all places."

The smell of food—or maybe plain old nerves—had her stomach churning, and an unwelcome choir in her head belted out its disapproval. *Bad idea, bad idea, bad idea.*

But she hadn't been able to tell him no when she'd encountered him in the hospital hallway. Not with such relief playing across his face. *"I can't believe you're here. You don't even know what an answer to prayer this is. I only have a few minutes now, but can we meet sometime? Please?"*

For a minute there, she hadn't seen the man who broke her heart but the teacher who'd fueled her creativity and pulled from her a love for storytelling she'd never known she had.

No, Gil hadn't always been a bad memory.

And so she'd agreed to meet today. She'd managed to put it out of her mind for most of the week, busy as she was running errands for Marcus and Hailey and entertaining Breydan, writing chapters of Colton's book in between. And talking to Colton on the phone, texting, whenever she wasn't writing about him.

"Definitely a surprise," she said now. There, she'd pushed words out. It was a start.

Gil smiled. Despite his obviously waning health, he still had those mesmerizing ash-colored eyes behind stylish thick-rimmed glasses. Still dressed like the fashionable college professor he was—black oxford, metallic gray vest.

"I thought you were a chemo-induced mirage when I first saw you. But no, it was really you."

Chemo.

He must've noticed her flinch at the word. Because his grin dulled. "I got the diagnosis seven months ago. It's . . . grim. Only reason I'm even doing treatment is for my wife. She needs something to hold on to."

Kate swallowed a drink of Coke, carbonation burning her throat. Maybe the mention of Gil's wife should sting. Maybe she should feel the same anger she used to when she played and replayed the night he'd told her their relationship wasn't working and—oh, by the way—he already had a wife.

And she'd wondered how in the world she could've been so stupid.

But looking at him now, all that just faded away. Because the man had just told her he was dying.

"Gil, I'm so . . . I'm so sorry."

"You know what's weird? When I tell people, I almost feel more sorry for them than myself. I've come to grips with it. Or maybe I'm just in denial." He shrugged, an uncanny nonchalance in the movement. "I mean, it's huge realizing you don't have much time left. But it gives a person a pretty sudden and intense dose of focus." He took a sip from his own glass—probably Sprite if his tastes, too, hadn't changed. "And that's why I've been trying to get ahold of you."

"I don't understand. Your email mentioned a script." Why would he care about an old script now?

"I want to finish it. Katie, that was some of my best writing, the writing I did with you. We were good together."

She had to focus not to wince. *"Good together."* She could still remember the first time he'd said those same words.

She'd felt so special, the way he'd singled her out at the beginning of her senior year at Iowa State. Truthfully, every female student in her class had developed a crush on their young teacher. They'd even made a game of it, taking turns leaving cans of Orange Crush on the podium each class.

Kate was the only one he'd ever caught in the act. She'd waited until he was deep into a conversation on literary versus commercial fiction with another student to reach into her messenger bag, wrap her fingers around the can . . .

And then he'd turned just as she pulled it out. His glance hooked on the can before traveling to her face, smile stretching enough to convince her maybe being caught wasn't such a bad thing. And soon she was completely under his spell.

Just before she graduated, he'd told her he'd taken a job at Northwestern University. He'd also just been contracted for his first Heartline script and begged her to move to Chicago so they could write together. With hardly a thought she had followed him, and soon they were brainstorming together at what would eventually become their favorite coffee shop.

Her fingers now closed around her ice-cold glass.

"Kate." Gil's voice was quiet and strained, as if he'd followed the trail of her memories. "I'm sorry. I'm sorry about everything. It was a thousand kinds of inappropriate, the way I acted. My marriage was in a bad place. I was pretty sure it was over. But even so, I was wrong to lead you on the way I did." He reached up to lower his glasses and rub the bridge of his nose.

"You told me not to take the internship."

His forehead wrinkled.

"That internship in DC. The one at the nonprofit. You told me not to take it, to move to Chicago so we could write together. Who knows where I'd be now—" She cut herself off. *Stop it. Stop playing the accuser. You're in a hospital, for goodness' sake. It was years ago.*

But instead of shrinking under her words, Gil sat straighter now, firm set to his jaw. "I have a lot to apologize for—I know this. But I'm not sorry I told you to skip the internship. I introduced you to the editor who eventually acquired and published your book, Kate. And co-writing that first script with me—that kicked off your career. If it's not the career you wanted, you could've switched direction anytime. But a six-month internship in DC was never going to be the thing that set you up for a glorious future. If you're still asking what-if about that . . . then I don't know what to tell you."

"Gil . . ." She tried to find words to respond, but they were lost under the sharp truth. *He's right.*

221

It stung to admit, but she had made her own choices. It had simply been easier blaming the man who hurt her.

He shook his head now, a sigh tailing the movement. "Look, I didn't want to dredge any of this stuff up. I just wanted to apologize and to ask your permission to continue with that last script we started. It was your story as much as mine, so I won't move forward if—"

"Go ahead." She pulled a napkin from the holder and wiped away the puddle around her glass. "Do whatever you want with it. I don't mind."

"At least fifty percent of that writing is yours."

"I'm not going to sue you or anything. Promise."

He folded his hands on the tabletop. "I think it could be a great story. And I need to do something great before . . ."

She could only nod, emotions too snarled to separate.

Not long later, they were standing and saying good-bye. She walked Gil as far as the elevator, stopping with him as he pressed the Down button.

"Gil, I . . ."

Understanding rested in his eyes. "Thank you for meeting with me, Katie. And for giving me the freedom to move forward with that story."

The elevator opened, and he stepped inside. The doors began to close.

Kate jumped to block them. "Thank *you*, Gil."

Surprise landed in his expression.

"You inspired me. You made me a better writer." Something freeing washed over her. "And everything you said back at the table . . . You were right."

Gil held out his hand, and she placed her palm in his. "Bye, Katie Walker."

Somehow the handshake was filled with warmth. "Bye, Gil."

And then she stepped out of the elevator and watched its doors close.

"Whoa, is that who I think it was?" Hailey's mystified voice sounded behind her.

Kate turned. Hailey stared at the closed elevator, bag of M&M's in hand.

"Yep, that was Gil. Long story." She held out her hand for Hailey to pour in a few M&M's. "Actually, it's not. He wants to finish a script we started years ago. I said okay." No need to tell Hailey the rest—not with her son battling the same disease as Gil.

"Tell me you laughed in his face."

"Uh, no. I said yes, and that's that."

Hailey popped a handful of M&M's in her mouth, studying gaze never leaving Kate's face. "You've changed."

"Not really."

"You have. A few weeks ago, just talking about Gil would've had you stress eating your way to a stomachache."

She reached for the bag of candy. "Well, I am eating all your M&M's."

"It's Colton."

Kate choked on chocolate, swallowed. "How's the weather out there in left field?"

"I'm serious, Walker. He's the only new element in your life since I saw you last. Thus, he must be the reason you're suddenly all zen about the Gil thing."

A nurse's voice on the intercom called a doctor to a patient's room. "I don't think so, Hail."

"He dropped everything to drive you here. I saw the way he held you when you were crying beside Breydan's bed—the way he refused to leave the hospital without you that first day. He's called you every day since he left. Texted constantly."

"Probably because he's worried I won't finish writing his book."

Hailey stiffened. "Don't do it, Kate."

"Do what?"

"Lock up before you even consider that maybe, just maybe, this guy back in Iowa means something to you." Hailey sighed. "Would it be so bad to admit there might be a little spark there? To try?"

"You think I don't try?"

"I think sometimes you close doors before you know what's on the other side . . . because it's easier or safer." She shook her head.

Kate's gaze traced the pattern of the gold flecks in the hard floor. "Even if there is a . . . a spark, like you said, how do you know I'm not just some rebound girl? There was another girl not that long ago. And he's still getting over not being able to play. So how do I know—"

"You don't."

Her focus snapped up.

"It's called taking a risk, Kate. Think about the characters in your movies. When they finally realize how they really feel— usually at the end—they act on it. The hero goes after the girl, or vice versa. Stop letting your characters be braver than you are. Be the girl who takes a risk." She paused before speaking once more. "It's okay to admit what you want. When you do, you might finally get brave enough to go after it."

Silence stretched between them, only the hum of the vending machines in the corner and the dinging of the elevator filling the silence, until finally, Kate looked up.

"You know, tonight's the homecoming game back in Maple Valley." She glanced at the clock on the wall. "If I left now . . ."

Hailey grinned. "Go. Now." She reached for her M&M's. "But not with my candy."

You walked out on the Sports Circle interview.

A gust of cold air that felt more like November than the last day of September whooshed over Colton as he read the text message on his phone. He didn't have to hear Ian's voice to pick up on his manager's ire. He'd probably done it for good this time.

No "probably" about it.

The only thing that didn't make sense is why it'd taken Ian this many days to confront him. Almost a full workweek since he'd blown the interview in Chicago. And while he felt bad for letting down Ian, he couldn't bring himself to feel much remorse over the job itself.

He wouldn't have been any good at it—he just knew it.

Halfway across the bleachers on the home side of the Mavericks' field, the marching band played their third or fourth pep song of the night, brass tones and drumbeats merging with laughter and voices and the rattling of metal underfoot. The buzzing stadium lights flickered occasionally, almost-dark sky cluttered with stars that seemed to watch in anticipation.

Anticipation. It was the perfect word for those elastic minutes right before a game, when time stretched right alongside your excitement until the moment the ref blew the whistle and the center snapped the ball.

Too bad Ian had to pick now to needle him about the failed interview. He glanced at his phone again. The last thread between them had finally frayed to its breaking point.

"Bad news?" Raegan must've read his face.

"Uh yeah, kind of." And he was the one delivering it. He typed a quick reply.

Yes, walked out. Extenuating circumstances.

"Letting my manager know that job in Chicago is a no go."

"Because you came back for Webster? Can't you explain? It'd be awfully hardhearted of them not to understand that kind of thing. I'd think they'd give you a second chance." Raegan pushed a streak of bright green hair—in honor of the Mavericks—behind her ear.

He tipped up the collar of his jacket. "I'm pretty sure I've already had a second chance." And a third and a fourth. Honestly, it was amazing Ian had held on this long. "I don't foresee a career in television in my future."

Didn't know what he saw anymore. Or wanted to see.

"I think God might have eleven more inches for you."

A month ago, Colton might've brushed of Case's words, countered the thought that he'd in any way limited himself in the past. All he'd wanted for months was a return to his old life. Now?

Eleven more inches.

Well, if God had eleven more inches, Colton sure didn't know what they held. All he did know was he would've made the same decision about walking out on that interview all over again, even knowing Webster was okay. The look on the kid's face when Colton showed up at the Clancys' house that night, when it dawned on him that Colton had dropped everything to come back to Maple Valley, it was worth losing the job.

He'd spent the evenings since then training with Webster. Running plays and finding moments to talk in between.

On the field, the Mavericks now broke from the lines they'd formed to warm up and jogged over to the sideline. Some gathered in clumps, others took a seat on the lone long bleacher running parallel to the near fence.

Colton's phone dinged again.

We need to talk. Call me.

Ian's clipped words signaled what Colton had known for days was now coming.

And maybe the best thing to do would be to make it easy for Ian.

Can't call now. It's been good working with you, Ian. I understand.

He slipped the phone into his jacket pocket and took a deep breath, inhaling the smell of nachos and popcorn, cold air and energy. It'd be okay. He'd figure out what to do next tomorrow. Tonight was about the game, about supporting Webster.

The bleachers shook with movement, and Colton looked over to see Case returning to their seats. He held a cardboard cup holder with three covered cups. "Hot chocolate for fellow game watchers."

He handed out the cups, then took a seat on the other side of Raegan and propped his feet on the bleachers in front of him.

"I wish Kate could be here." Raegan took the lid off her cup and blew over the steaming liquid. "After all the time she's spent talking football with you, Colt, I think this is probably the first time she'd actually get into the game."

He wished she was there, too. The phone calls and texts the past few days, emailing back and forth about the chapters she'd written, none of it was the same as seeing her in person. Although the calls had been great. Hours long and relaxed—conversation always starting at his book but wandering to so many other places.

When had he gotten so used to her presence in his everyday life?

His gaze drifted to the scoreboard. Six minutes to kickoff. He looked back to the team. Where was Webster?

There.

His focus hooked on the 73 on the back of a jersey at the end of the bench, *HAWKS* splayed above the number. Webster was hunched and alone.

As if reading his thoughts, Case leaned over Raegan. "Heard your boy might get more playing time than planned tonight, Colt."

"Really? Did you talk to Coach Leo?"

"No, but the mom of one of the starting receivers was working at the concession stand. She told me her son looked almost green when he left the house. Thinks it's the stomach flu. He insisted on trying to play anyway, but she said she had a feeling he wouldn't make it past the first quarter."

Which probably accounted for Webster's posture on the bench. Oh, he knew the kid wouldn't admit it for the world, but more than likely, anxious nerves were running a sprint inside him right now.

Eyes to the scoreboard again. Still five minutes until kickoff.

"Rae, could you hold my cocoa for a sec? I'm going to go have a talk with Web."

He shuffled past the people on the bleachers until he reached the aisle, then hurried down the metal steps. Several people tossed out greetings to him as he passed—Sunny from the hardware store, the Clancys, Seth and Ava, Bear.

How was it possible he'd come to know more people by name in Maple Valley than in all the time back in LA?

He jogged to the fence dividing the bleachers from the field. "Hey, Hawks."

Webster turned and Colton motioned for him to come over. Webster looked to his coach, who looked to Colton, then nodded.

Webster's helmet swung from his hand as he walked over. He stopped in front of Colton, circles of red in his cheeks and breath white against the cold. "You came."

Colton flopped his hands on the top of the fence. "Of course I came. Wouldn't miss it."

Webster didn't smile, and yet, if Colton wasn't mistaken, that was something close to gratitude in his eyes. "So look, I heard that one of the starters is sick."

"Yeah, if he yacks, I'm in."

"Well, I'm not gunning for him to go down or anything, but if he does, are you ready to move up the ranks?"

Webster gave an exaggerated eye roll. "That's the same thing Coach asked."

"So are you?"

Webster shrugged. "Won't know 'til I give it a go, right?"

Colton glanced at the scoreboard. Three minutes. "Remember all those running drills we did?"

"You mean how you made me run side to side and up and down the field 'til *I* yacked?"

Colton grinned. "Yeah. You know this field, Web—all one hundred and twenty yards long and fifty-three and a third wide. You can feel it. You know your routes. Now it's about finding open spaces. Dissecting the field and bringing that playbook to life."

Webster only stared at him, creases lining his forehead.

"Which is a lot of fancy talk to get across the point that you can do this. I'm rooting for you. As are the Clancys. I passed them in the bleachers, and I swear, Laura Clancy's so proud she's probably passing out buttons with your name on them."

Webster finally cracked a half smile then. Colton held one knuckle over the fence, and Webster lifted his for the fist bump, then returned to his spot in the sideline lineup. Colton turned, gaze instantly taking in the crowded bleachers, the sea of green and white—Mavericks colors—the dark blue backdrop where the faint outline of the moon hung.

His phone dinged once more and he pulled it out.

It was good working with you, too, Greene.

229

All right. Okay. That . . . was that. He nodded and climbed the bleachers.

～o

Stupid road construction.

Kate yanked off her seat belt before she'd finished parking in the football field lot. If not for the traffic hang-up around Iowa City, she would've made it to Maple Valley an hour ago.

But she'd listened to the first half of the game on the radio. It was nearly half time.

She reached for the blue scarf and matching mittens she'd stashed in the backseat, then hopped from the car. Scarf around her neck, mittens on, she tugged the yellow knit beret she'd found in her glove compartment from her pocket and plopped it on her head.

Not school colors, but at least she'd be warm.

Autumn cool wisped over her cheeks as she crossed the parking lot. She'd considered calling Dad or Raegan to let them know she was coming. But wouldn't it be more fun to surprise them?

Maybe . . . surprise Colton?

Somewhere between Chicago and Des Moines, she'd given up fighting the idea that it was Colton Greene, much more so than any game, that she was excited to see.

"It's okay to admit what you want."

Truth was, Hailey had made some valid points.

Truth was, maybe curiosity and interest and, fine, the attraction she'd been trying in vain to ignore for weeks might finally be winning out over the caution and guardedness she'd made her constant companions these past years.

Not that she had a plan or anything.

But she just might have a sort-of hope. A yearning that, once finally acknowledged, warranted at least a little exploration.

And that's what tonight was. The chance to explore her own heart while in proximity to the first man to tug at it in a long time.

She stopped at the ticket booth. The woman at the window glanced at the game clock. "Honey, if you wait three more minutes 'til half time, I can let you in for half price."

Kate looked at the field. Past the booth and the concession stand, the crowd in the bleachers stamped to the beat of the cheerleaders' cheer. After seven hours in the car, three minutes shouldn't sound like such a long time. But eagerness nettled her patience.

"That's okay, I'll pay the full five. My contribution to the athletic department."

The woman nodded and handed her the ticket. "Enjoy the game."

Kate glanced at the scoreboard as she left the booth. Still 7–10, Mavericks trailing.

"Kate!"

She turned at the sound of Raegan's voice rising over the buzz of cheers from the bleachers. Raegan walked over from the concession stand, arms full of snacks.

"Impeccable timing, sis." Raegan shoved a plastic tray of nachos at her. "I thought I could manage my and Dad's food on my own, but I clearly overestimated my abilities. What are you doing here?"

Kate stole a chip from the tray. "I came for the game, of course."

Raegan stopped, gravel crunching under her feet. "You drove all the way from Chicago so you wouldn't miss the homecoming game. You. The one who stayed home to watch *Casablanca* with Mom the night of your own senior year homecoming?"

"I can appreciate the sport as much as anyone." She started walking again.

Raegan scrambled to catch up behind her. "I'm sure."

She'd just choose to ignore that little morsel of sarcasm or the implication attached to it. Nothing was going to rankle Kate's spirits tonight.

Right as they reached the base of the bleachers, the crowd suddenly surged to their feet, cheers pitching to new levels. Kate spun around. "What's happening?"

The bleachers wobbled underneath them as they hurried up a few steps to get a better view. And there, Kate saw what had the crowd going wild. A player sprinting down the field with the football, the pair of defensive players he must've just crashed through running helplessly after him.

Raegan gasped. "That's Webster!"

Colton's Webster, apparently effortlessly edging around the last opponent who might possibly have a shot at slowing him down. The crowd went wild. Seconds later, Webster leapt into the end zone and the stands erupted. Raegan's "Whoo!" blared in her ear, and the scoreboard flipped—13–10. She could only imagine Colton's reaction.

Kate abandoned the tray of nachos on the bleacher, heart thumping like the stands beneath her and scanned the seats. She saw Dad, but no Colton. "Where's Colton?" The rumble of the stands drowned out her voice.

"What?"

"Colton?" she nearly shouted. "Where is he?"

Raegan's eyes were still on the field. "Press box."

"Press box? Why?"

"Half-time interview. Lulu from the radio station talked him into it."

She turned to Raegan as the team lined up for the extra point. "I'm going to find Colton."

She raced up the bleachers, the crowd erupting once more,

a signal that the kicker must've just added another point to the scoreboard. She caught sight of Colton through the glass of the press-box windows. He was giving someone a high five, expression beaming.

Nerves knocked around her stomach. *Go.*

She climbed over a bleacher, shuffled down a row, reached the door to the press box. *Do I knock or just—*

The door flung open, and Colton stood in front of her. "I thought that was you."

And if he was beaming before, he practically glowed now. Or maybe that was just the stadium lights washing over him. Or moonlight. Or . . . She didn't even care. She pitched forward the second his arms opened.

"Webster was amazing. And that's all you, all the time you worked with him."

His arms tightened around her. "No, it was all Webster. I knew he had it in him. And he needed this, you know? Something to boost his—"

Suddenly his arms went lax. He stepped back, gaze directed over Kate's shoulder.

She turned, saw a woman standing halfway down the row.

And from behind her, Colton's voice. "Lilah?"

13

"Hey, no loitering."

Kate's whole body jerked at the call of the voice over-head. The cold of the cement step at the corner entrance of Coffee Coffee seeped through the baggy cotton pants she'd convinced herself half an hour ago didn't look too much like pajamas.

But here in a blast of sunlight, they were most definitely pajamas.

And someone leaning out the second-floor window over the coffee shop had most definitely spotted her.

She leaned away from her seated perch against the storefront wall and lifted one hand to ward off morning's glare. "Excuse me?" She squinted in an attempt to make out the man's face. Bear, Seth's friend?

"What're you doing down there?"

"Waiting for coffee." *Avoiding Colton.* "And hoping I can get it in IV form."

He leaned his head out farther. Yes, definitely Bear. She hadn't talked to him much—but he seemed to show up wherever Seth did. Raegan, too. "You don't have coffee at home?"

She stood now, tucking her hands inside the puff vest she'd pulled on over her long-sleeved shirt when she'd left the house.

The clock in her car had glared the time as she'd slid into the driver's seat—5:13—and for a millisecond she'd considered the ridiculousness of leaving the house so early, so barely put together.

But all it took was one imaginary leap into the future—the thought of sitting around the breakfast table while that woman from last night smiled her belongs-on-the-cover-of-a-dentist's-brochure smile at Colton—and she'd started the engine and wound up here. Only to find the coffee shop closed.

"Yes, there's coffee at home, but here there's also pastries."

"Just a sec." Bear's head disappeared.

Kate folded her arms and turned a full circle on the sidewalk. Maple Valley still slept this early in the morning—grass glistening under a blanket of dew. Only the Blaine River across the street showed signs of life—swirls of blue and brown reaching perilously high.

"How do you feel about Toaster Strudels?"

Kate turned back and tipped her head. "What?"

Bear's face reappeared at the window. "Megan's been opening the shop later the past few days. You'll be lucky if she shows up by six-thirty. I've got coffee, just found a whole box of strudels in my freezer, and my toaster works just fine."

He was inviting her up to his apartment? "I hardly know you."

"This is Maple Valley. You pass somebody on the street and say hello and that practically makes you family."

He had a point. Besides, he was Seth's best friend. And Raegan's crush on the man couldn't be more obvious if she'd tattooed his name on her arm. Maybe Kate should take advantage of the opportunity to get an inside peek at the guy her sister liked.

Anyway, the Closed sign on Coffee Coffee's front door didn't look to be moving anytime soon. And it was chilly out. *And I'm not going back home.* Not after she'd practically thrown herself at Colton last night—only to turn around and see Lilah Moore.

"Promise you're not a serial killer?"

"Cross my heart." He motioned to the side of the building. "Stairs are over there."

Moments later, she'd rounded the corner and climbed the wooden steps leading up to a side door. Bear met her at the landing, and wow, up close his size fit his name. Same height as Colton but with even broader shoulders. And unlike Colton's cobalt eyes, Bear's were so dark it was hard to distinguish his irises from his pupils.

She stepped into a kitchen decorated in reds and blacks, from the towels hanging over the oven handle to the red-faced coffeepot, already gurgling to life.

Bear moved to the counter and pressed down on the toaster. "Probably should've mentioned before—if I *was* a serial killer, I wouldn't be inclined to tell you. That just wouldn't be effective."

"Is this how you usually find your victims? You lure them up with promises of strudels and coffee?"

Bear laughed and motioned to the table. "Take a seat."

She obeyed, slipping off her vest as she lowered. "Didn't realize there was an apartment over Coffee Coffee."

"I heartily recommend living above a coffee shop. Always smells good. I'd show you the rest of the place, but it's pretty bachelor-pad-y at the moment." He pulled a coffee mug from the cupboard.

"Your kitchen's nice."

He set a cup in front of her, steam rising. "That's your sister's doing. She came up here once for something or another, took one look at my sparse décor, and declared it unlivable. Personally, I couldn't care less if my dishcloths match my curtains, but you know Raegan."

The strudels popped up, and he stuck them on a plate, then plopped into the seat across from Kate.

"Don't you want any coffee?"

He shook his head. "Love the smell—hate the taste."

"But you already had it made?"

He made quick work of icing the pastries. "You ever wake up with a strange feeling today's going to be a different sort of day?"

"I usually just feel groggy."

"Well, every once in awhile, I wake up crazy early and pray and stuff. And that's what I did today, and I had a weird thought that someone might be showing up here. Since I'm one of approximately two people in all of Maple Valley who doesn't survive on caffeine, I thought whoever it was might want coffee. So I made it."

Intriguing guy, this Bear McKinley.

He pushed the plate of strudels to Kate. "Eat up." She took a bite, sugary warmth slicking down her throat, and reached for her coffee.

"Since you're here, Kate, I have to confess something—"

She sputtered on her swallow of coffee—like drinking water next to Dad's muddy brew. And the flavor . . . She flinched as her taste buds protested.

His dark eyebrows furrowed. "That bad? I don't make it often."

"Only when you get strange feelings?"

He grinned. "And when friends are around."

She set her cup down. "And they're still your friends?"

He laughed and reached for the remaining pastry on the plate. "But that wasn't what I was talking about." Something serious slid into his expression. "It's about Raegan."

A mix of curiosity and concern accompanied her nod. "Okay."

"She and. . . . we . . . you see, I think . . ."

Kate hid her grin behind another bite of her pastry. Not hard to understand why her sister liked this guy. Tall, dark, and handsome. Check. Cute when uncomfortable. Check. Kind, too, from what she'd seen and heard.

Even if he did make lousy coffee.

"From what I've seen of the two of you, there's more to the friendship than kitchen decorating." They were a match waiting to happen, chemistry practically tangible. Like perfectly arranged firewood just waiting for a spark. She should know. She'd written romances for a living for how many years now?

Of course, her understanding of her own romantic life was obviously in malfunction mode. Otherwise she wouldn't have found herself awake this morning before sunrise, wrestling with emotions she should've been smart enough never to let in, and . . . well, pining.

Yes, sometime between that conversation with Hailey yesterday and standing on those bleachers last night, taking in the appearance of the woman Colton had at one point planned to marry, she'd become the kind of woman who pined after a man she couldn't have. Because he was returning to California next week. And because of the stark reminder that was Lilah Moore's appearance—that Colton was oh so out of her league.

"Thing is, it'll never work."

Bear's words nudged her back to attention—*his* situation, not hers. "But . . . why?"

"By this time next year I'll be living in South America planting a church and staying there to pastor it until God leads me somewhere else. I'm leaving in the spring." He took a bite, chewed, met her eyes. "And Raegan . . . she loves Maple Valley more than anyone I know."

He had a point. Her little sister had always been a homebody, even more so after Mom's death. And Kate saw the truth in Bear's eyes as he looked down at her now, as if hoping she'd counter him but knowing she wouldn't.

"I don't want to hurt her." His words were soft, revealing.

"Thing is, once your heart's involved, I think a little hurt might be inevitable."

"You think?"

I know.

"But it would be better to pull back now, right? I mean, before she . . . we . . . you know, get even more invested. Draw a line in the sand and stop inching so close to crossing it. Just friends."

A few weeks ago, she might've agreed with him. Told him that was exactly what he needed to do if he didn't want to lead on her sister.

But turned out, lines in the sand were no match for greedy waves, their frothy waters reaching to wipe away safe borders.

"Tell me something—why South America?"

"That'd take one long, winding journey of a story to answer in full, but suffice it to say, it took me a while to land on a purpose or vision or whatever you want to call it. But I knew I wanted to travel and I knew I wanted to be in ministry." He laced his fingers together on the tabletop. "Pastor Nick's been a mentor of sorts, and he told me a while back that I didn't have to have a big plan for my life. I just needed to do the next right thing. Somehow doors started opening and South America became the next right thing."

"Sounds wise."

He tipped his chair away from the table, leaning against the wall behind him. "Oh yeah, it's great advice . . . until you aren't sure what the next right thing is. Might've helped me figure out my calling, but as far as relationships go . . ."

He shrugged and stood, reached for her coffee cup and walked to the sink to pour it out. Both hands gripping the counter edge, his gaze became distant as he faced the window.

There was a pensive bent to the man she probably never

would've noticed if not for these few one-on-one minutes. *He has a story to tell.* "Bear—"

He straightened suddenly. "Huh. She's still in her car."

"Who?" Kate stood and joined him at the window, spotted the yellow VW bug parked behind her Focus and the form behind the wheel. "Megan?"

"I saw her car pull up when I was pouring your coffee. Wonder why she's still sitting there."

Kate turned and reached for her vest. "Think I'll go check on her. Thanks for the breakfast and the coffee I didn't drink."

"Thanks for the conversation."

"Don't feel like I helped."

He lifted one shoulder. "Yeah, but . . . I get the feeling you understand."

Was she that transparent? Or was Bear simply that good at reading people? The questions followed her down the steps and out to the curb but cut off when she saw Megan's hunched form behind her steering wheel. Concern filled her, and she tapped on the passenger side window. "Hey, Megan, it's Kate. You okay?"

"Fine." But the muffled sob at the end of her words said otherwise.

Kate tried the door handle. Unlocked. Indecision stalled her for only a moment before she pulled it open. By the time she'd lowered into the seat, Megan's tears had erupted, shaking her whole body.

"Oh, honey, what is it? What's wrong? You're still sick? I can drive you to the doctor if—"

Megan shook her head, dark hair slipping over her face. "I don't need to go to the doctor. I went yesterday."

"Good. Did they get you on any kind of med—"

Another sob interrupted her. "I don't need . . . that's

not . . ." Megan took a shaky breath and finally looked over. "I'm pregnant."

~⌒~

The beat of his own footsteps on the gravel lane kept Colton moving even as his breath sharpened against the morning's chill. Case Walker's house came into view as he rounded the bend, golden sunlight dashing across the home's wooden exterior in broad strokes and glimmering in its windows.

And there on the front porch—Lilah.

His pace slowed to a jog, the ache in his bad knee fussing and cold air burning in his lungs. He hadn't expected Lilah to arrive so early. But his surprise now was no match for the shock that had sprinted through him last night when she'd showed up at the game. There'd been no uncoiling the mess of thoughts and emotion her appearance prompted—not as he'd sat next to her for the rest of the game, not when she'd tagged along to Frankie's Pizzeria with the team after, not later when he'd said good-night outside her hotel, when it'd been impossible to miss the harvest moon reflected in the diamond on her ring finger.

She waved now as he passed her rental car in the driveway and slackened to a walk. *Lilah. Here. In Iowa.* And where was Kate's little car?

"Since when did you become an early bird?" Lilah called as he approached.

He stopped in front of her and leaned one elbow on the railing leading up the porch steps, breath tight. "There's something about Iowa mornings. Fresh air. Early runs." The still and the quiet and autumn's whispers growing more pronounced each day. Watching the daily progress of farmers as harvest cut its path through one field after another.

"You said to come over for breakfast. I wasn't sure how early that was. I texted but you didn't answer."

Heartbeat finally slowing, he looked at Lilah now—really looked at her. Glossy black hair and lithe form unchanged since he'd seen her last. Her boots reached nearly to her knees, edging up to the hem of her belted gray dress.

Coordinated, fashionable, ever put together—that was Lilah. He'd never once, not even on the day she'd broken up with him, thought she looked out of place or overly uncomfortable.

Until now. She twisted her hands in her lap, and there was a pinch to her smile.

"I think I left my phone in the press box at the field last night." He lowered onto the stair below Lilah, leaning against the railing to face her. "As for breakfast, we've gotten into the habit of eating at seven thirty."

"We?"

"Whoever's home. Kate, Case, Raegan. Seth is usually at the restaurant early, but every once in a while he's around."

"Kate and Raegan are Logan's sisters, Case his dad. And Seth owns the restaurant, right?" She recited the names as if memorized from flash cards. "I didn't meet him yet, though, did I?"

Actually she had. Along with Ava and Bear and Webster and the Clancys, Sunny from the hardware store and her husband, Lenny, the woodshop guy, Alec the Scottish expat who ran the Chinese restaurant, Coach Leo, Pastor Nick from the church Colton had attended for three Sundays now—long enough that the Walkers' pew had begun to feel like his own.

"You met a lot of folks last night. Wouldn't expect you to remember all of them."

"You seemed to know them all really well. Did you hang out in this town when you were in college or something?" She fiddled with the long earring dangling from one ear.

"No, but Maple Valley is the sort of place that kinda reels you in whether you like it or not. One day you're new in town. The next you find yourself driving parade floats and organizing train pulls and going to town meeting after town meeting." Okay, truthfully, he'd only been to two town meetings. That first one at Seth's restaurant when he'd stood along the wall and wondered what he was getting himself into, and the second one earlier this week, when the mayor had announced the city would move forward with its Depot Day plans and keep the depot open through the rest of this season—and hopefully beyond—thanks to the success of the train pull in drumming up public interest.

The mayor had actually called him to the front of the room, credited him with the whole thing, made him stand there while the crowd clapped.

And he'd have been lying if he didn't admit he'd lapped it up. For a few minutes he'd almost felt like Colton Greene the admired quarterback again. The guy worthy of applause, or at least appreciation.

"You like it here." Statement, not a question. Lilah leaned forward, elbows on her knees. "You're different here. Calmer and steadier and all that good stuff."

Her words burrowed into him, tilling and turning over hurt he thought he'd finally buried under solid ground. Her words the day she'd broken things off sprouted anew. *"Yeah, it's the football, Colton—the lifestyle, the travel, all of it. But it's also you. I don't think you know how to live a normal life."*

"Why are you here, Lilah?" The question came out more abruptly than he'd intended, but maybe it was better this way. No more tiptoeing around the subject like they had last night. She had to have come for a reason. "If Ian asked you to try to talk me into—"

"He didn't." She reached behind her head to bunch her hair

243

together and then let it fall—a move he'd grown used to during the year they'd dated. "I need to resign from your foundation, Colton."

He exhaled as an angsty breeze reached under the porch roof to travel over them.

He should've known this was coming. With her political career on the incline, Lilah wouldn't have need for a part-time gig managing a foundation that'd never gotten off the ground anyway. He had been unable to give her direction, didn't really know what he wanted her to do with it. "You could've called."

She lifted one perfectly shaped eyebrow. "Like you would've answered." Her tone softened then. "Besides, I wanted to tell you in person. I felt like you deserved that."

"Well, thanks, I guess."

"I've got some recommendations for replacements."

He rubbed his fingers over his bad knee, trying to massage away the pulsing. "I don't know. Not sure there's much point to the foundation. It never really got going."

"I don't think you should just drop it, though."

"That's ironic, coming from you."

The comment raced out before he could stop it, and clearly it landed on target, because Lilah lurched to her feet, hurt and irritation in her expression. "That's not fair, Colt." She paced in front of him for several angry seconds. "You know what, that's the other reason I came. Ray has been practically begging me to set a wedding date, but I've been dragging my feet, and this week I finally realized why. You and I . . . we've never had closure."

"Not sure closure is possible."

She stopped and drilled him with a stare, voice notching up. "It might be if you'd let it. But it's like you're comfortable in broody, moody Colton-land."

"Nice rhyme—"

"I'm not joking here, and I'm tired of this. I'm sick of feeling guilty."

"You thought coming here to yell at me might alleviate that?"

Her impatience spilled into a scowl. "Don't do this. Don't turn off and refuse to hear me."

The sound of movement from inside drifted outdoors. Great, they'd woken others up. "I do hear you, Lilah. And I'm sorry you've felt guilty, okay? I don't blame you for the injuries or my retirement or any of that."

"But you obviously blame me for what happened with us. And that's not fair. I tried, Colt. I put my heart out there over and over, but you never let me in."

Now he stood. "Are you kidding? I was going to propose. I loved you."

"Because you *knew* me. But you never let me know you that same way. There was a wall you never allowed me past. It's not that I needed every detail of the decades before we met or diary-like monologues of your every thought. But I needed . . . something."

And the months and months of showering her with attention, affection, that wasn't something? "Did it ever occur to you that maybe it's painful for me to talk about my past?"

"Of course it did. But that's what people who care about each other do . . . they share their pain. They walk through it together." She folded her arms, voice lowering but fervent tone intact. "You can't have a marriage or a real relationship if one person insists on walking alone."

"I didn't—"

"You did." She tucked her hair behind her ears, something new landing in her gaze—clarity, resolve. "I realize there's no point in trying to convince you. If you don't want to take responsibility for your part in what went wrong, I can't make you. Maybe I just needed to say the words."

"Well, you said them." He heard the rigidity of his own tone, felt the stubbornness tightening through him. *You're handling this wrong. It's just like she said. You're refusing to hear her.*

But even if he wanted to correct course now, it was too late. Because Lilah had already returned to her car and slammed the door.

~⟋♢

"You are a hard man to track down, Colton Greene."

Kate's footsteps rattled on the bleachers as she climbed toward the press box that overlooked the Maple Valley High School football field. A pink sunset highlighted the web of peeling paint that wrapped around the makeshift building—no more than a rickety wooden box, really.

But it's where Colton had apparently decided to hide out for the evening. She could see his form—at least, she assumed that was him—sitting behind the press box's open window.

Wind flapping her hair around her face, she stood on her tiptoes to look in the window. "I've been trying to call you all day."

He held up his phone. "Left it here last night."

"So I finally learned from Rae. But she said you came out here looking for it two hours ago." And it wasn't all Raegan had said. Once she'd recapped the conversation she'd overheard between Colton and Lilah this morning, Kate had understood why they hadn't seen him all day. "Can I come in?"

His nod was absent an accompanying smile, but it was a nod all the same. "Door's locked. You'll have to come in the same way I did." He stood and held one hand through the window.

She stepped onto the closest bleacher, placed her palm in his, climbed through the window, and hobbled off the counter bordering the window. It was a small space—back wall plastered with game schedules and calendars with curled pages and front wall mostly windows that peered over a sleeping field.

"Decent place to kill a couple hours, I guess. Little cold, though."

Colton walked to the corner where a narrow space heater stood. He flicked it on. "Should help."

Colton pushed a ratty swivel chair toward her, its padding spilling out through ripped fabric. Once she sat, he unfolded a metal chair and lowered next to her.

The musty scent of old wood melded with the smell of stale popcorn—which made sense, considering the crackling of old kernels under her chair as she turned it to face Colton. "So."

Chin down, eyes on the field sprawling in front of them, he echoed her. "So."

"So Lilah went home."

He didn't say anything.

"Raegan told me."

"How much did she overhear this morning?"

"Not much."

He finally met her eyes. "So basically everything?"

"Basically yes."

The space heater's warmth began to fill the space, wrapping around her like a blanket and humming in tune with the wind. The first stars of the night were just beginning to peek through the sky's pastel canvas outside the shed's window.

"Rough day."

She offered what she hoped was a sympathetic half smile. "Well, I for one had an interesting day."

Something like relief washed over him, probably at the change in subject. "Tell me."

During their phone calls of the past week, she'd so many times heard him say a variation of those same words that, like magic, seemed to erase the miles between Maple Valley and Chicago. Just how many hours had they spent on the phone?

"You know Seth's friend Bear? It started with him serving me breakfast. Oh, and the worst coffee I've ever tasted."

His lips almost reached a grin. "I wondered where you were this morning."

"Eh, woke up early." *Escaped the house like a coward.* "Then I spent the rest of the morning and a good chunk of the afternoon with Megan."

"The scary barista?"

"She's not scary, Colt, she's just . . . prickly." She traced the cold metal of the microphone sitting atop the counter. "And also pregnant."

His eyes widened. "Whoa."

"Yeah. She had a momentary lapse in judgment with an old boyfriend a month or so ago. She's pretty upset. And I honestly don't think she has a single person here in town to talk to."

"Except you."

"I think she's still deciding whether or not she can stand me. But yeah, I'm probably the closest she's got—weirdly enough."

Cold air stretched through the window, arguing with blasts of warmth from the space heater. "I don't think it's that weird. You're a good listener, Rosie. Easy to talk to."

The space between them pulled taut, a delicate tension that dared her to ignore the resolution she'd come to this morning at Bear's. *Distance. Just friends.* After all, Lilah was gone now. Maybe the hope that had staked its claim yesterday at the hospital—wow, was it really just yesterday she'd still been in Chicago?—still had a place.

No. It just didn't make sense. Maple Valley was a bubble on its way to popping for both of them.

"So you had a wretched day. What do you usually do when you have a wretched day? What's your antidote? You once said your old social worker was awesome at cheering you up. What'd she do besides have you throw figurines at barns?"

His shoulders lifted just a bit. "Norah? We'd throw a football around."

Of course. Kate looked around the shadowed space, glance landing on the ball in the corner. "Jackpot. Let's go, Greene."

Without waiting for him to agree, she grabbed the ball, climbed onto the counter and out the window, football under her arm and bleachers clattering as soon as she touched down. Minutes later, she reached the field, Colton not far behind.

"Never thought I'd see the day when you'd willingly offer to toss around a football." He zipped up his hoodie as they walked to the center of the field. "We had to coerce you into it that Sunday afternoon."

"Actually, I should probably give you a little warning." Clouds rumbled overhead. *Please, God, not more rain.* Any more and the Blaine River's banks wouldn't hold its rushing waters any longer.

"Warn away." He took the football from her and tossed it into the air, the first hint of playfulness she'd seen in him tonight.

"When I was about seven years old, Beckett begged me to come outside and play Frisbee with him. I was writing at the time, because that's what I always did. Filled Mead Five-Star notebook after notebook with stories about pioneers and—"

He caught the ball. "Why pioneers?"

"Not relevant to the story."

"Yeah, but—"

"'Cause I thought going west in a covered wagon sounded cool or something. I don't know."

"Apparently the thought of Donner Pass didn't bother you too much."

She rolled her eyes. "So I tried to tell Beckett to go find Logan or Rae to play with him, but he insisted."

"Snake bites. Getting stuck in muddy rivers. Buffalo stampedes. All dangers along the Oregon Trail."

She pulled the football out of Colton's hands as if the act might shut him up. "He sends the Frisbee sailing at me. I catch it just fine, but when I throw it back it hits him in the face and knocks out one of his teeth."

Colton burst into laughter. "Was it a baby tooth at least?"

"Yeah, but that didn't stop my siblings from harassing me about it."

The sun's last hold on the sky had waned as she told her story, now lost to ever-darkening clouds. He pulled the football back from her. "Don't know why they harassed you. Not your fault. Beckett should've caught it."

"He was four."

"Well, then, for the sake of safety, do you know how to throw a football?"

"Um, with my arm?"

"There's technique, Kate."

"I'm okay winging it."

"Me and my teeth aren't. I'll teach you."

"Colt—"

"Hey, this was your idea, Rosie. Now, first thing you need to do is grip the ball." He reached for her right arm. "Don't palm it. And don't hold it too tightly. Your thumb and index finger should make an L." He placed the ball in her hand. "Index finger goes over a seam, ring finger over the laces." He fiddled with her finger placement. "Good."

"And now I throw it." She held her arm back, but he rounded behind her and stopped her arm before she could let go of the ball.

"Not so fast. Gotta get the rest of you ready." He placed his hands on both her shoulders and nudged the back of her left knee with his foot. "You want to face ninety degrees from your target and point your left foot toward the target."

"I don't even know what my target is." Only that his closeness had the same effect of that space heater back in the press box.

"Hold the football up by your ear." He moved her right hand. "Wind back." He covered her hand on the ball with his. "And then you'll throw in a half-circle motion and release the ball midway through." He moved her arm forward . . . then back . . . then forward.

"And my other arm?" He was enjoying this, wasn't he?

"Move it the other direction with your palm facing away. Like this." One hand still on her throwing arm, he used the other to pull her left hand back. "I'm just showing you the basics. It changes if you're throwing a Hail Mary or a short bullet pass or throwing while you're getting tackled."

Still in his grip, she moved her right arm in sync with her left, tilting her body just like he'd showed her, his movements matching hers . . .

And she released the ball.

Not quite a perfect spiral. But not a bad toss either. She turned, Colton standing so close behind her she almost knocked into him. As if on instinct, he reached to steady her, hands on her waist and laughter echoing around her.

Until, in a heady instant, he went silent—eyes searching hers and hands dropping to his side, even as he kept the space between them tight. And then, softly, "I can't remember it, Kate."

Distance. She ignored her conscience, refused to step back. "What?"

"My parents' death. I know what happened. I know the gruesome facts. I know, for some reason, I wasn't in the car. I can remember the hundred days before it, and I can remember everything after—every awful appointment with every well-intentioned therapist, drilling me with questions as if finally getting me to remember might solve all my problems. But it never worked."

The words tumbled from him, as if desperate for release. With the sun now tucked away under dusk's covers, only faint moonlight slanted in to outline the contours of his face, eyes that chose that moment to meet hers.

"And that's why I screw up every relationship in my life. Lilah said I wouldn't let her in, and she's exactly right. I wouldn't let her in because I don't *want* to remember. It's as if there's only a thin layer of ice between me and the memory, and if someone gets too close to me, the ice will crack and I'll . . ."

Plunge into a memory he has no desire to reclaim. Stark understanding ushered in such a welling of compassion it was all she could do not to pull him to herself. Attempt to embrace away the brokenness that displayed itself so clearly now in his face. *Oh, Colton . . .*

Distance.

Her conscience was barely a whisper now. And an irritating one, at that. Colton Greene had had too much distance in his life.

So she gave in, closed the last of the space between them, and wrapped her arms around his waist. She buried her face in the cotton of his shirt, felt his entire body slowly respond—his arms winding around her and tightening into a cocoon of shared emotion.

Forget distance.

This thing with Colton, whatever it was, maybe it'd end up breaking her heart. Here, right now, though, it wasn't about her heart—but about the heart beating against her cheek.

14

So tell me again what the point of this is. I've already been here once. Did the whole peeing in a cup thing."

Megan tapped her foot in a frenetic pace against the base of the patient bed in the Maple Valley Clinic.

Kate placed one palm on Megan's bony knee to still her fidgety leg. "Yes, but if I remember right, you told me you just up and walked out as soon as the doctor said you were pregnant. This time you might want to stick around long enough to get some info from Doc Malone. Maybe some vitamins. And a due date."

Megan slipped a chunk of black hair out of her face, revealing a line of silver hoops tracing up her ear. "I can figure that on my own. Chase and I . . ." She looked down. "Well, he was in town a whole two days. So X the date on the calendar and count nine months ahead and there you go."

"Hey, don't get all annoyed at me. You're the one who called and asked me to come with you."

It'd been a welcome interruption, really. Kate had been wrestling with the sixth chapter of Colton's book—too distracted by her own thoughts to make much traction with her writing.

It had been almost a full week since the night out on the

football field, some of it spent working at the depot to get it ready for tonight's kickoff to tomorrow's Depot Day, some of it spent working on the book. Nearly all of it spent in Colton's company. When she wasn't with him, she was writing about him. Or trying to.

Hard to write a book, though, when you were falling for its main character.

" . . . don't know why I did. It's not like you owe me anything. You didn't have to come."

Kate blinked, forcing her attention back to Megan. She slipped to the girl's side now and draped one arm over her shoulder. She felt Megan stiffen, but she didn't push Kate away. "Meg, have you called your parents?"

Her shoulders tightened underneath Kate's arm. "Are you kidding? If I was a nuisance to them growing up, can you imagine what their reaction would be to finding out I'm pregnant?" She shook her head and started with the foot tapping again. "No thank you. That is one lecture I don't need to hear."

"You don't think they should know they're going to be grandparents?"

"Oh, I'll tell them eventually. Maybe when he's five years old and rockin' the kindergarten thing."

The patient room door swung open then, and Dr. Malone came in, white coat swinging and stethoscope around her neck. The doctor wasn't more than five-foot-two, her tiny frame topped with Irish green eyes and red curls tinted with the faintest hint of gray. She'd been the Walker family doctor as long as Kate could remember, but it'd been years since she'd seen her. Probably not since Mom's funeral.

"Well, Miss Megan, nice of you to return." The doctor's smile held a tease and she glanced at the file in her hands. "We're looking at a May 6 due date."

Megan let out a slow breath, expression shielded as ever. There wasn't much to the rest of the appointment. Dr. Malone gave Megan a couple brochures, suggested a prenatal vitamin, and then had them stop at the front desk to schedule a ten-week appointment.

Kate waited until they were crossing the parking lot to ask her question. "Hey, earlier when you were talking about telling your parents, waiting until kindergarten, you said 'he.'"

Megan halted. "So?"

Kate rounded to the driver's side of the car and looked over its ceiling. "So was that a slip, or are you hoping for a son?"

Megan jerked open her car door. "I wasn't hoping for a baby at all." She thudded into the seat.

Okay. Kate lowered into her own seat slowly, tucked the key into the ignition, but paused before turning it. "You're not going to be alone in this, Meg. This is a great town with a lot of great people. And you, my friend, supply the coffee. If that doesn't earn you the support of everyone in Maple Valley, I don't know what would." She started the car.

"Yeah, well, you're not going to be here."

The comment landed with a thump, and Kate's fingers clenched the wheel. "It's true. I don't live here. But I'll come home to visit." Why, though, did the thought of not being here sting almost as much as the glare in Megan's expression?

It wasn't just Colton she'd been getting attached to this past month.

It was being in the same state as at least some of her family.

It was family breakfasts and daily trips to the coffee shop and weekend gatherings at The Red Door.

It was home.

When Megan didn't respond, only turned her focus out the window, Kate shifted into Reverse and turned the car toward the center of town. It was a stilted ride to Megan's house, the girl's *thanks* and *good-bye* when Kate dropped her off so wooden Kate wondered why Megan had asked for her company in the first place.

Instead of heading toward home, Kate drove to the depot next. She'd planned to spend the rest of the afternoon helping out with whatever final touches needed to happen before tonight's fireworks and tomorrow's big day. The sight of the depot and the scenery that wrapped around it brushed away at least some of the lingering unease from her time with Megan.

It was as if, with the turning of the calendar to October, autumn had thrown off any thought of a slow appearance. Instead of tentative pops of color, the tree-strewn hills behind the depot were awash in fiery hues. The depot building glistened in the sunlight, newly laid and newly stained boardwalk lining three sides and repaired track reaching into the rolling landscape.

If the outside looked this good, she could only imagine how great the inside looked.

Dad was walking toward his car when she pulled into the gravel lot to the east of the depot. "Hey, Dad."

He grinned and angled toward her car, pulling her into a side hug when she slid out of the car. "Hardly seen you this week, Katie."

"That's because you've been working longer hours than even the farmers."

A sling still encased his arm, but the scrapes and bruises he'd had when she first arrived home had faded. And a new energy warmed his eyes. "Worth it to see the old place sparkling again. You looking for Colton?"

"Not specifically, though I did text him earlier and tell him I'd come out and help with whatever's left to do after Megan's appointment."

Dad threaded her arm through his, then started toward his car again. "You remind me so much of your mother, Katie girl, the way you've taken Megan under your wing. You got her kindheartedness in heaping doses."

"Dad, I might feel bad for Megan, but I'm hardly making a real difference in her life. And I'm not doing what Mom did. Mom worked to save entire African villages. I gave a girl a ride to the doctor."

Gravel crunched under their feet. "You saw a need in front of you and you met it. That's what Flora did. Whether it was writing that grant proposal and starting a nonprofit or cooking meals and doing laundry and raising her kids. I don't think your mother ever saw one task as bigger or more important than the others."

They stopped at his car. "I like it when you talk about Mom."

The lines in his face deepened with his pleasure. "And I like that you like it. Not all your siblings do."

"Beckett?"

"Sometimes wonder if that's why he ended up so far from Iowa. If it's just too hard . . ." Dad shook his head. "I've hung up lots of hats over the years. My soldier hat, my diplomat hat. Won't ever hang up my parent hat."

She leaned onto her tiptoes to kiss his cheek. "We wouldn't want you to. Although, it'd probably be nice of us to stop giving you things to be worried about." Logan and Charlie in LA, still trying to heal from Emma's death. Beckett in Boston, so quiet sometimes—more distant than geography excused. Raegan, with perhaps more going on behind her claims of contentment than she let on.

And me. A years-old relationship still dogging her up until last week. A career that couldn't decide where to land. And a heart that'd made it clear she wasn't getting away with the easy route.

"Oh, hey, as long as you're here . . ." Dad opened his car door and reached for a pile of envelopes and papers on the dash. "Marty stopped by with a stack of mail for the depot, and since at it, he delivered my home mail. There's a big manila envelope for you."

She took the envelope from Dad, scanning the return address. The James Foundation. It was all the paperwork Frederick Langston had told her about. Copies of previous annual reports. Travel insurance forms, liability waivers.

She let out a long exhale.

"I take it this trip is getting real."

"Incredibly."

Dad leaned one arm over his car door. "And . . . you really want to go?"

"More than anything." The answer came out by rote. She'd been talking about it for a month, dreaming about it for years. Well, maybe not dreaming of this exact thing, but about playing some kind of significant role in carrying on the work Mom started. "Mom would be so happy I'm going." She looked up to meet Dad's eyes, an unexpected desire for affirmation.

"Your mother would be proud of you for going after what you want. You can be sure of that."

Wind rustled the papers in her hands, carrying with it a faint and lilting voice.

Dad grinned. "And that'd be Colton. He likes to sing if he thinks no one's within hearing distance."

She glanced toward the depot. Colton singing. It should make her giggle, send her skipping to the building with a dozen ready teases. So why couldn't she muster more than an unsteady sigh?

"Kate."

She turned once more to Dad.

"Don't assume saying yes to one dream automatically means saying no to another."

"I'm not sure what you mean."

He dropped into his car. "Oh, I think you do. Know how I know?"

They smiled at each other as Colton's voice raised and his song drifted in on the breeze.

"How?"

"Because I'm quoting a line from one of your movies." He grinned, closed his door, and waved as he drove away.

~⁓

"Well, if this doesn't smack of déjà vu."

Colton's glance slid to the right. That reporter, the one who'd shown up here his first morning of work at the depot. Amelia, right? He grunted as he hefted the oak door sitting behind the depot, waiting for installation. "Except you're not flashing a camera at me this time."

The woman patted the bag slung over her shoulder. "Not yet anyway."

Amelia close on his heels, he started walking toward the depot's entrance, the muscles in his arms tightening as he lugged the door into the building, familiar pang in his shoulder throwing a fit. Seven hours until tonight's fireworks kicked off the weekend's Depot Day events—and until this building where he'd spent as many hours lately as he used to on a football field was reintroduced to its community.

He angled around a freshly sanded wood pillar, the smell of sawdust still lingering in the air, and stopped halfway across the room, waiting as Seth and Bear carried in the repaired grandfather clock that would gulp up one corner of the room. Amazingly, they'd found the clock damaged but not beyond repair about two miles from the depot after the tornado. Somewhere around the place Kate and Raegan, probably Ava, too, were washing windows and glass display cases.

Amelia's footsteps picked up once more as Colton's did. "So I know this is a busy day for you," she said. "I'm doing a story about Depot Days, all the work that's gone into getting the depot and museum ready." She double-stepped to keep up with him. "I called Case, but he left to go home a while ago. He told me you could give me just as much info as he could—that you've done most of the work."

Colton set the door down, relief shooting down his shoulder, and leaned it against the pillar.

"So do you mind?"

He rubbed the dust from his hands onto his flannel shirt. "Mind what?"

Amelia rolled her eyes in exaggerated amusement. "If I ask you a few questions. About the renovations, all the work you've done."

"I haven't done that much."

"Right."

He followed the direction of her focus around the room. Fresh paint in rich hues of blue and gold. New glass displays in place of the shattered cases he'd seen that night he and Kate stopped by the storm-damaged building. Salvaged railroad relics and reprinted town photos in frames and on wall shelves all around the room. "Modesty's all well and good, Colton Greene. But you're just plain wrong. The place hasn't looked this good in years."

"Whatever you say." He hefted the door once more and moved it to the closet-sized ticket booth, its doorframe empty and waiting. "Ask away."

Amelia pulled a notebook from the pocket of her jean jacket.

"All right. For starters, did you really think you'd manage to get all this done in time for tomorrow's big event?"

Colton inched the door toward its frame. "Oh yeah. I mean, sure, there was a lot to do. But I've been in town long enough to know that around here, everyone pitches in. This week alone, we've had so much help from community members."

"But it was completely torn apart by the tornado—far worse damage than anywhere else in town. What all did you have to do to get it ready?"

Colton worked to fit the door into the open space while rattling off the list of projects he'd completed alongside Case in the past four weeks. But something was wrong. The hinges lined up, but the door itself was about a centimeter too tall for the space. Shoot, what now?

"Bet you never expected to find yourself pulling handyman duty in small-town Iowa."

"Guess not." He stepped away from the door, hands on his hips. Was there some other door that was supposed to go in this space?

Amelia stuck her pen behind her ear. "It's almost funny to think about. You, a former NFL quarterback. And not just any quarterback. You helped break a forever-long losing streak in major franchise. Last couple seasons, your team was the dark horse of the playoffs—and you were the jockey who made it happen."

He turned, brow furrowing. "In keeping with the metaphor and all, I'm the jockey who fell off his horse and hasn't been back on since. And I thought this interview—or whatever it is—was supposed to be about the depot."

Amelia shrugged, one corner of her mouth lifting. "Yeah, but when it comes to the depot, you're as big of news as its reopening."

He caught sight of Kate through a window across the room. She was scrubbing its glass, making faces at her sister, who wiped the other side.

Kate, who'd stood in the middle of the football field a week ago, arms knotted so tightly around him it was as if she'd hoped to squeeze any pain right out of him.

Kate, who'd filled his days and his thoughts ever since.

Who'd become so much more than a friend to him it was crazy to think he'd only met her four weeks ago today.

"Did I lose you?"

He blinked and swiveled his attention back to Amelia. "Sorry. Busy day. My focus isn't at record levels." And he needed to figure out what was up with this uncooperative door. Maybe there was a different one somewhere.

"Now that the depot's back in operation, when do you head back to LA?"

Why did the question feel intrusive? "Uh . . . originally the plan was early next week, but Kate and I still have some book details to work on." And he still hadn't bought a return ticket.

"You're probably eager to get back, though. Iowa has to feel so . . . small to you. Slow and unexciting. But then your book will come out and there will be signings and readings and a bunch of media stuff, right? You'll be back in the spotlight."

"Tell you the truth, Amelia, I don't miss the spotlight at all."

"You don't know how to have a normal life."

In the past week, most of the pricking from Lilah's words had worn off. But the words themselves had stuck around. Because a normal life was exactly what he'd begun to experience here in Maple Valley. And somewhere along the way, he'd started to like it.

Not started to. Did.

He liked this funny little town and all the characters that filled it up.

He liked *being* one of the characters.

And Kate . . .

He liked her best. Had stopped even trying to deny it.

Problem was, everything holding him in Maple Valley had an expiration date. Just like Amelia said, the depot repairs were about finished. He and Kate had planned out the rest of his book. She'd already written several chapters. She could do the rest on her own. And she'd be going back to Chicago any day now.

And Colton?

He wished he knew.

"Listen, Amelia, I gotta figure out what to do about this door. Any more questions . . . about the depot, that is?"

"I think we're good. Can I get a quick photo, though?"

"Of me?" He frowned.

"Yes. How about you and the door?"

Reluctance tugged at him, but he acquiesced, posing beside the door with a smile that probably screamed cheesy. Amelia lifted her camera, snapped the photo . . .

And with the flash of her camera, all went dark. The present stripped down to nothing. And in its place, a voice.

"Show me a smile, Colton. A great big smile."

An eruption of light.

Metal shrieking.

Crashing.

And a force pounding into him, thrusting his eyes open and his mind back to the here and now, and Amelia's stare, rimmed with worry and curiosity. "Colton?"

Rapid blinks. Heart pounding in his chest.

"Are you okay, Colton? You just . . . froze. You're completely white."

Why was this happening . . . again? First at the parade, then at that studio in Chicago.

"*Smile for the camera, Colton.*"

"I'm . . . I'm fine."

"You sure?"

Not at all. "Yeah. Sorry. Guess the flash messed with my head for a sec."

"All right, then." She replaced her camera in its bag and pocketed her notebook. "See ya around."

He mustered his own "See ya." Glanced at the door. Shook his head with enough force to strain his neck. And tried to convince himself the flashback meant nothing.

~~~

The first firework of the night rocketed into the sky and burst into ribbons of pink and purple and green, the boom echoing over the field in front of the depot.

Kate felt her whole body stiffen at the sound, even as she oohed along with all the community members gathered in clumps. Some in lawn chairs, some on blankets, others—probably the ones who didn't mind ladybugs scurrying over their shoes and up their pant legs—sprawled on the grass.

The distant scent of smoke drifted in a lazy fog over the crowd, along with the murmur of voices and the faint drone of country music from someone's vehicle. The scene should have been peaceful. But the noise in the sky and the disruption in her head—or maybe her heart—dissolved any chance of that.

"*Don't assume saying yes to one dream automatically means saying no to another.*"

"You don't like fireworks?" Colton leaned over from the lawn chair he seemed to dwarf.

"How'd you know?"

"You winced when that first one went off the way I do anytime someone suggests a round of golf."

Another eruption of color, fiery threads fingering every direction into the sky's midnight-blue veil before tipping toward the ground. "What's wrong with golf?"

"Nothing, if you like a sport that's basically the equivalent of a nap. Just thinking about it makes me yawn."

"Should I put that in your book?"

Those perfect dimples bracketed his smile like always. "We never did have that all-important discussion about what's on the record and what's off."

"Oh, it's all fair game, my friend."

"All of it? Everything I've done or said the past month? Anything could make it into the book?"

"I'm mad with power—the power of a writer's pen." The next firework barely fazed her.

"Well, if it's all fair game, then I think there's one moment from the past few weeks that definitely needs to make it into the book."

"Oh yeah?"

"Remember that time you kissed me back in Chicago?"

"Colton!"

"We've never talked about that, Rosie—"

"It was an accident." How did he make a smirk look so appealing?

"That's the thing. I didn't even know it was possible to *accidentally* kiss someone."

"Nice air quotes on the *accidentally*."

"And I just think it's a moment that needs to be recorded for posterity."

"You're incorrigible—you know that?"

"Nice vocab, Walker." He leaned back in his chair, the perfect picture of relaxed satisfaction, eyes fixed on the sky.

She lowered her voice then, even though Dad had abandoned

his chair next to her to go talk to someone across the field and Raegan had her earbuds in and Seth and Ava were so caught up in their own conversation there wasn't anyone else to hear her words. "But since you asked, I've never liked fireworks. They're pretty and all, but the color doesn't make up for the noise. Freaks me out."

He turned his gaze on her. "So why'd you come?"

"Because my dad runs the depot and I'm a Maple Valley native. Which means the idea of a Walker skipping any of the festivities is basically up there with, like, your not watching the draft."

"Have to tell you, I'm so proud of you, working football references into your everyday conversation." He leaned forward to tap her nose. "My little student, using all her new knowledge."

More colors sliced into the sky in an irregular rhythm of booms. How had her chair ended up so close to Colton's anyway? And why couldn't she unhook her attention from him?

"Let's bail."

She blinked. "Huh?"

"Ditch the fireworks. Got something to show you."

He stood and held out his hand to her. And despite every chiding voice grumbling in her conscience, she couldn't help herself. She took his hand and let him pull her to her feet, and when he still held her hand as he led her away from the lawn chairs, she couldn't make herself pull away.

It's okay to admit what you want.

What if she let herself believe just for today—maybe tomorrow, too—that whatever this was could work? That she wanted it to work.

And what if it really could? She was only leaving the country for a few months, after all. So what if they lived halfway across the country from each other? It was just . . . geography.

What about not letting yourself get distracted?

Well, Colton wasn't Gil. And she wasn't the same silly twenty-two-year-old, walking blindly into a doomed-from-the-start relationship. No, her eyes were wide open this time around.

Colton led her in a labyrinth-like path through the crowd and toward the line of trees at the back of the field, the blast of fireworks continuing overhead in a backdrop of wriggling colors.

"Think we'll find someone breaking in again?"

He tugged her closer to him as their path to the building cleared of blankets and lawn chairs. "Man, doesn't that seem like months ago?"

Yes. And it seemed like yesterday. Time was a funny thing in Maple Valley.

They reached the depot, and Colton unlocked the door and held it open for her. Dad must have planned to return to the depot before going home for the night, because the windows were still open—screens ushering in the night's cool breeze, tinged with the faintest ashy smell of the fireworks, their sound now muffled. Dim lighting from old-fashioned sconces on the walls muted colors and shadows.

Instead of turning on the lights, Colton led her toward one of the glass displays with a hand on her back.

"It's crazy to me what stuff survived the tornado. On the one hand, a half mile of track was torn up. On the other, stuff like that old clock and what I'm about to show you made it through."

He rounded the case and bent to pull out the old book she recognized as the depot's once-upon-a-time guest register. Long creases wrinkled down the grayish-blue cover that curled at the corners, and the pages creaked with age and possibly water damage as Colton unfolded the book.

She stood across from him, elbows on the case and eyes on

Colton's tousled hair. He found the page he was looking for, turned the book around, and slid it to her. "Look."

She gasped as her attention landed where he pointed. *Flora Lawrence.* She underlined Mom's name with her finger. And right underneath, Dad's. *Case Walker. 1979.*

"1979. That's the year the depot and museum officially opened after the Union Pacific donated a final mile of track. My grandma was part of the planning committee for the first ever Depot Days, so my mom came home from New York for the event."

"And your dad?"

His scribbled handwriting looked exactly the same on the page as it did now. "By that time, he was finishing up a two-year stint with the Foreign Services Office in London. He just happened to be between assignments on the weekend of the depot opening, so he came home. And that's when he and my mom finally got together once and for all, after years of starts and stops."

Colton leaned one elbow on the counter, attention fixed on her.

She perched her chin on her fists, moved her focus to the book once more. "It's a long story. Sometimes I think about writing it—it'd make such a good novel. Even with all their initial hits and misses, my dad likes to say that from the very start, he knew Mom was the one for him."

"Mmm."

At his bare response, she glanced up to find him still watching her, gaze intent and . . . Was that longing? "I'm sorry." Her words came out a whisper.

He squinted in question. "Sorry?"

"For flaunting happy memories when . . ."

"You're not flaunting."

His gentle tone, the warmth of his breath she could feel even from across the case, awoke every nerve inside her. She met his gaze, lamplight flickering in his eyes.

"Kate, I had a flashback today. Third or fourth time it's happened recently."

She straightened at his unexpected remark. "Of the accident?"

"I think so? I'm not sure."

"Tell me."

"I don't really . . ." He blinked once. Twice. Shook his head. "It's not really important—"

"But it is."

He rounded the case to stand in front of her. "No, what's important is, any other time and place and that flashback would've thrown me for a loop. I'd let it gnaw at me for days. But in Maple Valley . . . it just kind of fades away. Things feel normal for the first time in a long time."

Really? This intoxicating tension felt normal to him? "But about the flashback, if you're remembering . . ." If he talked it out, described the flashback itself . . . What if it was good for him? Healing in some way?

But she couldn't push the question to her vocal cords, each distant thought falling flat as he took another step closer to her.

"It's not just Maple Valley, Kate. It's you."

"Colton." His name came out a whisper, not at all the argument it should've been.

And then he kissed her—a tentative, feather-soft kiss, heart-fluttering enough on its own. But then as one heady second slid into two, he released her hands and wrapped his arms around her, his kiss becoming so much more that she couldn't stop herself from responding.

And every voice in her head finally silenced save one. The

one telling her if this was his kind of normal, she could stay wrapped up in it forever.

She slipped her arms around Colton just as he broke away, his eyes as dazed as she felt. And then he smiled. "For the record, Rosie, that kiss wasn't even close to an accident." His head tilted to her again—

But the door of the depot crashed open then, banging into the opposite wall. Footsteps accompanied the clamor, and as she and Colton shot apart, she was vaguely aware of the muffled pops of continued fireworks.

And Dad's voice. "The dam . . . It finally broke."

15

Pain sliced through Colton's shoulder as he heaved what had to be his hundredth sandbag onto the growing wall around the rising river. The first rays of sunrise colored the sky in curls of pink, and exhaustion rippled through him in waves.

But he'd never felt so perfectly in place. Even with damp clothing clinging to his skin and wind-thrown sand in his hair.

"You should go home, Greene. Get some sleep." Seth's friend, Bear, grunted as he hefted a sandbag. "First shift ended an hour ago."

"I'm good. Wouldn't be able to sleep anyway." Not knowing so many others were still out here defending the town against the river's marching speed. It'd be like abandoning his team to finish a game without him. According to the emergency response manager, they had less than a couple hours left before the river overtook the road.

"I can't believe it's flooding this late in the year."

Colton gritted his teeth as a spasm tore through his shoulder, then accepted another sandbag from Bear. "But we're making progress, don't you think?" He looked down the river, at the piles of bags and the assembly line of community members.

The main area of risk was the three-block stretch of businesses along the riverfront. Bags were already piled high in front of buildings.

A burly wind hurled itself against him now, carrying sand and pricks of water from lingering rain—or maybe from the river.

Bear inhaled as he lifted a bag. "If we're lucky, we'll hold her in." He shook his head. "Can't say the same for Dixon though. Has to be devastating."

News of the dam's cracking in the town forty miles north hadn't taken more than minutes to spread to Maple Valley. And just like that, the fireworks had ended and the community erupted into action.

And that moment with Kate back in the depot—suddenly it felt like days ago instead of only hours.

"It's not just Maple Valley, Kate. It's you."

His words had hammered him all night long as he worked, the truth of them spreading through him like the ache from his injuries. Ache was the perfect word for it, too. Without Kate, without the sense of calm and normalcy Maple Valley gave him, he'd go back to being the same old Colton, wouldn't he? Here . . . here he was a new man.

Except for the flashbacks. But even those weren't as bad, not with a hodgepodge of people who'd become like family faster than he could've imagined.

The sound of an engine rumbled in, and he turned to see a truck pulling to a stop, its bed loaded with more bags.

And Kate. She sat on a pile of bags in the back, holding on to the truck bed's side for balance. He was the first to abandon his post at the front line and meet the truck.

Kate jumped down as he reached her. "Special delivery."

"Katharine Walker, what are you still doing here? And why aren't you wearing your coat?" Her rain-soaked shirt clung so close to her skin he could see the flex of her arms when she lifted a sandbag. Her lips were nearly blue from the cold.

She lifted a sandbag. "Mrs. Jamison was shivering as she served coffee. She's seventy-five, if she's a day. Gave her my coat."

She would. Because that was Kate. The daughter who rushed home when her father needed her. The sister who kept an intentional pulse on each of her siblings. The community member who pitched in when the call came. The mentor who befriended a pregnant barista.

The woman who made him wonder what he'd ever seen in any other woman.

He reached out to accept a sandbag from her now, fingers brushing hers as he did, holding the bag in place between them. "First shift ended an hour ago. That's what Bear said."

Fatigue pulled at her eyelids. "*You're* still here."

The river's rushing roared behind him. "I am."

A slivered sun reflected in her eyes in flecks of gold. They still held the sandbag between them, caught in a moment not all that different from last night.

"Kate—"

Bear approached then, cutting off words Colton hadn't even fully formed in his mind yet. He glanced at the sandbag, then at Kate. She released it to Colton, who released it to Bear and stepped back.

"You know, I think you might be the new town hero," Kate said as he turned to grab another bag. "Everyone keeps talking about you. How you're not even from here, but you've worked longer and harder than anyone tonight. Or, well, this morning, I guess."

He gulped in the words *town hero* the way he used to *starting quarterback*, nourishing pride settling into the hungry spaces inside him. "Guess those years of running around in Superman pajamas with a red cape paid off."

"Did you wear your underwear over your pants? Please tell me you wore your underwear over your pants."

He turned back to her. "Not sure I'm comfortable talking about my underwear with you, Miss Walker."

She donned a properly contrite expression, underneath a spreading blush. "You're entirely right, Mr. Greene. So sorry for the impropriety."

"But yes, sometimes I did. And one time I was so sure the costume and cape were going to help me fly that I climbed onto the back of the couch and jumped and crashed into a lamp. That's how I got the scar over my eyebrow."

"Really? I always assumed it was a football thing." She lifted another bag, arms straining, and handed it to him.

"Kate, take a break, okay? Let us unload the rest."

"Not happening. I'm in this for the long haul. Plus, I can't go home until I get ahold of Megan. I've tried calling her four or five times already. The coffee shop's right in the path of the river."

"She's probably still sleeping."

"I know, but I'd feel better if I knew for sure."

Colton pulled the last sandbag from the truck just as another vehicle pulled up—this one an emergency response vehicle, its pulsing light glaring against dawn's shadows. Raegan jumped out of the SUV's passenger seat, wisps of blond hair fluttering against her cheeks underneath a newsboy hat. Just like Kate, goose bumps trailed her bare arms. Bear joined them once more as Raegan hurried over.

"River's over the Archway Bridge," she said.

Kate's eyes widened. "Already? Then that means the other bridges—"

"Yep, already barricaded."

"Emergency Management says we've done all we can as far as sandbagging. Now it's about safety, getting people home and away from the river. We need to spread the word—they're closing Archway down in an hour."

Which meant if they wanted to get home, they needed to leave soon.

Bear yanked the walkie-talkie from a hook over his belt. "I'll start passing on the message. But first . . ." He shrugged out of the flannel shirt he'd worn over a T-shirt and handed it to Raegan.

For just a moment, Raegan's grin chased away the tension of her delivered news. She pulled on the shirt and directed her next words to Kate. "I told Dad we'd head home in the next half an hour."

"I just need to get ahold of Megan first."

"Okay, see ya. Colton, make sure she does as she's told, all right?"

"I'll do my best." He turned to Kate and pinched his Henley away from his chest. "I'm not wearing another shirt under this, but—"

"I'm fine, Colt. You start wandering around here shirtless and that town-hero talk will take on a whole new angle."

"I'm going to finish piling the last of these bags. Meet at your car in twenty minutes? It's still parked up by the fire station."

She nodded and returned to the truck she'd arrived in. For the next fifteen minutes, he helped cover the line of people stretching downriver, spreading the news that it was time to close down the sandbagging effort. He caught a ride with Laura Clancy back to the fire station—learned Webster had been out all night working alongside everyone else. Couldn't help the shot of pride that tidbit of info produced.

But when Laura dropped him off, Kate wasn't at her car.

He waited. Five minutes. Ten. He tried texting, calling. Checked the time on his phone. Down to twenty-five minutes until the bridge closed.

Where are you, Kate?

～◦

Kate should've checked Coffee Coffee first. Why had she wasted time jogging the six blocks to Megan's house before coming to the coffee shop?

The sound of the river's whooshing pulse joined the slap of her feet in the puddles leading to Coffee Coffee's entrance. The bottoms of the sandbags around the corner door were already damp, and water was beginning to pool wherever the sidewalk dipped. And there, behind the glass windows fronting the shop, Megan's form.

Kate wrenched the door open and hurried in, breathless and irritated. "Do you have any idea how many times I've called you?"

Megan's attention jerked from the shop vac at her feet to Kate, dark hair swinging at the movement. "What are you doing here?"

"I've been trying to get ahold of you for hours."

"Yeah, well, I've been a little busy." Smudges of water dampened Megan's holey jeans and T-shirt with a band name in graffiti print. She wore only flip-flops on her feet, toes nearly blue.

And no wonder. Water had already begun seeping from the basement to stain the coffee shop's wood floor. Apparently Megan had been trying to keep up with it using the shop vac, but she had to know the effort was in vain. Once the river spilled over the road, together with the water leaking from the basement, it would only be a matter of time before it reached ankle-deep, or maybe even knee-deep, here.

Kate had seen it before. It's why all the businesses along the three-block riverfront stretch were all new or renovated within the past twelve years—since the last major flood gobbled up the area.

"You've obviously made a valiant effort here, but it's time to go home. You're exhausted and . . . and pregnant."

"Thanks for the reminder."

"You need rest."

"I need to save my livelihood." Her dark gaze shot bullets.

The musty smell of river water overtook the coffee shop's usual coffee aroma. "Megan—"

"Why are you even here?" The words exploded from her, and she flung her arms up. "Why do you keep showing up? Here, at my house, the doctor's office—"

"You called me—"

"You don't know me. You don't owe me. You're nothing to me. Why can't you just leave me alone?"

The anger in Megan's voice, the sharpness of her words—*"You're nothing to me"*—blocked any response. Kate hugged her arms to herself, cold and fatigue no match for the worry charging through her. *Oh, Megan . . .*

The girl's shoulders slumped then, her body going limp as she sunk down to sit on the shop vac, as if suddenly emptied of argument. "I put everything into this place—all the money I had left, every cent."

Kate pulled a chair away from a table, lowered. "I know you did."

"I made the mistake of calling my parents when I was thinking of buying it. So of course my dad called the Realtor—got him to admit the reason I was getting such a good price on the building was because it's on flood ground. I didn't care. Wasn't going to let the man who'd ignored me most of my life suddenly butt in and keep me from my future."

It was the most Kate had ever heard Megan say at once.

"So of course I ignored Dad and bought the place anyway. And now look—I'm going to lose it. And right when I need it most." She looked up, eyes hooking on Kate's from behind pooling tears and strands of hair that hung over her face. "I'm going to have to go home and tell my parents I lost everything—and oh yeah, I'm knocked up."

Kate leaned forward to brush the hair out of Megan's face. "You haven't lost everything, Megan."

She sniffled, swiped her sleeved arm under her nose. "I guess not. I have flood insurance."

"That's not exactly what I meant, but yay for that, all the same." She laid one hand on Megan's knee. "But what I meant was, you saw the way Maple Valley pulled together after the tornado, right? It's going to be the same way after this. I bet you'll be blown away at how this community comes around you and everyone else affected by the flood. Same way they did my dad and the depot."

"I've only lived here two years. I'm not your dad."

Kate allowed a lightness into her voice. "We've already talked about this, Meg. You supply the coffee. And that makes you a vital fixture of the community."

The faintest smile attempted an appearance on Megan's face.

"And it's going to be the same when you have this baby. If you let them, people are going to be there for you." Kate squeezed Megan's knee. "*I'm* going to be there for you."

Megan's hair flopped forward again when she lifted her head. "But—"

"Yes, I'm going to Africa, but I'm going to be home a couple months before your due date. Chicago's only five hours away. I can come home tons."

Maybe even . . .

Move home? Was it really a possibility? What if the trip to Africa turned into an eventual job offer from the foundation? Could she really say no to that to come back to Maple Valley?

See the need in front of you.

What happened when there were multiple needs in different places? How did a person choose?

How did Mom choose?

"Kate, I, uh . . . I didn't mean what I said before. You're not nothing to me."

She vaguely recognized the sound of the bells chiming over the coffee shop's entrance, the burst of chilly, damp air. She didn't turn. "I know you didn't mean it."

"A lot of people in this town are nice. But you're the first one who . . ." Megan gave a limp shrug. "Well, you know. I suppose I considered myself completely alone before."

She weighed her next words before speaking, a thread of a prayer running through them when she did let them out. "I'm going to say something, Meg, at the risk of sounding trite, but hear me out, okay?" At Megan's curious nod, she continued. "You were never completely alone. I don't know if you have any kind of faith or even believe in God—"

"I do. I guess." She shook the hair out of her eyes. "In a '*somebody* must have created the world' kind of way."

"All right, then. So if you can believe that—that there's a God who created a world out of nothing—then it's not such a leap to believe He's present in the here and now. And that He can pick up the pieces of your life—even when it feels like a flood-ravaged mess—and turn it into something brand new." She paused until Megan met her eyes. "Maybe . . . probably . . . something better than you imagined. Not easier, perhaps. But better, and all the richer for what you've been through."

"You believe that?"

She might be surprised at her own words, surprised they'd chosen now—in the middle of a natural disaster—to spring. But yes, she believed them. Maybe now more than ever. "Haven't always been the best at remembering it when I'm in the middle of my own messes. But I do believe it."

Megan's head tilted then, as a shadow drifted over them. "You."

Kate looked up. Colton. Warmth swept through her, a reaction to his presence that was becoming more familiar—more consuming—with each day that passed. "Hey, you. How'd you know I was here?"

"I asked about a hundred people until someone said they saw you jogging this direction. They'll be closing the bridge any minute. You have any idea how worried I've been?"

Megan laughed—actually laughed. "You two are echoes of each other. Kate said those exact words like fifteen minutes ago."

Kate stood, still swallowed up in Colton's shadow, awareness puddling inside her. "Sorry to worry you. But you found me. Let's go before the bridge closes. You need a ride, Meg?"

Megan rose. "Oh, I'm not leaving."

"But everything we just talked about—"

"I heard you, and I even believe you—that the town will pull together, I'm not alone, even . . . even the last part." She reached for the shop vac's hose. "But I still have to try."

"But—"

"In that case, we'll help," Colton said.

Kate's gaze flung to his face. "Colton?"

"We can at least minimize the damage. We'll pile as much of the furniture as we can onto counters. Or, wait, even better—Kate, didn't you say Bear lives upstairs? Maybe he'd let us haul some of it up there."

"The Archway is going to close in minutes. Once it closes,

it's like a domino effect downriver—all the roads and bridges for thirty, forty miles south of here will be barricaded, too. The ones north are already closed. If we don't leave now, we're not getting home today."

"Then we'll crash on someone's couch or get a couple hotel rooms."

"You'd do that?" Megan said.

Colton draped one arm around Kate's shoulder. "Of course we would. Right, Rosie?"

The grin on her face couldn't hope to contain all the admiration—or very possibly something much, much more—heating through her. "Of course."

❧

Colton leaned against the doorframe of Megan's bedroom, watching as Kate pulled the covers over the now-sleeping young woman. Band posters covered the walls, and dark clothing lay strewn around the room.

And yet, her comforter was patterned in bright pinks and greens and yellows. As if there was still very much a lingering little girl inside the twenty-one-year-old, business-owning, soon-to-be single mother.

Kate rose gently and padded to him. "She's asleep," she whispered.

Fatigue pulled at Kate's features, any makeup long since faded away and her hair a mess of tangles and . . .

And he was pretty sure she was more beautiful than ever.

She glanced over her shoulder. "I wonder how long it's been since someone tucked her in."

"She's lucky to have you."

Kate tipped her head toward him. "No, today she was lucky to have *you*."

"Both of us, then. We make a good team." Did his voice sound as husky to her as it did to him?

With one palm on his chest, Kate nudged him into the hallway and closed Megan's bedroom door behind her. "Megan has a guest bedroom. Thought I'd camp out here for a while, catch some sleep."

He nodded. "Bear said I could crash on his couch."

"Be careful driving back there. The roads . . . flooding . . ." She bit her bottom lip.

The narrow hallway was dim, afternoon sunlight shut out by the lack of windows. Despite his exhaustion, the last thing he wanted to do was leave Kate.

And if he was reading her right, the same hazy reluctance clung to her.

"Hey."

She tilted her head again. "Yeah?"

"Got any Saturday night plans?"

Amused interest joined her grin. "Originally I was supposed to be living it up at Depot Days. Eating cotton candy, taking a train ride."

He'd almost forgotten the now-abandoned event. "Well, after we both get some sleep, I was thinking, maybe we could go out on the town."

She stifled her laughter with a glance at Megan's door. "You do recall half the town is shut down due to the flood. And even if it wasn't, our options for 'going out on the town' are pretty much limited to antique stores—most of which close by five."

He stepped closer to her. "Oh, you are sorely underestimating Maple Valley's entertainment potential, Miss Walker. Agree to go out with me, and I promise, I'll find something fun."

"Okay, then. It's a date."

"All right."

"All right," she echoed him.

He started to turn, but she stopped him, grabbing his hand and then standing on her tiptoes to kiss his cheek. And then her voice at his ear. "Thank you, Colton."

"For?"

"Everything."

She released his hand and crossed the hall to what was probably the guest room.

"Hey, Kate?" He raised his whisper a notch.

She turned.

He pointed to his cheek where she'd kissed him. "Accident or intentional?"

She only rolled her eyes and disappeared into the bedroom.

16

*D*ude, what happened to 'strictly business'?"

Logan Walker's halfway-to-accusatory voice carried through the speaker phone of Colton's cell, propped up on the sink ledge in Bear's bathroom. Colton buttoned up the pale blue Oxford he'd borrowed from Bear. Everything he wore, down to the socks on his feet, on loan from the guy whose living room had become Colton's temporary bedroom.

"Uh, you might say it fell by the wayside." He buttoned the highest button. Thought twice and unbuttoned it. "Can you blame me? Kate's kind of amazing. And funny and talented and, like, the definition of attractive. Plus, a good kisser."

"Aghh, man, she's my sister."

Colton grinned at himself in the mirror. "Sorry." *Not.*

"If you mess this up, Greene—"

"I won't."

"It's not just me you'd have to deal with. It's my dad and Beckett and Seth and I'm pretty sure even Raegan would do some damage."

He lifted the phone and tapped off the speaker. "Speaking of Beckett, I got a text from him an hour ago. Fewer words but basically the same message you're in the middle of. How'd he get my number? I've never even met him." He left the bathroom and ambled into Bear's living room, now crammed with furniture from the coffee shop.

"We're a tight-knit family. There's very little we don't have our fingers in when it comes to each other's lives."

"So Raegan gave him my number?" He climbed past a table from Coffee Coffee.

"Probably. Though I wouldn't put it past Seth, either."

Colton lowered onto the couch, pulled Bear's borrowed leather shoes over, paused, and straightened before putting on the shoes. "Logan, so you know, I'm not . . . This isn't . . . I . . ." Clearly he should've slept more than four restless hours this afternoon.

"You're not playing around," Logan filled in.

"No."

"You really like my sister."

"I do." *Really*-really.

"Okay, then."

"And if you want to pass that message around to all the male Walkers, be my guest."

Logan laughed, and Colton reached for the shoes once more.

"Hey, sidenote: Kate sent me the first few chapters of your book. It's some seriously good stuff."

He tied the laces of Bear's shoes. "I didn't know she was sending it to you."

"Eh, we're both writers. We trade material a lot. It's almost weird reading it, because I know Kate wrote the bulk of it, but it sounds so much like you."

"She's talented."

"And you've spent a lot of time together. You'd have to for her to capture your voice so well."

But that was part of Kate's gifting—she was good not only at telling stories, but at sensing them, hearing them. Drawing a person out. Look at what she'd done with Megan.

"Anyway, I have a feeling this thing's going to be huge for you once it's published. It's going to make a splash."

Colton leaned back against Bear's leather couch, the same niggle of concern that'd been needling him for a few days now—especially in the past twenty-four hours—pricking him again. "Thing is, I'm not all that convinced I want it to make a splash."

He heard Logan whispering to Charlie on the other end. Something about crayons and not drawing on the kitchen table. Then his voice again. "Explain."

"Ever since the injuries, the new goal of this book turned into reviving my career, putting me back in the spotlight. But that might not be what I want. Not anymore. Truth is, I'm not sure why I'm even doing the book at this point."

"I guess I get that. Celebrity's not all it's cracked up to be. I've worked around politicians enough to know that. And yet, you do have a story, Colt. Don't you think it's worth telling?"

Not if it meant killing his chances at having a normal life—the kind of life he'd experienced the past month. All those things Amelia had mentioned during her interview—book tour and signings and publicity events—slipping back into that kind of life held about as much appeal as roasting in a polyester suit on a ninety-five-degree day.

Once upon a time he might've craved notoriety or success lived out in the public eye. But there wasn't a happily ever after to be had there. He was sure of it.

"Maybe the more important question is, if you drop the book, what are you going to tell Kate?"

And that right there—that was the question that'd made getting any kind of real sleep this afternoon almost impossible.

"I have no idea."

❧

"It's times like these I'm glad everybody knows everybody in Maple Valley." Kate touched the handkerchief Colton had used as a blindfold. "If we were somewhere else and people saw this, they'd think a kidnapping was in progress."

Her right hand was enfolded in Colton's as he led her from the car. A teasing wind tickled her nose.

"Careful. Curb."

Colton guided her up the curb and down a sidewalk toward who knew where. He'd insisted on the blindfold before they left Megan's, where he'd picked her up. She'd argued for all of fifteen seconds before giving in. Because it was just too hard to say no to the man when he wore that blue shirt that did amazing things to his already amazing eyes. And when he smelled of spicy aftershave. And when his drawn-out "please" was accompanied by twin dimples.

"I don't know, though, Rosie. For this to really look like a kidnapping I'd probably need to have a weapon of some kind instead of a blanket."

Yeah she'd wondered about that blanket he'd borrowed from Megan. Picnic? But there were few picnic areas unaffected by the flood.

Leaves crunched under their feet until Colton's steps slowed. "All right." He released her hand and moved behind her. She felt his hands near her hair as he worked the knot of the blindfold.

"It's a good thing Megan and Ava didn't see you tying that thing over my hair. They fought with my hair for an eternity trying to get it to behave." Ava had completely surprised her when she'd showed up on Megan's doorstep a couple hours ago.

"Raegan sent me. I've got clothes, hair supplies, everything. Have to admit, my closet is somewhat slim pickings. But I have a couple dresses."

They'd settled on a simple green wrap dress with a tie at

the side—brown boots, matching brown-and-beige scarf, and a jean jacket completed the look. Had Colton ever seen her in anything other than haphazard mixes of jeans and tees, hoodies and oversized plaid?

Her hair had finally ended up pulled over to one side, fastened with a flower-shaped clip the same shade as her hair.

"I don't think I messed it up too much," Colton said now. "But even if I did, I like your hair when it's messy." The blindfold slipped free.

Kate blinked and opened her eyes. Then blinked again as surprise wiggled through her. The old green house? The one she'd told Colton about that night at the corncrib. He moved around to stand beside her now, handkerchief dangling from his hand.

She glanced from the house to the ages-old For Sale sign in the yard to Colton.

"You remembered?"

"Of course. You said, and I quote, 'There's something magical about that old house on Water Street.' I wanted to see it for myself. Plus, I think it's sad you love the place so much but have never been inside."

She looked back to the house. With its wraparound porch and ivy running up the side, even old and run-down, it still felt exactly that—magical, somehow both quaint and regal at the same time.

"What are we going to do, break in?"

He reached into his pocket and pulled out a key hooked to a realty key chain. "Each day I'm here, I learn another perk about small-town living. I talked with the Realtor this afternoon, told her I wanted to use the house as a date locale. She thought it was romantic, and that was my in."

Romantic, indeed. "You're something else—you know that, Colt?"

He picked up the picnic basket and blanket he'd taken from the backseat, laced his fingers through hers once more, and led her to the house. The sidewalk in front of the property was cracked and uneven, bordered by overgrown grass from a lawn that clearly hadn't been mowed in weeks.

The porch steps groaned as they climbed, and in several spots gaps in the wood revealed years of neglect and damage. The porch itself was no better—boards knobby and unsteady, and the railing a mass of splinters waiting to happen.

But none of it ruined the stately feel of the property. It just needed a little TLC.

A porch board underneath her foot wobbled. Okay, maybe a lot of TLC.

Colton fit the key into the house's massive front door and wiggled the knob. "The Realtor said it's stubborn." He jiggled harder until finally the door heaved open.

A musty scent reached out to envelop them as they walked in. The arched entryway spilled into a spacious living room void of furniture but adorned with the kind of woodworking Kate loved about old houses. Some Old English could have this room sparkling in no time.

Colton set down the picnic basket and grinned at her. "Ready to go exploring?"

"Of course. But for the record, Greene, I know we're only a few minutes into this date, but it might be the best one I've ever been on." Not might be. Was.

The comment earned her one of his perfect smiles. And then, for the next twenty minutes, they wandered through the house. The creak of the hardwood floors tracked their movement, and their voices echoed in empty rooms. Rich wood pillars, French doors, a staircase with an ornate banister.

The bathrooms were old, and the kitchen needed more than a

facelift. Probably every window in the house should be replaced. And oy, all the wallpaper.

But for all its wrinkles and obvious signs of age, the house felt every bit as enchanting as it had seemed when she was a kid. Only even better now that she'd had the chance to see inside.

They ended up back in the living room. "So what do you think?"

"I think it's crazy someone with money hasn't already snatched this place up and gone to town on renovations. It's the coolest house ever."

He smiled and reached for the picnic basket. "Why don't you buy it?"

"You must've missed the part about 'someone with money.' Besides, I'm not sure there's much for me in Maple Valley. I mean, my family's here, but what would I do with a massive house?"

Colton handed her the basket. "I have a few things to grab from the car. Want to unload the basket?"

She nodded and he retreated, the sound of his footsteps loud on the porch.

She peeked in the picnic basket. Smiled as her stomach growled. He'd stopped at The Red Door.

By the time Colton returned, she'd unloaded the basket's contents—pulled pork in a leakproof container, sandwich buns, pasta salad, fresh fruit. Two delectable-looking pieces of blueberry pie. Plates, silverware, napkins.

Colton set an overflowing cardboard box in the center of the floor and started unpacking. A bedsheet? And . . . something plastic. An air pump. Computer and projector.

"I have no idea what you're setting up for, but I'm incredibly impressed at your preparation. Didn't you get any sleep after working all night?" Not that he looked tired. Oh no, he looked good. *Good* good.

"Eh, I'm fine. I'm going to need a little help with the sheet, though."

"Where are we going with it?"

He pulled a package of thumbtacks from his pocket. "Hanging it on the wall."

And that's when it started to make sense—the sheet, the projector. "We're going to watch a movie?"

"Yep. I have to admit, as far as movie selection, we're on Plan B. I originally wanted to get *The African Queen*. Figured it might be good to see the movie where your nickname came from. Alas, the library did not have that one. They only had one Katharine Hepburn movie, actually."

Kate tsked. "It's sad, the state of movie viewing in our country. And this is coming from a movie writer. People don't realize what they're missing."

"Well, thanks to you, I am done missing out on the greatness that is, apparently, Golden Era Hollywood."

She accepted one corner of the sheet. "I'd like to reiterate what I said earlier, about this being the best date ever."

An hour later, dusk had pulled all light from the room save the black-and-white movement on the makeshift screen in front of her. The plastic of the blown-up couch—the kind of thing that belonged in a pool or a college dorm room—squealed as she shifted. And Katharine Hepburn and Cary Grant bantered while chasing a leopard around a Connecticut farm—dialogue she had memorized from so many viewings with Mom.

Hepburn: You mean you want me to go home?
Grant: Yes.
Hepburn: You mean you don't want me to help you anymore?
Grant: No.
Hepburn: After all the fun we've had?
Grant: Yes.

Hepburn: And after all the things I've done for you?
Grant: That's what I mean.

"Man, is there any better screen pairing than Grant and Hepburn?" Her whisper slipped out while the movie continued.

"They are pretty great." Colton had stretched his arm around her not long after they finished their food. His fingers brushed through her hair now.

"Not great, Colt. Try amazing. If I could pull off something as witty and hilarious as *Bringing Up Baby* I'd totally keep writing romance scripts. Or maybe even another book." Something fun and romantic this time, instead of the heavy literary tome she'd attempted.

"You could. I know you could."

Perhaps. Between finishing his book and Africa, though, she wouldn't have time in the foreseeable future.

But maybe when she got home. She should be set financially for a little while, at least, right? That advance coming her way from his publisher would cover her bills while she was out of the country, yes, but there should be plenty left over. What if she took some time—tried her hand at writing not another Heartline screenplay but a book? See if she could pull in what she loved about classic rom-coms and come up with the kind of romance she'd like to read.

Then again, after Africa, surely she'd come home with ideas for a bigger story. Something heftier and intense. Wasn't that what she'd been telling herself for years she was supposed to write?

She glanced at Colton now, saw his eyes fluttering closed. Poor man could barely stay awake.

Amazing how he'd found a way to topple the wall around her heart. Not in a crazy dynamite-like explosion or with the force of a wrecking ball, but in a slow brick-by-brick dismantling. The way he poured himself into working with her dad at the depot. How he overtipped at Seth's fledgling restaurant when he thought no one was watching. The way he coached Webster and stuck around to help Megan today.

And tonight.

"You know what, Colt?"

His eyes drifted open. "Hmm?"

"I think agreeing to write your book was the best decision I ever made."

He shifted on the plastic couch, sudden discomfort playing over his face. "It was a good decision. We wouldn't be here otherwise."

"I'm sensing a *but*."

"I wasn't going to bring this up tonight, but since you mentioned it . . ." He reached toward the computer and paused the movie. "I'm having second thoughts about the book, Kate."

Confusion scratched through her. "Well, I'm only seven chapters along. There's plenty of time to change it."

He pulled his arm away from her shoulder. "No, not your draft. I mean the whole thing. It's hit me over the past couple days—I don't know that I actually want to do it. I'm thinking about calling the publisher, seeing what would happen if I broke the contract."

She tried to move away from him, but the size of the makeshift couch made it impossible. So she slid onto the floor instead. "I don't understand. All these weeks of work—"

"I know, I know. But it's like . . . like God called an audible in my life. I'm realizing I don't have to stick to the old play. And sure, I worried if I brought this up you'd feel like I wasted a month's worth of your time. But it wasn't wasted time, not if it led here. To us."

"Yeah, but . . ." But how to tell him it wasn't just the time? It was the fact that she'd pinned her hopes for the future on this book—on the financial security it meant, at least for a time. "You can't just drop it."

"Why not?" He shrugged. "I don't need it."

She jumped to her feet. "Well, I do." Her words came out harsher than she intended. But without a draft to turn in there wouldn't be any check from his publisher, which meant there wouldn't be any trip to Africa.

And she *had* to go on that trip. She might be reconsidering the rest of her life post-Africa. Might have played around in her mind with the idea of coming back home or trying her hand at another book or most appealing hope of all, finding a future with Colton.

But she couldn't do any of that without going to Africa first. Finally—*finally*—keeping her promise to Mom that she'd go, do, write something important.

Now, in one flippant thought, Colton could delete that opportunity from existence.

He rose now, slowly, wincing—from pain in his knee and shoulder or from her reaction? "Look, I didn't mean to upset you, Rosie."

"Kate." *Don't do this, Kate. Don't push him away. He doesn't realize . . .*

But it was his turn to stiffen. "Kate." There was a hard edge to his tone now. "At the end of the day, it's my story to tell, and it has to be up to me whether to tell it. I can't go through with it just so you can have your name on the cover of a bestseller."

That's what he thought this was about?

Hurt turned her away even as he seemed to sense the error in what he'd said.

"Kate—"

"Let's just finish the movie."

This wasn't how the night was supposed to end. Taut silence with only the huff of the car's heater for background noise.

Kate had hardly said a word the rest of the evening. Why they'd even bothered finishing the movie, he didn't know. Chances were Kate had heard as little of its final minutes as he had. They'd cleaned everything up while the credits rolled, the air squeezing out of the blown-up couch a frustratingly obvious metaphor for this date—from inflated and comfortable to flat and pointless.

Beside him, Kate ran both hands over her bare arms. Why hadn't she put her jean jacket back on?

"Cold?"

Only a wordless nod and he upped the heat a notch. *Can't take this anymore.* "I'm sorry I brought up the book, Kate."

Her hands dropped to her lap. "If you were thinking of backing out, you had to bring it up sometime. Might as well have been tonight."

Her barren tone stung. "Can't you at least try to understand where I'm coming from?"

When she didn't reply, he slung the wheel to the left.

"This isn't the way to Megan's."

"We're not going to Megan's. Not yet." He turned onto the road he knew led to the west edge of town—away from Megan's, the river, the lights of Maple Valley. "I'm not doing this—I'm not going to let you clam up and ruin what I think could be something great."

"*I'm* ruining it?"

There, finally. Maybe only three words, but at least she was engaging. "Yeah, you are. You're turning back into the Kate you were when you first came home—Chicago Kate, all reserved and closed off and—"

"I can't believe *you're* calling *me* closed off. And you ever think maybe that's just who I am? That Chicago Kate, whatever that means, is the real me?"

Pavement dissolved into gravel. "No, the real Kate gets into water fights in the bathroom and brags about her arcade basketball skills and climbs up corncribs."

"And ends up with a nail in her foot. Great fun."

Town lights faded in his rearview mirror, replaced by dark and shadows, only a sliver of moonlight slanting in. "It was fun. You were the star of the ER that night, cracking jokes and smiling your way through a tetanus shot."

Tracks of metal and wood sliced into the harvest-stripped field outside his window, the distant sound of a train's horn as it cut through town behind them drifting in.

"It was fun," Kate finally said. He felt her eyes on him as she exhaled. "And tonight was fun. It really was, Colt. You must've put so much work into it."

The train's honking drew closer.

"I don't think I ever explained to you my full situation . . . why I agreed to do the book. I was counting on the advance."

The admission softened the tension between them as realization settled in. "I knew you needed money for your trip, but . . ." Eight years of NFL paychecks, even without his being one of the multi-million-dollar players, meant he didn't often think in terms of what he could and couldn't afford.

Which meant he hadn't even considered the financial impact of hanging up the book contract. No wonder Kate had bristled.

Regret punched through him as the noise of the train's approach clamored in. "Kate, I didn't even think—"

Brash headlights flashed in his rearview mirror, and something heavy tightened inside him. *Weird . . . just like . . .*

The jolt lanced into him without warning. Razor-sharp and impossible to turn back from.

In less time than it took to slam on the brakes, the flashback yanked him in.

Only this time it didn't let him go.

He felt his breath quickening, heard Kate's faint voice saying his name, even as grainy images started forming.

It was dark and it was late.

And he was nine. He sat in the back of Dad's station wagon, arms crossed and ache swelling like a flood inside him. Anger and embarrassment.

"Colton, are you listening?"

Kate?

No, Mom. She was up in the front of the car with Dad. All three of them, riding away from the church like a happy little trio. Only Colton knew the truth. *We're* that *family.*

The ones who dressed in thrift-shop clothes and never took vacations. The ones who cleaned churches and office buildings three evenings a week just so they could make ends meet whenever Dad was laid off.

"I told you we should've gotten a babysitter, Joan."

"What's the point of picking up a few hours cleaning if we have to pay a babysitter while we're gone? Defeats the purpose."

Dad stared him down from the rearview mirror until Colton turned away, eyes on the trees lining the roads, streaked with sunset's orange. Dad flew down the gravel road as if it were a highway.

"Well, he's nine. He's old enough to stay by himself then."

"Not in our neighborhood. You know that."

If only he hadn't wandered onto the stage in that stupid church. But there'd been a lady playing piano, and when she'd spotted him, head poking out between a pew halfway back, she'd beckoned him forward. Asked him if he liked to sing. Handed him a microphone.

And for half an hour, he'd forgotten that he hadn't had dinner yet. That he'd been teased once again at school for how short his jeans were. That Mom and Dad had forgotten to come to his fourth-grade concert that afternoon.

The lady at the front of the church sang with him and laughed with him. Let him pretend to be a rock star. Pulled a camera from her purse and snapped some photos, flash cutting into the unlit sanctuary.

"Smile for the camera, Colton."

When she heard his stomach growl, she gave him a conspiratorial wink and took him to a room with a bunch of toys. She pulled a box of animal crackers from a cupboard and a juice box from a shelf.

Then he'd gone and spilled the juice. And that's when Dad had found him.

At least he'd waited to yell until they were in the car.

"Who knows what that woman thinks of us now. She's the pastor's wife, you know. We could get fired."

Colton saw Mom roll her eyes in her mirror. "We're not going to get fired because Colton spilled juice. It was in the nursery, for Pete's sake."

Colton's stomach churned for what felt like the hundredth time. He hugged his arms tighter to his body. A rock hit the window from the gravel underneath the station wagon's tires.

"Slow down, Alan. The last thing we need is a car accident. Especially now that we're down to one car."

"And why was she giving him food anyway? We're not destitute."

She was just being nice, Dad.

"That's just what we need. A busybody pastor's wife thinking we're a charity case."

"If the factory doesn't take you back soon, that's exactly what we'll be."

Dad slapped the steering wheel.

"The unemployment check, the cleaning, my hours at the hospital. They're not cutting it. We've got to figure something out."

"You don't think I know that?"

"I called the office . . . about food stamps."

No, Mom . . .

"How many times—"

"Don't start with me, Alan. Don't even—"

"Stop fighting." The words exploded from him before he could stop them, loud and angry and accented by his head hitting the back of his seat. "Stop it. You always fight. That's all you do. You don't take care of me like other parents do. You don't give me supper 'til it's dark." He felt like he might burst with the feelings knotting through him.

Sometime during his tirade, Dad had slowed to a stop, right in the middle of the road. And when the last word pushed past his lips, his father turned. Stone-faced, steely-eyed. "Get out."

"What?" The question was barely a peep.

"Alan."

"We're less than a mile from home. He can walk the rest of the way."

"You are not making him get out of this car. If you do I'm getting out with him."

Dad ignored Mom. "You know the way. Follow the road, over the railroad tracks, then up the alley to the apartment building."

When Colton didn't move, Dad shifted in his seat, stretching one arm behind him to open Colton's door. "Go. Now."

He glanced at Mom once more, waited for another argument. Mom reached for her door, but the glare Dad sent her froze her solid. Finally, he unhooked his seat belt and stepped into the near-dark.

"Al—" He heard Mom try once more, but Dad yanked the

door closed before she could finish, rock and dust erupting under the tires as he sped away.

Colton just looked down at his feet. Had Dad forgotten he'd taken off his shoes because they were covered with juice? He wore only socks on his feet underneath his too-short jeans. A mosquito buzzed past his ear and landed on his arm. In his shock he didn't even bother slapping it away.

He started walking, eyes to where the last sliver of sunlight beckoned on the horizon, refusing to look to his right or his left, where shadows floating in the trees threatened his imagination.

And then he heard it.

Honking—not a car, but a train. And the screech of wheels on metal, dragging and shrill. A crash. Unmistakable.

And he was running. And crying—the tearing of his feet and the pangs in his stomach forgotten. Because he knew . . .

The sun was gone by the time he reached the accident, sirens already sounding in the distance. Smoke and fire, someone yelling from inside the train.

And screaming, so loud it hurt his ears and pulsed in his head until he finally realized it was him. He'd sunk to the road, knees digging into the dusty ground.

"Colton!"

Someone shook his arm, but all he could feel was horror, waves of it, drowning him.

"Colton, you're scaring me."

More shaking, and in a moment that stretched until it broke, the flashback dissolved. His heart raced and head throbbed, but he was back in the present. With Kate looking at him as if he were a ghost.

And he was shaking, just like he had that day in the road, shock shuddering through him. When had he pulled to the side of the road?

"What happened? Was it another flashback?"

He couldn't force wind past his vocal cords, wouldn't have been able to find words if he could. With a jerk, he shifted the car into drive and spun around to face town.

The engine groaned. "Careful, Colt. We're on gravel and we're not the only ones on the road."

He ignored her.

"Please, talk to me. Tell me what just happened."

But before she could finish the word, a form leapt into the road in front of them. A deer?

Kate's scream collided with the sound of skidding gravel as Colton swerved, only to see another car approaching—its headlights barreling toward Kate's door.

Please, God. Please, please . . . no.

And then the impact.

17

"olton, we need to take some X-rays, see what we've got going on. It's your knee I'm most concerned about."

"Well, I'm not. I told you, it's an old injury."

The doctor's skeptical expression was focused on the jagged white scar over his kneecap. "Not that old."

Colton couldn't handle just sitting here anymore. It was bad enough they'd made him ride to the hospital separately from Kate. He'd stood there on that back road, numb and helpless, watching the ambulance race away, its wailing siren like an echo of his fear.

It could've been so much worse. The police officer's words hadn't come close to calming him. *The other driver is okay. And Kate's injuries don't appear to be life threatening.*

Had he *seen* her? Unconscious. Bloody. That protruding bone in her arm . . .

Colton had flinched, had to steady himself against what was left of Kate's car.

"We need to get you to the hospital."

"Case. I have to call Case and Raegan—"

"He's already been called. Emergency Management is helping them get across the river. I need you to come with me."

Colton now slid from the paper-covered table, the small patient room in the ER suddenly claustrophobic. The second his weight hit his legs, though, he couldn't hide his wince. Pain shot up from his knee, sharp as the glass shards the nurse had picked from his forehead only minutes ago.

But he didn't care about any of that. "I need to know how Kate is." He reached down to unroll his pant leg, trapped dirt now dusting to the floor.

"I told you, as soon as we have information—"

"I should be out in the waiting area when her dad gets here."

"He just got here," the nurse who'd reentered the room only seconds ago interjected softly.

"Colton, I don't—"

He ignored the doctor, ignored the pangs going off like firecrackers throughout his body, and limped to the door. Fluorescent lights glared from overhead as he followed the blue stripe on the wall toward the ER's waiting area.

He heard Case's voice before he saw him. "Katharine Walker. She was in a car accident."

"Oh yes, she's back—"

"Colton!" Raegan called the second she saw him, hurrying over to him, eyes betraying her dismay at the sight of him. He hadn't looked in a mirror, but he could guess how he appeared. Oxford unbuttoned—both it and the white shirt underneath stained with dirt and blood. Scrapes over his forehead where windshield glass had embedded itself. "Where's Kate? How is she? How are you?"

Case was at his side now, too, more concern than Colton deserved playing over his face.

"I don't know. They made me ride separately and took me to a room as soon as I got here. I keep asking—"

"Colton." The doctor's voice, his footsteps approaching from behind.

Colton's irritation expanded as he whirled around. "I told you, I'm not doing X-rays or anything else until we get some information on Kate."

Case stepped forward. "Dr. Woodard, good, I was hoping you'd be on duty tonight. How's my daughter?"

Of course Case knew the doctor. Probably knew most of the staff. Maybe his influence would gain them the update Colton's pushing hadn't.

But Dr. Woodard only shook his head. "I'm sorry, she's back with Dr. Morris now. I don't have an update yet, but I can go back and find out what's happening." He slid a chastising glance at Colton. "And in the meantime, if you can talk this one into letting us tend to him, that'd be good. His knee isn't okay, no matter what he tells you."

The doctor turned, white coat flapping behind him. And from across the room, the sound of a revolving door's whir ushered in more hurried footsteps. Seth, Ava . . . even Bear.

"How is she?"

Colton couldn't make out who asked the question. It was all he could do to stay upright, the numb rush of the past hour finally wearing off and leaving in its place such a revulsion he thought he might throw up.

But then Case's hand landed on his shoulder—not the bad one—a steadying presence. "What happened, son?"

Raegan was talking to the others, explaining that they were waiting for an update.

"I . . . we . . ." He gulped in a ragged breath. "We were just driving, talking. And then I . . . there was a train." It tightened his lungs all over again, the memory. "I had a flashback. I get them sometimes."

But never like he had tonight.

"And then I turned the car around and next thing I knew there was a deer and another car and we hit."

Oh, God, what did I do? If he'd just taken her back to Megan's.

"It's my fault." He could feel the eyes of everyone on him now.

Kate's dad and sister and cousin and friends and . . . "Logan. I should call Logan and Beckett. They—"

"We've already done that, Colton." Case spoke gently. "And no more talk of it being your fault. From the sounds of it, it was a deer. Those things cause more accidents . . ." He squeezed Colton's shoulder.

Colton didn't argue. Not out loud anyway. But he knew.

He'd been the one to insist they keep driving.

He'd been the one to pick then, of all times, to suddenly fully remember something he'd blocked out for twenty years.

He'd been the one to swerve the car back toward town, faster than he should . . .

It *was* his fault. And if Kate wasn't okay, he didn't know what he'd do.

"We should sit down." Raegan's tone was soft. "And you should get that knee looked at."

"Not until we know about Kate."

"Okay, good, this must be Kate's crew."

Colton spun, everybody bunching around him as a doctor appeared from around the corner.

"Dr. Morris?" Case stepped forward, hand outstretched.

The doctor shook his hand. "The good news is, she's going to be fine. She's going to walk again. Everything's fixable."

Colton could feel the whole group let out a collective breath.

"You say she's going to walk *again*," Case said. "That means she's not going to for . . ."

The doctor nodded in confirmation. "For a while. Her right arm was a clean break. We've already set it and it's almost done getting casted. Her right leg is a different story. She's going to need surgery, and I want to send her to Ames for that. So it'll be a while before she's up and about. Probably take some physical therapy for a few months after, but again, nothing we can't fix."

Months. What about Africa?

"I can give you more information on the surgery and how we'd like to move forward, but first I thought you might want to see her. She's also got a couple cracked ribs, so no tight hugs."

Relief fanned through their little group, but Colton couldn't grab hold of it. Broken arm, broken leg, cracked ribs. Kate . . . his Kate.

Not my Kate.

Not anymore.

"Of course, we want to see her," Raegan was saying now, her hand encased in Bear's. "Can we all go back?"

Dr. Morris smiled. How could he look so relaxed after the news he'd just delivered? "I think so. For a few minutes anyway."

The group began moving forward. Not Colton.

Case turned. "Colt?"

"You guys go on. I'm going to . . ." He closed his eyes. Opened them again. "I'll go get those X-rays."

"She'll want to see you."

"She's not going to be able to go to Africa, Case. You heard what the doctor said. She's going to be in PT for months." She'd already put her life on hold for a month, just so she could write his book—and then he'd gone and told her he was thinking of calling it quits. Now he wrecked the one thing she'd wanted more than anything? "I ruined it for her."

"You don't know that, son. Maybe the foundation will be able to postpone her trip. Maybe she'll recover faster than the doctor expects."

The rest of the group disappeared around the corner. "You should go."

"And you should come with." Case's voice hit a firm tone. But when Colton only shook his head, the older man finally sighed. "Well, okay. Then come back after your X-rays."

Colton nodded. But as soon as Case hurried out of sight, he turned and hobbled to the exit.

⤳⟆

"I. Love. Pain-killers."

Everyone in the room burst into laughter at Kate's declaration.

"What? If you had four broken bones—well, two broken, two cracked—not to mention enough glass removed from your skin to make a stained-glass window, you'd thank the Lord for modern medicine, too."

Raegan ran a brush through Kate's hair as she perched on the side of the hospital bed. "What I'm thanking the Lord for is that somehow you're cracking jokes just hours after a car accident."

Had to be the medicine.

Or maybe honest-to-goodness thankfulness. She was alive. Tonight could've ended so differently.

And now she was surrounded by family who'd left her room only long enough to buy flowers and balloons in the hospital gift shop, buy her every flavor of M&M's from the vending machine, and find her a jacket to put on over her dress until Seth and Ava got back from the house with clean clothes. Apparently they were getting a ride in the same Emergency Management boat that had delivered Dad and Raegan across the river.

If only Colton would walk through the glass door leading into her room. Where was he? She'd asked about him earlier. Dad said something about X-rays. But that was over an hour ago.

Dad was the only one who hadn't left her room even once. He watched her now from the vinyl chair he'd pulled to her bedside.

"I'm okay, Dad."

He had the same haggard look he'd had when she first came home weeks ago.

He leaned forward to grasp her fingers, extending from a gleaming white cast. "Of course, you are."

In the corner of her room, Bear held up her phone. "Megan texted back. 'WHAT?' That's in all-caps. 'Glad you're okay. Idiot deer. How's that guy?' I assume she means Colton?"

She wished she knew how Colton was. Dad said he didn't have serious injuries, but . . .

But they hadn't seen him in the car. Physically he might be fine. But something had happened tonight. The need to see him now coursed through her, overwhelmingly strong.

Pain-killers couldn't help with that.

"Can you text her back and let her know he's okay?"

Raegan finished brushing her hair and stood. "I'll go look for him, okay? He has to be done with the X-rays by now."

Her sister read her well.

Bear accompanied Raegan out the door, leaving Kate alone with Dad. Bobbing balloons filled the counter behind him. And behind that, a narrow window peeked on the black night. How late was it now? Had to be close to midnight, surely.

"So Dr. Morris filled you in on the surgery and everything?"

Dad nodded. "I'm afraid you've got somewhat of a long road in front of you, Katie."

"I know." She shifted on the stark white sheets of the hospital bed, her propped leg making any kind of comfortable position impossible and the cast weighing her right arm. "And the road definitely does not lead to Africa."

She'd known it before the doctor even started talking surgery and physical therapy. A feeling. She'd probably feel the disappointment more keenly tomorrow or next week or whenever the shock of all that'd happened tonight wore off. It'd sink in, eventually, that the open door she'd been so sure was from God had been so swiftly and forcefully closed.

But tonight . . . tonight she couldn't bring herself to think past her next conversation with Colton. If he'd just show up.

"You talked to Colton when you first got here, right? He told you everything that happened?" She licked her dry lips.

Dad lifted a glass of water from the bedside stand, held it for her while she sipped from the straw. "He told me what happened. In very monosyllabic terms, that is. He said something about a flashback."

"He remembered the accident that killed his parents."

It'd happened so fast. One minute they were talking—about his book. It'd seemed so important then. The next, a train was rushing past and Colton was going white and thank goodness he'd somehow managed to slow and brake in the midst of whatever turmoil had taken over his mind.

"You should've seen him, Dad. It was like his body was in the car but the rest of him wasn't. It was terrifying to watch. I can't imagine . . ." A pain much sharper than any of her physical injuries winded her. "It was almost scarier than the accident."

"At least you were with him."

"I don't think I helped at all, though. He didn't seem to hear me afterward. And then the accident happened right away and—" She cut off, jerked in the bed to face Dad. "He thinks it's his fault, doesn't he? That's why he hasn't come in. Oh my goodness, he's sitting somewhere in this hospital blaming himself."

"Kate—"

"We have to tell him it's not his fault." Her first real tears of the night finally started falling, streaming down her cheeks in hot trails. "That stupid deer could've jumped out in front of anybody."

"He knows that."

"I don't think he does. Otherwise he'd be here." She shook her head, sniffles clogging her voice, emotions now beyond her control. "Does he know I can't go to Africa?"

Resignation creased Dad's face. "I'm afraid so."

"H-he'll blame himself for that, too. We have to find him, Dad. D-drag him in here, if you have to. I have to tell him."

Dad handed her a tissue, but it wasn't enough for the rush of tears that'd turned into full sobs. "Tell him what?"

"That I . . ." *That I love him.*

Oh, Lord, I do, I love him. And he's hurting . . . and I'm . . . Losing it.

Or maybe the pain-killers were wearing off.

Or maybe this was a second round of shock.

Whatever it was, it shook through her. "I just need to talk to him."

Dad leaned closer, pulling her head to his shoulder. "We'll find him, honey. It's going to be okay."

She squeezed her eyes closed, letting her father's comfort wash over her.

"It's going to be okay," he repeated.

She sniffled once more, willed the sobs to stop welling in her throat. Deep breaths. Dad's fingers brushed the hair from her forehead, and he leaned her back against her pillows. "Why don't you try to rest for a few minutes."

She forced her eyes open. "As soon as they find Colton, you'll make him come in here?"

"I promise."

She let her eyes drift closed again, heard the creak of Dad's chair as he stood. Maybe the pain-killers hadn't worn off, after all, because she could feel her body finally relaxing, her thoughts releasing . . .

Until footsteps padded into the room. Soft voices. She strained to hear above the pull of her fatigue, tried to open her eyes.

"We think he left."

"Left the hospital?"

She gave in to sleep at Raegan's reply. "Left town."

310

18

*Y*ou've got two casts. You're sitting in a wheelchair. And you're attempting to rake leaves?"

At the sound of Megan's flat voice and her footsteps swishing through a blanket of gnarled leaves, Kate turned her wheelchair, dragging her rake with her. "Not attempting. Look at my pile."

Megan glanced over the leaves Kate had managed to sweep into a cluster—then over to where Dad worked. November hadn't wasted time making its mark this year, arriving in a bluster of cold temps and stripped-bare trees, turning Dad's backyard into a wash of burgundy and brown.

"Yeah," Megan said slowly. "Kinda like the Flint Hills up against the Rockies."

"Hey, if I had use of both arms and both legs, I'd have the Everest of piles going."

Megan thrust the covered coffee cup she held forward. "Here."

Kate could smell the coffee before she reached for it. "Pumpkin spice?"

"Obviously." Fingerless gloves covered Megan's hands, and she wore a tight black tank top over a hot pink long-sleeved shirt, black-and-white striped skirt, black leggings.

"Thanks for the coffee. You're looking very punk rocker today, Meg."

She eyed the chair. "And you're looking very Deborah Kerr at the end of *An Affair to Remember*. When do you get out of that thing?"

"Arm cast comes off tomorrow, which means I graduate to crutches." Kate followed her sip of coffee with a grin. "By the way, your classic movie education might be one of the greater accomplishments of my life." And a much needed distraction in the past four—almost five—weeks.

Megan shifted her weight from foot to foot, as if reluctant to spit out her next words. Finally she picked up Kate's rake and swept it over the ground, leaves crunching.

"You don't have to do that."

"If you want to get anywhere with your section of the yard, I do. Anyway, I came to tell you, I might not have as much time to watch movies starting tomorrow."

"What's tomorrow?"

Megan paused, leaned her elbow on the end of her rake, and raised her eyebrows. "Look at your cup."

Kate held it up, focus finally hooking on the Coffee Coffee logo on its side. "Oh my goodness, the shop. You're ready to reopen?"

"New flooring got installed yesterday. Furniture's going in today." She resumed raking. "Would've been done even sooner if the insurance claim hadn't taken so long to come through. But I guess considering everything, a month wasn't so bad."

Wow, had it really been a full month since the flood? Weird how quickly it'd all passed. First the surgery, a few days in the hospital, finally back home and halfway mobile thanks to the wheelchair on loan from the hospital. Somewhere along the way, the bruises all over her right side had healed and the scratches along her forehead had faded.

Sure, she had a couple months, at least, of PT ahead of her. But for the most part, her physical injuries were healing.

Just wished she could say the same for the emotional ones. "You still haven't heard from Colton."

For all her attempts at droll and uninterested, Megan read her awfully well.

"Only a couple emails." Letting her know he was back in LA, confirming that the publisher had let him out of his contract. But never any explanation about what'd happened in the car that night. Why he'd just up and left town.

Left her. Would a good-bye have been so much to ask? A two-minute stop by her hospital room to tell her in person whatever she thought they'd started had come to a swift and abrupt end?

"I can't believe I thought he was such a great guy." Megan's rake slapped at the leaves on the ground. "The way he helped that day at Coffee Coffee and all? I was convinced he was a regular Captain America type."

Kate couldn't keep following this line of conversation. "So the coffee shop reopening."

"That's some impressive segue skill you've got."

"Right up there with my raking skills." Kate wheeled herself out of the path of Megan's rake. "But seriously, you handled the whole thing like a pro, Meg. Not a lot of twenty-one-year-olds would've come through that on their feet."

Like every other business along the riverfront, Coffee Coffee's damage had been extensive. Flooring, plumbing, wiring—all of it had suffered. Its foundation had been compromised, its walls water-stained and stripped.

But Megan had found the determination to tackle the aftermath. The entire community had, really—just like after the tornado. It'd taken almost a full week for the river to recede, but once it did, they'd thrown themselves into piecing the town back together.

"So when do you head back to Chicago?" Megan asked.

"In a few days. Raegan's playing chauffeur. She's going to stay with me for a couple weeks. At least until my leg cast is off." Because Bear had finally talked to her about his plans. And though Raegan was still insistent on her desire to stay in Maple Valley long-term, she needed a temporary escape.

As for Kate, she didn't have a clue what Chicago held for her. She'd had to call Frederick Langston weeks ago and back out of the Africa trip—a conversation that'd left her mopey for days. She'd had such a perfect plan there for a while: Write Colton's book, go to Africa, come home brimming with project ideas . . . and then maybe, finally, write what she'd been born to write. Whatever that was.

Now she was jobless and idealess.

Heart muddled.

But the one thing she knew was, despite Dad's repeated offers, she couldn't stay in Maple Valley. She had to figure out what came next. Decide what she wanted and go after it . . . instead of waiting for it to come after her.

"I'll see you again before you leave, right?" Megan's hopeful voice cut in.

Kate found a smile. "Of course. Because I don't think I've, as of yet, fully convinced you to consider naming your baby after me. I'm not giving up."

"What if it's a boy?"

"Walker would make a great name for a baby boy."

Megan only smirked and kept raking.

Later, after she'd departed, Kate rolled her chair over knotty ground to where Dad was now gathering leaves into black garbage bags. The cool, the smell of fall, the brilliant blue of the sky against a backdrop of craggy brown trees . . .

Kate was going to miss this.

"You should be wearing a coat, Katie."

"Eh, heaving myself around in this thing keeps me plenty warm."

Dad tied a bag closed and dropped it to the ground. "I'm ready for a break. Care to take a walk with me?" He moved behind her chair and began pushing.

"I don't think crutches are going to be the most fun thing in the world, but they're going to be a major step up." Dad pushed her toward the line of trees where his yard ended and the ravine began. "Ooh, you're not going to push me down the ravine, are you? That seems dangerous."

"I may be pushing sixty, my girl, but I'm capable of controlling a wheelchair on a hill." Leaves and sticks crunched under her wheels and his feet.

"But why—"

"I never went down to see if our little bridge made it through the tornado. Didn't want to know if it didn't."

He angled her around trees, descending toward the twisting creek she could already hear. "I don't know how it could've survived." It'd been more crude walkway than actual bridge, just a few boards nailed together and reaching across the narrow creek.

Slivers of blue sky slanted through stretching trees. Kate gripped the arms of her chair as the ravine steepened and Dad's steps shuffled. Finally the ground leveled and they entered the clearing where the creek became visible.

And there, that little makeshift bridge. The one she'd told Colton about that night at the silo. Fully intact.

"Will you look at that? How in the world . . ." An awed reverence hovered in Dad's voice as he rolled Kate over muddy ground, cushioned by the creek that must've overflowed during the flood. He rolled her onto the walkway, set the brake, then sat down on the bridge, legs dangling over the side.

Kate cleared her throat. "I love this place, Dad. I love all the stories of yours and Mom's moments here through the years."

Dad chuckled. "Oh, I know that. You used to ask your mother over and over to tell you the story of the boy and the girl who met right here. How the boy decorated the bridge one night and how they danced until curfew."

"And they fell in love and she never stopped missing him when he went away to war," Kate picked up the story.

"And how even when her letters stopped, he didn't stop missing her."

Kate laid her casted arm in her lap. "And how they saw each other again when he came home. Then a couple years later. And a couple more years later."

Dad turned to her. "Until they finally both ran into each other once more, during the very first Depot Day event."

"And you asked her to marry you before she could get away again. And after a few years away, you moved back home and built her a house not far from the little bridge." Kate's hair tickled her cheeks in the breeze.

"Flora and I used to laugh about the fact that no matter how many times she recited our story to you, you never got tired of hearing it again. You were a romantic from the start, daughter."

"Or I just knew a good story when I heard it."

He shook his head and looked up at her. "I don't mind telling you, I've been a little worried about you."

"Dad, I'm going to be fine. My arm goes free tomorrow and my leg—"

"Not that." He tapped his heart. "This. I've been concerned you sort of turned off your heart. Maybe because of Gil. Maybe because seeing me lose your mom scared you. Whatever the reason, you lost sight of the little girl who so loved a romantic story that she begged her mom to tell it over and over."

Patterned sunlight filtered through the trees. "I write romance for a living."

"You write it. You sure don't live it."

"Dad!"

He spread his hands. "Sorry to be harsh, but you're going back to Chicago and I might not get this chance again. You're not getting up that hill on your own in a wheelchair, so I'm not losing out on the opportunity."

"You just told me I'm incapable of romance, and now you're bragging about trapping me down here?"

"You're not incapable, Katie. Your crying in the hospital proved that."

Great, she'd been hoping they could just forget her little sob fest the night of the accident. "I'm completely lost in this conversation."

He waited until she met his eyes, that Case Walker brand of gentleness and firmness mingling together in his expression. "You know the rules of romance, Katharine. You know the facts of what makes a romantic story work. But you haven't let yourself experience it." He moved to a kneeling position beside her. "And look, I don't particularly like seeing you hurt, but a life completely free from heartbreak? I can't want that for you. It'd mean your heart was hard. Steeled. Unmovable."

He set one hand on her knee. "But when you started crying that night in the hospital, I knew my girl was back."

"Because I broke down about a guy?" Her hair fanned against her cheeks and forehead, and she dug her uncasted hand into her pocket, fingers numbing in the cold.

"Because you'd fallen in love. Not in a wishy-washy, Hallmark card sort of way. But in a way that had you more worried about Colton's mental state than your physical state. You fell for him. Hard."

She could argue, but what was the point? Dad knew her—*oh*, he knew her. "Maybe I did, but look where it got me."

He grinned and stood, his shadow swallowing hers. "It got you right here. Softened. Flexible. Willing to consider maybe God knows better than you what your life should look like. And like this little bridge that weathered a slew of storms, ready to be used."

~~~

He should've called. Or emailed. A carrier pigeon with a handwritten note probably would've been better than just showing up on Norah Parker's doorstep.

But impulse had landed Colton here, standing outside a brick townhouse on a bustling LA street on a suffocating November day. Ninety degrees in autumn? It didn't feel right.

But then, there was little about the past month that had felt right.

A car with a grumbling muffler passed behind him, the smell of motor oil trailing behind it. He pulled his T-shirt away from his chest, wishing for a burst of cool air, then rang the doorbell.

Movement thumped from inside the house, and the front door swung open.

The sound of the noisy car faded down the street as the woman who answered the door stared, blinked . . . grinned. "Colton Greene."

"Hi, Norah."

"Colton Greene. Oh my word."

He stared at her while she stared at him. How was it possible she could've changed so little in over ten years? Same ebony skin and high cheekbones, the kind of beauty that even as a kid he'd known belonged in a magazine or something.

Not in a tiny office in a rundown building, dealing with angry kids like him.

But there was one difference. An obvious one.

"Oh come in and hug me already. I've still got a few weeks 'til the due date. I won't pop."

She stepped aside so he could enter the house, closed the screen door behind him, then pulled him into a hug. He leaned in for the embrace, a hundred memories skipping through his mind as he did. The first time she'd hugged him, when she'd dropped him off at the transitional home not a week after Mom and Dad died. That hug on the day his first foster parents sent him back, after they'd broken every last figurine from the box in her trunk.

The hug he'd stiffened through the last time he saw her.

Except—except that wasn't technically the last time he'd seen her. He'd finally figured it out—the voice he'd heard when he first woke up in the hospital back in January. He'd thought for so long it was Lilah. But it was Norah. He'd sent her tickets to that game—she'd seen him get injured.

And she'd come to the hospital.

She leaned back now, looking him up and down, letting out a slow whistle. "I knew when you were a teen you'd turn out good, Colt. Although you could use a haircut." The sound of laughter drifted from farther back in the house. "Come on back to the kitchen."

He followed her down a hallway, walls sprinkled with framed photos and prints from what appeared to be European countries. "You finally got to backpack through Europe?"

They passed an arched opening leading into a dining room, its floor scattered with toys.

"Two summers ago. Right before we adopted the boys, who you're just about to meet."

"And who's we?"

She led him into the kitchen. "My husband, of course. Waltzed into my life right on my thirty-eighth birthday. I was out celebrating with some girlfriends at this new restaurant, and of course they had to tell our waiter it was my birthday. Next thing I know, the chef is coming out from the kitchen with a dessert, singing some whackadoo version of the 'Happy Birthday' song. It was love at first sight."

Sunlight streamed into the kitchen through the window over the sink, white cupboards and pale yellow walls adding to the bright feel of the room. At the table in the corner, two identical toddlers giggled from their high chairs.

"Korean," Norah answered his questioning glance. "Henry and Lee."

"They're cute."

"Since I was almost forty when we got married, we just assumed adoption might be our best route. Lo and behold, three weeks after we get the boys home, I find out I'm pregnant . . . at forty-three. Funny how life works out."

"Yeah. Funny."

She beckoned for him to sit, and he lowered into a wooden chair with curved spindles at the back, while she dished cookies onto a plate and poured two glasses of milk. She set it all in front of him, then dropped into the chair beside her kids.

Norah pinned him with one of her leveling expressions then. "So tell me what you're doing here."

And it spilled from him, just like that—everything. The weeks in Iowa, the flashback on the gravel road. The accident. Kate.

At some point during his rambling Henry started crying, and Norah released him from his high chair, pulling him onto her lap.

320

"Now I'm back in LA, just tooling around doing nothing." Trying to forget Kate—and how he'd ruined everything for her.

And it wasn't just her he'd left behind. There was also Webster. And the town, finally recovered from one natural disaster only to face another. Case and Seth and Raegan—friends who'd started to feel like family.

"Well, that's stupid."

He about spit out the drink of milk he'd just taken. "Excuse me?"

Norah's flintlike expression pierced him. "Let me get this straight: You remembered your parents' accident. Then a deer jumped out in front of your car. And those two things together resulted in you walking away from the love of your life."

"I didn't say Kate was—"

"Didn't have to. I know you, Colton Greene. Shoot, at one time, I wanted to adopt you."

"What?"

She rubbed Henry's back as his eyes drooped. "When I picked you up from your third foster home and the look on your face . . . Every maternal instinct in me cried to do something about it. I walked into my supervisor's office and declared I was done yanking you around. I was going to adopt you myself. 'Course, she had to go and point out you were a preteen and I was only a few years out of college and it wasn't going to happen. Kind of hilarious to think about now since we're both adults."

He swallowed. "Well, thanks for the thought anyway."

Her expression firmed again. "Why'd you come here?"

"Had a hankering to be called stupid, I guess." He helped Lee take a drink from a sippy cup.

"I didn't call *you* stupid. Just what you're doing."

"Stupid is as stupid does."

"Colton."

He set down Lee's cup. "Okay. I thought . . . I thought you might have advice for me. I remembered when I was seventeen and had no clue what came next and you helped me fill out all those college and scholarship applications."

"That? We were just working with what you had, Colt. You had a talent for football." Henry fussed in her lap again, and she shifted him to the other shoulder. "So what do you have now?"

An achy heart that wouldn't allow him to forget the girl he'd left behind—in a hospital room of all places.

An inexplicable tug to return to a town that wasn't even his home.

"I guess I've got this foundation. It never got going, and the director resigned. I was thinking of closing it down at the end of the year, but I don't know, maybe I could do something good with it." He leaned his elbows on the table, first faint glimpses of what might be a future sliding in.

"There you go. You do realize you're in a much better place than a lot of guys who find themselves stuck, right? You've got financial security. You've got some options. Now it's a matter of figuring out where what you've got meets, well, what the world might need."

The hum of the refrigerator kicked in. "Case Walker—that's Kate's dad, the guy I worked with in Iowa—he told me this story about Raymond Berry, the football player slash coach. He said . . . I have eleven more inches."

"I have no idea what that means." When Henry started wiggling in her arms, Norah stood and paced beside the table. "But here's something else you have that you didn't before. You've got faith."

"Not a very strong one."

"Not sure it's so much about strong or weak. It's not like a

322

sport—you don't get injured and just stop playing. Not unless you choose to." She stopped walking. "You've had a lot stripped out of your life, Colton. But I think a lot of times, it's when the stuff we think we want is stripped away, we finally see what we need. And spoiler: It's not a career or a tidied-up past. It's not a place or a person."

In other words, not even Kate. Or Maple Valley. Or a normal life. Whatever that looked like. "Then what is it?"

"It's knowing you were created by a God who loves you. Finding your purpose in that and that alone. Maybe it sounds simplistic, but I think when you get to that place of security and confidence, your playing field's going to expand like you wouldn't believe."

"Eleven more inches." Just like Case said.

"I still don't know what that means."

"Not sure I do either. Not yet. But . . ." But maybe that was okay. Relief unfolded in him, rife with possibility. And promise—that there was more, even if he wasn't sure just yet what it looked like.

Yeah, maybe it was more than okay.

～？

"Okay, everything's in from the car. My stuff's in the guest bedroom." Raegan stood in the center of Kate's living room, hands on her hips, gaze scanning the space. "Your poor plants. You didn't have anybody come water them while you were away?"

"I watered them that week I came back when Breydan was in the hospital." Kate shuffled on her crutches to the couch. Man, what a relief it'd be to get the plaster off her leg. This hobbling thing was getting old.

"And that was nearly two months ago. Your whole place

needs a sprucing up." Raegan ran one finger through the dust covering the fireplace mantel.

"Good thing I brought a little sister home with me, then, huh." Her old couch whined as she settled in, and what was that crinkling underneath her?

"So between leaving Maple Valley and now, we've determined that in the next two weeks I will be your housekeeper, cook, chauffeur—"

"Don't forget laundress. Isn't *laundress* a great word?" She pulled a wrinkled paper out from underneath her.

"—and errand girl. Anything else I should be doing in all the gobs of free time I'm obviously going to have?" Sarcasm laced Raegan's tone.

"Well, you could finally talk to me about Bear." She unfolded the paper.

"Off-limits, Kate. Besides, it's not like you've been chatty about Colton."

To Gil. The words on the paper stared back at her. The dedication page from her book. The one Colton had torn out and wadded up. A familiar ache swiveled through her.

That and his voice from the night they'd sat in the big green house in Maple Valley, when he'd told her he knew she could write another book.

And Dad, calling her a romantic and assuring her a wounded heart just might be a good sign.

"Hey, where'd my laptop end up, Rae?"

"Kitchen table, I think. Need it?"

Kate set the creased page on the couch beside her and nodded. "I feel like doing a little writing."

19

Four months ago Kate had called this big green house magical.

And she just might be right.

"Which color, Colton?"

Raegan pointed to three streaks of beige paint on the otherwise white wall of the oversized living room. Or what would be a living room once he'd bought furniture and restained the hardwood floor and filled it up with people. "What do you mean which color? They're all the same, aren't they?"

Seth passed between Colton and Raegan, carrying two cans of varnish.

"No, they're not the same." Raegan rolled her eyes and pointed from brushstroke to brushstroke. "This one's On the Rocks. This one's Buff. And this one's Creamy Beige."

"I still say they all look the same. You pick."

She turned back to the wall with an overdone sigh. "Men."

He grinned and turned a full circle in the room. Seth and Ava were varnishing the ornate wooden banister leading upstairs, and Bear was sanding away the last of the grooves in the floor—while managing to avoid Raegan. *Hmm, wonder what that is about?*

And somewhere Webster was supposed to be collecting dinner orders. It was the least Colton could do, provide an evening meal for the people who'd given up yet another winter weeknight to help him renovate the house on Water Street.

Parker House. A home for young men transitioning from foster care to independence.

Had such a good ring to it.

He'd asked God for his eleven inches.

And in reply had been given the gift of a calling.

"You know, one of these days you're going to have to let us tell Kate."

Raegan. She'd abandoned her wall and now stood beside him, arms folded. He'd been surprised when he returned to Maple Valley in early January to see the streaks of pink gone from her hair. She'd seemed subdued at first—and not entirely overjoyed to see him.

He couldn't blame her. Not after the way he'd left. Not considering the thread of family loyalty that wove the Walkers together.

But once he'd explained his reason for coming back, his plans for this house, each member of the family had come to embrace his vision. Not only that, they'd helped him make it happen. Were helping him still. At that moment, Case was at a city council meeting to find out how the council was going to vote on Colton's zoning request.

"Hello. Earth to Colton."

He blinked. "Tell Kate. Right. I'll get on that right now." Or not.

And clearly Raegan wasn't buying. "She's going to find out eventually. You asked us to keep it on the down low, and we won't tell her, but we're not the only people she keeps in touch with. She talks to Megan at least once a week."

"If she finds out, she finds out. I'm not trying to keep a long-term secret here, Rae." He just . . . He hated the thought of intruding on Kate's life again. Would he love it if she showed back up in town—somehow forgot about all the hurt he'd caused her, the way he'd just left her in that hospital—and jumped into his open arms?

Sure.

But with everything that'd happened, the months of silence, he couldn't expect that. Besides, what had she said that night when he brought her here on a date?

"I'm just not sure there's anything for me in Maple Valley."

The heady smell of the varnish Seth and Ava were using carried through the room.

"On the Rocks."

He glanced down at Raegan. "Huh?"

"We'll go with On the Rocks. It'll look good with the woodwork."

So she was letting it drop. Good.

"Hola, people. Your friendly neighborhood reporter is here."

He turned to see Amelia Bentley traipsing into the room. She stopped in front of Colton. "After weeks of rumors, I had to come see for myself what you're up to here."

"Chasing a story?"

She laughed. "Something like that. And I found that guy on my way." She pointed over her shoulder to a man standing in the archway between the living room and dining room. Metro suit. Faux hawk.

"Don't recognize him."

She shrugged. "Neither do I, but he was at Coffee Coffee looking for you when I stopped in. I need to chat with Raegan for a second, and you should go figure out who Mr. Cosmopolitan is, but afterward, how about a little interview?"

"Sure thing."

"Really? No argument?"

Not at all. It's about time the rest of the community knew what he had planned for the old house. Hopefully, they'd welcome him and his new dream. It'd taken a couple months of thinking. Praying. But he'd finally done what Norah suggested. Pinpointed where what he had to give met what someone else needed.

And as soon as the seed of an idea had dropped into his mind, it'd developed roots, taking hold of his passion in a way nothing had since football.

Well, save the woman he still couldn't stop thinking about.

The stranger in the doorway moved forward and held out a hand. Couldn't be older than twenty-four or twenty-five. "Either you're Colton Greene or you're an amazingly accurate hologram."

Colton accepted the handshake. "Real thing, not hologram. I don't know you, do I?"

The man shook his head. "Not yet, but I have high hopes. Everett Corgin. Sports agent. Full disclosure: I'm new. I'm a junior agent with Glass & Drury, and neither Glass nor Drury know I'm here."

Colton rubbed the dust from his hands—leftover from helping Bear with the sanding, hoping the movement hid his skepticism. "If you're scouting for a client, I'm sorry to tell you, you've wasted a trip. But hey, we're getting dinner here in a bit. Since you came all this way, feel free to join us."

"You aren't even going to hear me out? I did spend six hundred dollars on a plane ticket and another couple hundred on a car rental."

Colton stifled an impatient sigh. "You have to know I'm not playing anymore. Can't."

"I know that." Everett pulled off his suit jacket and draped it over his arm. Apparently he didn't plan on leaving anytime soon.

"I do have a lot of work to do—"

"Five minutes. That's all I ask."

Fine. "All right. Let's go in the dining room. It's quieter there."

They backed into the dining room—just as stripped of furniture as the living room but with a fresh coat of paint on the walls. The room faced the house's sprawling back lawn, which edged up to a cornfield mantled by white snow that sparkled under moonlight.

"I had a whole speech worked up," Everett said as he halted in the center of the room. "But seeing as how you're busy and there's nowhere to sit and—"

"Sorry about that. There's a guy named Lenny, owns a woodshop in town, and he's making a table for me. It's going to be worth the wait, I think."

The guy—Everett, had he said?—only nodded uncertainly. "Like I said, I had a speech, but basically what it boils down to is this: You're not washed up."

Colton couldn't help a grin. "Uh . . . thanks?"

"You might think you are—"

"Used to. But I've had a perspective shift lately."

"—and Ian Muller might've thought so. But I disagree. He was so far off, it's not even funny."

Colton folded his arms. "Ian Muller is one of the best agents in the business." They'd mended their fences before Colton left LA. Colton had met up with him back in December, apologized for the way things ended, thanked the man for all his years of support. Thankfully, he'd had a chance to patch things up with Lilah, too.

"But I've got something Ian doesn't."

There was no hiding his skepticism any longer. "What's that?"

"Youth. And more time than Ian and his overflowing client

list will ever have." Everett smoothed back his gelled hair. "No disrespect, but Ian was doing everything backward. Probably told you to stay out of the limelight, right? What does that do other than get people to forget about you? You should be out doing commercials, traveling the interview circuit, going to fundraisers and galas and whatnot. And whatever happened to that book you were doing?"

Webster walked in then. "Got everybody's order but yours, Colt. We're ordering from the Mandarin. What do you want?"

"Kung Pao chicken. You want anything, Everett? This Scottish guy—weird, I know—runs the Mandarin. Best Chinese you'll ever have. I promise."

Everett only shook his head, traces of irritation in the move.

"Thanks, Webster. Let me know before you leave to pick it up. I've got cash." He turned back to Everett. "I really appreciate you coming all this way. But honestly, I'm done with that kind of public life."

"But why? I know you're not Michael Jordan on a Wheaties box—"

"Thanks for pointing that out."

"—but you could still be something. Your career could still go somewhere."

Colton glanced over the man's shoulders to the living room—the people painting and sanding and varnishing. Someone had started music, and the upbeat rhythm of a southern rock song drifted through the house. "It is going somewhere. It's going exactly where it's supposed to."

Everett must have heard it then—the resolve in Colton's voice—because he only nodded, resignation in his long exhale. "Well, then. Guess I'll head back to the airport."

"Unless you want to stick around and help us paint."

The man looked down at his suit.

"Right. Well, have a safe trip. And sorry I couldn't make it worth your while."

He saw the guy to the door, then reentered the living room. Amelia found him the second he walked in. "Interview time. I've caught hints of what you're up to, but not the full story. You're not just fixing up this house for yourself—that's for sure."

"Oh no. If I just wanted a place to live, I wouldn't have picked a place with four bathrooms. All of which need to be gutted and redone. Hope you've got your tape recorder handy."

Amelia held it up. "Always."

And then Raegan's voice piped in. "Just so you know, Colton, Kate subscribes to the *Maple Valley News*."

⌁

"You have to let me shop it, Kate. It's the best thing you've ever written."

Marcus's voice rose above the hum of an early February wind gusting over the sidewalk leading up to the Willis Tower entrance. Kate held on to one of Breydan's mittened hands, mimicking his stance—neck craned and eyes on the tower's stretched-out grasp for the sky, stomach close to somersaulting at the thought of riding its elevator all the way up.

But Breydan had insisted. And since it was not only his birthday but also the one-month anniversary of the day the doctor said the word they'd all been waiting for—remission—she'd have taken an elevator to the moon if he asked.

"Let me send it to a few editors."

With her free hand, Kate held the top of her coat closed, Chicago cold burrowing through her and gaze still tilted upward. "I need to polish it first. I've barely proofread the thing."

"So polish it." Marcus rubbed his hands together, blowing

into them. "But don't for a second think I'm going to let you get away with hiding it. I'm serious about it being your best."

"Lay off her, honey," Hailey said from Breydan's opposite side. "Didn't you promise no business today?"

"Yeah, no business today." Breydan broke free and hurried toward the building's glass-heavy entrance, bright blue letters spelling *Skydeck* overhead. So hard to believe a few months ago he'd been lying in a hospital bed, pallor the color of the sidewalk underneath her winter boots, fighting for his life.

Breydan was still small, peach-fuzz hair and bony frame tell-tale signs of all his body had been through in the past year. But the joy he'd somehow never lost showed through even more now. And the excitement in his eyes reached into the still-tender corners of her heart like a soothing balm.

Breydan waved them through the entrance and plopped into place in the line for elevator tickets. The lobby looked exactly like she remembered—cordoned-off lines, brightly colored walls and posters displaying facts about the structure, built-in monitors offering trivia while visitors waited.

"He's right, you know."

Kate turned to Hailey as Marcus caught up with Breydan. "About?"

"About the novel being the best thing you've written."

I know it is. She couldn't say it out loud. It'd sound cocky and boastful. But it *was* good. Just a simple love story, really, but it'd flowed like nothing she'd ever written. She'd taken cues from Dad—from all his talk of romance and his and Mom's journey—and it'd just poured from her.

It was funny . . . after years of wishing to write something besides romance, she'd come back to it with a new vigor. She'd refallen in love with love.

And each time the voice of her past hissed its way in—tried

to tell her this was just another wishy-washy story about fake people living fake lives who didn't really matter—she'd reread the last scene she'd written. Or scroll back to the beginning and read her first chapter. Or dream about the ending she couldn't wait to give her characters, the way their journeys would change them . . . and just might change the reader.

And somewhere in the process, she began to believe in her own story.

"You're okay with me having read it, aren't you? Marcus didn't think you'd mind."

She and Hailey waited off to the side as Marcus bought tickets. "No, of course not." She pulled off her gloves, one finger at a time. "You don't think it turned out overly sappy or sentimental?"

"Not at all, but it *is* romantic. Incredibly so. The tension, I could totally feel it. I laughed and cried and had to stay up half the night reading." She loosened her scarf. "It's your heart on the page."

"You just said every single thing writers want to hear."

"It has a different feel than your screenplays, too. Maybe it's because it's a book, not a script, but . . . it's like you finally figured out what you wanted to say and you didn't hold back. You said it. Something's changed in your writing, Kate."

Because something had changed in Kate. She still wasn't entirely sure what. So much about her life was up in the air right now. She'd done a little freelance writing here and there. Frederick Langston had thrown a couple articles her way for the James Foundation newsletter. Not the same as a trip to Africa, but at least she was involved.

But other than that, her days had mainly been filled up with physical therapy and writing her book. The only reason she'd even been able to afford the past couple months' mortgage payments had been the check she received in the mail back in November. From Colton.

She'd thought about sending it back. He didn't owe her. It's not like he'd forced her to spend that month working on his book. She hadn't finished it. It wasn't getting published.

But sending it back would've felt too much like a final goodbye. *Man, I miss him.* Missed him and wondered about him. Wondered what might've happened if everything hadn't fallen apart in one miserable day.

"Come on, Katie."

She reached for Breydan's hand. "Lead the way."

Within minutes they'd boarded an elevator and begun the initial ascent. The elevator stopped at the tenth floor, and they followed a maze of corridors to another elevator for the final stretch.

And then they were released onto the Skydeck, the bright white of a winter sun gulping up the space that circled around the elevators. Breydan immediately ran to a window.

She grinned even as her head fogged. The elevator hadn't bothered her nearly as much as she'd expected, but now, with only glass separating her from the sky's embrace and the Chicago skyline so, soooo far below, the muscles in her legs threatened to give out.

"You all right?" Marcus's smirk hovered between teasing and concern.

"I'm fine, smarty-pants."

"Braving your fear of heights. You're a good surrogate aunt, Kate."

Marcus joined Breydan at the window then, and Kate turned from the view to Hailey. "You don't have to stay back here with me."

"Oh, I'm not staying back here. I'm the support system that's going to get you to the window."

"Uh-uh. I promised to come up here. Not to go stand by the glass and lose my breakfast. Besides, I don't need to look out. I already know you can see Indiana, Wisconsin, and Michigan from here." She could recite tower trivia all day.

"That's a fact, Kate. Not the same thing as experiencing the view."

"You know all the facts of what makes a good romance, Kate. You don't let yourself live it."

Dad's words.

"Come on, just take a peek."

Hesitance weighing her steps, she let Hailey pull her to the front of the crowd. They stopped in front of a lanky window, and the second Kate felt the cool glass reaching for her, she backed away and closed her eyes. She could hear the click of Breydan's camera as he snapped photos.

"Open your eyes, Kate."

She forced them open, ignored the clenching in her stomach . . . and just looked. The Chicago skyline spread in smudges of gray and brown, winter white draping behind and in and around. And the clouds—it was as if she could reach forward to touch them. Even on the foggiest day, God's artistry breathed with life.

Breathless wonder dabbed away her fear.

"So what do you hear from Colton these days?"

Her gaze snapped to Hailey. "Uh, I thought we were admiring the view."

"I figure if I can get you to the window, then I can get you to talk about Colton."

"You figured wrong." She might think about him way, way more than the months of silence warranted. But if Raegan hadn't been able to get anywhere with the subject during her couple weeks staying with Kate, Hailey certainly wasn't going to.

"Oh, come on. You need to talk about it. Otherwise, he'll become another Gil and—"

Kate's laughter bordered on caustic. "Not a chance. Colton is nothing like Gil."

"So talk."

"There's nothing to talk about. I know Logan's seen him a few times. He told me at Christmas Colton's been busy with restarting his foundation. But other than that, I know nothing."

Hailey tilted her head, eyes turned back to the view. "Huh. I wonder how he's working with his foundation from Maple Valley. Maybe that's the kind of thing you can do from anywhere."

"Wait, what?" Kate turned to face her friend. "Colton's not in Maple Valley."

"Uh, yes he is. Breydan just got a package from him this week. Autographs of a bunch of old teammates and a really nice letter. And it was definitely postmarked from Maple Valley."

"I don't . . . I don't understand." If Colton was back in Iowa, wouldn't someone have told her?

"Come on, Kate. Come see me stand on the glass deck." Breydan pulled on her arm.

"You're a brave kid, B." She followed him across the room to where the glass deck jutted out from the building, watched him step onto the glass deck and play to the camera and pose like Superman.

"Maybe I'm crazy," Hailey said beside her, "but if the guy is back in your hometown, it must mean something."

"I have no idea what."

Breydan barreled toward her. "Your turn, Katie."

"Ha, good one. No thanks." Although, it had to feel a little exhilarating, didn't it, standing on the glass?

He rolled his eyes. "Don't be scared. If I can do it, you can."

"I like floors I can see, Breydan."

"Pleeease." He turned exaggerated puppy-dog eyes on her. "You know you want to."

Did she?

"Be the girl who takes the risk and goes after what she wants." Hailey had said that. Months ago, back when Breydan was in the hospital.

She took a breath, closed her eyes, felt Breydan push her forward. Then she opened her eyes and stepped onto the glass. But the view, the ledge, the fear she should've felt . . . none of it even registered.

He's back in Maple Valley. Colton's back.

And then she was moving off the glass and someone else was taking a turn and her heart was hammering for a reason that had nothing to do with height.

She whirled around to Marcus and Hailey. "Guys, I've gotta go. Sorry. Brey, thanks for forcing me to come up here." She leaned down to hug him, then turned toward the elevator.

"But where are you going? What are you doing?" Hailey called.

Kate spun as the elevator door opened. Grinned. "Calling an audible."

20

Had it really only been five months since the last time Colton gave a press conference?

And could this one be any more different? Fewer cameras, more familiar faces. And a sense of purpose so energizing, it could have fueled him for a year.

"We need to get moving, Logan. It's almost three."

"Five more minutes. The reporter from Channel 8 is still interviewing Webster."

Colton glanced around the packed living room. No, it wasn't nearly the crowd who'd flocked to his NFL retirement announcement. Mostly state and local reporters. And instead of the white walls that'd wrapped around that stadium conference room, this living room boasted warm tones—Raegan's choice, of course—and comfortable red-almost-burgundy leather furniture. Plants, bamboo blinds, new carpet, all of it completed the relaxed feel.

Not that he could claim credit for the décor. That was all Raegan and Ava.

So far, this was the only room to have gotten a complete makeover. There was still plenty more to do. And he'd have to wait until spring to tackle the exterior—replace aging siding and add a deck in back. Might have to completely pull off the existing porch and build a new one.

Logan waved at Charlie, who was perched on Case's shoulders at the back of the room. "I can't believe this came together so fast. I thought you'd spend forever working out zoning issues, getting permits, applying for tax-exempt status, all that."

Colton turned to his friend. "Wouldn't have come together even close to this quickly without the help of your family. And you. Seriously, man, thanks for coming home for this."

Logan brushed off the thanks just like he had every time Colton offered his appreciation. "I was going stir-crazy once election season was over. It was good to have an excuse to get back to Iowa for a couple weeks. Plus, Charlie's grandparents always love the chance to see her." He scanned the room. "You sure you're ready for all this?"

Tall windows ushered in streaming sunlight and peeked into the neighborhood whose residents had clamped on to Colton's vision as soon as Amelia's story ran in the paper two weeks ago. "More than ready."

His gaze moved from the window to the gathering of people behind all the cameras. Case and Raegan, Seth and Ava, Bear . . . Everyone had come to show their support.

"You know, if you would've let any of us mention this whole thing to Kate earlier—"

He shook his head before Logan finished the sentence. "I'm going to tell her." He had a plan . . . kind of. It started with the folder he'd rolled up in his back pocket.

"How hard is it to say 'Kate, I moved to your hometown. I bought that house you love. I'm turning it into a home for guys aging out of the foster system. I restructured and renamed my foundation and—'"

"Logan, can you let me do this my way?"

"Your way is annoyingly slow."

Maybe it was slow, but at least it wasn't reckless.

Thing is, he would do it all over again. Getting to know Kate—falling for her, even losing her—it had freed something in him. Led him to a place of honesty and shined a light on the shadows that once held him back.

Without Kate, he might still be desperately grasping for a future he knew now he wasn't meant for.

"Let's get started."

Logan gave up the argument and nodded. "I'll round up the troops."

The chatter of the group quieted as Logan collected their focus. Colton caught sight of Case Walker through the opening into the dining room. He still held Charlie, probably ready to make a run for it if her attention span waned.

Over in one corner of the living room, Webster Hawks straightened from his sprawled position on the recliner and stood. Did the kid realize his role in inspiring this day?

"Thanks so much for being here," Logan addressed the group. "We're keeping things easy and informal today. You should all have a packet of information about the Parker House, but here to tell you a little more about its purpose is its founder, former NFL quarterback and one of the finest men I know, Colton Greene."

The pride in his friend's voice warmed Colton as light applause broke out. His gaze landed on Raegan, who stood by a cherrywood buffet topped with platters of homemade cookies. And the Clancys, now flanking Webster. Coach Leo.

These people had become his family. This community, his home.

Assurance pooled inside him. If God could get him back to Maple Valley, fill him with a new dream, a new purpose for his life . . . well then, He could show him what to do about Kate, too.

He turned his focus to the cameras, none of his old fear of their stare left in him.

"When I was nine years old, my life changed forever. My parents were killed in an accident and I began a nearly decade-long journey through foster care." He couldn't help another glance at Webster, saw Laura Clancy place her hand on the teen's shoulder.

It hadn't been easy, facing the reality of what had happened with his parents. Such glaring light after so many years of darkness had felt like an assault. He'd taken Norah's advice—visited a Christian counselor back in LA for those couple months before moving to Maple Valley.

"It's not something I've talked about often because, frankly, it was a miserable time for me. But I realized something in recent months—in refusing to talk, I wasn't only silencing my story. I was missing out on an opportunity to honor someone who made an incredible difference in my life—even if I had too big of a chip on my shoulder to recognize it at the time."

He told them about Norah then. About her years of patience and persistence.

"The transition from high school to adulthood can be an iffy enough time for anyone. But for eighteen-year-olds aging out of foster care, it's a complete upheaval. The statistics about post-foster-care homelessness, addiction, and incarceration are staggering." He took a breath. "God used Norah Parker to keep me from becoming one of those statistics."

How he wished Norah could've been here today. But with a three-month-old, she couldn't travel. She'd sent a gift, though—a wall decoration made of old wood that spelled the word *Home*.

"I bought it at this shop where all the stuff is made of wood from old barns. Seemed fitting because you're in Iowa. But also because you and I have a history with barns."

He'd smiled and hung the thing over the front entrance—the house's first piece of décor.

"So that's why I've decided to name this home Parker House. My hope is to make the kind of difference in young men's lives that Norah made in mine. And if all goes according to plan, this home is the first of many just like it I hope to start across the country through the recently renamed Parker Foundation."

He finished his remarks minutes later. *This is right.* It was good.

And when the question-and-answer portion of the casual press conference ended in clapping, it wasn't the applause of those gathered in the room he heard . . . but the applause of his own heart.

He'd shaken at least a dozen hands before Laura Clancy wound her way through the crowd to reach him. "Colton Greene, I liked you when you were a football player. But now, I love you. And I can say that without it being awkward because I'm at least twenty years older than you."

She pulled him into a hug, then lowered her voice. "And just so you know, we're taking Webster out for dinner tonight. Asking him how he'd feel about adoption."

He stepped back. "Seriously? That's . . . that's . . ." The lump in his throat stole his words.

"I think the word you're looking for is *awesome.*" She patted his cheek and moved on.

Case Walker approached next. What started as a handshake turned into an embrace. "You found your eleven inches."

And a peace he couldn't begin to describe.

"Also," Case stepped back. "I think there's something you should see. Take a look out the window, why don't ya."

～

Just a house. Just a big, old house—but according to the article she'd read, Colton must have seen in it what she had.

Kate stood outside her Focus, car door still open, February breeze grazing over her cheeks. Her coat and scarf warded off whatever cold the tangle of nerves and jittery emotions heating through her didn't. She reached inside to grab the newspaper on her dash, the one she'd found in her mailbox yesterday after she'd raced home from the Willis. If she'd needed any other nudge to pack a suitcase and hit the road, well, she'd gotten it.

"Be the girl who takes the risk and goes after what she wants."

It sounded so good in her head back in Chicago, but now that she was actually here . . . she was a craggy, bare tree—stripped of cover and resolve, ready to crack, like an ice-covered branch.

But this was right. The thought had rooted inside her. It fueled her drive to Maple Valley, pulled her from the car, and tugged her gaze to the house.

She closed her car door now. There were no skyscrapers or city horizons here. Only fresh snowfall frosting the trees and a gleaming winter sun. And hope—the kind she'd craved for so long.

The kind that'd been there from the start, really, just waiting for her to notice it.

She started across the street, snow crunching under the white boots she'd tucked her jeans into. She wore the scarf Raegan had crocheted for Colton for the train pull. Would he notice?

Of course he'd notice. Because the man noticed everything. He'd seen the hurt underneath Webster's anger. The need underneath Dad's strength. The heart underneath a quirky, storm-torn little town.

He'd seen *her*.

Shovel tracks led the way up the sidewalk to the stairs that led the way up to the porch. The floorboards creaked as her steps slowed, white front door staring her down. She took a breath and rang the doorbell.

Nothing. No sound. Shoot, must be broken.

She was just lifting her hand to knock, when the door swung open.

And her heart knotted. "C-Colton. Hi."

"Katharine Rose Walker." Surprise and maybe delight—oh, she hoped it was delight—mingled in his voice. He was semi-dressed up. Jeans and a black sweater that couldn't hope to hide his football-player arms. Man, he had good arms.

Stop looking at his arms.

So she looked at his eyes instead—that same drenching, stunning blue as always, enough to sweep away her rehearsed words, leaving only quiet in its wake, hovering like the white of their breath.

Talk, Walker. Talk.

It'd help if he'd ask her why she was here. Or how she'd known where to find him. Something, anything, to tug from her the words she'd come to say. But he just stood there, watching her, his half grin tinged with uncertainty.

You know what you want to say. Now say it.

Just like she had with the book. Like Hailey said. Her heart on the page.

She held up the newspaper. "When were you going to tell me about this?" She blurted the words with all the grace of the clanging wind chime hitting against the porch corner.

Confusion flickered over his face. Oh man, he was cute when he was confused.

"You bought *my* house."

He pointed behind him. "You know, we could go inside—"

"And you revived your foundation and you didn't even ask for my help. You know I've wanted to write for a nonprofit. I could've helped. I haven't even been busy. Except, I guess I did write a new book, but—"

344

"You wrote a new book?"

"Yeah and it's good, too."

"I'm sure it is."

Why did he have to lean against the doorframe like that? All, amused and . . . and adorable with the wind fanning through his hair and leaving circles of red on his cheeks. Not to mention that faint scent of his cologne she'd gotten used to in weeks of living across the hall from the man.

Words and poise and confidence were lost under the sudden crazy-strong desire to launch herself at him.

His hands dropped to his sides. "What am I doing? You wrote a book. You've been trying to write another book for years and . . . "

He reached to pull her into a hug, lifting her feet from the ground and swinging her around just like a character in an old movie. Surprise stole her breath, and the newspaper in her hand dropped to the snow as she wrapped her arms around him.

"You wrote a book, Rosie."

"And you decided on a purpose for your foundation." She said the words against his shoulder, a giddy energy stealing away the last of her reserve. Why had she waited so long to come back? "I'm so ridiculously proud of you."

He set her down but didn't let go. "So proud that you came to scold me about not telling you?"

His arms were like a second coat, warm and perfect. "Yes. I mean no. I mean yes and no." It was too hard to think when she was wrapped in his arms. She forced herself to step back from their embrace. "My friend Hailey told me once that I needed to let myself want something enough to fight for it. To take a risk and go after it. Well, this is me, taking a risk and going after what I want."

"And you want . . . what?" he prodded her. "A job helping with my foundation?"

"Not a job." She met his gaze. *It's okay to admit what you want*. She swallowed, tasting the crisp cold in the air and the sweetness of honesty. "I want you."

His slow smile could have melted every speck of snow whiting their surroundings. But instead of saying anything, he reached around to his back pocket and pulled out a folded manila folder. He handed it to her. "Take a peek."

She opened it up, scanning the top page . . . then the next and the next. Lists of marketing materials—newsletters, appeals, brochures. What looked like a strategic plan—not just for the Parker House but for what he was now calling the Parker Foundation.

And the last page of the folder—a list of grant-makers and application deadlines. The word *Rosie* scribbled in the margin in Colton's handwriting.

"If I want to grow this thing, I'm going to need to find some new revenue streams. Word on the street is, there's some grant-writing history in the Walker family."

She looked up from the folder, tears—the best kind—pooling faster than she could blink.

"You're not the only one who knows what you want, Rosie."

When he pulled her to him again, the paper fluttered from her hands. He kissed the tip of her nose, soft as the snowflakes drifting from the porch roof and landing on her cheeks, and then her lips, warmer than the pale sunlight that wove through the lattice.

She melted into the moment. *Better than any happy ending I could ever write.*

Not an ending at all, really. And maybe that was the best part. The beautiful peace that came with living her own story, knowing every turn of the page and tug of the heart was a new beginning.

"Kate," he whispered as he pulled away.

"I thought we'd moved past the talking part."

"Yeah, but . . ." He looked over her shoulder.

She circled around, hands sliding down to connect with his, still hooked around her, and saw what he saw: a crowd gathered in the front door, some now spilling onto the porch. Cameras. Grins. One lone flash.

"You could've told me I was interrupting a party."

"Press conference, actually. Hey guys, check it out, the foundation just got its first employee." He pulled her to him and touched his forehead to hers. "Rosie Walker came home."

"You better not welcome all your staff this way, Colton Greene."

"Nope. Only the ones I'm crazy about."

And then, to the tune of applause and cheers, the glitter of snowfall like a wink from above, Colton lifted her from her feet and kissed her once more.

Acknowledgments

True story: I didn't know much at all about football when I started writing *From the Start*. That fact and a few other circumstances made writing this book ~~slightly~~ reeeeally challenging. Let's be honest: Previously, football was, to me, basically just a good excuse to eat inordinate amounts of snacks on Super Bowl Sunday. But guess what, I think I finally appreciate the game!

But I appreciate the family and friends who helped me through this book even more:

Mom and Dad, thank you for everything, but especially for those last couple weeks before both rounds of deadlines. Thank you for praying with me, feeding me, brainstorming with me, and putting up with the moodiest version of me ever.

Amy, Nathanael, and Nicole, thanks for unknowingly loaning some of your coolest traits to the Walker siblings. Grandma and Grandpa, as always, thank you for your constant encouragement and prayer.

My editor, Raela Schoenherr, and my agent, Amanda Luedeke—thank you both for being awesome. Raela, thank you for helping shape this story and in doing so, nudging me into being excited about it again. Amanda, thank you for being a voice of calm and direction and levity.

Editor Karen Schurrer, your feedback, editing, and advice are awesome. I can't thank you enough for that. And everyone at Bethany House—I couldn't ask for a more wonderful group of people to usher this story out the door.

Clay Morgan, thanks for being the best football source ever, for answering all my questions, and especially for that Raymond Berry story. By way of thanks, I will try to cheer for the Steelers now and then.

Beth Vogt and Rachel Hauck, your phone calls on that deadline day when I needed it most meant so much to me. Lisa Jordan, thank you for months of cheerleading texts and emails and cards. And Susan May Warren, your voice is so often in my head as I write—I don't even have words for how thankful I am for that or how much I look up to you. Thank you for reading my opening scenes and pushing me to take them further.

Lindsay Harrel, Gabrielle Meyer, and Alena Tauriainen—you know how much I love you, right? Thanks for the brainstorming, prayer, and amazing friendship.

Thanks to Denise Hawks for loaning out your last name and coming up with Webster's first name, and to Rachel McMillan for coming up with the cutest name ever for little Charlotte.

Readers, you add crazy amounts of wonderful to this writing journey. Bear hugs to those of you who've sent kind notes, been a part of my launch team, or taken the time to review my books. I'm truly beyond grateful.

Also, at the risk of sounding like a total fangirl (which, let's face it, is exactly what I am), I have to thank the band NEEDTO-BREATHE, whose album *Rivers in the Wasteland* is probably the best thing ever to happen to music. I may have listened to it a few hundred times while drafting this book.

Finally and most importantly, I'm so thankful to God for giving me a love for stories in the first place . . . and for opening the doors to let me tell them.

Melissa Tagg is a former reporter and total Iowa girl. In addition to her homeless ministry day job, she is also the marketing/events coordinator for My Book Therapy, a craft-and-coaching community for writers. When she's not writing, she can be found hanging out with the coolest family ever, watching old movies, and daydreaming about her next book. She's passionate about humor, grace, and happy endings. Melissa blogs regularly and loves connecting with readers at www.melissatagg.com.

More Romance to Enjoy

Blake Hunziker has finally returned home to Whisper Shore, and he's planning to stay. Local inn owner Autumn Kingsley, on the other hand, can't wait to escape. When the two of them strike a deal to help each other out, they may get more than they bargained for.

Here to Stay by Melissa Tagg
melissatagg.com

Miranda Woodruff, star of the homebuilding TV show, *From the Ground Up*, has built a perfect—but fake—life for herself onscreen. Will it all come crashing down when she falls in love for real?

Made to Last by Melissa Tagg
melissatagg.com

Dr. Ryan Tremaine is trying to pick up the pieces of his life, and reconnecting with his kids is the first step. He thought hiring Carly Mason as a nanny would be the key to his success, but the growing attraction between them threatens to send his plans into chaos. . . .

Together With You by Victoria Bylin
victoriabylin.com

BETHANYHOUSE

Stay up-to-date on your favorite books and authors with our free e-newsletters. Sign up today at bethanyhouse.com.

Find us on Facebook. facebook.com/bethanyhousepublishers

Free exclusive resources for your book group! bethanyhouse.com/anopenbook

an open book

You May Also Like . . .

After his spontaneous marriage to Celia Park, bull rider Ty Porter quickly realized he wasn't ready to be anybody's husband. Five years later, when he comes face-to-face with Celia—and the daughter he never knew he had—can he prove that theirs can still be the love of a lifetime?

Meant to Be Mine by Becky Wade
beckywade.com

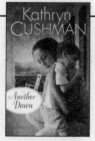

Grace Graham has been given one last chance to redeem herself. But when tragedy strikes her son, will she have the strength to resist running and stand strong?

Another Dawn by Kathryn Cushman
kathryncushman.com

Ben has always known just how to get under Bea's skin. When their friends decide to play matchmaker, can these two stop bickering long enough to realize the true source of the "spark" between them?

Becoming Bea by Leslie Gould
THE COURTSHIPS OF LANCASTER COUNTY #4
lesliegould.com

⬥ BETHANYHOUSE

Stay up-to-date on your favorite books and authors with our free e-newsletters. Sign up today at bethanyhouse.com.

Find us on Facebook. facebook.com/bethanyhousepublishers

Free exclusive resources for your book group! bethanyhouse.com/anopenbook